Veronica Stallwood was born in London, educated abroad and now lives near Oxford. In the past she has worked at the Bodleian Library and in New College library. Her first crime novel, *Deathspell*, was published to great critical acclaim, as were the ten Oxford novels which followed, all of which feature Kate Ivory, and her atmospheric suspense novel, *The Rainbow Sign*.

When she is not writing, Veronica Stallwood enjoys going for long walks, talking and eating with friends, and gazing out at the peaceful Oxfordshire countryside from the windows of her cottage.

Praise for Veronica Stallwood:

'Stallwood's speciality is adroit plotting set in a vividly realised Oxford locale, and this is vintage stuff' *The Times*

'For readers who are missing Inspector Morse' *Oxford Times*

'Dreaming spires updated, a fetching, formidably erudite heroine matching minds with an egomaniac? Sayers would give it the nod' *Good Book Guide*

'A deceptive and atmospheric tale' *Time Out*

'Stallwood . . . can produce shivers even in a heatwave' *Daily Telegraph*

'The author has produced another cracking read, packed with plausible characters and a believable plot with dark undertones' *South Wales Argus*

'A cleverly drawn mys entry *Evening Telegraph*

'Engrossing fiction fi her niche' *Good Book Gu*

Also by Veronica Stallwood

Deathspell
The Rainbow Sign

Kate Ivory Mysteries

Death and the Oxford Box
Oxford Exit
Oxford Mourning
Oxford Fall
Oxford Knot
Oxford Blue
Oxford Shift
Oxford Shadows
Oxford Double
Oxford Proof

OXFORD
REMAINS

Veronica Stallwood

headline

First published in 2004
by HEADLINE BOOK PUBLISHING

First published in paperback in 2005
by HEADLINE BOOK PUBLISHING

10 9 8 7 6 5 4 3 2 1

ISBN 0 7553 0074 2

Typeset in Times by Avon DataSet Ltd,
Bidford-on-Avon, Warwickshire

Printed and bound in Great Britain by
Clays Ltd, St Ives plc

Headline's policy is to use papers that are natural, renewable and
recyclable products and made from wood grown in sustainable forests.
The logging and manufacturing processes are expected to conform to the
environmental regulations of the country of origin.

HEADLINE BOOK PUBLISHING
A division of the Hodder Headline Group
338 Euston Road
London NW1 3BH

www.headline.co.uk
www.hodderheadline.com

For Annabel

i

I was six years old when my father died.

You would think that after all these years the events of that night would have faded from my memory but they are still lurking there in all their colourful detail, waiting in ambush like the pirates in my childhood dreams. One reason for their tenacity is that I remember my childhood in images rather than words (which is strange when you consider the importance that words have had throughout my adult life).

'Wake up!'

It was my mother's voice, piercing through the layers of sleep, her hoarse words stirring the air close to my ear and interrupting my restless dreams. I was dreaming of breakers pounding harshly against a hostile shore; of a fragile craft, like a splinter of jet against the granite waves, whipped by wind and rain on to the rocky teeth of a storm-lashed cove, while I strove vainly to save her hapless crew. For I had espied two figures in the boat, mouths agape with soundless cries for help, white hands fluttering in supplication. But, valiantly as I strained against the inertia of sleep, my limbs refused to obey my will, and my voice, like theirs, was drowned by the screaming of gulls far above my head.

'Wake up,' my mother was saying. She spoke in a rasping whisper and kept repeating the same phrase: 'Wake up!' as she shook my shoulder.

I was a heavy sleeper in those days and, besides, I was loath to abandon the boatmen to their watery fate, and so I fought against her efforts to rouse me. At that moment those two unknown people in the boat were so much more real to me than my mother and father. Why was it necessary to wake up in the middle of the night

1

to join my parents' shadowy world when I was needed so urgently in my own vivid one?

'Go away!' I mumbled. I doubt whether she could hear my actual words, but she said crossly, 'Get dressed, Joseph. You have to get dressed and come downstairs.'

'Why?' If I had been fully awake I would never have dared to question my mother's orders like that.

'It's your father,' she was saying. 'You have to help me.' And then, most worrying of all, she added, 'I don't know what to do.'

Her words made me feel as though all responsibility for the family were being heaped upon my inadequate shoulders. How could I possibly bear such a burden?

My eyes were open by now and I was struggling to sit up in bed. My mother had switched on the light, a bright central bulb that shone straight into my still blinking eyes. She was sitting on the edge of the bed, very close to me, so that I could smell the mixture of perfume and fear that oozed from the soft folds of her body. The sweet scent of her perfume mingled rankly with that of acrid perspiration.

As I blinked, her face came into focus, too close to mine. And now I could smell, too, the wine on her breath and see a thin red arc crusted on her lower lip where the wineglass had rested. As she spoke again I saw that the wine had stained her tongue with a matching splash of dark red, bisected by a forked white line like the fangs of a snake.

'Get dressed, like a good child! You can do that, can't you?' Her voice had softened and there was a note of pleading in it. I sat and watched as she took the pile of folded clothes from the chair and placed them beside me. She smiled as though to encourage me to do what she wanted, and then she left the room. As she closed the door in her firm way it set my dressing-gown swaying on its hook and I stared at it fearfully. Sometimes its dark blue shape seemed to me like a man hanging there, his shrunken, hunched form hidden in its dark folds.

But, in spite of my nervousness, I did not dare to disobey her. I forced myself to swing my feet out from under the blankets and over the side on to the cold floor (for even in summer there was a chill in our unheated bedrooms, as though the winter cold could never quite escape).

Slowly I began to pull on the school uniform I had removed just a few hours before. Perhaps it was not the middle of the night after all, for at that age I would have been in bed at seven, well out of the way so that my parents could enjoy their evening meal in peace. I would have been asleep by seven-thirty.

My eyelids kept sliding closed and I had to thrust my chilled feet into recalcitrant socks. At last there remained only my shoes, and I fumbled them on, but could not quite manage to tie the laces. I hoped that no one would notice.

There was a small, oval, walnut mirror on a table by the window, intended to encourage me to brush my hair every morning. As I stood up I saw my reflection unexpectedly so that for a moment I thought I saw a stranger – a boy whose huge dark eyes stared back at me from a white face, topped by a thatch of dark hair that certainly needed the attentions of a brush and comb.

I hesitated. I wondered whether I could take my teddy bear to keep me company. He was still lying on my pillow, his single eye watching my every movement. He would be some kind of ally in whatever ordeal awaited me downstairs, but I knew that my mother would be irritated by the sight of her son clutching such a babyish toy. I touched his paw for luck.

Unable to put off the awful moment any longer, I stumbled out of the bedroom and made my way along the landing to the head of the stairs, my shoelaces whispering behind me.

The stair rods were a dull copper and the third one down had pulled away from its bracket so that I had to be careful not to trip over it for my feet felt larger than usual, flapping at the ends of my white legs like alien appendages. There was an awkward corner a third of the way down. On, down the beige runner I went, following the four-petalled flowers and the rust stripe right to the door of the drawing room, like a diminutive Theseus drawn towards the Minotaur. I stood there for a moment, staring at the ribbed brass doorknob, knowing I had to turn it and enter the room. But this was not my territory. This was my parents' domain, kept free of childish things.

When I became a man, I put away childish things.

I had heard the school chaplain read those words to us and they had stayed in my head. It appeared that I was not to be allowed to wait until I was a man.

I only ever ventured into the drawing room by invitation, and now I waited anxiously for a voice to prompt me to enter. After a few moments, I pushed at the knob and the door swung wide; I suppose it had not clicked shut when my mother went back inside. My father would not have liked that. He would always complain at the slightest draught.

'So you're here at last,' said my mother. She sounded odd, as well she might, I realise now. She wore a long, blood-red scarf, knotted low so that its ends reached below her waist. Its colour drew my attention back to the wine stains on her lip and tongue. 'Go over there.' She indicated the chair on the opposite side of the fireplace. The logs had burned down so that only the heart of the fire still glowed red, and the room was turning chilly. 'What can you see?' She did not attempt to accompany me, but stood quite still before the big mirror over the fireplace so that two images of my mother followed my progress.

Obediently, I approached the silent figure in the red velvet armchair which was reserved always for my father. He was sitting there now but his shoulders were slumped and his head lolled to one side so that for a moment I wondered if it was really him. I expected him to sit up straight, as he always did, and to speak to me. He still had not complained about the open door and this unwonted silence was disconcerting. I looked into his face and saw that the skin around his mouth was tinged with blue. It felt as though a lump of ice had dropped down inside the collar of my shirt, and I shivered. I looked up and saw my mother's face in the looking-glass above the fireplace, staring at me, waiting for me to do or say something. I turned back to the figure in the armchair.

'Father?' I enquired, but there was no reply. My quavering voice set up a faint echo, but still there was no response. I stared at him while he in his turn stared at the floor close to my feet. My own eyes followed his gaze towards my school shoes with their trailing

4

laces. And then I saw that in my haste I had put them on the wrong feet. They looked so peculiar, with the toes pointing quaintly east and west, like a clown's, that I felt the laughter rising like nausea from deep down in my chest, pushing upwards, trying to break through my rigid throat and stiff lips. I pressed my hands to my mouth, wishing I had a handkerchief with me to use as a gag. Finally, against all my efforts to prevent it, laughter erupted like a volcano and I heard the loud, hysterical 'Tee hee hee!' bursting from my lips.

The laughter rebounded from the high ceiling and echoed around the striped walls as though it existed quite independently of me, bleating on and on, though by now I was praying for it to stop.

Put away childish things . . .

I stuffed my shirt-sleeve into my mouth, for I was desperate to stop the terrible sound, but still it hiccuped out through the flimsy barrier of the cotton fabric.

I can still see the scene reflected in the mirror of my memory: me with my hands over my mouth, Mother's white face staring at me with disbelief, and, impervious to us both, the silent figure of my father. By then, of course, I had realised what had happened to him. There could be no other explanation for his total disregard of my wanton, unseemly behaviour.

I looked again at my mother, thinking she would give me some instructions, tell me what I should do, but all I could see was the blood-red arc of her lower lip.

If only I had left it there, if I had departed from the room and returned to the cooling nest of my rumpled bed but, no sooner had the echoes of my laughter faded away (though my father's whisky glass still resonated, bell-like, with the sound), than I felt compelled to speak.

'He's gone away. He's dead, isn't he?' I said. The words were simple enough, if a trifle insensitive to my mother's feelings. But it was as though that clanging laugh of mine had released something inside me, opening the door to all the wretched, pent-up feelings of my young life. For, instead of my usual breathy treble, I spoke in the voice of Stentor: a vibrant, low-pitched voice that carried to every corner of the room.

5

My mother's eyes were still upon me, and to her expression of contempt was added, fleetingly, something that I thought for a moment was fear, but which was gone too quickly for me to be sure.

'Wait here,' she said. 'Don't move.'

She left the room and I could hear her lift the receiver of the telephone on the hall table and dial. I heard her speaking, but I have no idea what she was saying.

I can still remember how I felt at that moment. It was as though I was suddenly split into two separate people. One self floated away and remained suspended just below the ceiling, observing my other self standing there by the fireplace. The original 'me' was staring at my father, waiting for my mother to finish speaking and to return to the drawing room. But the second 'me' had nothing to do with any of it. He just floated there, ten feet above the carpet, and watched.

Sometimes I wonder whether he and I were ever completely united again. Sometimes it seems to me that I'm forever standing apart, a spectator, watching that other self live my life.

1

It was an early morning in October and a light mist drifted up from the canal, shrouding hedges and buildings, and muffling the sound of traffic. The sky was growing lighter, but the street lamps still glowed, golden and muted in the mist.

Kate Ivory wrapped her towelling robe more tightly around her and ventured out through the back door of her newly-acquired house, a tin of cat food in one hand and a teaspoon in the other.

'Susanna!' she called cautiously, and tapped the spoon against the tin. *Ting*. She kept her voice low enough not to wake up any neighbours who might still be sleeping at that hour, yet at the same time tried to make it carry far enough to reach the missing cat. *Ting ting*. She thought this was the sound that would bring her cat scampering back to its anxious owner, but there was no response. She walked up the path to the front gate and tried again.

'Susanna!'

She looked down the road towards the canal, hoping that Susanna hadn't strayed in that direction and come to a watery end. Kate had been so careful, keeping her cat indoors for a week until she grew accustomed to the new house. But Susanna had been missing now for nearly eight hours. That's not so long, Kate told herself. Susanna would be back at any moment. *Ting*. It was cold standing out in Cleveland Road in her robe. She really must return to her warm kitchen and drink her coffee while it was still hot. Yet she remained by the gate, hoping to see Susanna.

She tapped the tin of cat food one last time with the spoon, then gave up.

Cleveland Road was to be found in that part of Oxford called Jericho, the city's first suburb, built in the ancient Walton Manor during the nineteenth century. The area was bounded on one side by the Oxford Canal and on the other by Walton Street, where the Oxford University Press raised its new home in the 1820s. Most of the houses in Jericho were terraced and the streets constructed on a grid pattern. Situated so close to the city centre, and convenient for the railway station and buses, Jericho was a very desirable place to live.

Kate Ivory had bought an end-terrace house, tall and thin, in one of the streets running down towards the canal, larger than those built in the early 1800s. Cleveland Road dated from later in the century, when perhaps its inhabitants were expected to grow taller and need more room for their possessions.

Kate had moved in only recently and there were still unopened boxes of books standing in every room, waiting for her to decide where to build shelving to hold them. The furniture that she had brought with her from Agatha Street had been placed in the correct rooms, but hadn't yet been arranged to her satisfaction.

The house had been on the market for an unusually long time when she made her offer for it, but Kate decided that there was nothing much wrong with the house itself; it was the previous owner's taste that was to blame.

'Dark blue and muted pink do not form part of my favourite colour scheme,' she had said to her mother, when she came to look round. Roz was dubious about Kate's choice of property.

'And I don't think I can ever look at another flower. Well, not on a wall, anyway. But that's all that's wrong, isn't it?'

'There's a funny smell,' said Roz, wrinkling her nose.

'I'm sure it's just the dog. Once the owner's removed his bedding, and I've taken up the carpet and opened all the windows to air the rooms, it'll be fine.'

'If you're sure,' said Roz, unconvinced.

The funny smell had not appealed to any of the other prospective buyers either, nor had the colour scheme. The overall effect was gloomy, yet at the same time whimsical. Busy flowers bloomed over the walls. More, but different, flowers rambled along borders. The elaborate, dark-patterned curtains displayed ruffled edges and swagged valances.

'Dust traps,' observed Roz, who was not enthusiastic about unnecessary housework.

'I'll put up blinds, and simple curtains,' said Kate.

She didn't tell Roz that the house had been even worse, the first time she had visited it: the sofas were overstuffed, the woodwork dark, and every surface was covered with china figures of dancing ladies of some indeterminate era. The carpets downstairs were dark red with a sculptured pattern. Upstairs they were a patchwork of different pinks and blues. The main bedroom was decorated in shades of pink that up to now Kate had associated with the women's underwear section of an old-fashioned department store. More dancing china ladies simpered in rows along the walls. Quilted pink satin cushions lay in a heap on the bed, a fluffy white toy dog nestling among them. At least, Kate took it for a toy, until it bared its teeth at her and snarled as she approached. She quickly retired to inspect the bathroom.

No wonder so many viewers had been put off. The effect was of small, dark rooms, invasive vegetation and an aggressively feminine atmosphere.

But in spite of her mother's negative reaction, Kate checked the measurements of the rooms and saw that they were more generous than she had expected, then she closed her eyes and made a huge effort of imagination to picture the house the way it could be. Once she had closed her eyes, the funny smell became more noticeable, but she convinced herself that this had more to do with the badly-disciplined dog and too many over-boiled vegetables than to dry rot, faulty plumbing or some other expensive cause. And since she had already made an offer, and it had been accepted, it was really too late for second thoughts. A full, expensive survey would put her mind at rest.

'Don't ever let me accumulate that many belongings,' she said to her friend Jon, when he came with her on her next visit to the house. 'Remind me to donate unworn clothes and unloved ornaments to charity, or put them in the bin.'

'I thought you did get rid of anything you no longer needed, as a matter of course,' said Jon.

For a moment Kate wondered whether he was referring to George, or maybe to Paul, or to Liam. (Had she told him about these previous lovers of hers?) 'It's just that I never want my own house to become this cluttered.'

'It *is* a bit oppressive,' said Jon.

'You think I'm stupid to consider buying it?'

'You have a better imagination than me,' he said diplomatically. 'As long as you don't think you're taking on too much work.'

'The work's mostly cosmetic,' she had answered airily.

Cosmetic it might be, but it was also hard. She had blunted three scrapers before hiring a machine that steamed off the wallpaper. Underneath the pink and blue flowers had been green and yellow stripes, and she had removed those, too, finally reaching a sad shade of green paint. She couldn't wait to start applying her own choice of emulsion on the walls. The whole place would start to look more cheerful, more like *her*

10

house. She had removed the wallpaper from the two main downstairs rooms, but there were still an awful lot of pink and blue flowers left to be demolished.

Oddly enough, although Kate was normally a very organised and orderly person, she found she was enjoying this unfinished state of things. It left her options wide open. Anything seemed possible. Just for the moment her life was in a fluid state and she needn't make any decisions about pattern or colour – or anything else – for a week or two. It reminded her of the time when she sat down to dream about a new novel, before she decided on plot and characters, and before the reality of settling down at the computer every morning had taken away the gloss. Her house could be a model of minimalism, or rural chic, or witty eclecticism. It was just waiting for her to decide which one.

The ceilings in this house were higher than those in the house she had left in Agatha Street, the rooms were a little larger, and there was an extra bedroom; she hadn't entirely decided what to do with it yet. The layout was vertical rather than horizontal, which was another change from Agatha Street. Kate was very happy that this house was so different from her previous one. It was time to move on, and once she had decided on her style, fitted fresh sofa covers, bought herself some new bed linen and decided where to put her books, she would be able to start a whole fresh chapter of her life.

ii

My sister returned home the next day, summoned by my mother
from her boarding school.

Selina was eleven at the time – the five-year difference in our
ages was so much more significant in childhood than it would have
been later in our lives. When she arrived from the station – in a
taxi, an unusual luxury – she was swept into my mother's embrace
and could barely manage to throw me an encouraging smile over
her shoulder before she was whisked away to the drawing room.
My mother was speaking to her, her voice high-pitched and
unceasing, and when the door clicked shut behind them I could still
hear her loud complaint, though I could not distinguish her words.

What had she expected from me the previous evening when she
roused me from sleep and ordered me to come down to the drawing
room? I do believe she wanted me to take on the mantle of the man
of the house (whatever that might mean). I think she resented the
fact that, as the only adult present in the house, she was expected to
ring for the doctor and then deal with all the unpleasant things that
would need to be done. I understand now that, since she had taken
no responsibility for her own life up to that point, she saw no
reason why she should start to do so now. She must have been
angry with my father for dying in such a way and leaving her to
cope with all the fuss. At the time, of course, I understood none of
this and felt only a generalised shame that I was failing her in some
unspecified way. But at least Selina was here. From the perspective
of a six year old, she seemed almost grown-up.

My mother made it plain that I was not wanted now that her
daughter had arrived, so I returned to the kitchen, where a little
earlier I had discovered a hidden packet of biscuits. I was in the

habit of looking through all the cupboards, making an inventory of their contents, playing a version of Kim's Game, checking to see that I was correct in my memorised lists. (Of course, sometimes the contents were used up, or replenished, but I knew when this happened and did not confuse it with a mistake of my own making.) But on my secret trawls through the kitchen cupboards it was not often that I found anything as interesting as this. In the normal way of things I would have left it where it was, or removed a single biscuit, eating it carefully so that I scattered no crumbs to give myself away. But that morning I stood at the table and methodically ate my way through the entire packet. I had some idea that if I ate all the biscuits and then hid the empty packet at the bottom of the rubbish bin, no one would discover my crime. (In the circumstances, I need not have worried. No one was interested in biscuits that week.) Even as I chewed, I felt guilty, though. I know now that this was not because I had failed to ask whether I might take a biscuit (or five) but rather because I felt no sadness for my father's death.

In fact, if I am honest (and I have no reason to be anything else), I felt relief. He had been a large, loud and terrifying man. Without him the life of the house seemed more manageable, less likely to erupt into unheralded shouting and rage. There were no more masculine rumblings behind closed doors to make me feel even smaller and more insignificant than I was. I suppose that I felt more comfortable in a house with only women around me. I am not proud of my lack of feeling for my father's demise, I am simply recording the truth as I see it. My adult self is certainly not going to blame the child that had not learned how to respond to the death of a parent.

I remember little of the remainder of that first night. I must have turned my back on the stiffening form in my father's chair. I must have walked across the room towards the door. I might even have bent down and placed my shoes on the correct feet. Who knows what a child in shock will do? When did I stop laughing? I do not know.

Certainly, I returned to my bed. I must even have closed my eyes and slept. I believe that I left my bedside light on, for I remember the loud click it made as my mother switched it off in the morning.

13

Did that mean she had not looked in on me during the night, or that she had, for once, taken pity on me and left me with a talisman against my likely nightmares? I would like to think it was the latter. I do not know.

When I had eaten all the biscuits and hidden the evidence of my theft, I returned to my room and to whatever book I was reading at the time, hoping to escape into someone else's world, as was my usual habit when I could no longer cope with my own.

In the hours since Father's death I had caught my mother watching me in a calculating way, as though working out just how far she could manipulate me into being her support, transforming me into the new man of the house. At the end of each inspection she would look down her nose and pull her mouth into a pout, as though disappointed with what she had learned. It appeared that I had been considered and then discarded for this role. But it did not matter now. *Selina* had come home. *Selina* would solve all our problems. Unlike me, *Selina* was just what my mother needed at this time. Now it did not matter that I had been weighed and found wanting.

Nowadays I think of an eleven year old as being a child, even in today's precocious generation. A girl of eleven might wear make-up and unsuitable clothes, but you would not think of depending on her in a family crisis. Selina was different: she was emotionally mature for her age. You invariably felt better about life when she was present in the house. I do not think it is just because she was my big sister and I looked up to her, in every sense, that I remember her this way. I believe she really was exceptional, and wise beyond her years.

2

Kate hadn't moved more than a couple of miles from her old house in Agatha Street, but this new neighbourhood even smelled different from Fridesley. It must be the presence of the canal, hidden behind a row of houses, and the lack of diesel fumes from the Fridesley Road. Although she was now much closer to the centre of the city, the rumble of traffic was more distant. In the early morning silence she heard a muffled voice announcing the departure of a train, then, a few moments later, the clacking of its wheels passing over the points as it pulled away from Oxford station and made its way northwards out of the city. During the day she would hardly notice it, but at this hour she could hear every slight, unfamiliar sound: the whine of the milkman's electric-powered float and the clang of the bottle on her front doorstep, a car engine starting up further down the road and the gear change as it disappeared round the corner into Walton Street.

Back in the kitchen, Kate returned the cat food to the fridge, then put on the kettle for fresh coffee. Perhaps she would have more luck when it was light and the sun had burned through the morning mist. She thought how good it would feel to go for a run across Port Meadow. Somehow, with the house move, she had given up her usual morning run. It would do her good to turn her back on cardboard cartons and unpainted walls and get outside for a while. After finishing her coffee, she went upstairs to put on her running gear, then set off down the road towards Port Meadow and the towpath. She wanted to call out for Susanna around the neighbourhood as she ran, but on the other hand she didn't wish to gain a reputation for eccentricity this early in her life as a Jericho resident. This thought didn't stop her from peering over walls and into hedges, however, hoping for a glimpse of marmalade fur.

Cleveland Road seemed to have a wide mix of residents. There were houses that had been spruced up and whose open blinds showed off polished wooden floors, pale modern furniture and imaginative lighting. There were the houses belonging to older residents: dark brown paint on the doors, beige or yellow rendering, and net curtains pulled tightly closed to deter nosy people from inspecting the lives going on inside. And then there were the houses with bicycles leaning against the dustbins in the front gardens, a couple of modest cars outside, and brightly-coloured, uneven curtains pulled most of the way across the windows: students.

Half an hour later, when she turned the corner back into Cleveland Road, walking the last couple of hundred yards so that her heart slowed back to its normal rate, Kate saw that there was more movement in the street as people edged cars out into the narrow street, or collected the milk from their doorstep. As she approached her house she saw a young man opening the gate next to hers.

'Morning,' she said.

'Hi,' he replied. Then, 'Bin day,' he added, smiling.

Binday? Was this a traditional Jericho greeting? Then she remembered the dustbins out on the pavement, which should have given her the clue, but she had been too busy searching for a glimpse of ginger cat to register what they meant. 'Oh! Thanks for reminding me.'

'We were always forgetting ours the first few weeks we lived here,' said her neighbour. 'And there's so much to throw out when you've just moved in.' He looked older than a student, but younger than Kate herself.

'I'll write myself a note so that I don't forget,' she said. Another note to add to the dozen or so that already decorated her fridge door.

'I'm Brad, by the way,' said her neighbour, who didn't seem in a hurry to return to whatever it was he did during the morning. Brad had copper-coloured skin, black hair and dark brown eyes with enviably long lashes. He must have been used to the surprise at his prosaic name, for he added, 'My real name's Rohan and my surname's difficult to remember. People asked me where I came from and when I said "Bradford", they called me Brad.' The explanation sounded well-rehearsed.

'Kate Ivory,' responded Kate. 'I work at home, so I expect you'll see me around quite a bit.'

'You do? Me, too. It will be nice to know there's someone else beavering away next door. My partner's out all day, of course, and it can get lonely, working on your own, don't you think?'

Kate's reply was guarded. She didn't want to get involved in chatty coffee sessions, at least not until she knew her neighbour a little better. 'Mostly I'm too busy to notice – I get very involved in my work. What do you do?' she asked.

'I'm an architect,' he said. 'Small-scale projects – conversions, things like that. And you?'

'I'm a writer,' she said.

'Should I have heard of you?' He smiled as though he knew what a cliché this was.

'Definitely!' There was no point in being modest about these things.

'I'll have to look you up in Blackwell's.'

'It's very possible that I don't write your sort of book,' Kate conceded.

'You never know,' said Brad, giving her the full advantage of his eyelashes. 'I have very wide-ranging tastes.'

Kate was just turning towards the side path when she had a thought. 'You haven't seen my cat, have you?'

'The marmalade one with the long legs and white feet?'

'That sounds like Susanna.' This was promising.

'I saw her yesterday evening, cautiously inspecting the hedge, but I haven't seen her this morning, I'm afraid. Has she run off?'

'She's only been missing for nine hours or so, but I'm worried she's lost her way, or returned to the old house.'

'I'll keep an eye out for her. Patrick and I are both cat lovers.'

Patrick must be the partner he mentioned, thought Kate. 'Thanks,' she said, and went indoors for a shower and a well-deserved breakfast before returning to the apparently endless business of making the house into a home.

Although she hadn't yet made any decisions about the decoration of the rooms, she had bought tins of light, warm yellow paint for the hall and stairwell. There was something so bleak about the sight that greeted her as she opened the front door that she had opted to civilise this space before doing anything to the rest of the house. So far she had painted the wall that led down past the sitting room to the kitchen. It wasn't much, but already it made a difference to the feel of the place. She would get the second wall finished today. Kate looked at her watch. She really didn't have time to get enough done, before leaving for her morning class, to make all the messy brush-cleaning worthwhile. She would fill the time by taking a look at the boxes in the spare room to see if she could find the rest of her kitchen equipment.

Upstairs, she looked around the back bedroom. She couldn't decide whether to make this her workroom, or whether to use the second reception room downstairs, that was intended by its architect to be used as a dining room. She rarely produced a meal that was formal enough to need a special room in which to eat it, after all, and it would be handy to be so near the kitchen, where she could regularly top up her caffeine levels.

The spare room was lighter and airier, certainly, but even when she had removed all the cardboard boxes, it lacked character. Downstairs there was a small, working fireplace and she quite fancied settling down by a cosy fire on a winter's day. Kate set about opening cartons and noting their contents.

Twenty minutes later, having unpacked the box she had been looking for, she screwed a hook into the recently-painted wall downstairs, then hung the new mirror on it. ('New' was a relative term in this case, since the mirror was second-hand, but not too badly spotted, and with a mahogany frame which she had cleaned and polished.)

She stood a couple of feet away from it and looked at herself. There was still a streak of white gloss paint across the front of her hair making her look older than usual (or more distinguished, she amended), but the mirror itself was excellent. A slight fault in the glass made her look taller and slimmer than she knew herself to be. This was just what she needed before leaving the house, she considered – something to give her an extra boost of confidence before facing the outside world. It was not necessary, in her opinion, for mirrors to adhere to the strict truth.

The hall was wider and brighter than the one in her house in Agatha Street, with sunlight streaming in through the glass panels of the front door. It occurred to Kate that the sun was rather higher in the sky than she had expected and she went into the kitchen to check the time. She had been so involved with the house that it had nearly slipped her mind that this was the first morning of her literature class. She just had time to find a black bin-liner and stuff all the strips of wallpaper lying on the floor into it. She might as well take advantage of the fact that it was bin day, after all.

Then she splashed her face with warm water and rubbed the dust off on a hand towel, pulled on a clean pair of jeans and sweatshirt, grabbed a fresh A4 pad and her copy of *The Mill on the Floss*, before setting off in the direction of Summertown.

The gate was only a few steps away from the front door, but Kate turned and looked back at her new property. The door was painted dark green. She would have to change that. The outside was rendered and painted white. It was not exactly shabby but she could see that by the time next summer arrived she would have to budget for a paint job. Cream linen curtains downstairs, she decided, and a dark red door. A red with a touch of brown in it. And a tub of geraniums on either side of the steps.

Happy with her vision of the front of the house, she walked briskly down Cleveland Road, then turned left in to Walton Street. It was a fine, sunny day now, with just enough freshness in the air to make a walk a pleasant prospect.

Perhaps a literature class was too close to her everyday work to rate as relaxation. Maybe an author should take a Wednesday-morning class in something entirely different: musical appreciation, or archaeology. But Kate had never managed to rid herself of the sneaking feeling that she was an impostor in the world of letters, lacking all the necessary degrees, and completely ignorant of Chaucer and even Wordsworth. And so she had signed on for yet another literature class. This year's offering looked particularly interesting, with a reading list that covered novels from the middle of the nineteenth century right up to the early years of the twenty-first. She didn't recognise the tutor's name, but trusted the university's Continuing Education department to find someone interesting to teach the course.

There was no time now to look into any of Summertown's shops. She still hadn't got used to the fact that there were so many shops to visit, both in Jericho itself and in Summertown, just a little further away. When the class was over she might find herself something interesting to eat for her lunch, and maybe pop into the bookshop, too. Meanwhile, she had better put a move on, she thought, as she turned in to Ewert Place and entered the modern grey building.

There was always a lift to the spirit, as well as a slight frisson of nervousness, in entering a new class for the first time.

iii

I was not a prepossessing child.

I understand that this is one reason why my mother did not like me. I do not blame her for it. I do believe she felt the love that all mothers feel for their offspring, whether they want to or not, but 'liking' is something else. There are some people we can never like, however hard we tell ourselves that they are intelligent and virtuous.

By the time I was five I had come to the conclusion that liking someone was easier if they were good-looking. Perhaps if I had been a good-looking child my mother would have liked me, too. She would have looked at me and smiled, and touched the top of my head, the way she did to Selina. Selina's hair was a soft and silky blonde, inviting a caress, while my untidy thatch was coarse and brown. Occasionally my mother would pat it gingerly, as though it were a dog that had been known to bite the hand that fondled it.

My mother had a great appreciation of beautiful things. She had taken William Morris's advice to heart and liked to surround herself with objects that were aesthetically pleasing. She had nothing in her house that she did not believe to be beautiful. (The merely useful she ignored as not being her concern.) Even my father was a handsome man, as well as an intelligent and successful one, and in social situations she would watch him with pride, as though his fine looks were the most important aspect of the man. Perhaps I am underestimating her. I never knew her well enough to appreciate her deeper feelings – or even to find out whether she possessed any – but that was how she seemed to me.

She owned two delightful little landscapes by Cotman, hung in the downstairs hall, well away from direct sunlight, where one might come across them by chance, and a lovely little bronze by Adams that she kept on her Victorian work-table. She liked to pick it up, I remember, and run her hands over its burnished surface as though polishing it. She looked after these *objets* herself. The cleaning woman was not allowed anywhere near them. She washed her delicate china in a special bowl, using a soft linen cloth with which to dry it. And she would let no one else wash her underwear, either. For this she had a special white soap, unperfumed and finely grated, which she dissolved in tepid water in the basin in her own bathroom. The garments were made from silk crêpe de Chine in the palest coffee colour, trimmed with cream lace. She sprinkled a few drops of rosewater into the final rinse so that I always associated its scent with my mother's appearance in the mornings. The first thing she would do after breakfast would be to arrange the flowers in the vases throughout the house so that the eye would be caught by beautiful, sweet-smelling things.

I can see that I did not fit into this carefully constructed idyll. I was plain, with pale, freckled skin and hair that would never lie smoothly against my head but which stuck up in tufts as though an electric current had just passed through it. I would catch my mother's disapproving stare upon me and then my feet and hands would grow larger and my shoulders hunch forwards to protect my narrow chest.

My father was a barrister, and a successful one. It would be difficult to imagine my mother marrying a man who was not successful. He dressed well and wore his clothes like an actor. He held himself upright without any conscious effort, and he moved like an athlete.

My mother would comment, with a sigh, that she might have had a brilliant career on the stage, but she had given it all up for marriage with my father, and for me.

'Yes, for *you*, Joseph,' she would say, sorrowfully.

As she mentioned my name she would frown, and her gaze would rest on my recalcitrant tufts of hair, then drift down to the freckles on my nose, the blush that suffused my cheeks and the socks that lay in folds around my ankles, and I would know that in my case, if not in my father's, the sacrifice of her career had been a bitter waste.

Now, all these years later, I wonder just how good an actress she would have been. She had a commanding presence, it's true, and a carrying voice, but she moved without grace, her feet in their narrow shoes planted squarely on the ground with every step, her knees always a little bent, her chin pushed assertively forward. The range of roles she might have played was narrow, though I think she might have made an impressive Lady Macbeth. But as for something more modern, or even a comedy, I just cannot see her managing it. She was aware of her clothes, and she could arrange her features into smooth lines in front of the mirror, but she did not really *inhabit* her face or her body.

What made me say that? I had never noticed it before. But now that I see the words on the page I believe they are true.

She would have been so angry if she could have read them. Oh, but she would never have forgiven me for seeing through her like that.

I can hear her voice quite clearly, even now. 'What *do* you look like? Take that stupid expression off your face immediately. I can't imagine how I ever produced such a ridiculous child!' It was not that she set out to be unkind, rather that her exasperation with me simply overflowed into words. These moments of devastating honesty were more frequent when she was drinking, I realise, looking back at it. Just before she spoke she would tap the rim of the glass with her long fingernails. That faint, repetitive *ting* fills me with apprehension even now. And when I think of my mother, I am always a child.

It is funny how she always preferred red wine. I would have thought her choice would be something flinty and dry, and very, very pale. But no, she always chose the red. Perhaps there was more warmth inside her than I ever imagined, finding some fellow-feeling in the rough tannin and voluptuous fruit. Perhaps she felt in need of its nutrients. Certainly she cupped the goblet between her narrow hands as though absorbing warmth from the wine it held, rather than imparting her body's warmth to it, as another might do. She sipped slowly, savouring every delicate mouthful, acquiring the red arc on her lip that I had noticed on the night of my father's death, and the serpent's trail down her moist pink tongue.

3

Kate found the lecture room on the first floor. There were already half a dozen students settling themselves into place and so she took a seat to one side, close enough to the front to contribute any intelligent comment that might occur to her, but far enough away not to be too conspicuous if she could not think of one. She recognised one or two faces from previous courses, but no one she knew well enough to talk to. She appeared to be the youngest person there, presumably because most people her age had a proper job instead of being free to take the morning off if they felt like it. And, as usual, there was a solitary man, sitting in the corner and trying to look invisible.

The time was coming up to ten o'clock and she looked towards the desk at the front, then checked the leaflet in her file. The tutor should have been male, but the person standing at the front of the class was definitely female. With a slight shock, Kate recognised her as Faith Beeton, a member of Bartlemas College, and a friend of hers. She was sure that Faith was an expert in her field and a perfectly competent teacher, but she was not at all sure that she wanted her teaching *this* class. She brought back too many uncomfortable memories.

They had met first a few years ago when Kate was helping with a summer school at Bartlemas. On that occasion one of the Development Office staff had been pushed from the college tower and Kate herself had been threatened and attacked. More recently, she had met more members of the college whom she hadn't taken to at all, and the subsequent death of one of her neighbours, also a colleague of Faith's, had prompted her to leave the house in Agatha Street and move to Jericho.

At the sight of Faith, standing there ready to begin the class, it all came flooding back, and she couldn't help wondering whether the woman wouldn't bring some new catastrophe into her life. Then she realised that Faith had seen her, had recognised her, and was looking at her in a friendly way, so she forced herself to smile in return. Having made eye-contact, Faith returned to the business in hand.

'Good morning, everybody. Those of you expecting Dr Jones will be surprised to see me here instead. Let me introduce myself. My name is Dr Faith Beeton, and I am a Fellow of Bartlemas College and a University Lecturer in English Literature. I have taken over this class at short notice from David Jones because I'm afraid that the poor man was involved in a motor accident while he was on holiday in Italy. He's out of danger now, thank goodness, but it looks as though he'll be unable to take any classes for the rest of the term, at least.'

'Will he be all right?' asked one of the students.

'He's doing very well, his wife says. She flew back to England with him last weekend, so he must have been well enough to travel.'

'Send him our best wishes. We hope he'll be better soon,' said a second.

'Certainly.'

Kate noticed that Faith had changed since she first met her, several years ago, in Bartlemas Chapel. Then, Faith was a newly-appointed Junior Fellow, with a three-year contract, who covered her insecurity with a spiky, rather abrupt manner and a habit of regaling anyone who would listen with a series of abstruse facts. Now she looked much more self-assured, without a hint of self-deprecation, though Kate was pleased to note that she still had the same quirky dress sense.

'I know you're all disappointed that Dr Jones can't be here this term, but I'll do my best to deliver an interesting course. When we've got through a little necessary admin. work, we'll get straight on and consider the first book on our reading list.' Faith hadn't taken the chair behind the tutor's table but was pacing up and down the grey carpet, looking at each student in turn as though committing their faces to memory. Several students were staring at their notepads as though they found the experience unsettling and were studiously avoiding making eye-contact with her. 'Has everyone finished reading *The Mill on the Floss*?'

If anyone had failed to do so they didn't have the nerve to confess the fact to Faith Beeton. In spite of her friendly opening remarks, they all recognised that she was a formidable person. Kate watched her as she handed out various sheets of paper and asked whether people wanted to take a mid-term break. What was it about her, she wondered, that she always found disconcerting? There was nothing out of the ordinary about her short, dark hair and small, pointed face, her slight, wiry figure. Today she was dressed in a black suit with a crimson top visible in the vee of its neckline, and there were long gold earrings swaying beside her angled jawline. It must be the intensity of the stare from those dark, brilliant eyes. And she was looking thinner, too, as though she had too many things on her mind.

Faith returned to her desk and referred to a page of notes. The vertical crease between her brows was more pronounced, but it was a little soon in the term for her new class to be a cause for concern – and the row of grey-haired, middle-class women didn't look as though they'd be causing much trouble, anyway.

'I'm afraid that this term we have a new regulation,' Faith was saying, waving a sheet of paper at them, and Kate realised it was time to stop her flight of fantasy and return to the matter in hand. 'If we are to continue to receive funding from the Department, everyone will have to produce a piece of written work each term – an essay, in fact. This need be only fifteen hundred words or so, and I'm sure it shouldn't prove too onerous.'

Is this what I need, wondered Kate: just when I want to get on with decorating my house, someone produces a request for yet another piece of writing with a deadline. And it's not as though they're going to pay me for it. Doesn't the woman know I'm a professional? But Faith was explaining that class fees would double if they didn't do what she asked, and Kate supposed she would just have to get on with it.

'Now, let's turn to the first page of *The Mill on the Floss*.'

Kate was pushing her notes into her bag when Faith joined her, as quietly and unobtrusively as ever.

'Have you time to talk?' she asked.

'Now?'

'Yes.'

'I should be decorating the hall,' said Kate, picking at the yellow paint on her thumbnail, but then she noticed that up close, Faith wasn't looking well: there were new lines around her eyes and grooves beside her mouth. There was obviously something wrong. 'But I could put off decorating for half an hour or so. I need a break,' she added, ignoring the fact that she had already spent two hours at the class. Faith, after all, had given her a room in her house for a couple of weeks while Kate was house-hunting, so she owed her at least half an hour of her time. 'I can't ask you back to my place, though. It's in no state to receive visitors yet.'

Faith, whose notes were already packed away inside her burgundy leather briefcase, waited while Kate stowed the rest of her belongings, then led the way out of the lecture room, locking the door behind her.

'My place is too far. Shall we go to the café round the corner, the one behind the pâtisserie?' she asked. 'I shouldn't think anyone we know is likely to go there. No one will be interested in what we're saying.'

If Kate wondered why they needed to be so discreet, she kept her own counsel. As they crossed the Banbury Road, she thought she saw a friend of hers.

'Isn't that Emma?' she asked.

'Who?'

'You remember. Emma Dolby – Sam Dolby's wife.' She noted the disapproving expression on Faith's face: one should never define a woman by her marital status, Kate remembered, a little too late.

'She organised the "Gender and Genre" study fortnight at Bartlemas,' she added quickly. 'And she writes children's books, and teaches creative writing classes, and has about eight children of her own.' Now she was making Emma sound like Superwoman, when she was really a scatty, disorganised person who never quite caught up with the details of her own life.

'She sounds marvellous,' said Faith drily. Faith, of course, had produced no children of her own and, as Kate remembered it, had had no success with her attempt at writing a novel, either.

'I haven't seen her for ages,' said Kate, refusing to move, since Faith appeared inclined to stride on towards the coffee shop and forget about Kate's fecund friend.

Emma had emerged from a shop just ahead of them and paused in front of the wine merchant's, inspecting the special offers on the board outside. Kate was about to call out a greeting when she stopped herself. Was that really Emma? She was so used to seeing her friend encumbered with small children and supermarket bags, looking dishevelled, that she thought she must be mistaken. This Emma lookalike had well-cut hair and smart black trousers worn with a fitted casual top. And wasn't she slimmer than Emma? This woman held her head high and had an air of self-confidence about her. This could only be the Emma that Kate knew if she had been through some makeover show on the television.

At that moment a tall, tweedy man with thinning brown hair came out of the wine merchant's carrying a bottle-shaped bag and joined Emma. They turned and started to walk away. They looked as though they were together, thought Kate. And that wasn't Sam, Emma's husband, or George, his brother. In fact, she had never seen the man before.

'Well?' Faith was asking impatiently.

'I must have been mistaken,' said Kate weakly. 'I thought it was Emma Dolby.'

'That's what comes of having a novelist's imagination, I suppose. Come on.' Faith actually took Kate's elbow as though determined that she shouldn't escape. 'The café I was thinking of is down this way.' She spoke briskly, as if Kate was being indecisive and, well, *stupid*.

Kate gave one last puzzled, backward glance as the other woman and her companion disappeared northward, and then she followed Faith as she walked away from the Summertown shops and into a back street. Perhaps she really was mistaken about Emma, but the woman, in spite of her elegant appearance, had been carrying a Tesco's plastic carrier bag, bulging with special offers, instead of the shiny leather handbag that one might have expected.

But if it really was Emma, what had happened to change her so radically since Kate had last seen her?

iv

There was scarcely a week remaining of the school term after my father's funeral and so Selina had stayed at home with us, missing those last few days and returning to school only after the long summer holidays.

Our mother had fallen into what I would now term depression. A Slough of Despond. This wasn't just grieving, or sadness at her loss, but rather a complete negation of everything she had once been. She sat, sometimes smoking a cigarette, sometimes drinking a glass of the smoky-dark Côtes-du-Rhône she favoured. Many evenings she failed to change out of her dressing-gown, sometimes not even combing her hair, apparently sprawling all day long on the couch, doing nothing. I was so used to seeing her wearing what she called her 'face', with bright lipstick on her lips and all natural shine removed from her nose and cheeks, with her eyes carefully outlined with a dark pencil, and mascara on her lashes, that I scarcely recognised the pallid figure she had now become. Her smart clothes were left hanging in the wardrobe, and her polished court shoes abandoned in favour of flat-heeled mules. Even her legs were bare.

How could she stand this languor, day after day? Didn't she get bored? Didn't she wake up some mornings feeling that she had to leave the house, stretch her legs, move in the fresh air, talk to other adults? Apparently not.

She was incapable of dealing with the smallest practical problem – a dripping tap in the bathroom, the fact that we had run out of sugar, the ringing of the telephone. She sat there, frowning at her chipped nails and waiting for something to happen, for some wonderful person to arrive through the front door and deal with all these annoying problems for her.

'Be patient,' she kept telling Selina when my sister suggested anxiously that such or such a task needed to be undertaken. 'I can't do everything at once.' And then she carried on staring into emptiness. If we had been older we might have recognised her depression for what it was, and called a doctor. But we were too young, and I doubt whether she would have taken any notice of anyone, doctor or not, who tried to jolt her out of her passivity, and she was really not ill enough to be removed against her will to some mental hospital.

She'll snap out of it in time, is what we thought.

We think of depression as being a kind of sadness, but it isn't, it's a lack of motivation, a draining away of energy and the will to accomplish anything at all. Is it the listlessness that medieval theologians wrote of with such condemnation? Sloth. Torpor.

The synne of Accidie, as Chaucer called it.

Certainly there was something of despair in her mood. And children, like Chaucer, are liable to see depression as a sin, freely chosen, rather than as an illness. Later, many of us, through hard experience, learn to be more tolerant.

An uncle arrived, some half-brother of my mother's whom I had never met before. He dealt with the funeral arrangements and then disappeared out of our lives, looking bemused. I don't believe I have ever seen him again. I don't even remember his name. For a short time, while he was there, the house resounded to his masculine voice, and life felt familiar. I think that Selina was as relieved by his arrival as my mother: at last some of the responsibility was being taken from her shoulders.

On the whole, when an outsider was present, my mother did make an effort. She would curl her hair, put on a suit or a smart dress, paint her face, varnish her nails. As the doorbell pealed and the door opened, she was like a marionette jerked into life by a pull on its strings. She would put on her bravest smile, rise to her feet, allow hands to grasp hers, accept the proffered comfort. If her visitors noticed that the flesh was sagging beneath the paint, they were too kind to mention it. And in any case, no one stayed long.

'You don't want me here, chatting on as though nothing had happened, you poor thing,' I heard one woman say. She picked up her handbag and went away, leaving my mother looking like an overdressed doll in her corner of the sofa, fuming at being addressed as a 'poor thing'.

For of course she did want just that: someone to sit there and chat inconsequentially to her, as if nothing untoward had happened in the previous week. For a half-hour at least she would be able to pretend that her life was not overturned. I think she believed that if she could just sit it out, patiently and stoically, her life would return to normal. I'm not sure whether she missed my father as a *person*, as a companion, even. What she resented was the fact that her status, as a widow rather than a wife, was now lower than it had been while he was alive. She hated the expectation that now she would have to cope with any matters to do with money. She was old-fashioned enough to think that all such problems were for men to deal with, not women. Perhaps she even thought they rendered her unfeminine in the eyes of the world – and this would be one of the worst insults you could pay her. But did she really miss him? I'm not sure. And I'm not sure about my own feelings either.

On the one hand, I quite enjoyed the extra attention I was getting, not to mention the extra sweets and biscuits that people thought would make up to me for the loss of my father. I felt at that time, as at no other in my life, that my unfortunate looks and awkward mannerisms were being overlooked and I was being treated with an unwonted indulgence by every adult who crossed my path.

At the funeral my mother looked magnificent, exactly as a widow should, as though she was an actress who had studied and rehearsed for this part for her entire life.

Perhaps she had.

I retain a vague impression of the coffin, though I looked at it only once before averting my eyes. It was of some dark wood – mahogany, perhaps – and there was a formal wreath of yellow and white flowers, very stiff and artificial-looking, on top. They reminded me of a heap of scrambled egg on a white china plate. A card with my mother's spiky black handwriting scrawled across it was stuck into its outer rim. I'm sure she had written something entirely appropriate. It was the kind of thing she was good at.

After that first quick glance, I looked away from the coffin, for I had a secret fear that my father might change his mind and push the lid open and reappear in our lives, only this time in an even more ghastly form. Again, in my mind's eye, I saw his livid face with the blue skin around his lips, the way he sat slumped half out of his chair, his fingertips brushing the carpet.

What else do I remember of that day? The smell of flowers and candles was overpowered by that of expensive scent and aftershave. The pews were full of dark suits and black coats. Many of the women wore hats, some with short, spotted veils. There was a low hum of greeting and conversation, not quite covered by the gentle notes of the organ as we waited in the porch for the hearse to arrive. I hardly remember the short walk down the aisle as we preceded the coffin and took our places at the front, just the sense that so many eyes were upon us.

In fact, I can remember few details of that day, or of the funeral itself, just the disjointed impressions I have written above. I wish that I could recall something more, something of the importance of the occasion. The death of my father had a profound effect on my future, and his funeral was the most solemn event in my young life, and yet I can't even remember what the weather was like. The month was July, but was it hot and humid, or one of those grey, blustery days with squalls of rain between the spells of sunshine? What hymns did we sing? To which prayers did I add my dutiful 'Amen'? What did the vicar say in praise of 'our brother, Arthur Greville', his excellent parishioner?

I recall wondering for a moment who 'Arthur Greville' was. Then I remembered that my father's name was 'Greville'. It was what my mother called him. 'Arthur' sounded like a stranger. Much later I wondered at what point he dropped his first name. Did he, or more likely my mother, consider 'Greville' a more distinguished name than 'Arthur', or had the name been given to the infant to flatter some rich relation, while the child was always addressed as 'Greville'? I don't know, and there is no one left alive now who could tell me the answer.

Mr Evans was there, slipping his arm through my mother's in his usual helpful manner, assisting her into the car. I see him leaning forwards, his face inclined towards hers; I hear his voice, a low, sympathetic murmur in her ear. I see the lift of her shoulder, the pettish rejection of his over-solicitous manner. And Selina must have been standing near him, her arm, too, a steady support for my mother's faltering steps. Certainly I was the least important person present that day. I spoke to no one, it seems to me now, and no one offered me more than a brief nod of the head in acknowledgement of my existence. Perhaps one doesn't offer formal condolences to a six-year-old boy. And if not condolences, then what can one possibly offer?

During the service I stood next to Selina, who stood between me and our mother, supporting both of us. She held my hand for some of the time. She was wearing her school uniform, which was of some dark colour, and the shallow crown of her hat had been decorated with a black grosgrain ribbon. I wore my grey flannel suit, with short trousers, and a black tie. This tie was lent to me by the same uncle who had arranged the practical details of the funeral, and was too wide and too long for a small child. I tucked the ends into the top of my trousers to keep it out of the way.

As I undressed that evening, I realised that I had omitted to return the tie. The uncle had left. I didn't want to bother anyone with such a minor problem on a day that was full of its own, major ones so I rolled it up neatly and placed it in the top right-hand drawer of my chest. I still have it. I wear it sometimes to dinner in Hall. It is a very nice tie, if a little sombre for every day. It is still useful for wearing at funerals, too.

4

Kate and Faith were seated at a small table in a steamy café in a narrow street in Summertown, ordering coffee and vacillating over the choice of pastries. Think of it as an early lunch, Kate told herself as she decided on a particularly large, cream-laden confection. Faith chose a plain flapjack, but then she had a puritanical streak, Kate had noticed before. Kate, on the other hand, believed in a certain amount of self-indulgence.

'What's up?' she asked, before plunging her fork into sweet, buttery pastry.

'College business, as usual,' said Faith gloomily. 'I sometimes envy your lonely work at the word processor. You don't have to deal with awkward people every day, do you?'

'Not *every* day, certainly,' said Kate judiciously. 'What is it this time?'

'A student is making trouble.'

Kate had imagined this to be a daily occurrence, not something to make a fuss about. 'Isn't it a bit early in the year? I didn't think the university term had started yet.'

'This is Noughth Week—'

'What sort of week?'

'It's what we call the week before term starts. Don't you remember?'

Kate had never got the hang of referring to the weeks of term by their ordinal numbers. She suspected that it was one of the ways in which Oxford let the rest of the population know they were outsiders; they didn't belong to the select few.

Personally, she saw nothing wrong with a straightforward date, like 9 October, rather than 'Tuesday of First Week' or whatever they wanted to call it. 'I'd forgotten,' she said. 'But do go on with your story.'

'Well, since it is Noughth Week, the students will be turning up in a few days' time, and this particular trouble concerns a second-year student. Apparently her grievance has been festering all summer and now she feels she wants to bring it out into the open before the new term starts. I could deal with her, of course, if things were normal, and I could squash her nasty accusations before they had time to do any harm, but the fact is that her case is mixed up with college politics.'

Kate had worked one summer vacation at Bartlemas, Faith's college, and hadn't enjoyed the experience. Lunch in Hall every day had been spiced with malicious gossip. Nearly every member of staff had been on the make, some of them even involved in serious fraud. But that had been a few years ago, she reminded herself, and the situation must have improved by now. 'The nasty accusations aren't against you, are they?' she asked.

'No, someone else is in the frame. But I'm Dean for Women Students and so the complaint lands on my desk.'

'And you can't decide who's in the right?'

'I'm pretty sure I know the truth of it, but that won't be good enough for some of the Fellows.'

'This is getting too complicated. You'll have to explain.'

'It all depends which faction you belong to,' said Faith, which made nothing clearer as far as Kate was concerned.

'Faction? Aren't you used to dealing with factions and cliques by now? I thought Bartlemas had always operated like that.' Kate stopped herself from glancing at her watch, but this could well take more than the half-hour she had originally allocated for coffee with Faith.

'This might take a few minutes more of your time, or even longer,' said Faith, confirming Kate's view. 'How much do you remember about the college? Aidan Flint was Master in your time, wasn't he?'

'And I met his successor, Harry Joiner, a couple of years ago, too. The word was that Joiner made a fortune from double-glazing and then decided he wanted to buy himself the kudos of an Oxford Mastership.'

'That sounds like the generally accepted version,' said Faith.

'I can't say I liked Joiner any more than Aidan Flint.'

'You're as forthright as ever, I see. It's refreshing after my mealy-mouthed colleagues, I have to admit. But even Aidan seemed quite civilised by comparison with Harry Joiner, though he narrowly avoided being arrested over some fraud to do with Development funds.'

'I hadn't realised he was involved,' said Kate, who had learned something of the affair from a policeman friend of hers.

'The Development Office was raising so much money from old members of college for worthy building projects that it proved to be too much of a temptation for Aidan and one or two others. They skimmed off a substantial proportion of the funds into their own accounts, I'm afraid to say.'

'But they weren't arrested?'

'They were all persuaded to take early retirement.'

Of course, thought Kate. That would be how it was done at Bartlemas.

'I don't think Harry was much of an improvement, in terms of moral principles,' Faith was continuing. 'Though he did bring even more money into the college. Well, Harry's left now, too – head-hunted by some global corporation or other. I'm sure he's happier with his fellow board members than he was in the Senior Common Room.'

'I suppose that little in the outside world prepares you for the bitchiness you'll meet in an Oxford college,' said Kate.

'And now we have a new Master,' said Faith, as though Kate hadn't spoken. 'His name's Oliver Crowson and he's a very different character altogether. The Fellowship felt that we should elect someone whose reputation was as the unblemished snow, and whose views on borderline criminality were censorious. We've lost our wonderful chef, of course,' she added, as though this told Kate everything she needed to know about the college under the new regime. 'Do you remember his raspberry bavaroise?'

'Vividly,' said Kate, forking in another piece of pastry.

'There's nothing like that any more, even at High Table. But there are compensations. College life's been comparatively calm, and we've managed to get on with some proper work without wondering what hideous revelation about us will be splashed over the tabloids this week. Our reputation is creeping back to its previous height and I suppose we can look back on the past few years as just a little blip in our six centuries of history.'

No, it took more than a few financial misdemeanours to dent the reputation of an Oxford college, thought Kate. Bartlemas would always survive, no matter what happened there, and some of the brightest young people in the land would still be queuing up to join its undergraduate body. And if the epithets 'smug' and 'self-satisfied' came into her head she managed to repress them and give her full attention to Faith's problems.

'But you hinted that there is still friction in the Senior Common Room.'

'Some of the members of the SCR are still fighting the Civil War.'

Seventeenth century, remembered Kate. But as close as yesteryear to the Bartlemas Fellowship, no doubt.

'Oliver Crowson, whose name so unfortunately resembles that of the late Protector, has introduced his no-frills, no-nonsense regime to the college,' continued Faith. 'Did you ever meet young Agnew, the new Maths tutor? No? Well, he's a little under-awed by college politics and he's pointed out that we're divided neatly into Roundheads and Cavaliers – or Roundies and Cavs, as he puts it. In the seventeenth century the college supported Charles I, of course, and melted down its silver to donate to his cause, but the present-day Fellowship isn't as united as it was then.'

'So the Cavs want raspberry bavaroises, while the Roundies won't even have a teaspoon of jam on their rice pudding,' said Kate, translating Faith's story into terms she could understand. 'But apart from giving everyone indigestion, what other effect does this argument have? And, if it isn't a rude question, which side are you on?'

'If we have to use these ridiculous terms, I'd have to say I'm a Roundhead. Couldn't you guess?'

The crimson blouse Faith was wearing was silk and matched her lipstick; her earrings were heavy gold. On the other hand, she had eaten only half her plain flapjack and then laid her fork neatly on her plate, while Kate had chased down every last crumb of sweet pastry so that she shouldn't miss any of it. But Faith had never been simple to read.

'There are still a few of us left who believe in upholding academic standards as well as enforcing reasonable levels of discipline,' said Faith, as though she were some ancient, grey-haired don. 'I would like to think that an Oxford degree still stood for excellence.'

'Sounds reasonable,' said Kate cautiously.

'But the others, and I fear they are now in the majority, see our undergraduates as "product", as though we were all marketing men, looking to get the greatest profit from our teaching operation.'

'And how would they do that?'

'Students pay fees, and accommodation costs as well if

they live in college or in one of the college student properties, but that's just the start of it. They —' and Faith spoke the pronoun with the deepest contempt — 'have calculated how much an Oxford graduate can expect to earn over his or her working lifetime, and just how large a proportion of it the college might expect to receive back in donations over the next thirty or forty years.'

'I'd heard that that was how they operated. It's not unexpected, is it? And I don't suppose it's even dishonest.'

'But what does it lead to? Discipline breaks down because you mustn't alienate the little darlings. And we've long since stopped expecting them to be able to spell or punctuate, let alone know anything about syntax and grammar. Look at this,' she said, reaching into her bag and handing over a scrap of lined paper, torn from a notebook.

Dear Ms Beaton, I cant get my essay
finished in time this week, I did'nt find the
Sidney book in the library, someone else
must have borrowed it, so will hand it in
next week, if thats alright. K. Kettleby

'And this is a student of English Literature?' asked Kate.

'She's expected to get a 2.1,' said Faith. 'And she couldn't even get my name and title right.'

'Irritating,' agreed Kate. 'But surely that's not what's keeping you awake at nights.' She looked regretfully at her empty plate. The tables around them were filling up with women shoppers tucking into chicken salads and cheese and biscuits. Lunchtime. Perhaps she should offer to get them both a ham sandwich? But Faith waved away the suggestion. She seemed impervious to hunger.

'As I said, some of us try to keep to the old standards, but you always get a few stroppy students who use the system to their own advantage. They know there are certain senior Fellows who will support them, and that makes them think they can get away with outright insolence! How can we keep any discipline if our authority is constantly undermined?' She paused. 'Maybe we should have that sandwich after all. Make mine an egg salad,' she added.

Faith's anger at her colleagues used up as much energy as her own jogging session round the streets of Jericho, noted Kate, as she queued to pay for their sandwiches.

'And you're having trouble with one particular student,' she said, before biting gratefully into her chicken roll.

'Daisy Tompkins,' confirmed Faith, using her knife to divide her egg sandwich into eight tiny portions. 'She comes from rural Oxfordshire and she's the first of her family to go to university. She's hard-working, I'll give her that, but I get the impression she's used to being the little princess.'

Kate could see that was an attitude that would get up Faith's nose. Faith, as far as she knew, had reached Oxford the hard way, with no helping hands or encouragement along the road. 'And you mentioned that she's made a formal complaint about someone?'

'That's right. She's complained about a colleague of mine, Joseph Fechan. That's spelled F-e-c-h-a-n, but pronounced to rhyme with vain. Not that he is, mind you.'

Kate tried hard not to feel prejudiced against a man who spelled his name one way and pronounced it in quite another. What had Fechan done, she wondered, for Daisy Tompkins to put in a formal complaint and for Faith to get in such a state of anxiety? Had he made sexist remarks, or placed his damp hand on her bare knee? Faith was looking at her least forthcoming, but she chanced a question anyway. 'What's she complaining about?'

'Unfair assessment of her essays. And she says he picks on her in tutorials. He's sapped her confidence, apparently. And she claims he discriminates against her because she has a working-class background.'

'I should have thought that last was a cause for celebration. Didn't I hear that you're supposed to be attracting more students from state schools?'

'Yes. Which makes it even more awkward. If Daisy chooses to make all this business public, we shall look like complete bastards, maltreating the poor little outsider. It doesn't help, of course, that Joseph comes from a posh background, has an old-fashioned educated accent and has no intention of converting to modern sloppy speech patterns.'

Kate amended her image of Joseph Fechan from leering lecher to elderly ascetic with long white hair and a prim mouth. Now she considered it, even his name had an antique ring to it. 'Your friend Mr Fechan is getting near to retirement, I suppose?'

'Not at all. He's only a couple of years or so older than you.'

'Mid-thirties, you mean?'

'*Late* thirties,' said Faith, with her usual honesty. 'I have to admit that he's not the most prepossessing man I've ever met, but underneath the awkward manner – he's shy, of course – there is an excellent mind and a highly-principled person. And did I mention it? He is, in fact, Daisy's Moral Tutor.'

Kate addressed herself to the rest of her sandwich in silence, thinking about this young-old man who had fallen foul of a pert little thing like Daisy Tompkins. She had met one or two men resembling Faith's description of Fechan. She thought they were a dying Oxford breed, but apparently there were still some of them around. And what did a Moral Tutor do, for goodness' sake? It sounded like a hangover from Victorian days.

'Don't write Joseph off as an anachronism,' said Faith fiercely. From the expression on her face, she must have read Kate's thoughts. 'We need more like him, not fewer.'

'If you say so.'

'This business with the student is just an excuse, of course. It's hard to get rid of a college Fellow, but if they can make Daisy's accusations look as tacky as possible – and can make them stick, too – they might be able to achieve it. At the very least he will be rendered powerless and sidelined.'

'But shouldn't your Fellows be accountable for their actions? If Fechan really has been harassing this student, he should be made to pay for it.'

'Let me tell you a story. You can think of it as a metaphor, if you like.'

'Go on.' Faith couldn't help sounding like an English teacher, supposed Kate. She wondered whether she should get them both a second cup of coffee, but she didn't want to sit in this coffee shop for the whole afternoon.

'I was out walking in the countryside around Garsington last weekend. Do you know it? You can see for miles from the top of the hill. It was a beautiful day, the air clear, as it so rarely is in this part of Oxfordshire, and above my head I saw a majestic bird with black and white bars on the underside of its wings. It soared with grace; it rode the air currents with authority. I knew from its forked tail that it must be a red kite, and a big one, at that. When I lifted my own arms out to the side to measure myself against its wingspan, I reckoned that we were about the same breadth. I watched it for a while, taking pleasure in its mastery of the sky, and then I saw that a group of smaller black birds – crows, they could have been, or perhaps rooks, I can't tell the difference – but whatever they were called, they were harrying my kite, trying to chase it away. It – no, I'll call it "he", for I'm sure the bird was male – *he* bore the harassment for a while, merely moving this way or that to avoid the teasing of the lesser birds. But they persevered, and eventually my kite slipped sideways and downwards through the air, until he was free of them. Then he disappeared from my view behind a fold in the hill. The rooks, if that was what they were, returned to ground and to whatever it is that rooks do there. Why did they do it? Why did they chase him away, out of that patch of sky? What was the point? Was it because they couldn't bear to see a bird more magnificent than themselves without bringing it down?'

Kate wasn't skilled in bird psychology so she said: 'And you believe that Joseph Fechan is a noble creature, like your red kite, and your fellow dons are as petty as the rooks?'

'You think I'm being fanciful?'

'I don't know a lot about red kites, but I think they may be more handsome than they are noble. Don't they live on carrion?'

'Perhaps,' Faith said huffily.

'And worms, and stuff they find on rubbish tips.'

'All right! But even if you don't agree that they lift the spirit, you have to admit they *look* fantastic.'

'Like so many other worthless males,' said Kate, a little more forcefully than she had intended. From Faith's disgusted expression she judged it was time to change the subject.

'I'm getting some idea of what Joseph Fechan's like,' she said. 'Now, tell me about Daisy. Isn't that what you said the girl's name was? What's she like? I don't have a picture of her at the moment.' As soon as she had spoken, Kate realised that she was making a mistake. She had wanted to escape back to her own house, but now she would have to listen to the other half of Faith's story. Before she knew it, she would be involved in whatever it was that Faith wanted her to do. Her trouble was that she had a weakness for this kind of gossip. She told herself it was all good research for the characters in her next book, and provided an insight into the psychology of academics.

'Daisy Tompkins is a pretty little thing,' said Faith with a slight downturn of the mouth. Jealousy or dislike, wondered

Kate. 'She just misses being good-looking, in my view, but I'm probably in a minority of one, as usual.' Kate raised her eyebrows at her. 'You want me to be more precise? Well, she has fair hair which she coaxes into blonde, and large, light-blue eyes, and she's very slim – to the point where I suspect she may have been anorexic in her teens. I assume that she's ashamed of her teeth since she often keeps her mouth closed when she smiles.'

'Does that follow?'

'Oh yes. And I believe that anorexics have bad teeth, so that proves it.'

Kate wasn't so sure, but she let Faith continue with her description of Daisy, biased though she suspected it to be.

'That closed smile gives her a sly look that doesn't endear itself to me – but I'm sounding mean and jealous, aren't I? She's a blue-eyed blonde with a heart-shaped face and small features, and she wears skirts short enough to show that she has good legs. She attracts a lot of attention from men, I imagine.'

So I was right, thought Kate. A pert little thing. She could imagine the uncomfortable tutorials with Fechan in his moth-eaten gown (did Oxford dons still wear them to give tutorials?) and the mini-skirted Daisy with her burnished blonde hair and rural accent, leaning back in the shabby sofa and showing too much leg.

'I'm sure it's not a question of jealousy,' said Kate, not wishing to offend Faith any further. 'What about the girl's character?'

'I ought to tell you that officially she's a woman, not a girl, but with Daisy I'm afraid that "girl" is the term that comes to mind when you meet her.'

Kate stole another quick glance at her watch. She was keen to return to her nest-building back in Cleveland Road.

'This is really interesting, but I don't quite understand what it is you want me to contribute to this argument,' she said. 'I can sympathise with you, of course, but that doesn't help you much, does it?'

'What I really need is an unbiased opinion – that is, the opinion of someone who isn't a member of college and therefore a member of one or other party. Someone who is familiar with the college, but also has a good knowledge of life outside it. In particular, I'd like the opinion of someone who doesn't want Fechan off the premises for selfish reasons of their own. I have to admit that the man isn't very popular with a good number of my colleagues, and they, as a result, will take the side of Daisy Tompkins, whether she is justified in her accusations or not. I, and one or two others, on the other hand, think that Miss Tompkins is a sly little minx who is determined to make trouble.'

'Why?'

'For the fun of it, I imagine,' said Faith. Kate wondered whether Faith herself didn't enjoy doing the same thing.

'Perhaps she's looking for attention,' she suggested.

'I wish she'd do it by producing some outstanding work, rather than by ruining the reputation of my colleague. There, you can see how biased I am! I wanted to give you the file on her complaint so that you could read it through. I was hoping that you could look over the facts for me and tell me whether I'm being unfair.'

'Is that allowed? Should I be looking at private stuff like that?'

'Probably not, but you're not going to go running to the Master to complain, are you?'

Kate couldn't just leave Faith in the lurch. Somehow the fact that she had been listening to her for the past hour meant that she was already committed to helping her, she realised. And anyway, if she was honest, she was longing to get her hands on Daisy's file and see what all the fuss was about.

Faith had been skirting around the meat of the question for so long that Kate wanted to know the facts.

'And there's not a thick file to wade through, by the way,' Faith said, 'just a few sheets of A4. It won't take you long to read.'

The request reminded Kate of the eager writers she had met who had urged their short stories, or the first few chapters of their novel, or even the rough notes they had made towards this novel, into her unwilling hands, and asked her for an opinion. The reading of these works hadn't taken long, but working out how to comment on them in a positive and encouraging manner had been a lot more difficult. She had the impression that this task was going to be similar.

'I have to get back to college now,' Faith was saying. 'Are you at home this afternoon?'

'Yes. But I still don't understand why you want *my* opinion,' said Kate, making one last attempt to extricate herself. She had a wall to paint, hadn't she, not to mention a new book to plan. 'What can I do for you that you can't do for yourself? You're an intelligent woman and you have more experience of this than I have. What is it you want from me?'

'I thought I'd explained,' said Faith, surprised at Kate's vehemence. 'It's just because you're *not* involved that I want your opinion.'

'There must be lots of other people you know who could do it just as well, if not better.'

'You know the college, but you're not a part of it, and you don't know the people involved, so you have no preconceptions about the case.' Faith was repeating her argument as simply and as patiently as she could.

'This Daisy Tompkins sounds like a spoiled brat to me. She's succeeded in getting to Oxford, lucky girl, and now she's making a fuss about things not being fair. She should count her blessings.'

'What's wrong with you, Kate? You're not usually bitter like this.'

'Oh, put it down to my hormones,' said Kate, who actually meant every word, but now felt a little ashamed at having spoken her thoughts out loud to Faith. 'Take no notice,' she added, knowing that Faith would take her at her word.

'Then I'll just pop round with the folder later this afternoon. Don't worry, I'll just hand it over and disappear. I won't waste any more of your time. I know you must have a lot to do.'

And so at last Kate escaped back to her house. On her way through Summertown she looked out for Emma Dolby, but Emma, if it had indeed been her, was nowhere to be seen. And why wasn't she doing her shopping in Headington, where she lived, wondered Kate.

Before changing into her painting jeans she made herself more coffee and sat down in the kitchen to mull over what Faith had told her. By the time she had finished drinking her coffee she had come to the conclusion that, even if she didn't mind reading Daisy's file to find out what had been happening, she really didn't want to be involved in the messy business of college politics.

She might have worried about Faith's problem for even longer, but luckily the phone rang to distract her from it.

'Kate? Estelle here.'

Kate just managed to stop herself from saying, 'Estelle who?' She hadn't contacted her agent for several months and hadn't been expecting a call from her.

'Estelle, how nice to hear from you,' she said politely. 'How are you?'

Estelle, as usual, was rushing onwards and not listening to Kate. 'I'm just touching base, as it were, Kate. It's ages since we spoke. How are you getting on? I'm sure you're settled into your new home by now—'

'Not—'

'Excellent. I'm so glad. And you have plenty of ideas for the new book?'

'A few,' said Kate cautiously, looking at the modest number of pages in her new notebook that were actually covered with her handwriting.

'I'm so glad to hear it. I expect we'll have a first draft to look at quite soon, won't we?'

'I'm not—'

'Good. That's very good to hear, Kate.'

'I'm glad—'

'I won't keep you away from your work any longer. I just wanted to know that everything was fine with you.'

'I—'

'Goodbye, Kate.'

And Kate said 'goodbye' in her turn to a receiver that was emitting a dialling tone.

V

Six is very young to be sent away to boarding school, and it was considered too young by most reasonable people, even more than thirty years ago. But after nearly a week in that house, shut in with my mother and me, Selina had seen how things were, and had talked it over with me. I suppose it must have been true that I was being neglected, though being left to my own devices was something I would never object to. It's true, too, that I was getting over-involved in making my lists. I listed the contents of drawers and cupboards; I was cataloguing the books in my father's study; I even copied down the titles and artists of the pictures on the walls of the house, in my large but neat handwriting.

'It's not healthy,' I heard my mother telling Selina. 'Why is that child always reading and writing? He's nothing but a little bookworm.' But I couldn't understand what she was complaining about. I was a perfectly healthy child, even if undergrown and pale of complexion.

Selina had her own methods of dealing with the problem.

'Look at your shoes,' she said a day or so after her arrival.

I was sitting on an upright chair and my legs were sticking straight out so that I could see the toes of my shoes. They were a little scuffed, I suppose, but nothing too dreadful.

'Your big toe's trying to push its way through the leather,' she said. 'You should have had a new pair weeks ago.' She stared at me critically, allowing her light blue eyes to travel up and down my body and ending at the crown of my head.

'You must have a haircut before the funeral,' she said. 'And change that pullover. You've spilled something disgusting down the front of it. And why are you squinting?'

'I'm not.'

'I'll take you to have your eyes tested,' she said firmly. 'I think you need spectacles.'

I would have sulked at this for I had no intention of being addressed as 'four-eyes', but Selina had left the room, telling my mother what should be done, and when she received no response, set about doing it herself. If she couldn't solve my psychological difficulties, at least she could apply herself to the practical problems of my life. I think there is a lot to be said for that approach. There is something very comforting for a child to have its growing feet acknowledged in that way, while its increasingly compulsive behaviour is ignored.

Selina applied herself to the question of my education immediately after the funeral. Young as she was, I believe she was the one who chose my new school. She phoned her friends and asked discreetly where their brothers were educated and whether they were happy. (Selina must have been the only person who ever cared about my happiness in that way. I can't imagine that this would have been my father's main criterion when choosing a school for his son.)

She made notes on her friends' recommendations and acquired prospectuses. I expect she telephoned school secretaries and bursars to make her enquiries, for her voice could sound mature when she wanted it to. But she could hardly visit a school on her own, for no one would have mistaken her for anything but an eleven-year-old child when they saw her. She could have persuaded my mother to accompany her but I think she feared a sudden switch to vivacious mode, for my mother was liable to these abrupt changes of mood, frightening in their suddenness and energy. Selina was resolved to keep everything in our lives under control, and as normal as possible, and this meant that my mother had to be excluded from all practical matters.

And so she studied photos of playing fields and ivy-clad buildings, of scientific laboratories and music rooms. She repeatedly quizzed her friends and their brothers, and when she had made her choice she presented my mother with a short list of one. When my mother expressed reluctance to make a decision she argued the advantages of having me out of the way (though she didn't put it quite like that). There was no doubt in her mind that my mother would accept her decision. She sat by her side and encouraged her to write the necessary letters. I expect she even urged her to write out the appropriate cheque, but I didn't see this. She oversaw the shopping trip where my uniform and equipment were bought, ignoring my mother's sigh of exasperation every time she charged another expensive brown corduroy item to her account. But the only comment I heard her make out loud was: 'I don't know why you're making such a fuss about him. He's never any trouble, you know.'

And that was the highest praise I ever received from my mother. At the time I was proud to think that I never caused her a moment's anxiety, but now I can see that it is a judgement both of my own lack of spirit and my mother's lack of understanding of her child.

Yes, Selina was certainly an exceptional girl for eleven. She had seamlessly changed roles with our mother and now she was in command in the house. It was immensely comforting to know that things were once more under control, the way they had been when my father was alive, and this time without the undercurrent of fear which had flowed when he was in the house, alive and threatening.

Have I managed to convey at all the people in my life? My mother and Selina? My father?

I couldn't write much about Greville, my father, because as a child of six I couldn't begin to understand him. There must have been more to him than good looks and a healthy bank account. I see now that he was a passionate man. I don't think he would have been such a success at the law if it were not for that. He, rather than my mother, was the one who felt deeply. *He* was the one who might have been an actor if he had harboured such an ambition.

I only had to look at Selina to see that Mother and Father were good parents. My own shortcomings cannot be laid at their door. The genes they passed on were superior; their care of me, if sometimes severe, was exemplary.

The corner of my father's life that I saw was a very tiny one: he rose at six-fifty in the morning, he breakfasted with Mother on toast, marmalade and coffee, he left the house for his Chambers and I didn't see him again until, briefly, during the evening, he wished me 'good night' with breath that smelled of whisky and tobacco. Many weeks, when he worked late into the evening, I saw him only at weekends. How could I know who this man was?

If my father had lived, say, another ten years, I would have come to know him better and I would have appreciated his many good qualities. As it is, I remember him only as the loud, frightening presence in the drawing room, his voice booming up through ceiling and floorboards to reach me as I lay awake in my bed.

5

It was nearly five o'clock when Faith rang the doorbell. As she didn't immediately offer to hand over the blue folder she was carrying, Kate had to say, 'Please come in,' and lead the way into the kitchen, which still had its original tea-coloured ceiling and paintwork, but at least didn't have strips of blue and pink paper lying in heaps on the floor. Faith, she noticed, had stared into the two rooms they passed on their way to the kitchen.

'I think you'd better clean your hands before I give you the folder,' she remarked.

Kate obediently found white spirit and a cloth and set about removing the paint from her hands. At least she was spared from offering the other woman a cup of tea.

'It must have cost you a packet,' said Faith conversationally, watching as Kate scrubbed at her fingers. 'However did you manage to afford it? I hadn't realised you were so successful.'

That was Faith for you: direct, to the point, and inadvertently revealing her own jealousy and insecurity. Knowing just a little of her background, Kate didn't blame her for being that way.

'My father died when I was a child,' she replied evenly. 'Roz—'

'That's your mother, isn't it?' interrupted Faith.

'Yes. The scatty redhead. I think you probably met her.'

'I remember the hair and the scattiness. It was her name that eluded me.'

'It so happens that my father was well-insured, so the mortgage was paid off and Roz had enough for us to live on in a frugal kind of way. By the time she was ready to take off to parts unknown, house prices were soaring in the area and she was kind enough to give me half the proceeds when she sold the family home.' And now her own insecurity and bitterness were peeping through, thought Kate.

'How old were you?'

'Seventeen.'

'So, instead of joining your mother on the hippie trail, or even searching for your own club scene, you invested your share of the loot in sensible Oxford property.'

'Not immediately,' said Kate defensively. 'I waited for a few months and then I bought myself a studio flat in Kidlington.'

'Really wild,' said Faith drily. She stared at Kate for a moment and then added, 'I suppose that does explain some of the things about you I was puzzled by.' But what 'that' and 'the things' were, she didn't elaborate.

Kate finished wiping paint from her hands and washed them under the tap. 'I'll take it upstairs straight away and put it in what will one day be my workroom,' she said, taking the folder from Faith.

Faith, inevitably, followed her upstairs, taking mental notes on everything she saw.

'Why don't you use the front room upstairs to work in?' she asked.

'Because I've chosen that to be my bedroom,' said Kate firmly. Really, Faith would take over her life if she let her. 'How's your own novel going, by the way? I think you were doing a major rewrite last time we spoke. Did Foreword take it on?'

'I should have known better than to attempt to become a novelist. But it's the fashion, isn't it? Everyone thinks they can write a novel – and they can't. It's a complex structure – well, I suppose you must have found that out over the years.'

'Yes, I *had* noticed.'

'There are so many aspects to think about all at the same time: theme, setting, structure, dialogue. Not to mention choosing the point of view.'

'And then there is the plot, keeping up the suspense, and developing the characters,' said Kate, who didn't usually think about her work in such a cerebral way, preferring to improvise such things as dialogue and setting as she went along. As for themes, she believed that they became obvious once you'd finished writing your novel.

'I just haven't got the knack. Though, of course, I do know quite a lot about the theory.'

'It's odd how people who are really good at theory often can't manage the practical side,' said Kate.

She picked up a rag and wiped the dust off her desk, then placed the folder on it.

'I'll give you a call as soon as I've read it through and formed some kind of opinion.' And then she managed to usher Faith downstairs and towards the front door.

'What colour are you going to paint it? I expect you'll be using creams and neutrals,' said Faith, managing to look into the sitting room. 'Those colours seem to work best in an old house, don't they?'

'I haven't decided yet,' said Kate, who didn't wish to get into a discussion about her decorating ideas with Faith.

'Thanks a lot, Kate,' said Faith, finally, as they reached the door. 'I do appreciate what you're doing, really.'

When she had closed the front door, Kate returned to her careful application of ivory gloss paint to the outside of the sitting-room door. She would read the information on Daisy Tompkins later, after dinner maybe.

* * *

There were only three rooms that were habitable in Kate's new house in Cleveland Road: the kitchen, the bathroom and the bedroom. Consequently, when she had cleaned her paintbrushes for the last time that day, and eaten some salad and a cheese omelette, washed down with a glass of white wine, she took herself off to her bedroom, where she lay propped up on the bed, surrounded by the books she wanted to read (so much less demanding than writing her own) and within reach of the remote controls for her radio, CD-player and television set.

After a few minutes she realised she lacked only two things, so she went back downstairs for a packet of chocolate biscuits and a glass of water, then padded back upstairs to the bedroom. She looked up the television programmes to see if there was anything worth watching, decided there wasn't, at least for the next hour or so, and chose herself a book to read instead. Faith's folder on Daisy Tompkins had definitely lost its appeal.

She bit into the first chocolate biscuit. One of the good things about chocolate was that, like coffee, it smelled just as good as it tasted. Her mouth was full of chocolate biscuit when the phone rang. It was as well that she had had the foresight to bring it upstairs with her. She answered it on the fourth ring.

'Kate? It's Jon.'

Jon Kenrick had got into the pleasant habit of phoning her every evening. Kate settled back on her pillows and smiled at the receiver.

'Good to hear you,' she said. 'How's your day been?' They always started off this way, rather as though they were an old married couple. At least, never having been part of any sort of married couple, she imagined that this was the way they behaved.

'Busy,' he said. He sounded tired, she thought. She could

try asking him for details, but she knew he would tell her practically nothing. He was a very self-contained man, unlike other menfriends of hers who were only too happy to chat on for an hour or so about their working day if you gave them their cue. Kate picked up a second chocolate biscuit and looked at it.

'Do you want to tell me about it?' she asked, and took a surreptitious bite of biscuit.

'It involved one boring meeting, three abortive telephone calls and a large amount of paperwork. How about you?' he asked quickly, as though knowing that she would ask him for details, given half a chance.

I've half-finished painting the hall,' she said, choking on biscuit crumbs.

'Are you all right?'

'Fine.' She swallowed a mouthful of water to wash down the remaining chocolate. 'At least I get a glimpse of civilisation now when I open my front door. But the other rooms are little better than when you last saw them.'

'You have to go through the stage where it looks worse before it starts to improve,' he replied.

Yes, they were definitely getting too domesticated for comfort, thought Kate. 'And I went to my first literature class of the term,' she added brightly, just to show that she still had a brain.

'Was it good? Did you enjoy it?'

'Yes and no. Yes, I enjoy analysing the structure of other people's novels, and the other class members seem a pretty bright bunch, but there was one small snag: the usual tutor is incarcerated in hospital following an accident and his replacement is Faith Beeton.'

'Isn't she the one you stayed with for a couple of weeks or so when you were house-hunting? The one with the Spartan fridge contents?'

'Puritan, even. Yes, that's the one. She's a Fellow of Bartlemas College, where Jeremy Wells—'

'Ah, yes. I remember.' Jeremy Wells was one of Kate's neighbours in Agatha Street who met an untimely end in a car crash. It was memories like this that Kate was hoping to escape from when she moved to Jericho. This must have occurred to Jon, too, for he added, 'Still, I expect she's pretty knowledgeable about English literature. And you don't have to socialise with her if you don't want to, do you?'

'That's what I thought, but she asked me to join her for a coffee after the class and I could hardly refuse.'

'Not too onerous, though. I expect you could manage that all right. You probably needed time off from stripping wallpaper.'

'And then she asked my unbiased opinion of a student of hers. She dropped off the file on the girl this afternoon and now she wants to know what I think.'

'That sounds less of a good idea. Do you really have to get involved?'

'Faith can be very persuasive, and I suppose I owe her a favour for putting me up for that fortnight.'

'I'm sure you told me that you paid her rent in exchange for the use of her spare room. I don't want to criticise a friend of yours but I did get the impression that Faith Beeton could be quite manipulative.'

Kate had the impression that manipulating people was what Faith did best. 'I think you're right, but somehow I always get sucked into her schemes.'

'Have you read the file yet?'

'No. I've been putting it off. Maybe I'll do it tomorrow morning.'

'You've got a heap of things to do tomorrow. I should get on and read it now and then tell Faith you have no idea at all about this student of hers. The problem is outside your experience. You leave it entirely to her excellent judgement. It's not your responsibility, after all. It's hers. And you need to relax in the evening.'

'That sounds like good advice.' She spoke slowly, as if wondering whether she really enjoyed being bombarded with so many suggestions as to how she should conduct her life.

'And I suppose that as usual you'll ignore it.'

'I might find it easier to relax and ignore all other calls on my time if you were here with me,' she said. 'You can be even more persuasive than Faith, as I remember.'

'I wish I were there with you, too. I'd drive straight over to join you – it sounds as though you're eating chocolate biscuits, by the way – if I didn't have such an early start in the morning.'

'How did you know they were chocolate? I could save you a couple, if you like.'

'I must be getting old: I don't fancy rolling out of bed at a quarter to five in the morning, not any more.'

'That's not age, it's just good sense.'

'If you can't get rid of this chore Faith's landed on you, at least put your feet up for the rest of the evening.'

'As a matter of fact, they are up, physically if not meta-phorically. I realise I'm not good at saying "no" to Faith. But I'll take your advice about getting the file read and done with. And you're right: I needn't come to any conclusion about it, need I? Daisy Tompkins and Joseph Fechan are Faith's problem, not mine.'

'What funny names you go in for, in Oxford.'

'There's nothing wrong with Kate Ivory, is there?'

'Nothing at all.'

The name 'Kate Kenrick' flashed through Kate's mind, as though Jon had sent her a silent message, and then it disappeared again. She wasn't going down that route, even in imagination.

'I'll go and get the file and deal with it. I might even promise myself a glass of wine as a reward, just to celebrate getting shot of it, and then I'll watch something mindless on the box.' The thought of watching television with her cat draped across her knee reminded her of Susanna's absence. She'd been so busy all day she'd almost forgotten about her. 'And there's one more thing: the cat's disappeared,' she said.

'When did you last see her?'

'Yesterday evening. I've walked all the local streets looking for her. I just hope she hasn't tried to make her way back to Fridesley.'

'It's only one day so far,' said Jon. 'I expect she'll turn up tomorrow. You'd been keeping her indoors for a week or so, hadn't you?'

'I thought that would be long enough, but I was wrong. I've met one of the neighbours, though, and he's promised to keep an eye out for her. He seems to be a cat lover.'

'I'll ring you again tomorrow evening and you can tell me whether she's turned up.'

'You haven't told me how you are and what you've been doing,' said Kate, realising that she'd been talking about herself all the time.

'It was just a standard day, and I'm fine,' said Jon. Then he added, 'Oh, there was one thing. I had a letter from my sister.' He sounded apologetic, as though he couldn't possibly expect Kate to be interested in his affairs.

'And?' she encouraged him.

'She and her husband seem to be having some kind of argument at the moment. She's looking for sympathy from me, as far as I can make out. But I don't really want to take sides in their quarrels.'

'Maybe you should ask me to look it over and give you my unbiased opinion,' said Kate mischievously.

'If you're not careful, I'll take you up on that.'

Was this glimpse into his sister's affairs a sign that Jon was starting to relax and allow her further into his life? He usually kept his work, his family and his girlfriend in separate boxes. She wondered what had happened to him in the past to make him so unwilling to give anything of himself away. Sometimes she felt as though she was being held at arms' length, emotionally if not in reality. It was possible that one day she might want more from a relationship, but with Jon she wasn't sure that she would ever have it.

Before picking up the folder Faith had left with her, Kate went to the back door and called hopefully for Susanna, but no small cat appeared, yowling for her supper.

vi

I went away to school at the beginning of the following term. My mother drove me there and inspected the plain white bed in its cubicle, identical to all the other cubicles in the dormitory. Selina had already left for her own school, otherwise I am sure she would have been there, too.

My mother left, first giving me a peck on the cheek and telling me to be a 'good boy' and do what I was told. I watched her car disappear down the long drive, accelerating as it neared the gates and leaving a puff of blue exhaust smoke to remind me that she had once been there.

Going away to school may have made my relationship with my mother more remote than it had been previously, but it hardly changed things between Selina and me. For the past couple of years we'd only ever seen one another in the school holidays. And now on Sunday evenings when we were expected to write letters to our parents I could write the conventional one to my mother – even at six I could dash such a thing off in five or ten minutes, with accounts of the house cricket match and my pleasure at early steps in Latin – and then I could write a letter to Selina that contained more of my real thoughts.

There was a belief among the boys that a junior master read our letters before they were posted, but I didn't believe he paid much attention to them. They must have been tedious reading for an adult. Perhaps there were one or two troublemakers whose missives were examined, but I don't think anyone bothered with those from the pen of a child as quiet and mousy as I was.

This weekly letter became a habit with us, for Selina always wrote to me in her turn, from her own school. It felt like a luxury, the only luxury in my life, to be able to spend twenty minutes every week talking, uninterrupted, to Selina, telling her everything that had happened, confiding my small triumphs and my many humiliations to her without fear of derision.

And on Tuesday morning her reply would arrive without fail. I would save her letter for the brief half-hour after Prep. and before bedtime, when we were allowed to pursue our own hobbies and amusements.

And so I learned about Selina, for I suppose that she, too, needed someone to confide in and at the time she had no one better than a small brother for her confidant. I think that in those letters we forgot the distance between us, and the difference in our ages.

Her letters were light-hearted and amusing, and they cheered the heart of a small boy marooned in a strange place. She told me of the choir competition – Selina sang with the altos – where her school came third. She wrote of tennis matches lost and won, of her friends and of her teachers. And, always, she wrote with a light touch, with never a word of complaint for an injustice. She saw only the best side of every person and she searched for the blessing to be found in every small failure.

This correspondence of ours was like talking to myself, or to God, only with Selina I knew that someone was listening and taking notice of what I had to say.

6

Next morning, as she drank her coffee, Kate was rereading the notes she'd made on the class discussion of *The Mill on the Floss*, wondering how much effort it would take to turn out an essay on George Eliot for Faith Beeton. She had a copy of Gordon Haight's biography of Eliot in one of the boxes upstairs, and she supposed she should reread it before attempting the essay. She had to remind herself that she couldn't just launch into a piece of work like that the way she could into a chapter of fiction. Faith would soon spot the fact that she had based it on little but her own imagination, she was sure. She'd get on with it this evening, though. If she had to write an essay, she might as well get it done so that it wasn't hanging over her head all term.

Meanwhile, she had the other piece of work she had promised Faith, the one concerning the student, Daisy Tompkins. She had skimmed the contents of the folder the previous evening, as Jon had suggested, but she was tired and hadn't concentrated properly, so she hadn't yet formed an opinion about them. Jon was right about one thing, though: thoughts of Daisy Tompkins would prevent her from getting on with anything productive in the house, so she'd better read through the notes again. She pushed her literature file to one side and took out an A4 pad. The kitchen table was starting to look like her study, she thought, and it was all down to Faith Beeton.

She opened Daisy's file and looked again at the contents.

They were sparse enough. She listed them on the pad. There was a typewritten sheet, signed by Daisy Tompkins, setting out her complaint. Then there was a handwritten report by Joseph Fechan, DPhil, in a hand so small and cramped that Kate had had difficulty in deciphering it. Dr Faith Beeton had written a very brief report as Dean for Women Students, which Kate guessed must be a draft since it was so skimpy. In addition there was a statement by someone called Kim Kettleby, who appeared to belong to some militant feminist organisation and who was supporting Daisy, as far as Kate could make out, on the grounds that she was female and therefore part of an oppressed underclass and by definition quite blameless.

Kate reread Daisy's complaint. She had to push her coffee mug to one side to make room for the contents of the folder. The kitchen table was getting very crowded but at the moment it was the only working surface she had and it was having to accommodate her breakfast and her literature course homework as well as Daisy's file.

Daisy asserted that she had come up to Bartlemas as a hard-working and successful student, with excellent references from her A-level teachers. Bright-eyed and eager to learn, Kate translated. (Stated baldly, it sounded quite brash, but Daisy managed to write diffidently, putting forward other people's opinions of her work rather than her own.) She had applied herself to her studies since arriving at college, finding, as she had expected, that the work was more advanced and that there was a certain amount of pressure to get through the reading and essay-writing that was expected of her. According to Daisy, everyone was satisfied – even pleased with both her attitude and her work – everyone, that is, except Joseph Fechan. It all seemed quite petty to Kate, but she read on. Daisy and Jan Rooling, a student who was following the same course, saw Joseph Fechan for a tutorial every Tuesday morning.

At this point Kate was forced to put to one side her expectation that this complaint was all about a pretty young student and a lecherous old tutor. Unless he had managed to dispose of Jan Rooling, it looked as though there would be no opportunity for any sexual moves on Fechan's part. So what had he done that was so dreadful that she had to lodge a formal complaint? Dr Fechan, Daisy alleged, had 'picked on her'. He had 'made her look a fool in front of Jan Rooling'. He had marked her essays consistently lower than she was expecting and he had undermined her confidence by his snide remarks so that she lost confidence in her own abilities and consequently had difficulty in all areas of her life. Her social life had suffered. She lost interest in running, an activity she had previously enjoyed. (Well, anyone could lose interest in running, Kate believed. She had done so herself for months at a time, and she had no Joseph Fechan to blame for it.) Daisy wrote that she had eventually visited the college doctor who had been concerned about her mental state and had prescribed a course of antidepressants.

So, on the face of it, Daisy had changed from a bright, happy young woman to an introverted depressive, lacking in self-confidence. And all due to the nasty Mr Fechan. In addition, according to Kim Kettleby, Daisy Tompkins was a saint. Kate doubted it. Few humans, if any, were saints, in her experience. And there was something about the simple certainties in Daisy's account that she distrusted. Life was never that straightforward; cause and effect were never that obvious. She would have to go through it again.

Kate applied herself to the sheet of paper as she would to a chapter of George Eliot's *The Mill on the Floss*. The piece was well-written, she admitted, even a little more succinct than Eliot's. Spelling and grammar were conventional and free from errors. The argument was neatly laid out and well-presented. And that was where the flaw lay.

There was something *too* neat, *too* organised about it. Each effect had been thought out before Daisy wrote it. It reminded Kate of a particularly well-conceived and executed chapter of one of her own books. In her own case, she would have sat down and worked out what she wanted to say and what effect she wanted to produce in the reader before putting it on to the computer. Is that what Daisy had done?

Or was she, Kate, being influenced by what Faith had said? It was all very well expecting her to be an unbiased observer, but Faith had planted the seeds of doubt in her mind before Kate had even opened the file. She looked at Daisy's statement again and noticed that, although the girl wasn't accusing Dr Fechan of any sexual impropriety, she still managed to give the impression that there was something creepy, or a little unsavoury, about him.

> I dreaded my tutorial. Whenever I had to go to his room, I felt awkward and anxious about what would happen. I was always apprehensive about what he would say. I could feel my face turning red even before I sat down, and I was shaking with nervousness. I was glad I had Jan Rooling with me, even if it was embarrassing to have her listening to what Dr Fechan was saying about me. But I wouldn't have been able to face it alone; I would have been too frightened.

Was Daisy a simple, put-upon girl or was she, in fact, much cleverer than Joseph Fechan was giving her credit for?

Kate glanced at the supporting evidence provided by Kim Kettleby. Again, if she believed Faith, this young woman was hoodwinked by Daisy into saying what was necessary to assist her case. Daisy would have known the right words to use, the right attitude to take – the right buttons to press? – to make Kim leap to her defence. Faith had provided no background information about Ms Kettleby. It would have been useful to know something about her and her background before believing (or disbelieving) every word she wrote.

And the important item that was missing from the file, it occurred to Kate, was any sort of report from Jan Rooling. If she was present every time, surely she could have corroborated what Daisy said about Fechan. Was she browbeaten, too? Or did she collude with the tutor and send Daisy into a state of depression? Was it pleasant for her to sit there and witness Fechan tearing the other girl to shreds every week while she played the Good Student? Kate leafed through the papers just in case she had missed something, but there was nothing from Ms Rooling.

Or perhaps Daisy *was* just a naïve little thing who was overwhelmed by Oxford and was then made to feel a fool, with the result that she lost confidence in her abilities and could achieve nothing. What had Faith said about her background? Daisy came from rural Oxfordshire and was the first of her family to go to university, let alone Oxford.

Kate had some brief experience of rural Oxfordshire and knew that its inhabitants could be very – well, *rural*. She had lived for a few months in Gatt's Hill, south-east of Oxford, and had come to know quite a few of the locals. From her brief acquaintance with them she had learned that the neat, picturesque village was riven with factional arguments, and longstanding feuds.

There must have been something about the village, sprawling along the hilltop, with its wide skies and inspiring views, that could turn your brain and cause you to lose your sense of proportion, she had concluded. In a town, you were protected from the extremes of weather by buildings and pavements. The rain and cold were mere inconveniences, they weren't thrust into your consciousness by being *there*, present all the time, above your head, in front of your eyes: grey clouds scudding past, pushed by the bitter winds; black velvet skies at night, pierced by a million unfamiliar stars which were invisible in the city. Oh yes, she had learned that you could go mad if you spent too much time out there in the country, instead of safely cocooned in concrete and bricks.

She thought of Donna, who had looked after the garden belonging to the cottage she had borrowed in Gatt's Hill. Donna appeared streetwise and sophisticated, with her body piercings and her unconventional love-life, but underneath she was a simple country girl who was taken advantage of by someone older and nastier. Was Daisy in a similar situation? She had liked Donna, even though she had known her so briefly, and she liked the idea that Daisy Tompkins had the same uncomplicated character.

Kate returned to the opening of Daisy's account. No, there was something about it that argued against that idea: this wasn't the complaint of a girl who didn't know her way around. For one thing, Daisy had taken real care with her words. And surely, if she had produced a page of writing without a single spelling mistake, or a slip in punctuation or grammar, it showed that she had worked at it. This was no spontaneous outpouring, but a second, or even a third, draft. Novelists, after all, Kate told herself, knew about these things. She reminded herself that there were computer programmes to ensure the accuracy of one's prose style, but she had found that though they might correct some of your own mistakes, they subsequently compensated by adding at least an equivalent number of their own. And anyone who relied on a spellchecker was asking for their prose to be turned into gibberish.

She looked again at Fechan's comments. His writing wasn't untidy, but it was difficult to read. It was small, and very black, and the words were squashed tightly together so that they often merged in a confusing way. If she had set up her computer she would have transcribed his notes on to it and printed them out so that she wasn't held up by attempting to read his handwriting. As it was, she copied a few key sentences on to her pad in her own clear, near-Italic hand.

Kate was no handwriting expert, but Fechan's spoke to her of a tightly-controlled personality, one who was older than his years. A fussy old woman, she concluded, and one who didn't find it easy to express his emotions. This last was perhaps an unwarranted conclusion, but Kate didn't care about that. She read over the sentences she had transcribed. The man was hurt as well as angry. He didn't see that he had done anything wrong. More than that, he was convinced that he had done his duty. He had pointed out Miss Tompkins's mistakes and inaccuracies, not in an unkind way, but rather in an attempt to lead her into better methods. She was bright, he conceded, but she needed to develop a more mature approach to her work.

So far, it was just a case of which of them you believed. Of course, Kate could understand that if Daisy had been bullied, something ought to be done about it, but she couldn't help thinking that she had been drawn into a very minor disciplinary matter. Why couldn't Faith sort it out for herself? She answered her own question: college politics. Your view of the matter depended on whether you wanted Joseph Fechan to continue as a Fellow of Bartlemas, and on your attitude to students from state schools and how much latitude you should allow them. Faith was right in thinking that Kate was neutral on both counts.

She turned back to the folder. There were two statements on Daisy's side, just one on Fechan's. Why had no one asked Jan Rooling for *her* account? Or perhaps they had, and she had refused. Why? Was it because Ms Rooling couldn't agree with Daisy's version of events, and yet didn't want to be disloyal to a fellow student? Or that she didn't have the time, or didn't want to get involved? These were possibilities, too.

Kate dipped into the file to pull out Faith's brief note – not that she thought it would be any use at all to her. As she did so, she saw that there was a Post-It note stuck to the back, as though it had become detached from some other document and had affixed itself to this one.

The note was in Fechan's cramped black hand. Kate squinted at it. How on earth did Daisy know that his comments on her work were unkind when she could hardly read them?

> *Faith, I've tried to be fair to the girl, but she is a* monster. *She wilfully misinterprets everything one says to her. She dominates the unfortunate Miss Rooling. Her essays are slick and clever – and* shallow, specious, *and possibly* plagiarised. *She has no business being a member of this college. Are we still an educational establishment, or do we simply dispense valuable degrees in return for a modicum of State money? JF*

It was just as well that Fechan's outspoken comments were confined to this small sticky-back note. Now *these* words, she recognised, certainly *were* spontaneous. There were no second or third thoughts here, and she was pretty sure that the message he had written for Faith hadn't been worked over and revised the way Daisy's had been. She wondered what to do with Fechan's note. It would be a mistake to have it floating around in the file so that anyone might read it. In the end she stuck it to Faith's own report where she would be able to see it and could then dispose of it (or not) as she thought fit.

Kate started to write on the A4 pad. She could at least give Faith her thoughts on the matter, even if she had reached no firm conclusion.

DAISY TOMPKINS V. JOSEPH FECHAN

1. Daisy's complaint against Fechan contained more inferences than facts.
2. It appeared to be a carefully contrived piece that had been

worked over by a skilled writer who knew just the effect she was aiming for.

3. Kim Kettleby's support for Daisy had no weight since she hadn't been present at any of the tutorials.

4. Where was Jan Rooling's account of what happened?

After another few minutes she found she was doodling a bunch of small flowers on her pad, no nearer a conclusion.

vii

My father was a brilliant man. Everyone said so. I heard them saying it as they shook my mother's hand or kissed her powdered cheek on the morning of the funeral. 'Such a brilliant man.' One or two even turned to me and repeated it, in case I had not heard the first time. 'You must always be proud of your father. He was such a brilliant man.'

Perhaps he was. From my perspective as a grown man I am not sure that I would describe him thus. He had a quick mind, certainly; he could not have succeeded in his career if he had been slow and plodding. But I think he may have been flashy rather than brilliant. Down the long corridor of the years I can see him glinting and sparkling in every company, and I can hear the laughter rising from the group surrounding him, so that they seemed set apart from the rest, transcendent.

When we were alone with him he was not so genial a figure. He was like a magician who gives a resplendent performance on the stage, with coloured smoke and mirrors, who then puts his paraphernalia away in its box in his dressing-room and departs, a commonplace figure in a raincoat, out of the stage door and into the city streets.

Our paths did not cross often. We met at breakfast, where none of us was expected to make conversation, or only of the 'Please would you pass the marmalade' variety. If the marmalade was not his preferred brand, we would hear about it. If the news in his daily paper was not to his liking, he would emit growling noises from behind its screen, like an angry bear.

We tiptoed around his temper, Selina and I, trying to make ourselves as unobtrusive as possible. By the time he came home in the evening we were expected to be in our rooms, invisible and silent.

The greatest test was during Sunday lunch, a conventional meal, served formally in the dining room. And then, over the roast lamb and boiled peas he would bark questions at us, aimed, or so I believe, at ascertaining whether we were working well at school and had learned those things which he thought it appropriate for a child to learn.

I do not suppose the witnesses he cross-examined in court found him any more genial than Selina and I did, but I was too young ever to see him in action.

I see now that he lived his life in a permanent ferment of anger, but where the anger came from I shall never know. Perhaps he never reached the eminence in his profession of which he felt himself capable, or received the recognition which he felt to be his due. Perhaps he nursed some secret ambition – to be a musician or a comic actor? – which he refused to acknowledge. But his unfocused anger was like some malevolent stranger living with us in the house, poisoning our childhood.

They said he was a brilliant athlete, too. This must have been when he was a young man, at school or at university, for he never indulged in any sport that I can remember during the six years of our acquaintance, though he certainly took the greatest interest in my own sporting career, such as it was.

Perhaps I would have developed some physical co-ordination with encouragement; perhaps I might have found a sport in which I could demonstrate reasonable competence and which I might even have learned to enjoy. But I was no natural athlete, not at the age of six, and not afterwards, either.

My father did turn up to the very first sports day at my day school and watched me trail in second to last in the fifty yards dash. I did try, I remember, arms and legs flying out sideways with the effort. He was not pleased. 'Child looks like a windmill,' he said to no one in particular as he turned away.

At home he tried to teach me to throw and catch. I seem to remember that he presented me with a small bat, hoping I would learn to be a competent cricketer. Perhaps I am imagining this, the discomfort as I tried to hold it in the way I was instructed, and hit the rubber ball he bowled to me. Again, I did my best, for I was desperate to win his approval, but I had no natural talent for the game and he was expecting too much from a child of my age. I gained the impression that I bored him with my lack of skill. He had expected his son to be a credit to him, a child he could parade in front of the other parents and say, 'Yes, that's my son. He's a bit young to be captain of cricket, but he seems to be making a decent fist of it, nevertheless.'

If only he had asked me about the things at which I excelled. But he was not interested in the books I read, or even in my stamp collection, the nucleus of which had once belonged to his own father.

But I am forgetting. This story belongs to Selina, not to me. I do not need my story to be written down for I am still living my life. It is Selina who needs to have a memorial in words written on paper. If I were a craftsman she would have something solid in wood or stone. I would plant a garden, perhaps. But my only skill is with these words on this paper, attempting to tell the truth, even if it is only the truth as I see it. Which of us can do more than that?

I'm sorry, Selina, if this memoir will never see the light of day. Can you read these words, I wonder, or are they part of the endless dialogue that circles inside my head? Are those dull physicists, with their talk of multiple dimensions and alternative universes where all our possible selves lead their lives just a membrane's width away, right after all? Is there another Joseph Fechan who listens while I speak, or who reads my work over my shoulder as I write? Perhaps there is another Selina, too, who lives a contented life as a wife and mother in that alternative universe.

I wish I could believe that were so.

7

Kate might have wasted a lot more of her time but luckily she was interrupted by the ringing of the telephone. She picked it up with relief.

'Hello, Kate? It's Neil here. Neil Orson,' he added, just in case Kate had forgotten, in all the excitement of moving house, the name of her editor at Foreword.

'Neil, how are you? It's been ages since we spoke.'

'Sorry about that. I've been unusually busy for the past couple of months.'

'You're sounding very cheerful.'

In fact, he sounded as though he had returned to his normal, confident self. Only a few months ago Neil had had his bank accounts raided by identity thieves, and huge bills run up in his name. The experience had been devastating for him, especially since he had also been suspected of the murder of one of the thieves. Neil, Kate reckoned, was someone who defined himself by his possessions and status. When these were whipped away from him, he had collapsed. Presumably his money had been returned to him now and everything was sunny in his garden. Perhaps he had even found himself a nice young woman to fall in love with. Kate liked Neil and she was glad that things were going well for him. It made her life easier, too, to have an editor who was happy and successful.

'I've put in an offer for a house, so I shall be able to move out of my dreary rented place soon. That would cheer anyone up,' he said.

'I hope for your sake it doesn't need as much work doing on it as this one.'

'Oh, I've found a small firm of builders and decorators who are going to do the hard work for me.'

'That's good,' said Kate, trying not to sound jealous.

'And my social life's looking up, too. I'm not missing London quite as much as I did at first.'

'You've found some agreeable female company?'

'How did you guess?'

'It wasn't very difficult, Neil.'

'Her name's Verity, and she's small and dark-haired with big brown eyes. We must all have lunch together one day.'

'That sounds lovely. But Neil, I'm sure you haven't rung me up just for a gossip.'

'Well, I was wondering how the new book was going.'

'I haven't got very far with it yet,' Kate said warily. It was several days since she had given the new book a thought. Did he expect her to produce a proposal for it while she was in the middle of sorting out her house and finding places for all her belongings?

'It's all right. I haven't rung to nag, really I haven't,' he said, as though reading her mind. 'I know you're still settling into your new house, but I just wondered whether you'd had any ideas about it at all. Can you give me a clue, perhaps? I'll need something fairly soon to put in the catalogue.'

'I might be able to put a hundred or so words down on paper,' said Kate dubiously, 'but the finished product might be rather different.'

'I don't suppose you've got round to doing much writing yet; I do understand that.'

'Oh, you know me,' said Kate. 'I manage to get a couple of hours' work done first thing in the morning, before I turn my hand to paint-scraping and furniture-shifting.'

'Really? I'm glad to hear it.' Neil sounded relieved.

'I'm writing longhand in a notebook at the moment as I haven't quite finished my workroom, and my computer is still in a corner of a bedroom, which is why my ideas are rather fluid.'

'I can tell you're keeping yourself busy.'

'And I've signed on for a literature class. It's as well to keep the critical faculties sharpened, don't you think?'

'I didn't think yours needed much honing.'

'I always feel at a disadvantage in Oxford. Everyone seems to be so much better-educated than me. I feel I have to work harder, just to keep up.'

'Really? I can't say I've ever felt like that.'

'Every time I walk through an arched gateway into an ancient stone building, I feel positively intimidated.'

'It sounds like a problem with an authority figure,' said Neil astutely. 'What's happened? Have you fallen out with your father?'

'Oh, there are no problems there,' said Kate, omitting to mention that her father died when she was a child.

'So, is there anything you can tell me about the new book?'

Kate pushed aside the jottings on Daisy Tompkins and glanced down at the page of notes on *The Mill on the Floss*. Just for the moment, all new ideas had left her. She thought rapidly. 'I was throwing together some ideas about a story centred on an intense brother-sister relationship,' she said, putting as much enthusiasm into her voice as she could reasonably manage. 'It's a theme that fascinates me and I feel I could develop a powerful storyline around it. Of course, I'm still developing the characters at the moment, but I was thinking about setting the story around a family feud and torn loyalties.'

'Sounds promising,' said Neil doubtfully. 'And of course, I wouldn't want to interfere with your creative processes, but perhaps it would be as well to keep your options open for the moment. See what else occurs to you over the next week or two. That's if you're not entirely committed to this brother-sister idea, naturally.'

He hates the idea, Kate inferred. And he hopes I'll drop it and come up with something better and more saleable. 'I'll keep working on it,' she said.

'Good. You'll get back to me when you've written an outline, will you?'

'Of course. But give me time to organise my workroom and set up my computer. Working in longhand is so much slower, I find.'

'There's no pressure on you, Kate. Like I said, I didn't call to nag you about producing a completed manuscript quite yet. You get your house sorted and then I'm sure you'll come up with something exciting for us.'

Perhaps the second, or even the third book on her reading list would provide a more fruitful idea for a modern novel, Kate thought hopefully, as she pulled on her goggles and went to find her sanding block and paint-scraper. For the moment it was more satisfying to put *The Mill on the Floss*, her second-hand idea for a novel, as well as Faith's problem with a student all to one side while she concentrated on a task that would produce a tangible result.

As she worked, she found that thoughts she had pushed to the back of her mind surfaced and confronted her, as though there was a second, bossier person living inside her head.

Well now, Kate, I heard all that stuff you were talking about with Jon. So, you're longing for him to be here, are you? You miss him. You'd like it if he came down for the weekend. Yes, she told herself firmly, that's all true. I would be delighted if he gave me a hand with these rooms. I am growing tired of scraping off endless layers of paint and steaming off wallpaper. It's hard work on my own. And I'd enjoy the company. *Oh, really?*

There was silence in the room, apart from the rasp of her paint-scraper. Well, *was* it true? Did she really want another person there in the house with her? Even the decorating she preferred to do by herself. She could play old pop music, she could even sing if she wanted to. She didn't have to make conversation or listen to someone else's suggestions. Not that there was anything wrong with the other person's suggestions. It was just that she wanted to do this by herself so that it would truly belong to her, and anyway she didn't want to have to justify her choice of colour or fabric all the time.

Was there something wrong with her? Would she never be able to share her life with another person? And what about children? She was rapidly coming to the age when she needed to make decisions about such things. Surely sharing your life with a baby (not that it stayed a baby for long, she reminded herself: baby turned into toddler, into child, into stroppy teenager) couldn't be all that difficult? Look at Emma Dolby! And how old would she be when she had to cope with teenage tantrums and sulks? she asked herself And what if her child went seriously off the rails? Drugs. Shop-lifting. Car theft. Joy-riding. She would be in her fifties, maybe even sixty by then.

But it had been hard enough getting to know her mother all over again after Roz's years away. Could she really face taking on a child? They said you felt different when it was your own, but then 'they' said all sorts of things which were plain wrong.

And what about Jon? What were his feelings on the subject? They had never talked about the possibility of having children. Perhaps he didn't see her as a long-term prospect. Perhaps he knew how brittle her feelings on the subject of parents and children really were. Maybe it was time she brought the subject up.

Were her parents' generation right after all? Get married in your early twenties, don't stop to wonder about having children, just get on with it. If you thought about it for too long, they said, you'd never do it. True enough. As she looked around her, this seemed to be true. But then, most of her parents' generation got divorced in their thirties or forties, and some worn-out woman was left to bring up the children, however dysfunctional, all by herself.

And what was Neil suggesting about her problems with an authority figure? Roz could hardly be said to count as one and, as Kate had failed to tell Neil, her father had died more than a quarter of a century ago. She hardly ever thought about him, if she was honest, so their relationship really couldn't be described as problematic.

Kate put down the scraper and went back to the kitchen to turn on some music. She would bring up the question of children, very vaguely and in a general way, when Jon phoned that evening. And she would telephone Faith Beeton after six o'clock, when she might be found at home, and tell her that she had come to no firm conclusion about Daisy Tompkins. Though, knowing Faith, that would hardly satisfy her.

But before she could put this plan into operation, there came another interruption.

viii

I did not like the look of the house from the first moment I set eyes on it. It was tall and thin and had narrow, mean windows. Any light and movement within were hidden from my view by the thick curtains drawn vehemently across the panes. They were a rich cobalt blue, I remember, an attractive enough colour for a scarf, or even a tie, perhaps, but not one that appealed to me for use in the decoration of a room.

When my aunt appeared, she was tall and thin, like her house, and had an air as forbidding.

'Come in,' she said, but there was no warmth in her greeting. 'And make sure you wipe your feet properly on the mat. I don't want any dirty little boys traipsing mud across my floors.'

I was offended. I might have been small for my age, but I certainly was not dirty. My mother would never stand for dirt in her house, at least before the death of my father. I have to admit that her standards slipped progressively downwards after that unhappy event, but I was left with a horror of dirt and mess, an obsession, one might almost say, with neatness. On that chilly afternoon it seemed as though I shuffled my shoes on the brown doormat for a good five minutes before my aunt would let me into her house. She removed my holdall from my grip, placed it at the base of the staircase and ushered me into the back room.

This room was gloomy, due not only to the waning daylight but to the 40-watt bulb that hung, encased in an ochre shade, from the centre of the ceiling, casting its baleful light into a small pool on the carpet and throwing shadows on to the dark colours of the walls. I remember a lot of olive green on walls and chairs, and several mustard-yellow cushions with a pattern of rust-red splotches that made me feel quite queasy to look at.

'Your sister will be arriving here late tomorrow afternoon,' said my aunt. 'It is a great pity that her school finishes its term one day later than yours, but that cannot, apparently, be helped. You will, therefore, amuse yourself in a quiet and decorous manner until she gets here. When she does, I expect that she will take over your care and amusement. I have never wished for children of my own and it is only as a favour to your poor mother that I am welcoming you into my own home at this difficult time.'

Even at that age I was aware that she was misusing the word 'welcoming'. There was nothing of welcome in what she said then, or at any time in the future. She was not cruel, I am glad to say, but 'welcome' was certainly not what I was feeling in her home that day.

To my surprise, given her somewhat forbidding appearance, my aunt did enjoy something of a social life. That first evening, after I had eaten my tea and been tidied away into an unobtrusive corner of the sitting room, several people presented themselves at the front door and were invited in with what, for my aunt, appeared to be quite effusive pleasure.

Why were they there? My aunt, it turned out, was a keen player of card-games. Although they played with counters, I noticed from my dim corner of the room that these were purchased with real money before the play began. I watched the visitors carefully. There were two women of about my aunt's age. This, I realise now, must have been forty-something, fifty at the most, but they all seemed quite ancient to me, and certainly they would have had none of the youthful appearance met with in women of that age nowadays. There were also two men, one of them grey-haired and desiccated, wearing a white shirt, grey trousers and a grey knitted cardigan over the top. The other, however, was younger, or at least appeared so. He had gingery hair and moustache, was wearing more colourful clothes (that would not have been difficult), and had a loud, braying laugh.

I could tell that the others were not keen on this last man's attempts at jolly conversation; they were too intent on their cards and the intricacies of whatever game it was that they were playing. Still, in spite of the gloomy interior of that house, they were a convivial enough group.

Eventually my aunt remembered my presence and sent me off to bed. I need not add that there was no offer of a bedtime story, let alone a good-night kiss for a lonely small boy.

Next afternoon, as promised, my sister arrived, and I was greatly cheered by her presence. I think that, though we would not admit it (for its admission would express disloyalty towards our mother), we were secretly relieved to be away from her. It was now some months since my father had died, but the atmosphere in our family home had not lightened at all with the passage of time.

Selina arrived, as promised, at about five-thirty that afternoon. She was allowed to wash her hands and face, and unpack her few possessions from her small suitcase, and then we both sat down to what my aunt considered to be a proper meal for children, called 'tea'.

That evening we spent with just the three of us, reading, talking, listening to the radio when my aunt considered that there was a suitable programme. We retired early.

But the next evening, our aunt's friends again arrived. On this occasion there were only three of them, as one of the ladies was, apparently, 'indisposed'. My sister, therefore, was invited to join them at their card play, once they had ascertained that she had some knowledge of whichever games it was they were used to playing. I am not sure whether she, too, exchanged some of her pocket-money for counters. What I was watching so intently was the behaviour of the ginger-haired man.

All his amusing tales were aimed at my sister. Perhaps he was merely pleased to find a new audience for them. When my aunt served refreshments (of the sausage roll and triangular egg-and-cress sandwich variety, I fear), he was assiduous in pressing my sister to partake of them, although she protested that she had already eaten her evening meal. He urged my aunt to allow Selina a single small glass of sherry. I was glad to note that my aunt was sensible enough to refuse this request.

I learned that his name was Owen. Since that time I have never liked the name. Somehow, when Owen assisted my sister when she was introduced to an unfamiliar game, his hand strayed to hers. His arm stretched itself familiarly along the back of her chair. I saw her shoulder twitch. She was not comfortable with this unasked-for proximity.

I wondered what I could do to help her, but I was too shy to intervene. I feared they would have laughed at me and, reminded of my presence, would have sent me to bed, their laughter following me upstairs. As it was, my aunt noticed me far too soon, and I was banished from the sitting room, away upstairs to clean my teeth, wash my face and ears, put on pyjamas, climb into bed and put out the light, all by myself. As a matter of fact, I enjoyed the feeling of independence that this gave me.

Next morning brought great disappointment. After our breakfast of lightly-salted porridge and weak, sugared tea there was a telephone call, which my aunt answered. She returned to the dining room with a look of surprise on her face.

'Well, Selina, you are a very lucky girl. My friend, Owen Salter, has asked whether he might take you out on a boating trip on the river this morning. It seems that he has a day's holiday from his office and would be grateful for your company on an expedition which he would otherwise undertake alone.'

She managed to make it sound as though Selina's company would be only slightly preferable to a morning spent on his own, but I was not fooled. Owen Salter had *asked my sister to go out with him*. And both she and my aunt had assented.

I don't know what it was about Selina that made men who were old enough to know better invite her out. She was obviously attractive to them. I do not believe that they were necessarily the sort of men who liked the company of very young girls in preference to women of their own generation. There was a languor about Selina, a sense that she was waiting for something to happen to her, that drew these men to her.

All I knew at the time was that I felt shut out and neglected. I was, I confess it, *jealous*. And what was my aunt doing, allowing Selina to go out, unchaperoned, with a man more than three times

87

her age? Selina returned from her outing some time in the evening. To my young eyes she looked flushed, with a pink rash on her chin, and a little feverish.

There was more to my aunt than met the eye, I realise that now. On the one hand she was the vinegary spinster who did not want to be bothered with the presence of children. On the other she was a woman who had never married and who had suppressed her passions beneath a thick carapace of respectability. I believe she liked to flirt with danger – or at least with temptation – but vicariously. At the time I saw it as one further betrayal by a malevolent Fate.

8

Someone was knocking at the front door. Kate pulled off her gloves, pushed her goggles up on to the top of her head and went to see who was there.

She was greeted by a beaming Brad, holding a ginger cat with white paws and a white bib.

'Susanna!'

'I hoped I'd got the right one,' he said, supporting Susanna's back legs and gently extricating her claws from his pullover. Little threads of blue wool were standing up on the surface of what Kate could only hope was not a cashmere sweater.

'Come in! Is she all right? Has she been hurt?'

'She seems to be fine,' said Brad. 'She could be hungry, though.'

'Where did you find her? Where's she been all this time?'

'I found her in the garden of number twenty-seven. It belongs to a couple who are out at work all day, so I couldn't ask them about her. She was crouching under the hedge in their front garden. Lucky she has such distinctive fur or I might not have noticed her.'

'She's a bit dusty,' said Kate. 'Do you think she got herself locked in somewhere?'

'Could be. It would explain why she didn't turn up when you called.'

'Susanna?' enquired Kate, putting out a hand. And then Susanna made it quite plain that she was indeed Kate's cat by leaping from Brad's arms on to Kate's shoulder.

'She hasn't scratched you, has she?' she asked anxiously.

'Not too badly,' said Brad, dabbing at his forearm.

A true cat lover, thought Kate gratefully. 'Come into the kitchen. It's the only place where we can sit down at the moment, I'm afraid.'

She found a clean hand towel so that Brad could deal with the scratch on his arm. 'I'm sorry about that,' she said. 'I'll put the kettle on for us and find her some food.'

Still holding Susanna, she filled the kettle, then took a packet of the very best, most expensive cat food from the cupboard.

'I'll open that, if you like,' said Brad. 'You won't want to put her down just yet.'

A few seconds later, Susanna jumped down to her bowl and wolfed her food as though she hadn't eaten for a couple of days. Maybe she hadn't, at that. Kate watched her fondly for a few moments, then belatedly remembered her visitor.

'I really should be going,' Brad was saying.

'You deserve a coffee, at least.' It was too early to offer lunch, and anyway there was nothing but a couple of eggs, some cheese and a few tomatoes in her fridge at the moment. 'Or would you prefer tea? I have herb teas, too.'

'I've had my quota of coffee for the day,' he said regretfully. 'But maybe I could just force myself . . .'

'Coffee it is, then,' said Kate, secretly pleased since she, too, had tried to cut down on her caffeine intake, but had failed. She measured dark Italian roast into the cafetière and topped it up with near-boiling water. Then she opened a new packet of chocolate biscuits for Brad. The man had earned them.

'Do you need a bandage for that?' she asked, looking at his arm. 'Or how about some surgical spirit?'

Brad shuddered. 'It's hardly bleeding at all now,' he said bravely.

Kate passed the plate of biscuits to his end of the table. 'Have some of these to keep your strength up.'

'How's the decorating getting on?' asked Brad politely.

'It's still at the stage where the place looks worse than when I started,' replied Kate. 'I'll be glad when I've got my workroom sorted out, though. At the moment this is the only table I can use.'

'And it looks as though it's doing duty as a desk, too.'

Kate remembered that Brad was an architect. He was probably used to working in well-designed, orderly surroundings. 'The only good thing about it is that I really can't be expected to produce a new novel until I have a civilised space in which to work. I'm enjoying taking a few weeks' break. I'll write twice as fast to make up for it later.' Well, she'd try, anyway.

They each took another chocolate biscuit and watched as Susanna chased the last few crumbs of food around her bowl. Her meal finished, she looked for a suitable place to wash herself, finally choosing to sit on top of the pile of clean laundry which was waiting for Kate to get round to ironing it. As Kate and Brad were finishing their coffee, she walked across the kitchen, passing Kate without a glance, and sprang up on to Brad's knees, where she sat with her eyes closed, purring.

'She hasn't forgiven me yet for moving house,' said Kate.

'She will,' said Brad, gently stroking the fur between Susanna's ears.

'More coffee?' asked Kate, since she didn't want to disturb Susanna now she appeared to be settling down. If Brad stayed for a little while longer then maybe Susanna would, too.

'Please.'

Before pouring the coffee, Kate moved the blue folder that was on the table by Brad's elbow. Daisy Tompkins's folder, she remembered. She shouldn't have left it out like that, but at least it wasn't open, and the word CONFIDENTIAL was printed firmly across the top, then PERSONAL FILE, above the label that identified it as belonging to a member of Bartlemas College.

'Bartlemas?' said Brad idly. 'I haven't seen one of those for months.'

'Why? Were you a student there?'

'No, but Patrick worked in their Development Office until a few months ago.'

Kate moved the blue folder into the middle of a stack of papers, just in case Brad felt like taking a look inside. 'Oddly enough, I worked in their Development Office one summer, too. Just for a few weeks during a summer school; I wasn't a permanent fixture.'

'Poor old Patrick was supposed to be raising money for some expensive new building work. He had to cold-call half a dozen rich old college graduates every morning and persuade them to part with a large pile of their loot.'

'I remember that the Development Officer and his assistants were very successful at that,' said Kate. She remembered that they were equally successful in siphoning off a modest proportion of the funds for their own use. She only hoped that Brad's partner hadn't been one of the guilty ones.

'Yes, they all did very well – all of them except Patrick,' said Brad, and Patrick went up in Kate's estimation. It sounded as though he was an unlikely embezzler. 'He was working on a one-year contract, but at the end of it he left to study for a professional qualification,' Brad added.

'What's he doing now?'

'Learning to be an accountant.'

There seemed little one could respond to this, but Kate filed the information away in case she needed some help with her next tax return.

'Well, I'd better be getting back home,' said Brad, as he finished his second cup of coffee. 'I warn you, you may hear me practising this afternoon. I hope it doesn't disturb your work.'

'You play a musical instrument?'

'I sing in a chamber choir and I really need to go over my part before this evening's practice. Bernstein can be quite tricky, especially if you have no knowledge of Hebrew.'

This left Kate mystified, but she was glad that his music practice didn't involve using a drum kit. 'I look forward to it,' she said cheerfully. 'Though I doubt whether I'll hear much through the noise of my paint-scraping.'

On his way out, Brad looked into the room Kate was working on.

'Have you decided on the colours you're going to use?' he asked.

'Cheerful creams and yellows,' Kate replied. 'And then I'll think about adding more colour in the curtains and cushions.'

'As long as it isn't red,' said Brad.

'Why not?'

'When added to cream and yellow it makes the room look like a classic trifle. It's a mistake people tend to make.'

Nothing wrong with trifle, thought Kate, as she led the way to the front door.

When Brad had returned to his own house, Kate attempted to make friends with Susanna. She could see that she would have to allow the cat to sleep on her bed for the time being, at least until the house started to look like a civilised home again. She filled a tray with cat litter and took it up to her bedroom, then she tucked the cat under one arm, picked up her basket and settled her in a warm and draught-free corner.

'Just don't expect to live up here for ever,' she said, before closing the door. She wasn't proposing to lose her cat again for the present.

Before returning to work on the living room, she visited her computer. It was time she checked her emails. She hadn't done so for several days and there might be something important waiting for her. In fact, there were three offers to sell her Viagra via the Internet, two people who wanted to design an animated logo for her, and five people with unlikely names who wished to send her large sums of money in exchange for her bank details.

She deleted all these and looked to see what remained. Just two, and the first of them was a message from Faith Beeton.

Dear Kate,

I hope that by now you have found time to read the file on Daisy Tompkins. Since I have not heard from you, I assume that you have as yet come to no conclusion on the matter.

As it happens, Bartlemas will be holding a reception for their second-year undergraduates on Tuesday of First Week. This, as you have probably worked out, is to welcome them back to college after the Long Vacation and encourage them to turn their minds to their work once more. It's all part of the process to make them feel kindly disposed towards us and remember their dear old college when they are loosed upon the world and earning big bucks in the City. Some of us are not convinced, however, that this will be the inevitable result of our effort.

What is more to the point is that both Daisy Tompkins and Joseph Fechan should be present, together with other colleagues and students of mine. Would you like to join us, as my guest? We meet at six o'clock in the Lamb Room and move into Hall for dinner at seven-fifteen. I believe I mentioned that we have lost our excellent chef, and I really cannot recommend the offerings of the man who has taken his place. If your taste runs to over-cooked minced beef under a heavy, varnished pastry crust, accompanied by boiled carrots and thick-cut chips, then you are welcome to join us for dinner. On the other hand, if you prefer to slip away after the New Zealand Sauvignon and Chilean Merlot, I will quite understand.

Yours,
Faith Beeton

Faith's style in an email was exactly the same as in a letter, noted Kate. She made no concessions to the relative informality of the medium. Once Kate had worked out that Tuesday of First Week was in five days' time – why couldn't Faith just *say* so, for goodness' sake? – she considered her options. Did she really want to attend a reception at Bartlemas? She didn't have the happiest memories of the place. But still, most of the people she had known in the past had left – or been removed from their posts – and she had to admit that she would like to meet the famous Dr Fechan, not to mention the sly Miss Tompkins. And what about Jan Rooling? Would she be there, too? If she shared a tutorial with Daisy, she must be a second-year, too. Kate wondered whether she would be able to pin her against a wall and ask her why she had written no account of what had happened during the joint tutorials. But she wasn't supposed to have seen the confidential papers in the folder, so it was difficult to see how she could lead up to such an interrogation in a casual, off-hand manner.

She typed a brief email reply to Faith, accepting her invitation to the reception but turning down the offer of dinner. It was always her luck to get stuck next to the most boring Fellow on such occasions and she would hardly be allowed to bring up the subject of the Tompkins-Fechan contretemps over the boiled carrots.

She opened the second email, noting with surprise that it came from Sam Dolby, Emma's eldest son. She had made his acquaintance the previous year, when he had helped her with some research on the Internet, but she hadn't thought she would hear from him again. The subject of the message was 'Emma'.

Hi, Kate

I know you've been a mate of Emma's for years, and you probably know her as well as anyone, so I thought you were the one person I could talk to about her. Certainly I can't discuss the way she is with Dad. Have you seen her recently? Do you think she might have gone off her head, or is it just something that happens to women when they're middle-aged?

Let me know what you think.

Cheers, Sam

Kate didn't know what to make of it. If that *had* been Emma in Summertown yesterday, looking slimmer and smarter than usual, with a decent haircut and wearing make-up, she didn't see that the change in her was anything other than an excellent thing. It was definitely an improvement on Emma's customary imitation of a bag lady. Why should Sam think that his mother had gone 'off her head' or, presumably, entered the menopause? Wasn't Emma a bit young for that, in any case? It seemed like only yesterday that she had been producing her last infant.

Kate thought carefully and then sent Sam a reply.

Hi, Sam

As a matter of fact, I haven't seen Emma to speak to for a few weeks as I've been really busy moving into my new place. I did think I might have caught sight of her in Summertown yesterday, though, looking very slim and well-dressed.

If you're really worried about her, why don't you drop in one day after school and we can talk about it?

Cheers, Kate

As she sent the emails winging their way through cyberspace, Kate reflected that at least she needn't ring Faith that evening, after all. She might even give Emma Dolby a ring instead, and find out whether she had really had a major makeover, or whether the woman she had seen in Summertown was someone entirely different. And she would try to find out what it was that was so worrying Sam.

ix

I suppose that most twelve-year-old boys develop an interest in sex. That is what books and television programmes, even pundits on the radio, tell us. In my own case, all I can remember of that age is my developing interest in vernacular architecture.

It happened like this.

Although I was only six when he died, my father had attempted to enthuse me with his own love of English country churches. We avoided any form of religious service, of course, but on Sunday afternoons he drove me to villages in Oxfordshire and Buckinghamshire and then took me on a tour of their churches. He lectured me on Saxon towers and Norman decoration. I learned the correct pronunciation of 'clerestory'. I stared at stone fonts and read the inscriptions on eighteenth-century memorials.

After his death I gave up these visits, for my mother was not interested, and I was still too young to set off on my own. But once I was old enough to cycle more or less safely around the leafy Oxfordshire lanes, I remembered my former interest, and took up the hobby once more. I can see that as a hobby it would bore most boys of that age: bicycling around the Oxfordshire countryside at the weekend with a packet of sandwiches, a bottle of water and an apple in my saddle bag, exploring some village, visiting the church. I had a notebook in which I carefully copied down the details given in the guide book (usually written by some former vicar), and made drawings of the more interesting details of the interior. What was I escaping from? That is what I wonder now, as I think back to those days. I must have been cycling away from *something* or *someone* when I turned my back on my mother's house and pedalled away into the sunlit morning.

The notebook I used was a small one, and I reduced my handwriting down to fit its narrow lines. When I see some note I have written, even today, I see how I have shrunk my handwriting as though to fit the page of that distant notebook.

Why was I so different from my contemporaries? Perhaps there was too much interest in sex all around me at home, what with the various men sniffing around my mother, and the way my sister was developing into a young woman. I think her attractiveness to the opposite sex was something Selina found uncomfortable. I do not believe she welcomed it. Certainly she did not display her figure to its best advantage.

In the six years since our father's death, Selina had grown tall. She was two or three inches taller than our mother, and proportionately rounder. Our mother had the slim-hipped, boyish figure which displays 'fashionable' clothes to their best advantage, while Selina's feminine curves made her 'tsk!' with annoyance at the way her daughter's clothes draped themselves in an unfashionable manner. Perhaps the fault lay with the clothes rather than with Selina, but our mother did not see it that way, and neither did my sister.

And there were men who came calling, asking to take Selina out for a walk, or to a concert, or to some meeting devoted to a worthy cause. They were not the sort of young men who drove expensive cars, or who dressed well, or who had witty small talk. Really, they were little better than Owen Salter. Mother looked down on them. Selina learned to feel ashamed when she was seen in their company. I simply walked out of the house and rode my bicycle off into the countryside, looking at old buildings. Perhaps I should have stayed at home and taken more notice of Selina's admirers. But what could I do?

9

'Hello, Emma. How are you?' To her own ears, Kate's voice sounded falsely jolly.

'Kate? Is that you? Did you want something?'

So Emma had noticed the false note, too. 'Nothing special. It just occurred to me that we hadn't been in touch for weeks, well, months even, and I wondered how you were.'

'I'm fine. Just the way I always am.' The trouble with Emma was that she had no small talk, and really wasn't capable of gossiping about nothing much on the phone for half an hour, in a friendly way.

'And the children?' enquired Kate.

'They're all fine. Are you *sure* there isn't something you want? You're not looking for gainful employment, are you?'

'I'm happily employed in achieving a civilised background for myself at the moment.'

'Oh, of course. You've bought yourself a new place in Jericho, haven't you?'

'Yes,' said Kate smugly. 'It's lovely, but it does need some work doing on it.'

'If that's what you rang me up to tell me—'

'Oddly enough, Emma, I thought I saw you in Summertown yesterday,' Kate put in hastily before Emma could hang up on her.

'Really? Well, just because I live in Headington doesn't mean I can't shop somewhere else whenever I feel like it,' said Emma, sounding a bit huffy.

'Of course you—'

'What time would this have been?'

'Just before lunch. I'd been to the first of my literature courses at Ewert Place.'

'Oh, I see,' said Emma thoughtfully. 'But I didn't see *you*.'

'You were a little distance away and you weren't looking in my direction. If it *was* you,' Kate added quickly.

'It might have been someone else,' suggested Emma.

'Quite.'

'And was this woman,' she paused for a moment, 'um, on her own?'

'Er, I really couldn't be sure,' Kate lied.

'Well, I don't suppose it was me at all,' said Emma firmly.

'I don't suppose it was,' said Kate. 'I must have been mistaken.'

'Are you intending to go to these literature classes *every* Wednesday morning?' asked Emma, just as Kate was going to say 'goodbye' and hang up.

'Yes. There are another nine this term and a further ten after Christmas. Why? Do you want to join us?'

'No. I haven't got the time, I'm afraid. But I just wondered.'

'Well, I'm sure you're busy now, Emma. I won't keep you any longer.'

'Goodbye, Kate.'

And Kate was left looking at the receiver and wondering what all that had been about. Emma was usually a painfully direct person but she had just been evasive. And she had obviously been in Summertown, in the company of another person, and she hadn't wanted Kate to know about it. And, of course, she had been looking most unlike her usual untidy self.

Kate looked at her watch. Sam should be back from school by now. She could check to see whether he had answered her email yet.

Sure enough, once she had blocked and deleted the messages from the spammers who wanted to sell her a Master's Degree, or Viagra, or who promised to pay her for her opinion on a range of subjects, she saw that there was a new message from Sam.

Thanks, Kate. I could drop by tomorrow, about 5, if that's OK with you. Sam.

She sent him a reply straight away.

That's fine, Sam. I look forward to seeing you tomorrow. Kate.

But suppose Emma was seeing another man? How could she discuss the possibility with her teenage son? But no, Emma was the last person who would carry on a clandestine affair with someone, surely? She just wasn't the type.

Later, when she was talking on the telephone to Jon, she wondered whether to bring the subject up with him. But he didn't really know the Dolbys, and anyway, she didn't think he was keen on gossip. Jon, it seemed, had problems of his own.

'Have I mentioned my sister?' he said.

'Yes, you told me that you'd had a letter from her, but I don't think you told me her name.' What was it he had said about her? Not very much, and he had spoken apologetically as though not expecting Kate to be interested in his family. He had mentioned something about a letter and an argument with her husband, as far as she could remember.

'Her name's Alison and she's younger than me. She got married young – too young, in my opinion – when she was only twenty-two.'

'The marriage must have lasted a few years, though,' said Kate, doing a rough calculation.

'I suppose so,' he said grudgingly. 'She has four children, at any rate. Alexander – Sandy – the eldest, must be fourteen now. Or fifteen, maybe,' he added. 'And the little one, Elspeth, is only three.'

'Is your brother-in-law Scottish?'

'How did you know?'

'I took a wild guess when I heard their names.'

'Oh, yes. I see. Her husband's name is Iain, by the way, with an extra "i". He's a farmer.'

'Sounds pretty solid to me.'

'Iain is certainly a solid character, and with a traditional view of family life.'

'Difficult to imagine a radical farmer,' said Kate, then added quickly, 'I'm sure he's a sterling character and with four children they must be committed to their marriage, in spite of the argument.' Now she was sounding like an agony aunt. What did she know about these things? But she tried to sound concerned and supportive.

'I hope you're right.'

'So what seems to be the matter?'

'She wants to know if she can come and stay with me "for a wee while", as she puts it. What do you think she means?'

'I'm not sure I can understand the way another woman, in an entirely different situation, is likely to think,' said Kate cautiously, and tried not to cringe at the use of the word 'wee', which she associated with nursery rhymes rather than Scotland.

'Well, I don't understand her, certainly.'

'But she's *your* sister. How can I offer an opinion? I've never met her!' This sisterhood of women stuff was all very well, but was she supposed to be able to read another woman's mind? Alison's life sounded a little dull to Kate, but that didn't mean that Alison felt the same about it. After all, many women would find Kate's life boring, and Alison's perfectly delightful.

'Maybe she's just tired. Maybe she needs a holiday,' she suggested.

'Maybe she's a mental case.'

'That, too, is a possibility. You know your sister better than I do.'

'Now you're being frivolous again.'

'It's my nature, I'm afraid. But your sister sounds a much more serious character than me.'

'Who knows what my sister is? Getting married at that age, she didn't have the chance to know who or what she was. Maybe she's decided it's time to discover herself.'

'Well, let's hope for your sake, and for Iain's, that she manages to do so in the space of a week or two. She can't just walk away from four children and a farmyard full of chickens, can she?'

'I don't think she keeps chickens,' said Jon doubtfully. 'But I get your meaning.'

'I can't believe that a sister of yours would walk out on her responsibilities,' said Kate.

'I do hope you're right.' Jon didn't sound so sure. 'Look, Kate, how are you fixed for this Sunday? Why don't I come down to Oxford and give you a hand with removing old wallpaper, or whatever it is you're doing at the moment?'

'Or why don't I take a few hours off, and we could find a suitable pub for lunch?' she countered.

'Good idea.'

As she put the phone down five minutes later, it struck Kate that Jon knew, or guessed, more about his sister's intentions than he had let on. And if he had brought himself to talk about her and her situation to Kate, it was because he was truly concerned about her.

Well, she thought, as she settled down with Susanna on her

knees, there's no way I can invite her down to Oxford for a few days' sisterly get-together, not unless she's an expert carpet-layer or decorator, and if she doesn't mind sleeping on the floor, of course.

She had decided to get ahead with her reading for the literature course and had taken the next book on the list up to the bedroom, as well as the cat. She opened *Emotionally Weird* and started to read.

Half an hour later she put the book down and contemplated her own next project. She would ring Neil Orson tomorrow morning and put her latest ideas for a sparkling new novel to him. George Eliot was wonderful, of course, and she still liked the brother-sister relationship as the central theme for her own story, but Eliot was hardly up-to-date in matters of style. She *could* learn something from Atkinson, however, and tomorrow she would try out her latest brainwave on her editor. But first, she must read a little further.

'Hello, Neil. It's Kate Ivory.'

'Good morning, Kate. And don't worry, I do recognise which Kate you are from the sound of your voice.'

'Oh, good.' That was a relief. She found it discouraging when she rang her agent, Estelle, and had to spend the first minute of the conversation reminding her who she was. And Estelle never did sound really enthusiastic, even when she connected Kate's name with the novels she had written. 'Neil, I wanted to try out an idea of mine on you. See what you think.'

'Fire away.'

'Well, I still like the brother-sister story, but how do you feel about my writing it in lots of separate sections, from a lot of – well, several, anyway – points of view?'

'It sounds all right so far,' said Neil doubtfully. 'Not *too* many viewpoint characters though, Kate. It confuses the reader.'

'Ah, but the clever thing is, we can vary the *look* of each narrative. Set it in a different font,' she added, in case he hadn't taken her point.

'Very interesting, Kate. Very clever, I'm sure.' Was there a note of desperation in his voice? 'But why don't you keep it simple? One or two narrative voices, all in the same font. Looking just the same. I'm sure your readers can work out the different perspectives for themselves.'

'Do you think so?'

'Yes. But I'm so glad you're thinking about the new book. It sounds as though you'll be able to get it all down on paper in no time at all once you've finished painting your walls.'

Just a bit of simple wording-in, is what he means, thought Kate, giving up her bright idea with great difficulty. In the end that's all my work comes down to.

At 4.45 p.m. Kate closed the door on the sitting room and went upstairs to wash her face and run her hands through her hair. She took off her grubby shirt and replaced it with a clean T-shirt, ready for Sam Dolby's visit. She didn't think he would really care how she was dressed, but she did feel a little more civilised now she had made this minimal effort.

What should she offer him, she wondered. Tea? Coffee? *Beer?* She put out the packet of chocolate biscuits on the kitchen table and found a couple of clean mugs, deciding that she shouldn't lead Emma's son astray, and anyway, five o'clock was much too early to be drinking beer.

Sam turned up on time, since he was a well-brought-up lad underneath the standard expression of boredom, and teenage slouch.

'Coffee?' she offered.

'Yeah, thanks. Instant's fine,' he answered.

'You'll have to make do with real,' she said cheerfully. 'I only use the other stuff in an emergency.'

While they waited for the kettle to boil she passed the biscuits across the table. Sam took one and crumbled it on to the table, as though his mind was elsewhere.

'You'd better tell me what's on your mind,' said Kate, hoping he wasn't going to demolish her entire stock of chocolate biscuits. She didn't fancy eating them with a teaspoon with her coffee tomorrow morning.

'It's Emma,' he said, having rejected 'Mum' the previous year, remembered Kate.

'I gathered that,' she said, since Sam had stopped. He seemed incapable of coming out with more than four words at a time, though in a noisy, competitive family like the Dolbys, he would probably revert to their articulate, verbose style when he had grown out of his current laconic phase. 'Tell me more,' she encouraged him in her most teenager-friendly tone.

'She's changed. She just isn't like herself any more.'

'Slimmer?' queried Kate. 'Smarter?' *More devious*, she wanted to say, but wasn't sure that Emma's son would appreciate the description.

'Not just that. After Flora, I think she and Dad agreed not to have any more babies.'

'How old is Flora now?'

'Must be a year, maybe a bit more. She still can't talk. She's very boring. Not that Emma likes to hear me saying stuff like that.'

'So you're not too keen on babies. That's normal at your age, I should have thought.'

'I don't really mind baby-sitting the little ones now and then, but she's been taking advantage. Of me *and* Abigail, if it comes to that. She gets fed up, too.'

'I can see Emma might need some time off from her domestic chores, though I gather it was her choice as much as Sam's to have lots of children. I expect she wants to be an attractive woman, as well as a mother. It's only natural.'

'It *was* about time Emma smartened herself up a bit. Not that she didn't look fine before,' he added hastily. 'But she's not as old as all that, even if she is getting on a bit.'

'She's only about a year older than me!'

'Really? You look quite a bit younger.'

'Thanks, Sam. So what else have you noticed that's different about her?'

'She disappears off without any good reason.'

'That's still not particularly odd. She's probably had enough of all the domestic chores. She must have been doing them for about eighteen years.'

'She likes that stuff,' said Sam dismissively. 'At least, she used to. I know she still comes and shouts at us to pick up our shoes from the hall, and do our homework, and clean our teeth and get to bed at a reasonable time, but her heart isn't in it, somehow. I don't think she cares whether our teeth get holes in them or not.'

Now that Sam had started talking it was going to be hard to stop him, Kate saw. She poured the coffee and passed the biscuits across again. She was glad to see that this time he ate his biscuit instead of reducing it to crumbs.

'I don't get it. What's so different?'

'She's still there at the times we expect her to be, getting our tea, and Dad's supper, and everyone's breakfast, of course. But it's as though her head's somewhere different. Sometimes she kind of smiles, as though she's listening to someone else, not to Tris banging on about his football shorts, but more like some radio station the rest of us can't hear.'

'OK. I'm getting the picture.'

'Well, what do you think? Is she normal, or has she gone off her head?' Sam was tracing patterns in the biscuit crumbs on the table, then licking his finger. He wasn't looking at Kate. And he hadn't mentioned the most likely explanation of his mother's behaviour. Emma, she reckoned, sounded as though she had fallen in love. Much as Kate liked Sam's father, the other Sam Dolby, she couldn't imagine that he was the one that Emma was dreaming about as she ironed her children's school shirts or stuck a couple of dozen fish fingers under the grill.

'I told you in my email that I thought I saw her on Wednesday, at lunchtime, in Summertown,' she began. 'She was walking away from me, so I didn't see her face properly, and she didn't see me, so we didn't say "hello". I wasn't absolutely sure it was Emma, because she had lost weight, and had a new haircut.' She was going to say that for once her friend wasn't weighed down with Tesco's carrier bags, and didn't look harassed, but thought this was tactless. She made no mention of the male companion. After all, she could have been mistaken.

'Was she wearing her new blue coat? It has some kind of stand-up collar thing,' he added helpfully.

'As I remember it, she was wearing well-cut black trousers and a fitted top in a rather pleasant shade of plum.'

'That's her other new outfit,' said Sam glumly.

'So it *was* Emma I saw. When I talked to her on the phone she seemed rather keen to persuade me that it couldn't have been, but she didn't do a very good job of it.'

There was a pause as though both of them were trying to think how to say the unsayable.

'She'd have been on her own, I suppose?' asked Sam eventually.

'Oddly enough, Emma asked the same question.'

'But she must have known!'

'She asked if the woman who looked like her, but most likely wasn't, was on her own.'

'Well, was she?'

'I don't know, I can't remember,' Kate said hastily. 'She could have been.'

'That's not very helpful.'

'Sorry. I thought she was talking to someone who came out of the wine merchant's, but they might have met just by chance. It could have been anyone – a friend of your father's, or a colleague of Emma's.'

'Or she might have been meeting a man,' said Sam.

'I suppose it's what we've both been wondering about,' she said unwillingly.

'You've been wondering too, haven't you? Do you think she has found herself a bloke?' supplied Sam.

'On the one hand it looks like it,' conceded Kate. 'On the other hand, I can't think of anyone more unlikely to find herself a bloke than Emma Dolby. She and your father are devoted to one another – everyone knows that. Not that she couldn't find someone if she wanted to,' she added swiftly, in case Sam should take it the wrong way. 'It's just that it would be totally out of character.'

'Yeah. That's what I used to think.'

'What about your brothers and sisters? And your father, if it comes to that. Have they noticed anything different about her?'

'Dad's just pleased that she seems to be looking good, and is more cheerful about the place. Abigail's not interested in anyone's love-life except her own. Hugo lives in *his* own world. I think he's in love with his bicycle. And the rest of them are too young to understand.'

Kate noticed that he'd reverted to calling his father 'Dad'. Maybe he wasn't feeling as adult about the situation as he liked to appear. 'So it's just you and me, Sam?'

'Yeah.'

'Best to keep it that way, don't you think?'

'OK, but what are we going to do about it? Can you arrange to meet her for tea or something and get her to talk to you?'

'She didn't seem very keen on swapping confidences last time I spoke to her.'

'You could say *you* had a problem you wanted to talk about. Get her to meet you in Blackwell's coffee shop. I know she likes that place, and she can buy herself a couple of paperbacks on her way out and tell herself that she needed them for one of her courses.'

'You know her too well,' said Kate. 'OK, Sam. I'll give it a try. As a matter of fact there is something I'd like to talk to her about, but I'm not sure whether I should.'

Sam showed no interest in this typically devious piece of adult thinking.

'I'd better be getting back,' he said. 'Thanks for the coffee. I seem to have finished off your biscuits, I'm afraid. I'll bring you a new packet next time.'

So there was to be a next time. Certainly she owed young Sam something for the help he'd given her over Internet searches. When she'd watched him cycle off up the road, she checked the time. No point in ringing Emma now. She'd be scrubbing the babies and preparing food for her older children and husband. How on earth did she find the time to keep a lover happy as well?

X

I was sitting in an English class at school, letting the master's words wash over me, waiting for the others to catch up. The lesson moved so slowly on that summer's afternoon, with a fly buzzing vainly against a windowpane and the slow *tock* of the classroom clock counting off the laggardly seconds. And then his words caught my attention and I tuned in to what Mr Rank was saying.

'Shakespeare attended the Grammar School in Stratford when he was seven years old. The school day stretched from six in the morning until five-thirty in the afternoon, with a break for lunch. And the boys learned prodigious amounts of material, *by heart*.' He paused to let this fact sink in, and since he was not about to enlighten us as to the method of memorising used by these Elizabethan schoolboys, I returned to my own thoughts. But I was, in spite of myself, intrigued. How did they do it? In our time, even if a seven year old were willing to apply himself to such a task, how would he ever achieve it? My own ability to list the contents of my mother's cupboards paled into insignificance by comparison.

By this time my interest in churches had developed into a fascination with vernacular architecture. Perhaps it was because I believed that the architecture of the houses of ordinary people would teach me something about their lives. At the time, the lives of ordinary people were a mystery to me. I didn't understand how they thought, how they felt. Describing a cross passage or noticing the placement of the chimney in relation to the doors seemed as though it would offer me a glimpse into a normal world.

If I could remember what I saw, if I could analyse it, I would hold the key to the secrets of life. It seems ridiculous to me now, of course. I never did find the key. I do not hold it today.

As I cycled round the Oxfordshire villages, visiting churches and noting down details of vernacular architecture, this problem of remembering, of sorting and classifying my observations, lay at the back of my mind and I worried away at it every now and then. Like William Shakespeare I, too, wanted to be able to remember all the details I had seen, to quote the inscriptions I had copied down from tombstones and monuments.

The idea of a mind stuffed full of facts and figures, of diagrams and maps, of details of cornices and brick patterns, filled me with excitement. It would be as though I carried a massive reference library around with me, only instead of weighing me down and hurting my shoulders, this one would be weightless and I would be able to retrieve whatever fact I wanted, faster than ever I could from any physical tome. But was it because Shakespeare was a genius that he was able to do this mammoth feat of memory? Would I, with my puny little brain, ever know what it was to pull out remembered facts at will? But Mr Rank had said that *all* the children were expected to do it. For a moment, I saw a trembling wrist held out for the *thwack* of the master's ruler. There would have been many who did not fulfil his demands. What was the secret? How to learn the knack of it?

The obvious solution eventually came to me: I asked Mr Rank, the master who had told us about Shakespeare. One day, after our English lesson, I waited behind in the classroom until the other boys had left for their mid-morning break.

He looked puzzled for a moment. 'Shakespeare?' He had given the introduction to the playwright's early life more than two weeks previously.

'How did he learn so much by heart?' I pressed him. I really wanted to know.

'They had a method, learned from Classical antiquity – by which I mean the Ancient Greeks, who passed the method on to the Romans,' he explained kindly but superfluously, straightening the pile of books on his desk, glancing at the clock on the wall. I realise now that he was eager to reach the staffroom and his packet of Embassy cigarettes but at the time I was thinking only of what he could teach me, if only he would agree to do so.

'The Renaissance, you know,' he added, unwilling to expand on the idea, longing for his cigarette. He would barely have time to smoke it now before his next lesson. He picked up the books and moved from behind his desk, turning towards the door.

I followed him, saying, 'But, sir—'

'*Ad Herennium*,' he said dismissively, hoping this would silence me.

After one last encouraging smile, he reached the door at last, opened it, left the classroom and hurried away down the corridor before I could delay him any longer. I stayed behind and copied down the Latin title he had given me. I checked the clock: I had twelve minutes before my own next lesson – just time for a preliminary search in the library. I was determined to find the secret of remembering that those boys of a past age had acquired as a matter of course. I had great perseverance as a child, or perhaps it was only that I had no close friends and nothing more interesting to do with my time. And so it was that I set to work.

10

By half-past five, Kate was feeling in need of a break. She tidied away the coffee things, mopped up the rest of Sam's crumbs, then went upstairs and changed into sweatpants. She put on her running shoes and set off down Cleveland Road towards the canal. It was a fine evening, and people were arriving home from their day's work, or setting out for the shops or perhaps for their evening's entertainment.

She started slowly, moving at a brisk walk rather than a run, persuading herself that she was warming-up, though in reality she was already feeling weary after a day's work, much of it physical. She raised a hand in greeting to Brad, who had just arrived at his front gate, bearing a supermarket carrier bag. She skirted round a man walking a dog, keeping out of snapping distance of the dog's teeth, then carried on down the road, picking up her pace and feeling happy that she wasn't quite as unfit as she had feared.

It was as she approached one of the houses that she had mentally written down as being let to students, that it happened. The houses in this part of the road were tall and gabled and had only about two or three feet of scrubby garden between their front wall and the pavement. They had large sash windows upstairs and down, with ragged posters stuck on to the glass.

Something prompted her to look upwards, and she was just in time to see a large object balanced on the window sill above her. Two people, invisible behind it, were having a loud argument. As she watched, disbelieving, the object – wide and

115

substantial – was pushed through the open window space and over the edge, hitting the narrow strip of garden and toppling over to measure its length on the pavement in front of her.

Now that she was really running she had no time to stop. Her right foot caught the edge of the object and she went flying, her arms stretched in front of her in an attempt to break her fall.

To her relief, Kate found she had landed face-down on something soft and resisting.

Once she realised she was still alive and breathing, she lifted her face from the musty-smelling surface and pulled herself up on to her knees. Her left arm had scraped along the low wall and was grazed, and her trousers were spattered with dust. She stood up carefully, finding it difficult to balance on the unstable surface. She hoped she'd done herself no more than minor damage, and looked down to see what had caused her fall. She had landed on a mattress.

She looked up at the large sash window above her which was gaping wide open. In the room beyond she could see two figures, naked and arguing, who seemed quite unaware that they had nearly annihilated Kate Ivory.

A couple of young people, fully-clothed, probably both male, though she couldn't be sure, were at her side a moment later, sounding worried.

'We're really sorry about this,' one of them said. He was medium-sized and sandy-haired.

'Are you all right?' asked the second one anxiously. He, or maybe she, was shorter and slighter and dressed in a baggy sweater with ragged cuffs, and equally baggy jeans.

'I'm afraid they were having a bit of a row,' said the first.

Kate was moving her legs and feet. Nothing seemed to be broken, or injured, though she thought she'd probably acquired a number of bruises down her leg and on her elbow, as well as the graze on her arm.

'Do you live far?' asked the second student.

'Just up the road.'

'That's good. We haven't seen you around before,' said Sandy-hair.

'I've only just moved here.'

'Not much of a welcome to Cleveland Road, then.'

'Why don't you come inside? We could clean up that arm and make you a cup of tea,' said the smaller one.

'Though I'm not sure we've got any drinkable milk,' said Sandy-hair. 'How about coffee?'

'I can drink coffee black, if necessary,' said Kate, hobbling towards the front door behind the two young people.

Inside, the house reminded her of her own before she started to renovate it. There was a smell of curry, and coffee, and there were a couple of bicycles leaning against the wall in the hall.

'I'm Dan Jones, by the way,' said the sandy-haired young man. 'And this is Rollo Persse.' So the second figure *was* male, thought Kate. 'Come on through to the kitchen.'

The kitchen had been opened out by the owner, so that it now incorporated the old dining room. There was room for a table and half a dozen chairs, as well as the usual stove and fridge, washing-machine, ironing board, microwave and cupboards of the standard kitchen.

Rollo moved a basket of laundry from one of the chairs and pushed aside a collection of ballpoints and pads from a section of the table. Kate sat down while he went off to find something to clean up her arm.

'Anyone got some cottonwool?' she heard him shouting up the stairs.

Someone must have responded because he reappeared with cottonwool, as well as a bowl of warm water smelling of antiseptic.

'Thanks,' she said a few moments later. 'That's fine.' Her arm was stinging from the antiseptic and she thought

117

that fresh air would probably do it as much good as anything.

Dan had put the kettle on to boil and found a couple of clean mugs into which he spooned a supermarket's own brand of coffee. 'You'll have to wash up a mug for yourself if you want one,' he said to Rollo. Rollo dutifully rinsed a mug under the tap and cleaned it up and dried it with a grey tea towel. Kate tried hard not to shudder. She had forgotten how insanitary student arrangements could be. Still, it probably strengthened their immune systems, she told herself hardily.

'That was rather an extreme method of getting rid of an unwanted mattress, wasn't it?' she said.

'Oh, Tom and Rebecca have one of those dynamic, confrontational relationships,' said Rollo. 'Tom was expressing his feelings of anger and frustration, I imagine.'

'Rollo's studying Psychology,' said Dan. 'What he means is that those two fight all the time, and this time it was probably something to do with sex.'

'They'll be down to apologise when they've put some clothes on,' added Rollo.

'How many of you are there in the house?'

'Well, there's Ethan and Holly, as well, though they're not an item. And Yan, though we hardly ever see him.'

'He might as well move in with his girlfriend full time,' said Dan. 'I don't know why he bothers to pay rent here.'

'That would be making a statement about their relationship that he's not prepared to make just yet,' said Rollo.

'You mean Daisy likes to keep her options open,' said Dan.

'I don't believe she really screws around all that much.'

'Sorry, Kate,' said Dan, interrupting him. 'You can't be interested in this stuff.'

Kate was longing to ask Daisy's surname, but at this moment two more young people entered the kitchen – Rebecca and Tom,

Rollo told her – and so her remaining time was spent listening to profuse apologies and assuring people that, really, she was perfectly all right and they weren't to worry one little bit about her.

When she had left them, she walked slowly back up the road. As she got near to her own house, she found herself the object of intense inspection by a small, mousy woman, who could have been any age over sixty-five. She had seen her once or twice before, putting out her rubbish bin, picking up discarded cartons from the pavement, shouting at children riding their bikes on the footpath, always scowling, and she remembered that Brad had mentioned that this was Mrs Janet Morrison, self-appointed Chief of the Moral Police. Kate would be wise to give her a wide berth, he had warned. 'She mutters about Sodom and Gomorrah whenever she sees me or Patrick.' When Kate had laughed, he had said, 'Don't worry! She'll find something to disapprove of about you, too.' Now, the small, pouched eyes were fixed on Kate, and she found it difficult to walk past without acknowledging the woman's presence.

'Good evening.'

'I expect those students nearly killed you, didn't they?' she said eagerly, obviously wanting to hear the worst.

'Really, I'm—'

'You ought to see a solicitor. Sue the little buggers. They should be taught a lesson.' The scowl was in place, Kate saw, but there was a light of pleasure in the old woman's eyes. This was something she could really get her teeth into and complain about. It would keep her going for weeks.

'I don't think—'

'Those boys are nothing but a pack of tomcats. And the girls are even worse. Have you seen the one with black varnish on her fingernails and a skirt so short you can see her arse?' She put a thin, veined hand on Kate's arm and clutched it tightly. Kate had to fight the impulse to move smartly backwards out of her grasp.

'I can't say I—'

'No better than a prostitute, she isn't, that one.'

'I really have to get home,' said Kate, finally managing to complete a sentence.

'You take my advice. You sue them.' The vindictive words followed her up the road. 'And don't have anything to do with those two sodomites, either!'

By which Kate assumed that she meant Brad and Patrick.

It was true that Kate did want to get home. She wanted to take off her dusty clothes and soak herself in a hot bath. She could wash away the memory of that foul old woman's words, too. Life in Jericho was just a little more exciting than she had been expecting.

At about eight o'clock, when she was feeling better, and when Emma might be supposed to be relaxing, Kate phoned her friend.

'Emma, it's Kate again.'

'Twice in one week? What have I done to deserve this honour?'

This was a little unfair, Kate considered. She usually kept in touch with Emma. It was just that she had been unusually busy these past few weeks.

'It's ages since we met for a chat,' she said. 'Why don't you take half an hour off from the family and come out for a coffee?'

'At your place? I thought you were knee-deep in stripped wallpaper.'

'I am. I'd like to escape from it. Why don't we meet in Blackwell's coffee shop? I wouldn't mind browsing my way through the latest novels.'

'When do you suggest?' Emma had softened. Sam obviously did know his mother very well.

'I'm free after the weekend. How about you?'

'Fairly free,' said Emma carefully. 'What about Wednesday?'

'Sure. What time?'

'Two-thirty? I know it's a bit early, but I'll have to be home in time for the children returning from school.'

'What about the little ones?'

It was wiser not to try to remember their names, Kate had learned from past, embarrassing experience.

'Jack was five in February, so he's well settled into school,' said Emma reproachfully. 'So there's only Flora, and I have a girl – a young woman, I should say,' she corrected herself hastily. 'She comes in to help me every day, so I can take a little time off for myself. I need to get away and be my own person occasionally, you see.'

'Good idea,' said Kate. 'Every woman needs time for herself. I'll see you on Wednesday, then.'

Sam had got it right again, she thought. Emma appeared to be searching for herself. Though whether she would find this nebulous entity waiting for her, after all the years of child-rearing, laundry and housework, Kate wasn't at all sure. She did think, though, that Emma was a bit late catching up with the trend towards self-knowledge and self-fulfilment. Didn't that sort of thing belong to the selfish 1980s? But then, she shouldn't begrudge Emma the chance to make up for her lost decades. Her numerous children, and her rather dull husband, had had their full share of Emma for the best part of twenty years.

She realised, with surprise, that she had never before admitted to herself that Sam Dolby Senior might be just a tad boring.

xi

It was an unusually warm September morning. The summer had been hot and dry and the signs of autumn were well advanced. The landscape was made up of bleached yellow fields and rusting foliage, yet the sun was warm on my bare forearms.

It was the perfection of that particular morning, a morning of freedom before the return to school for the new term, that I was compelled to remember. I needed to fix for ever the tender blue sky, streaked with silver trails where planes had passed, the feel of the warm, humid air on my neck, the chattering and dry, staccato runs made by the unseen birds. They sounded busy, preoccupied. Swallows and martins gathered in shrill queues on rooftops and telegraph wires. 'Not cold enough yet,' I imagined them saying. 'Stay awhile here.' Even as I watched them, they dispersed, swooping and turning just above my head, to chase the lazy insects.

As I followed the footpath across the field, empty now of its summer crop, the pale green of the recent sowing just visible in the furrows, I felt it give beneath my feet, crumbling and friable, like a living thing. Perhaps for the first and last time in my life I felt close to the earth, at one and at peace with the natural world.

In the slanting morning light the hills seemed closer than usual. There was no haze, in spite of the season. Even a skylark, forgetting that this was September, practised a few notes of his spring song. The landscape was autumnal, but the feeling in the air was of a beginning, not of the dying of the year.

The footpath skirted a field of maize. The dead leaves and yellow stalks rustled as though a herd of small, running animals were passing through. I knew that in reality it was only the breeze clattering like a noisy brook, but I preferred to think of those hastening forms, scurrying along their secret pathways.

I can recall it all: the ceaseless, underlying hum of the motorway, a few miles to the south; above it, the whine of a small plane, unfurling the silver banner of its vapour trail across the sky; miniature clouds like soap bubbles blown from beyond the Chilterns; the creaky squawk of a lone duck flying towards the village pond. I can even remember the acrid smell of the muck that the farmer had spread on a nearby field.

I remember the details of that day so easily, when so many others have fused into an undifferentiated cluster of cottages, barns and church towers, for that was the morning when I put into practice what I had learned. I hung every detail of what I saw and heard on to an item in my imaginary marble palace, adorned with its courtyards and fountains, its statues and paintings. The sky, with its clouds blurred and streaked as though a sable brush had been drawn through them, I spread across the domed roof of the entrance hall. The skylark and the duck, frozen in their flight, I perched in niches in the wall. The songs that the birds sang are repeated over and over into the air as I stand before them in my imagination. The bi-plane putters once more across the sky and I can hear the insistent hum of its engine, just as I heard it that September morning.

What strikes me now, as I pass again along those corridors and past those statues in their niches, is that there are no people in my house of memory. Were there none visible on my morning walk all those years ago, or did I edit them out of the picture? I can remember only the items that I set myself to remember. All the rest is a mystery.

Certainly, I preferred a world without other people in it, one that was entirely under my own control, one which contained no one passing judgement on me.

Over the years, I have often strolled through those corridors and taken my leisurely tour of the palace I constructed. I look at the statues in their niches, count the pillars in their colonnades, and thus bring back the shimmering details of that perfect morning.

Was that really all I saw? I stop at the end of the colonnade, there where the skylark is singing. But what else lies around the corner? What memories did I attach to the paintings in my picture gallery? The first picture I come to has a heavy gilded frame, and shows a maiden sitting in a flower-strewn field, embracing a unicorn. Did I know even then the association between maidens and unicorns?

The picture dissolves and the actual scene in the churchyard is superimposed on the canvas. I have never needed any prop to aid my memory of what I saw.

The churchyard wasn't particularly large, but it was enclosed in a tall stone wall, still covered in fading heads of red valerian, even so late in the year. There were small groves of dark cypress, and hidden corners where the gravestones were splashed with lichen and their inscriptions worn away. Thus it was quite possible to round a buttress and come unexpectedly upon some other visitor to the place.

The grass was longer in that isolated corner, as though the custodian of the lawnmower had given up and returned home before venturing so far. It was an ancient, secret place. Against the grey stone of the buttress a couple of poppies still bloomed, their red petals like crumpled paper. A bumble bee hovered above them, appearing enormous, flying erratically. There were flowers too, many of them faded, in the glass jars or vases on the nearby graves. The bright, artificial colours stood out against the greys and greens of the churchyard. Just to my right, a bulbous blue vase lay on its side, its water spilt, its flowers withered.

She was reclining there, my maiden – though I very much doubt that that is what she was – in the grass. Her skirt was black and her blouse was white, patterned with small pink and blue flowers. For a moment I was disappointed that she didn't wear the pure white of my favourite lady with the unicorn. Her hair was fair and fell to her shoulders. Her lips were scarlet. And she was straddling the hips of a youth wearing T-shirt and jeans. Her pale legs were bare, her skirt pushed up over her thighs.

I stood and stared, unable to move. I think it was the fact that she was in charge of what was happening that shocked me the most. She was no passive victim of a seduction or ravishment, in need of a knight on a white charger, riding to her rescue.

They must have heard me at last, or at least sensed my presence, for the girl turned her head to look at me. She seemed not at all discomforted by the sight of a boy pushing a bicycle, staring down at her.

She stared back at me and at that moment I saw her face in detail: an oval face with small, delicate features. Her eyes were the clear blue of the sky, with well-drawn eyebrows. The lips, painted with scarlet lipstick, were full and pouting.

She bore a strong resemblance to my sister. Selina even owned a black skirt and flowered blouse like those that this girl was wearing and, for a terrible moment, I thought it *was* my sister who was riding the uncouth lad in the grubby T-shirt and the unbuttoned jeans. He had wiry, reddish hair, and reminded me of Owen Salter. I don't suppose they were really much alike, for I doubt whether I had a clear picture of what that man, seen only once or twice, had looked like. But it *felt* like him.

I stood, rooted to the spot, my heart thumping, my head filled with the whine of the aeroplane engine, unable to speak, to move, or even to think. Selina. My sister!

Then I realised I was mistaken. Of course I was wrong. The thought that this could be Selina was ridiculous. My sister would never behave in this way. And anyway, this girl was plumper and her hair wasn't cut the way that Selina's was. The expression on her face, lascivious, jeering, was one that my sister's could never display. *This was not my sister*. It couldn't be. How could I ever have made such a mistake?

It seemed as though I stood there for an hour, but it can't have been more than a minute or two. Then, at last, I turned, stumbling in my haste, and mounted my bicycle. I rode away down the path and away from the church, veering from side to side in my haste, back into the village with its interesting mixture of vernacular architecture.

A cottage with a cruck end. Another that demonstrated a box frame. A third looked like a longhouse, but this was too far to the south and east of the country for this to be likely. Tiled roofs. Thatch. A nineteenth-century terrace decorated with a pattern of yellow bricks.

But it was no good. However hard I tried, noting and cataloguing in my head, I couldn't remove the picture of the couple in the graveyard from my mind. And what was worse, when the scene came unbidden to the screen of my memory, it was no longer the young woman with the painted face whom I saw. It was Selina's face that smiled the malicious smile, Selina's fair hair that was falling on to her shoulders; it was Selina's pale thighs that were pressed against the red-faced, sweating man.

I strove to forget what I saw. I still strive to erase the false picture from my memory, but it is always Selina that I see in the flowery field, instead of the lady with the unicorn.

I said nothing of any of this when I returned home in time for my lunch.

11

On Tuesday evening, dressed in a decorous jacket and skirt, with a teal-blue silk shirt and plain pearl earrings, Kate presented herself at the lodge of Bartlemas College as instructed by Faith Beeton. She was wearing one of her least eye-catching outfits as it was her intention to observe Faith's colleagues and students in the English department rather than to attract any attention to herself.

'Kate Ivory?' queried the porter.

Kate nodded.

'I have a message here from Dr Beeton asking you to proceed to the Lamb Room without waiting for her. She's been delayed for a few minutes and she will meet you there.' He looked down at the scrap of paper. 'She suggests that you try to get hold of the red wine rather than the white, for some reason.'

Kate promised to take heed of the suggestion.

'Do you know where the Lamb Room is?'

Kate assured him that she did, and set off round the Front Quad towards an archway in the opposite corner.

It was a beautiful evening, the sky streaked with lemon yellow and lavender, and the boisterous wind had dropped, as it so often does in the early evening. As she walked through the next quadrangle, past the famous Bartlemas magnolia tree, then through an eighteenth-century doorway, and heard the murmur of voices coming from the room on her left, memories of previous parties in the Lamb Room came flooding back to

Kate. She paused outside the perfectly-proportioned sash window. The curtains had not yet been drawn and she could see that the room was filling up with people.

The room was a large one, large enough to hold those who would have been invited to this evening's party of welcome. She couldn't see the whole room since there were slender columns, presumably helping to support the decorative ceiling, blocking her view. She had thought she was arriving at the very beginning of the reception, but students and staff alike appeared to have arrived before her, eager, no doubt, to take advantage of the free food and wine.

Kate took her time to study them, standing outside the lighted window – looking in, she thought ruefully, like a child with its nose pressed against a display of toys in a shop window. They looked like the standard Oxford assortment, with a few of the young people rather better-dressed than their elders. Students of English Literature had the reputation of being lively and attractive, and stylishly dressed, as though prepared at any moment to be talent-spotted by a casting director. She was glad she hadn't decided to compete.

It was difficult to tell just how many people had assembled in the Lamb Room, but although the space was a large one, it was nearly full. She would have guessed that more than a hundred people were already there. What had Faith told her about the party? Oh yes, this was a welcome-back bash for the second-years. Bartlemas was one of the smaller colleges, but even so, there must be about a hundred in each undergraduate year. Add on the teaching staff and their assorted partners, not to mention guests like her, and she could expect to find around a hundred and fifty beneath the elegant ceiling of the Lamb Room.

But it was time for her to join in instead of standing aloof outside in the quadrangle. She opened the door and went inside.

A blast of conversation hit her. It sounded as though everyone had already drunk their first glass of wine, and was well into their second, for the noise level had risen above the gentle murmur of the totally sober. Remembering what the porter had said, Kate took a glass of red wine – though hadn't Faith promised her New Zealand Sauvignon? She watched the tray of white wine move away with regret. She looked around the room over the rim of the glass and waved away a plate of snacks. She wasn't about to drop flakes of pastry down her new silk blouse.

Members of Bartlemas College had been sipping their wine, nibbling on collapsing pastry and exchanging venomous gossip for some two hundred years in this very room, she reflected. With its convenient columns and shadowy corners it was ideally suited to conspiracy. Roundheads and Cavaliers, Whigs and Tories, Marxists and reactionaries had probably muttered together behind these columns and plotted their take-over of the college by electing their own choice of Master. As she looked around her for a familiar face, she wondered for a moment what she might see. For a few fanciful seconds she imagined that the room might be full of gentlemen in periwigs and knee-breeches, talking of the latest findings in astronomy or physics. (She was a little vague as to what these would have been two hundred years ago – or even yesterday.) But then she looked again and saw the usual assortment of Oxford academics and students. The students looked and sounded inordinately pleased with themselves but then, she supposed, they always had.

Kate noticed that she was as well-dressed as any of the women, though she hadn't yet caught sight of Faith, who had a habit of looking pretty good herself. Most of the staff belonged to Faith's generation, but unlike her friend, they had the hunched backs and puffy faces of those who spent too long in front of a computer screen. The women wore their hair long and straggling untidily over their shoulders. Their party tops were dun-coloured and shapeless; their legs, when she could see them, were bare.

Even as she watched, she heard their voices rising and saw their faces, devoid of make-up, growing pinker and shinier. She sipped at her own drink, confident that any untoward rosiness or shininess her own face might acquire would be hidden beneath a discreet layer of Dior's matt foundation.

She was annoyed with Faith. Shouldn't she be here to greet her guest? But there must be someone else she knew! She had worked at Bartlemas for several weeks one summer and surely there must still be one or two people in the college she would recognise. She looked around. No one. She thought about approaching one of the chattering groups and introducing herself. But her boredom threshold was remarkably low and she was sure that most of the people present would cross it with no trouble at all.

She eavesdropped on the conversation behind her left shoulder.

'Of course the tragedy of serious music has been its eager embracing of Modernism,' said a woman's voice.

Kate wondered how the woman's companion would respond to this sweeping generalisation.

'As in literature, do you mean?' The man's voice was younger. 'Just as, at the end of the nineteenth century, education brought about near-universal literacy, so at the same time the intelligentsia scorned storytelling, excitement and linear plot formation in favour of—'

'Precisely! And composers discarded melody, rhythm and harmony – everything that people look for in music'

'And so it is only genre fiction that carries on the nineteenth-century tradition of storytelling in literature,' put in the man.

Kate wasn't sure if she was pleased to have confirmation of her prejudices in this way. Although she herself was a practitioner in the field of genre literature, in her experience, people who spoke so authoritatively about the theory of writing could rarely produce anything of any merit themselves. She turned slowly to see who had been speaking and saw a sour-faced woman in a dull blue sari talking to a greying man in baggy beige trousers and sandals who, in his turn, was looking over her shoulder, presumably in the hope that someone younger and more attractive would appear and tempt him away.

'You don't know who the girl in the silver knitted thing is, do you?' he asked.

'Holly Eaves? Unoriginal mind, but a hard worker,' said his companion, as though she had judged and summarised all her students.

'Good, um, presence, though,' said the man.

At this moment a young woman walked past Kate, and although she was quite plain, and moved clumsily, she felt the man's eyes follow her wistfully until she passed out of sight behind another column. In a few more minutes, emboldened by the freely-flowing wine, he would start to move in on one of the more nervous-looking students, Kate thought, whether it was the unfortunate Holly or someone else.

But she reminded herself that, pleasant as it was to observe, she was supposed to be looking out for Daisy Tompkins and her friends, as well as for Joseph Fechan. How was she supposed to recognise them in this crowd? Did any of the people around her fit Faith's descriptions of Daisy and her Moral Tutor? And what *had* Faith told her that might help her to identify the girl? That Daisy was fair-haired, blue-eyed, pretty. There were half a dozen who fitted that description. And Joseph Fechan, she gathered, was unprepossessing. Well, there were more than enough men to choose from who fitted *that* description.

Unless Faith appeared soon she would really stand no chance of knowing who was who. Since this was supposed to be a college affair people weren't wearing name badges, and Kate was relieved that she didn't have to peer closely at the present collection of bosoms and chests, even if it did mean she didn't know who anybody was.

Where did Daisy fit in to this group, wondered Kate. Was she one of the supremely confident young people, loud-voiced and laughing, or one of the mice, hiding in a corner, or behind a column, gazing at her own feet and drinking orange juice? And what about Joseph, if it came to that? Was he hidden in a group of similar middle-aged men, or was he one of the predatory ones, his narrow eyes glinting behind his varifocals, wondering which of the students he could seduce tonight?

At this moment she saw Faith, elegant as ever in cinnamon-coloured wool crêpe, approaching through the crowd. Hot knife through butter just about described her progress, thought Kate admiringly.

'Kate! I'm so glad you could make it,' Faith called loudly, her voice rising above the clamour around them. Then, 'Have you introduced yourself to anyone yet?' she asked, bending close to Kate's ear so that no one else could hear what they were saying. 'Have you met Daisy and her friends?'

'I've only been here for five minutes,' replied Kate. 'I haven't had a chance yet. And I wasn't sure who I was supposed to be talking to. I wouldn't want to waste my time, not to mention my intuition, on the wrong people.'

'What was that?' Faith had obviously caught very little of what Kate had just said. Kate decided to keep it simple.

'Which one's Joseph Fechan?' she asked. 'I couldn't recog-nise him from your description.' There were plenty of odd-looking men, certainly, but no one quite as peculiar as the man Faith had told her about.

'Fechan, did you say? He's only just come in. He likes to avoid these affairs if he can, but I told him he really should make the effort this evening. It's his chance to start the new academic year on the right foot. He should chat to people, make himself pleasant. He needs all the friends he can get.' Faith's lips were only an inch away from Kate's ear. She seemed determined to keep their conversation confidential. It occurred to Kate, though, that if Joseph Fechan had to be told these obvious truths about the advantages of shmoozing, then he must be particularly socially inept.

'So where is he?' she asked.

'He must still be somewhere over near the door,' said Faith vaguely.

At that moment, above the clamour of the room, Kate heard something that she thought at first must be a fog-horn. Then she distinguished separate words. Not a fog-horn, then, but someone speaking and, such was the volume and penetration of his voice that the whole room could do nothing but pay attention.

'None of the sweetened gnat's pee, thank you *very* much. Haven't you any of the *Sauvignon blanc* left? That New *Zealand* wine that you served last Friday was really *quite* drinkable.'

Warned off the white wine herself by Faith, she could sympathise with his words, but the man's voice sounded as though it was being broadcast through a loudspeaker. As it rose effortlessly above the hubbub, everyone in the room must have heard what he said. On certain words he placed an unnecessary emphasis, which added to the strangeness of his speech. Heads began to turn, shoulders twitched with embarrassment, then people apparently realised who was speaking, and made a palpable effort not to stare at him. There was a two-second hush and then, as though at a signal, everyone began to chat again, more loudly than ever, as though to drown out the intrusive voice.

'That sounds like Joseph,' said Faith. Kate couldn't imagine that he could be mistaken for anyone else. Surely no one other than Joseph Fechan had such a voice?

'I thought that once we'd got rid of that oaf Harry Joiner, things would start to improve,' the voice that was Fechan's continued.

In spite of the increased background noise, his words were still quite audible and, what's more, he appeared to be moving in their direction.

'I believe he filled the wine cellar from the shelves of some supermarket,' the voice continued inexorably. 'Understandable on grounds of economy, perhaps, but *hardly* on taste. Perhaps he holds *shares* in the nasty establishment.'

Kate wondered who he was talking to and whether that person had yet dug a hole in the floor and disappeared through it. Maybe everyone at Bartlemas was used to Fechan, but if that was so, why had so many shoulders twitched?

The crowd shifted at that moment.

'Can you see him?' asked Kate.

Faith pointed at a figure halfway between where they were standing and the door. Kate studied the man Faith was indicating, knowing that she would not be the only one to stare at him. And anyone who spoke like that must be used to the attention of strangers, surely?

To her surprise, he wasn't bad-looking, at least from a distance: over six foot tall, with a lean, slightly stooping figure, and a shock of dark hair in which there was practically no grey. Strong features, pale skin. She guessed that the rounded shoulders made him look older than he was. He appeared to be at least forty-five, but Faith, she remembered, had told her that he was in his late thirties. He was dressed in an old-fashioned tweed jacket, as far as she could see – the kind that had leather patches on the elbows and could be picked up for a tenner in a charity shop. She moved closer. Maybe Faith had exaggerated his unattractiveness. He really wasn't that bad, by Oxford standards.

'If we can edge across the room, I'll introduce you to him,' said Faith, following closely behind her.

'Just a minute! Why would he want to talk to *me*? What on earth can I talk about?' Kate was panicking at the idea of being on the receiving end of that voice. And everyone in the room would turn and stare at *her*.

'Oh, ask him about the nineteenth-century correspondence he's reading at the moment. Men are only ever interested in themselves and their own work, aren't they? You have the great advantage of not being a member of this college, anyway. That alone would make you attractive in his eyes.'

As they got closer, Kate heard that Fechan appeared to have left the subject of the wine, but was in no mellower a temper, for he was saying, 'Why on earth do we have to have all these *students* present? Don't we see enough of them in tutorials and so forth? Why do we have to *socialise* with these dreary young people as well?'

A man in an expensive dark suit on their left looked put out, Kate saw. He had stopped whatever he had been saying in mid-sentence and was frowning at Fechan. She wasn't sure, but she thought she heard him mutter, 'Bloody Fechan!'

'The Master,' Faith informed her. 'Oliver Crowson.'

Leader of the Roundheads, Kate reminded herself. The man didn't look as though he had stinted himself when it came to choosing a suit, and there was nothing plain and Puritanical about his silk tie, but he did have a very short haircut, certainly.

'He's not looking pleased,' remarked Kate.

'Let's see if we can join Joseph and get him to shut up,' said Faith. 'He only gets like this when he's feeling uncomfortable. He doesn't shine in social situations, I'm afraid.'

And you can say that again, thought Kate.

'I think it's a good idea to meet our undergraduates in an informal setting,' a brave man was saying to Fechan. 'And it does help them to feel that they really *belong* to the place, don't you think?'

'You mean you want their *money* once they start earning their inflated salaries. Surely you don't have to pour Merlot down their throats and make ridiculous small talk in order to impress upon them their responsibility towards their college?'

'Well, I don't look upon this evening as such an onerous duty. Do you, Joseph?'

Faith insinuated herself between groups of people and made her way across the last few yards separating them from Fechan, Kate following in her wake. With the press of warm bodies, the temperature in the Lamb Room was rising, and the faces around her were growing ruddy with the heat. Kate was confident that her own glowing complexion was the result of cosmetics, but the women around her hadn't been so well-prepared. Funny how academics even smelled different from other people, she thought, as she squeezed between warm tweed shoulders. She wasn't sure whether the aroma was that of old books, ink and scholarship or, more prosaically, a disinclination to visit the dry cleaner's.

Kate saw Fechan's mouth open again, as though to tell his companion exactly how he felt about socialising with *hoi polloi*. He had large, yellow teeth that reminded her inevitably of the wolf in *Little Red Riding Hood*. She hoped that he wasn't about to launch into a personal comment on another of the people present. Why couldn't he criticise the many members of staff who had left under a cloud in the past few years? There were enough of *them* to keep him talking for the next hour or so. The man to whom he had been speaking had backed away, Kate noticed, looking around for another, more conventional group to join.

'Who on earth is *on* the Wine Committee these days?' he

enquired of the room as a whole. 'Isn't there *anyone* in this college who has a *palate*?' He had reverted to the subject of the college wine, apparently.

'Though I suppose that any decent wine would be entirely *wasted* on the lager-swilling louts that we let into the college these days.'

He had what sounded to Kate like an old-fashioned, affected Oxford accent, but she was willing to admit that in his case there was no affectation whatsoever involved. This was simply how he spoke, and always had done, reared in this way of speaking since he was an infant, no doubt.

'Once upon a time, this college had Fellows who knew the difference between a drinkable wine and *total crap*,' he continued. 'But evidently such days are long past.'

To Kate's ears there was something particularly shocking in hearing the word 'crap' pronounced in such a refined accent. And the man seemed impervious to the effect he was having on other people present. As she looked around, she could see three people whose faces were turning red. She was surprised that anyone present was still young and sensitive enough to be capable of blushing, but then, if she had been a member of the Bartlemas Wine Committee, she would probably be blushing by now, too.

'I should have thought,' the stentorian voice continued inexorably, 'that after the *débâcle* of last year's Christmas lunch, when that *execrable* Chilean Merlot was served, certain people might have quietly *removed* themselves from the tasting panel, but I can see, or rather *taste*, should I say, that their presence on the committee is only too current. And if that were not enough, they were overcharged, of course,' he added.

'I believe this wine was quite competitively priced,' put in someone else, gamely. 'I'm sure it came out at under a fiver a bottle with the discount they negotiated. Give them their due.'

'Six pounds and fifty pence a bottle,' said Fechan inexorably. 'That's seventy-eight pounds a case. And the discount was seven and a half per cent, which means that we paid seventy-two pounds and fifteen pence for a case, or six pounds and one and a quarter pence per bottle.'

'Nothing wrong with your mental arithmetic, certainly!'

'I don't need to work it out. The figures were in the Minutes of the committee meeting.'

'Well, there's no need to be quite so nit-picking about it, is there?'

'It's a pity that the members of the Fellowship don't pay more attention to such important details in their dealings,' insisted Fechan.

He was by now addressing the backs of several heads, but at least he appeared to have reached the end of his comments. Was there anything more he could possibly add on a subject Kate had thought long exhausted?

'Come on,' hissed Faith. 'It's time I introduced you to him.'

'Must you?' muttered Kate. 'I'd really rather not.'

'Don't be silly. He's a lovely man once you get to know him.'

Kate wondered whether she and Faith understood quite the same thing by the term 'lovely'.

Faith was already pulling her through the remaining yards separating them from Joseph Fechan. There wasn't much resistance to their passage, she calculated: not many people were disputing their right to talk to the most unpopular man in the room. There was, after all, no way that Fechan's victims could pretend not to hear, and they must be aware that everyone else had registered their humiliation. They might even have the suspicion that everyone agreed with Fechan and that they were secretly laughing at them. She only hoped that she would never have the bad luck to be on the receiving end of one of his devastating comments. It was unfortunate that Faith was leading her into a meeting with the impossible man and, inevitably, into the line of fire.

'Gnat's pee!' Fechan repeated, but his voice had returned nearly to normal. Having inadvertently filled her glass with the white wine of which he was complaining, Kate had to admit that Fechan was in the right of it when he criticised the tasting panel of the college Wine Committee, but that didn't mean that she agreed with his way of expressing his opinion.

'Joseph!' Faith was exclaiming. 'You must meet my friend, Kate Ivory.'

'Must I?' he replied, apparently unaware that this was less than polite. And if he echoed Kate's own thoughts on the matter, at least she hadn't voiced hers aloud.

'Stop behaving like a bad-tempered old bear,' said Faith, in a joky manner that Kate could only think was positively reckless in this company. But, oddly enough, Fechan appeared to mellow under Faith's influence. Perhaps his anti-social behaviour had been in response to what he felt to be the antipathy of most of the people present. 'Be kind to her, Joseph. She isn't used to our uncouth college ways,' added Faith.

Surely he would respond adversely to such a suggestion.

But he simply repeated, in a normal voice, 'Kate Ivory. I'm delighted to meet you.' And he gave her a smile of such sweetness that for a moment she began to understand what Faith saw in him. 'And why would you be gracing our uncouth company with your presence this evening?'

Which, however pedantically he expressed it, got to the nub of the matter, thought Kate. But she couldn't very well inform him that she had come to suss out his treatment of young Daisy Tompkins so that she might give Faith her opinion on both of them – as a disinterested spectator, of course.

'Why, I'm here as the guest of my friend, Faith Beeton,' she said, giving him the benefit of her own most charming smile.

'And I would hardly describe the company as uncouth.'

'The present generation of undergraduates . . .' began Joseph grimly, his voice starting rise, but Faith placed a hand on his arm and he subsided again. 'Are you a member of this college?' he asked, making a visible effort to attempt polite small talk.

'No.' There was no point in adding that she was not a member of any other Oxford college, nor yet of any other university.

'We met when Kate was helping with the "Gender and Genre" summer school,' put in Faith. 'But I don't think you were involved, were you, Joseph?'

'I try to absent myself when our college is invaded by hordes of ignorant young North Americans,' said Fechan.

'Not so young,' recalled Kate. 'More like mature students, I would have said. And as I remember it, some of them were pretty canny.'

'And did you enjoy the experience?'

'Not a lot. They weren't used to nineteenth-century plumbing, apparently.' Fechan's tactless honesty was catching, she found.

Fechan treated her to his laugh, an experience which blasted Kate's ear-drums and made her determined never again to crack anything approaching a joke in his presence. When she had recovered, she tried to study his face, aware that she was here this evening to make an impartial appraisal of the man. Why else would Bartlemas be plying her with Chilean Merlot? But after his apparent friendliness, Fechan had retreated inside himself again. He was avoiding her eyes, and he was studying his shoes, as though they were the most fascinating objects in the whole room. To Kate they looked like standard Clarks' lace-ups, in a standard shade of mid-brown. But Fechan was staring at his feet as though he expected them to double in size at any moment, or sprout feathers.

It was no good, she thought, after a minute's uncomfortable

silence. He might have a lovely smile, when he remembered to use it, and he smelled pleasantly of sandalwood soap, but he was certainly a very strange man. He looked like a caricature, not a real person, as though he had wandered into the Lamb Room from a Harry Potter movie. He would be one of the losers. A baddie. Maybe one of Draco Malfoy's gang, though she didn't really think he was that evil – or even that tough.

Kate was uncomfortably aware that from all over the room eyes were watching her. She couldn't believe it was her they were interested in, but rather that they would stare at anyone who voluntarily spoke to Fechan, 'the madman'. Staff and students alike sipped their wine and peered at Kate over the rims of their glasses. She found herself pushing at her hair in embarrassment, just in case she'd forgotten to put a brush through it earlier. Some of the attention she and Faith were attracting might be sympathetic, she thought, but most of what Fechan said was being heard with ill-disguised pleasure. Kate could imagine some Fellows returning to their cronies and relaying his diatribe with glee: 'Guess what old Fechan was on about today!'

And if *she* wasn't enjoying her meeting with Fechan very much, what, she wondered, would the effect be on a young and naïve student from an Oxfordshire village? Especially if he decided to give his uncensored opinion of her essay. Kate started to understand what Daisy had been through in one of her tutorials, as the recipient of adverse criticism delivered in that unnaturally loud voice. It wouldn't have been Jan Rooling alone who heard Fechan's criticisms of her essay. If his performance this evening was anything to go by, the whole college would have been aware of his opinion of her work.

Kate realised that Faith was speaking again, presumably to fill in the silence. 'Kate's a novelist, you know,' she was saying. Joseph Fechan came out of his reverie and looked interested, Kate noticed to her dismay. She really didn't think that her efforts in the field of historical romance, or even the rather more serious novels she had been encouraged to write recently by her new editor, would in any way interest an old-fashioned academic like Joseph Fechan. She had a nasty feeling that the word 'crap' might echo round the Lamb Room once more, delivered in his loud, precise accents.

She interrupted Faith before she could be more specific about Kate's literary output, remembering something the other woman had said before. 'I believe you know something about nineteenth-century letters,' she said quickly.

'Didn't you mention you were reading the Horsley Papers?' prompted Faith.

'You're interested in the Callcott family, too?' he enquired politely.

'Well—'

'Of course she is,' put in Faith forcefully. 'You were telling me about it, weren't you, Kate? This is the book that's going to make her name, Joseph.'

'I don't believe I've ever seen you in Room 132,' said Joseph.

'Where?'

'It's the Bodleian reading room for those of us who study modern manuscripts,' he said, still in a normal tone of voice, to Kate's relief. 'If you're interested in the Callcotts you'll find their correspondence in MSS.Eng.c.2243 to 45.' Kate still looked blank, but he added, 'And at MSS.Eng.c.2203 and 56.'

If Kate had been going to say that she didn't consider that the nineteenth century was what she would describe as 'modern', she was luckily interrupted by Faith Beeton.

'That's just what you wanted to know, isn't it, Kate? Why don't you jot down the shelfmarks?'

Kate opened her mouth to ask why, but felt a sharp blow to her left ankle and said hastily, 'Yes, of course. Thank you.' As usual, she had a small notebook and pencil in her bag and as Fechan repeated them, she obediently wrote down the shelf-marks.

'And you won't mind if Kate drops in to pick your brains about the, er, Callcotts, will you?'

'If there's anything I know that might be of use, I'll be delighted to assist you,' he said politely.

Kate couldn't be sure if he was being genuinely helpful, or whether this was merely a polite reaction to a request from a colleague. At least she could be grateful that he hadn't trumpeted his half of the conversation to the whole room.

'Joseph, I'm going to have to drag Kate away, I'm afraid. I've just seen the woman she came here to meet.' Thank goodness that Faith came to her rescue just before she made a stupid remark and gave herself away as an ignoramus who had never looked at a modern manuscript, and Fechan announced the fact to the whole room. 'I'll see you later, Joseph,' Faith said, taking Kate's arm and leading her towards the opposite side of the room.

Kate felt that people were eyeing her covertly, wondering who this woman might be who had held a conversation with Joseph Fechan (and without being shouted at, apparently).

'I'm not sure that I learned anything at all of any use to you from that brief conversation,' said Kate as they moved out of Fechan's orbit. 'Why did you let me in for that? And what on earth am I supposed to know about the Horsley Papers? You might have briefed me about them before.'

'Don't you see?' hissed Faith into her ear. 'It gives you an excuse to go back and see him again.'

'Why would I want to do that?'

'I thought you said you'd help.'

Kate was at a disadvantage. It was difficult to turn down a request from a friend when you were in the middle of enjoying their hospitality – even if you weren't enjoying yourself. On the other hand, drinking Bartlemas wine and watching other people making fools of themselves did make a change from stripping wallpaper.

'Yes, of course, you're right,' she said.

She thought of ringing Neil Orson the next morning and proposing a novel based on the correspondence of a rather pleasant Victorian family. No one had mentioned any scandal, she would have to say, or anything exciting at all. No? Neil didn't think it sounded very promising? She was sorry about that. She'd just have to keep on searching for a likely plot, then.

She looked back. Joseph Fechan was studying his feet again. His full glass of wine was clasped in both hands and he was making no attempt to drink any of it. No one approached him. She felt sorry for him, abandoned and isolated like that, but she couldn't blame people for leaving him alone. He might have behaved perfectly properly towards Faith and her, but the man was unpredictable, and unpredictability, after all, was what people feared most in others.

'Don't worry about Joseph now,' said Faith, noticing who she was looking at. 'It's time we found Daisy Tompkins and her friends.'

xii

Mr Evans was there. Have I mentioned him before?

He was there at my father's funeral, helping my mother out of the car, offering his arm as she walked up the aisle. A stocky man, to my child's eyes an old man, though I doubt he was much past forty. He wore dark suits and equally dark ties and his hair was cut short, greying at the sides, with a perfectly straight parting on the left-hand side. I used to wonder about that parting. How long did it take him in the morning to achieve that perfectly straight line? Did he stand very close to the mirror and check that there were no errant hairs straying over on to the wrong side?

There were flakes of white dandruff on the dark shoulders of his coat and he would brush at them in irritation when my sister handed it to him as he was leaving. It's strange the details I remember about this man. Perhaps it was my hatred of him that made me watch him so closely. Right from the beginning, I didn't trust him. I thought he was too solicitous towards my mother, too proprietorial. He was usurping my own position in the household, I thought. I didn't mind being bossed around by my mother and Selina – I was used to it, after all – but I certainly didn't want some strange man taking his seat by the fireside (my father's seat, I remarked to myself) and suggesting to my mother some improvement in my upbringing.

As a matter of fact, I needn't have worried about this. My mother had no great interest in the details of my upbringing, just as long as I never inconvenienced her. She would certainly not put herself out to bring in any innovations in my routine. Mr Evans had miscalculated in this.

I watched them closely, but to my relief Mr Evans left at

nine-thirty every evening. Selina accompanied him to the door, so I wasn't afraid that he and my mother had spent any time together, unchaperoned. I'm sure they all thought I was asleep by then, but I waited, awake and attentive, for the sound of the two sets of footsteps across the hall, the polite murmur of Mr Evans's thanks and the answering murmur from my sister. Sometimes I would crouch on the first-floor landing, peering through the banisters, making sure that the man was safely off the premises, and it is on these occasions that I saw Selina take his coat from its hanger and hold it out for him to put on. He brushed at the shoulders and took just a little too long to place his arms into the sleeves, to pull the fabric across his rounded chest. There was no impatient shrug to indicate that he was tired of my sister's ministrations.

Selina's solicitude appeared to me to be the action of a daughter towards a father, or perhaps it was that of a mother towards her son. It stays in my mind because it was so kindly done, and so typical of Selina.

12

The party was growing livelier. Although a few people had already left, the remainder were making more noise, and there was louder laughter and the particular noise of young people showing off to their contemporaries.

The second-years were greeting the friends they hadn't seen for three months and catching up on the news of their activities during the vacation. Alliances were being renewed, Kate registered, and love affairs were being planned or rejected. It was likely that the older generation were all doing the same thing, but a little more quietly.

As they passed the couple she had eavesdropped on earlier, she heard the man ask, 'Do you know the girl with the blonde hair over there, Raji?'

There was a note of pleading in his voice, but his companion answered shortly, 'She's much too young for you, Matt. Don't be so ridiculous!'

'I was only asking!'

'And that young woman is off limits. Don't you know that?'

'All right. Don't get so worked up about it. I only wondered who she was.'

He wasn't having much luck this evening, Kate guessed. She glanced across to where he had been staring and saw another pretty girl with blonde hair who looked much as she imagined Daisy must look. The girl, sensing that Kate was staring at her, stared back, as though committing her features to memory.

'Who's the blonde girl over there?' Kate asked Faith. 'She fits your description of Daisy Tompkins.'

'Where?'

But the crowd had shifted and the blonde girl was out of sight again.

'I can't see her at the moment,' said Faith.

'Never mind. Tell me who all these people are. I thought I might recognise some of them from my time here at the summer school.'

'Well, I know the students look the same every year, but we do lose one lot after Finals and acquire a new set of first-years a few months later,' said Faith reasonably.

'I meant the others. I thought there'd be one or two I'd recognise from the Development Office or the Bursary. It's not so many years ago, after all.'

'Bursary and Development Office staff weren't invited,' said Faith shortly, so that Kate remembered just how hierarchical the college was. The Fellowship were jealous of their status, obviously, and didn't invite administrative staff to their reception. 'But we've had a pretty high turnover recently,' Faith was saying.

'Yes, I suppose you have.' Better not to refer to the unsavoury happenings in the college over the past few years. 'Who are those two?' she asked, indicating the couple whose conversation she had listened in to earlier.

'The woman in the sari is a medievalist, I believe.'

'The man addressed her as Raji,' put in Kate.

'That would be her. Yes, she's some kind of historian, anyway. She disapproves of us all, as far as I can make out, and really doesn't count in college politics,' said Faith dismissively.

'And her companion?'

'The man in the beige cargoes is Matt Agnew, our new Maths Tutor.'

'Roundie or Cav?' asked Kate.

'He hasn't made up his mind yet. He's neutral.'

'No such thing in wartime,' said Kate.

As she watched, she saw Agnew dart away from the medievalist and catch up with the girl in the knitted silver top who, having placed herself with her back to a column, was easy to pin down.

'I suppose Holly knows how to look after herself?' said Kate.

'She should have learned her way around by now,' replied Faith.

'Carry on with the cast list, then,' said Kate.

'The young gentleman in black velvet who is just joining the sari-clad historian is Hilary Flyer, who teaches Economics.'

'He has to be a Cavalier,' said Kate, finding it useful to fit these people into such simple categories.

'You're right. But stop playing silly games. I've just spotted Daisy Tompkins and a few other students of English. Hurry up, I doubt they'll stay much longer. Some students seem to be slipping away already. The young always have such busy social lives.'

Reluctantly, Kate stopped taking in the details of the young man in black velvet – Hilary Flyer, did Faith say? He was far more her type than anyone else in the room. Then she reminded herself that she was not in the market for stylish young men at the moment. She had a solid, dependable man of her own and Jon would look quite ridiculous in such flamboyant clothes.

They skirted round a gang of students who seemed to have snagged themselves a bottle of red wine and were busy emptying it as fast as possible.

'Come on, Dan, don't hog the lot!'

'Wait a sec, Rollo, Jan's in greater need than you!'

'Can't you find us another bottle to take to the party?'

'Go on, Ethan, you're the expert.'

Kate stopped. These were her rescuers from the mattress incident in Cleveland Road.

'Hi!' she said, as Faith melted away behind a column. Faith would have to wait. Kate had heard the name 'Jan' and wanted to find out if this was Jan Rooling.

She managed to swipe another bottle of wine from a passing waiter and hand it across to Rollo. That should buy her a little time with the students, she calculated.

'Hey, thanks!' he said. 'That was well good.'

'And are these your house-mates?' she asked, looking at someone with long, dark hair and an oval, intelligent face who was filling her glass to the brim from the purloined bottle of wine. She might kill off several million brain cells this evening, but she looked as though she had a few to spare.

'This is Jan,' said Rollo. 'She's another brainy English type, aren't you, Jan?'

The girl nodded, and looked silently into her glass.

'She's only interested in words printed on paper,' said Dan. 'Not a great one for the light conversation, are you, Jan?'

Jan didn't answer.

Well, thought Kate, I can see why they found it difficult to interview her over Fechan's behaviour in the tutorials.

'Are you better? Did you recover from your mattress adventure?' asked Dan.

'Yes, I'm fine,' said Kate.

'Kate's the unfortunate woman who was passing by when Rebecca and Tom had one of their little arguments and chucked their mattress out of the window.'

There was general laughter, brought on by the consumption of wine as much as the actual words, Kate reckoned. Everyone seemed to know about Tom's 'anger and frustration', she noticed.

'I'd better be moving on,' she said. 'I'm Faith Beeton's guest and she's standing over there looking impatient.'

As Dan and Rollo turned back to their friends, she heard one of them say, 'Anyone seen Daisy and Yan?'

'She's on her own this evening,' said Rollo.

The one they called Ethan laughed and said, 'She's on the pull, you mean!'

'Poor old Yan. He doesn't know what he's latched on to.'

Well, well, thought Kate. Maybe Faith is right about Miss Tompkins, after all.

'Would the dark-haired girl be Jan Rooling – Daisy's partner in her tutorials with Fechan?' she asked, when she had rejoined Faith.

'Yes,' replied Faith. 'She's expected to do well, but I can't say that she takes her work as seriously as one might wish.'

'She looked serious enough to me,' said Kate.

'Don't be fooled. She socialises with engineers and medics,' said Faith, as though this said all one needed to know about the girl.

Kate took another hard look at Jan Rooling. She was demonstrating to her companions her ability to drink a full glass of wine in under fifteen seconds, as far as Kate could tell. She didn't look as though *she* would be reduced to rubble by spending an hour in Fechan's company, but then, you never could tell. Perhaps he was one of those people who could always find your weak spot, push the button that reduced you to hopeless incompetence, let you know you were inadequate. Kate had met a few of those in her time.

'Come on!' said Faith, pulling her away. Glasses clinked merrily behind them as they made their way towards the next group.

'I'm sure I saw Daisy here somewhere,' said Faith. 'She'd feel it was politic to be seen to stay until it was time for Hall. And you won't find her stealing off with a bottle of college Merlot, either. I told you she was a calculating little thing, didn't I?'

Apparently the unfortunate Daisy couldn't do a thing right in Faith's eyes, either. Kate felt sorry for her students: if they worked hard they were calculating; if they enjoyed a good social life they weren't serious.

Kate had managed to swap her empty glass for a full one from a passing tray. Couldn't she slip away soon herself? She was growing tired of this party. She was too old to enjoy the company of the students, and not quite serious-minded enough for the teaching staff. She was glad she had turned down the invitation to dinner. A visit to her mother's was a more attractive prospect. It was time she caught up with what Roz was doing with herself these days. Too long a silence and Kate began to worry that her mother was getting herself into trouble again. Irresponsible, that's what she was, and that was inappropriate in one's mother; it was surely time that she grew out of it.

'Come on, I spotted her over in this direction. We'll grab hold of her before she disappears,' said Faith.

'And what's my cover story this time?'

The crowd was thinning now and it was easier to hold a conversation without bellowing. 'Cover story?' queried Faith. 'You've been reading the wrong sort of books, Kate, quite obviously.'

This could well be true, but Kate felt that a familiarity with the more lurid variety of thriller was holding her in good stead this particular evening. She was convinced that a thorough knowledge of *Jane Eyre*, or even of *The Mill on the Floss*, would be of no use whatsoever.

'Daisy!' cried Faith, halting beside a slightly-built young woman with fair hair and round blue eyes, who was just a couple of inches shorter than Kate. Yes, thought Kate, that's the girl I noticed earlier. Daisy was dressed in black, which set off her fragility, her clothing somehow giving the impression of being diaphanous and of moving in a light breeze. Kate thought the impression was carefully contrived, but then wondered whether she was being unduly influenced by Faith's opinion of the girl. Faith, after all, had even objected to the fact that she wasn't stealing the college wine.

'I'm glad you're still here, Daisy,' Faith was saying. 'I did so want you to meet my friend, Kate Ivory. Kate, this is Daisy Tompkins.'

Daisy gave Kate a shy smile. (Did someone of Daisy's generation really feel shy in the presence of a woman in her thirties, wondered Kate.) 'Hello,' she said.

Daisy Tompkins had small features in a heart-shaped face. Kate thought she was the same girl that Raji had described as 'off limits' to Matt Agnew, but she couldn't be absolutely sure. There was a softness about her, a vulnerability, that would make her extremely attractive to a certain sort of man. But maybe that sort of man would be a bully, someone who enjoyed hurting the innocent. For there was also innocence in Daisy's face, or at least a lack of worldly wisdom.

'And these are my friends, Tom and Rebecca,' added Daisy. Tom had thick brown hair and rimless glasses. Rebecca's hair was auburn and she was wearing green-tinted lenses that made her look like an alien. They each took a step backwards, as though to indicate they didn't wish to be included in the conversation, but didn't quite leave their small group.

'Hi, Kate,' mumbled Tom, looking embarrassed.

'Are you OK now?' asked Rebecca. 'After, you know, your fall.' She avoided the word 'mattress', Kate noticed.

'I'm fine,' said Kate. 'I've forgotten all about it.'

They looked relieved that she didn't want to chew over the incident again. They'd already done quite enough apologising for their behaviour, and now they moved away a little, opting out of the rest of the conversation but remaining on the fringes.

'Kate's a real, published writer, Daisy,' explained Faith. 'And that's what you want to be, too, don't you?'

In Daisy's place, and at her age, Kate would have cringed with embarrassment at such an introduction, but Daisy kept up her shy smile and advanced an equally shy hand. Kate shook it, but it was limp and slightly damp and she released it as soon as she could.

'I'm so pleased to meet you,' Daisy said in a polite, little-girl voice. 'I'm sorry I haven't read any of your books, Miss Ivory, but they keep us very busy here, you know. We don't have much time to read for pleasure.'

Oh no, thought Kate. I don't quite believe this. This young woman is just too good to be true.

'Please call me Kate,' she said. 'Miss Ivory' made her feel old enough to be the girl's grandmother.

'Weren't you talking to Dr Fechan just now?' asked Daisy. Kate felt that she wanted to ask what they had been talking about but was too polite to do so. She had been aware, while she was talking to Joseph Fechan, that this girl had been watching her, her head turned in their direction, the blue eyes fixed upon them, even from the further side of the room. Maybe she had simply wondered who Kate was, since she must be one of the few people in the room who wasn't a member of the college.

'Just briefly,' she replied. 'He seemed very concerned about the quality of the wine that the college is serving.' She looked at her near-empty glass. 'But it seems perfectly satisfactory to me.'

'I stick to orange juice at this time in the evening,' said Daisy primly. Which puts me in my place, thought Kate.

'I'm sure Daisy would like to discuss your books with you,' said Faith. 'Why don't I leave you together to talk shop?' and she disappeared as sinuously as ever, before Kate could stop her. Kate looked at Tom and Rebecca, hoping they would join in the conversation and introduce a different subject, but they both avoided her eyes.

'What do you write, Kate?' asked Daisy as Tom and Rebecca sipped at their wine.

'Historical novels,' said Kate. At least Daisy hadn't asked whether she wrote under her own name. 'I used to write romances, but I've progressed to something a bit more up-market recently. How about you? Do you know yet what you want to write?' At least this conversation was easier than the one with Joseph Fechan, but she wasn't sure she was learning very much about Daisy Tompkins. How could she get through the layers of convention and meet the real person in five minutes flat, she wondered. The task was impossible.

'I suppose I just want to be a novelist,' said Daisy simply. 'I don't much like the description "literary novelist", it seems too pretentious. But then, I haven't reached anywhere near the stage where I have to put labels on myself. I've only written short pieces – you know the sort of thing: versions of my own life, oddments of poetry, incomplete short stories. But one day I'll make it, I'm sure.'

'Determination is what it takes, as I expect you know,' said Kate, sounding pompous to her own ears. Was this a contest to see who could produce the most conventional sentiments?

'I'd like to hear some time how you got started,' said Daisy.

'You would?' The story, in Kate's view, was a dull one.

'Yes. I've never had the chance to speak to a professional writer before. We study dead authors, on the whole, and we concentrate on the text, but I'd like to know what really goes on inside a writer's head.'

'I'm not sure it's anything very complicated,' said Kate apologetically.

'It must be. Think about the process: you have to take the raw material of your own life and then transform it into Art.' She stopped, as though embarrassed by her own enthusiasm. Or perhaps she was thinking she'd given too much away about the things that went on inside her own head.

'Well, we must meet for coffee, or lunch or something, and compare notes,' said Kate.

'Could we really do that?'

'I'm a bit busy with house-painting at the moment,' said Kate, watching the light of interest in Daisy's eyes extinguish itself, as though she wasn't interested in any writer who had to do mundane chores. 'But do keep in touch. Please.'

'It's been really interesting talking to you, Kate,' said Daisy, glancing at her watch, as though she had given Kate her attention for long enough. 'But I'm afraid we're going to have to leave. This is First Week and some of us are getting together to catch up on what we've been doing since the end of last term.' Kate felt as though the animated person she had been speaking to only a few seconds ago had disappeared, leaving the well-behaved little girl in her place once more.

'It's lovely to have met you, too, Daisy,' she said. 'And I do wish you the very best of luck with your literary career.'

There was a flash of something in Daisy's clear blue eyes. Was it scorn? Surely not. But her face was no longer pretty. She's like a character in a fairy story, thought Kate. Though I'm not quite sure which one.

The girl gave another of her shy smiles, then turned back to her two friends as Kate walked away. She paused, pretending to examine a plate of smoked salmon snacks, hoping to hear what they would talk about when she had left. She wasn't disappointed.

'Daisy the creative writer,' she heard Rebecca say softly.

'Always good for a story,' added Tom.

'Future winner of the Booker Prize.'

'Destined for screenwriting success in Hollywood.'

'Or maybe it's OUDS you should join,' said Rebecca.

'Faith Beeton takes me seriously,' said Daisy defiantly.

'Faith Beeton takes everything seriously,' said Tom.

'I've never met anyone who was more in earnest about absolutely everything than our Mrs Beeton,' said Rebecca.

And Kate knew that Faith would have hated to be called that. She was, in any case, a really bad cook. Kate helped herself to a small parcel of salmon mousse wrapped in an envelope of smoked salmon. As she looked around for Faith she noticed that Daisy and her two friends were leaving the party, and were walking away, out of the Lamb Room. As Kate watched, they were joined by another tall young woman with chopped scarlet hair and a plunging v-neckline.

What did she make of Daisy? At one moment she appeared to be talking quite sincerely about her writing, then she slipped into what could only be an invented character who was off to a jolly get-together with her chums, chatting together over cocoa and digestive biscuits, no doubt. That's the impression you're determined to give me, Miss Tompkins, but I bet your little party will be a sight raunchier than you're letting on, in spite of your nice manners and demure clothes. Daisy was playing a part, she was sure – Rebecca had implied that – but she didn't know how far removed it was from her real character. And surely most of the people in this room were playing a part, too? Daisy wasn't alone in that.

But then there had been the revealing comments about Daisy in the student house. She was sure now it was Daisy Tompkins they were talking about. And even her friends had hinted that she wasn't the little innocent she appeared to be.

It was five past seven, time for her to say her goodbyes and leave, too, if Faith was to get her dinner in Hall. Kate herself was going to walk up the Cowley Road to her mother's house. Roz had rung that afternoon to offer her a meal.

'You need a night off,' she had said. 'I'm sure you're sick of the smell of paint by now.'

'Just a little,' Kate had admitted. 'Faith's invited me to a do at Bartlemas, so I'll come straight on from there. About seven-thirty?'

'Just right.'

If she left Bartlemas now she would have time to walk up the Cowley Road to her mother's house. She found Faith near the door and thanked her for an enjoyable evening.

'No need to be so effusive,' said Faith drily. 'I thought you might be interested to meet the people involved in our little *fracas*, though.'

'They were certainly an interesting crowd.'

'Well, and what did you think of Joseph Fechan?'

Kate glanced round. No one was within hearing distance. 'He's . . . different,' she said guardedly.

'Well, yes. But do you mean we all have to be the same as each other? Surely Oxford has room for all sorts. We should welcome the presence of people with original minds.'

'Is his mind original?'

'He often talks good sense,' said Faith.

'That's not what I asked.'

'We all specialise so narrowly, it's difficult sometimes to know anything at all about a colleague's area of interest.'

'Faith, you don't often avoid saying what you mean. What is it you're not telling me about your friend Joseph?'

'When it comes to Joseph,' she replied slowly, 'it's sometimes difficult to separate what he's saying from the way in which he expresses himself. It's his manner that puts people off. If they could get past that and listen to the point he's making they would find he's full of good sense.'

And if this didn't exactly answer Kate's question it did at least give her something to mull over later. If she hadn't known that Faith went for good-looking, muscled men some ten years her junior, she might have suspected that she fancied Fechan.

'Do you know who the young woman with the scarlet hair is? She seemed to be another friend of Daisy's but I didn't get to speak to her,' she said, changing the subject since she didn't think she'd get Faith to give away anything more on the subject of Fechan.

'It could be Kim Kettleby. She's quite startling-looking. Was she wearing shiny plum lipstick and black nail varnish?'

'Dark lipstick, certainly. I didn't notice the nails.'

'It was probably her, then. Our resident loud upholder of women's rights.'

'I'd have thought you'd approve of her, then.'

'It's the loud and self-publicising part I'm not so keen on. But you found it an informative evening?'

'I did,' replied Kate truthfully, wondering just how much use to her in making up her mind the evening had been. 'I must be off now, though. I'm having dinner with my mother.'

Faith looked surprised. 'I never had you down for such a conventional person,' she said.

'If you knew my mother a bit better you wouldn't say that.'

And with that, Kate escaped from the Lamb Room.

She looked at her watch. She was in plenty of time. As she walked back through the stone archway and across the quadrangles towards the lodge, she noticed that undergraduates were leaving the modern building – a hall of residence, she remembered – on the far side of Pesant Quad. Since they appeared to be carrying wine bottles or six-packs, she assumed that Hall would be poorly attended this evening, and that a party would soon be in progress. In her own experience, these things didn't really get going until the pubs closed, but maybe today's students were a more abstemious bunch.

As she passed through into the next quad she heard the bass thump of music start up. The noise came from the direction of the Student Union bar, in what must once have been the cellar where food was stored. She thought sadly that she must be leaving her youth behind: she would rather be eating a meal at her mother's house than join the noisy crowd at Bartlemas.

xiii

I believed that if I wrote down all the thoughts, all the conversations that were taking place inside my head, that I would be finally quit of them. Isn't that the principle that all the famous talking cures are built upon? But for me it hasn't worked out that way. Round they all go in their never-ending dance. I write them down and close my eyes and there they are, whirling and spinning behind my eyelids. Laughing at me.

I've tried to write things down in order. Some sort of order, at least. I started at the beginning, or at least I started where I thought it all began, with my father's death. Perhaps I was wrong. Perhaps I should have started further back, or much, much later, when I had become the person that I am now. We start where we have to, I suppose. The moment chooses the man. But I am aware that I have digressed, that I have moved backwards and forwards, darting like a mayfly across the surface of my life's history.

I'm doing my best. It's all I can do. I've bent my head to Discipline all my life and now Discipline itself appears to be cracking and crumbling away, leaving me with the chaos of a rubble-strewn landscape, as in the aftermath of some war.

Is it because I'm so good at remembering? I hang new facts on to the hooks inside my mind. I visualise them; I give them a special place in which to live and have their being. When I want them, they come running to my call, like obedient dogs. But often they come running up, demanding my attention, when I don't want to be bothered with them at all.

Why can't I see a field of daffodils without some obvious line by Wordsworth filling my mind? Everything I've ever read is stored inside my head, just waiting for its moment to emerge. Throughout the years, from my childhood onward, these little nuggets of information, these poems and proverbs, have embedded themselves in the cells of my brain and now they emerge, in dribs and drabs, chasing themselves forever in spirals, never getting free.

It wasn't so bad when I was a child, of course. Then my eye was still naïve, my vision quite fresh. My observations were original instead of being the second-hand thoughts of another man. These days, is there any such thing as an original observation to be made? As I study the literature of the late twentieth century, I doubt it. But then, do any of my students need a teacher with original thoughts in his head? The undergraduates have their minds set on passing examinations, gaining qualifications and proceeding to lucrative jobs. And as for my colleagues, I am sure that they would consider anything approaching an original thought as highly suspect.

I should have asked Mr Rank whether there was a way of getting rid of all the accumulated bric-à-brac which litters my brain and which lies around like junk in the attics of an old house, of no further use to the owner, waiting only to be consigned to the rubbish bin. If I could enter a church in order to pray, if I could believe that there was anyone or anything who might listen to that prayer, then this is the gift that I would ask for.

I would pray for the priceless gift of forgetting.

13

It was good to get out of the confined and overheated atmosphere of the Lamb Room and into the fresh autumn air of the High. Kate walked down the broad, empty street towards Magdalen Bridge. Nearer Carfax there were a couple of hotels that looked as though their customers were still awake, but the colleges all slumbered behind their high grey walls.

As she crossed the Plain and turned into the Cowley Road the mood of the city changed: here there were people on the pavements, cars passing, and lights and noise from the restaurants and shops. Ten minutes later, she turned into a quiet side street, walking away from the main road, then into the narrow road, lined with cars, where her mother lived.

Roz's house was in an Edwardian terrace, its walls of yellow brick, its roof of grey slate. Kate pushed open the gate and walked up the short path to the front door, painted dark red and set within an arched porch.

'Have you walked all the way from Bartlemas?' asked her mother when Kate had accepted a glass of red wine and settled herself in front of the glowing cast-iron stove in the sitting room. It was a decent Spanish wine, she noticed, and better than anything they had served at Bartlemas.

'It took me only about twenty minutes. And I enjoyed the exercise after being cooped up in the Lamb Room with all those . . .' She found it impossible to describe the guests at the Bartlemas party without boring her mother rigid for the next

162

half-hour. 'And I didn't think much of the atmosphere either,' she finished lamely.

Certainly the atmosphere in Roz's small house was a lot more relaxing. The solid-fuel stove was in keeping with its period, though Roz's décor was neither Victorian nor particularly English.

'The odd thing is, that although it's more relaxing here, it's somehow more stimulating, too.'

'I'm glad you approve,' said Roz.

'But you've changed things in here.'

'I've done more than that, actually.'

Kate looked around her more carefully. When Roz moved in, six or seven years before, she had filled her house with objects that she had picked up on her travels. These, intriguingly, had arrived in boxes of various sizes from places around the globe, apparently forwarded by friends who had been looking after them for her. They weren't, on the whole, artefacts that were normally bought by tourists, but everyday objects that simply looked 'foreign' in their Oxford setting, especially in contrast to the Lamb Room: the plates and bowls, dark-glazed and decorated with abstract burnt-sienna patterns, that Roz used at every meal; cast-iron cooking pots and smoked-glass wineglasses also used as a matter of course; the cushions, embroidered and tasselled, that she scattered along the back of a plain, dark red sofa; the oriental rugs on her polished floorboards; the duvet covers and pillow slips in dusky paisley patterns, or scattered with golden, exotic birds, on the beds in the two bedrooms upstairs.

'There are fewer things around,' said Kate eventually.

'Is that all you've noticed? I thought you were my literary, observant daughter.'

'You've reduced the clutter, then.'

'Clutter? My house was never cluttered!'

'Have you changed the colour of the walls? Weren't they a darker gold last time I was here?'

'Now, that's the first thing you've got right so far.'

'Why have you changed this room? I liked it perfectly well the way it was.' She recognised the mild complaint in her voice, as though she was a child objecting to some alteration in the family home that challenged her sense of security.

'I liked it too. But I've been here long enough and it's time I moved on. I'm thinking of selling.'

'You're not off on your travels again, are you?'

'I've lived in this house for years now – longer than I usually stay in one place, certainly, but I haven't the urge to go travelling again just yet. But I do want to move on.'

'And you think you should make the place look bland for the prospective buyers?'

'Not bland, exactly.'

'That's good, because you're scoring very low indeed on "bland".'

'I'm glad to hear it. But I am reducing the number of my belongings on view, since I'm trying to appeal to as broad a spectrum of buyers as possible, rather than limit myself to those who like the eclectic, exotic look.'

' "Cluttered" is the way we literary types describe it. But I still don't understand why you're thinking of selling. I thought you'd decided to settle down in Oxford after your years as a wanderer.'

'I'm as settled as I ever will be, here in Oxford. But I could move a mile or two away, couldn't I? You needn't worry, I'm not going to abandon you all over again.'

'Huh!'

'Have you any idea how this house has increased in value since I bought it?'

'It must have doubled, I imagine. But then, so has every

other house you might want to buy in its place. You have to live *somewhere*.'

'I'm not as scatty as you seem to think, Kate,' said Roz. 'Of course that thought has occurred to me, but I also know that this is a city with high employment and thousands of students and academics, a city where people want to live and where there will always be a shortage of property to buy.'

'You're going to become a landlady? I'll help you write the Rules of the House, if you like.'

'No, *not* a landlady. I'd hate to have to worry what other people were doing to my furniture.'

'Or a property developer? Don't tell me you've been watching too many television makeover shows.'

'I've met several people recently who have been very successful at buying property, modernising it and then selling it on.'

'These must be new friends of yours,' suggested Kate.

'I like to extend my circle of acquaintances, certainly.'

'You'll need a fair bit of capital, surely, if you're going to buy up property in this area.'

'You're about to tell me that the value of houses can fall as well as rise, like the lugubrious voice at the end of the financial ad. Yes, Kate, I know *that*, too. But I've made a perfectly good living for the past twenty years or so by buying and selling goods of various kinds.'

'You have?' She had never been entirely sure how her mother had financed her peripatetic lifestyle. 'The only job I've seen you hold down was the one where you had to make thousands of sticky pastries for your friend Leda's restaurant.'

'All that honey! All those almonds! These days I gag at the slightest whiff of orange-flower water! If those months taught me anything at all it was that I would be a lot happier if I gave up cooking and took to trade once more – bartering, haggling, being an old-fashioned merchant.' Roz stood up, as if to indicate that the subject was closed. 'Now, Kate, I think I'd better dish up our meal. Take your glass to the table and then make yourself useful by bringing in the vegetables.'

From which Kate gathered that her mother would tell her no more on this occasion about her plans. She only wished she could tell how serious Roz was about sinking all her capital into some dubious property business. And who were these new friends who were apparently encouraging her in the venture?

'Now, tell me what you've been doing this evening,' said Roz, once they had cleared a reasonable amount of food from their plates. 'You're dressed up for a respectable party, but you turn up at my house for dinner at seven-thirty.'

'Faith Beeton invited me to a reception at Bartlemas.'

'Oh, yes. I believe you did mention it when we spoke on the phone. Why should she do that? I didn't think you were on such close terms.'

'It's a long story.' She wasn't sure she wanted to tell Roz how she had got involved in something that really didn't concern her. Her mother might point out that she tended to do this sort of thing a little too frequently.

'There's plenty of wine left in this bottle and you can have second helpings of your dinner if you like, so we're really not in any kind of a hurry.'

There was no getting away from it, apparently, so Kate said, 'Faith Beeton's having problems with one of her students and she thought I might be able to give her an unbiased opinion on the matter.'

'Really? It sounds most unlikely. Do you really want to involve yourself in her professional work? But then, I seem to remember that Faith is a very forceful young woman. She manages to boss even *you* around, after all.'

'I'd say she was more manipulative than forceful,' said Kate with feeling. 'I really don't know how she managed to persuade

166

me to get involved. But that's why I was at Bartlemas this evening: I was supposed to be giving the people involved the once-over. And she seemed to think it would be helpful if I got the general flavour of the place.'

'I suppose it could come in useful as background material for one of your books.'

'That's what I always tell myself when I have to do something I don't want to.'

'And did you come to any conclusion?'

'Not really. There were so many people there that I only met each of them quite fleetingly. The "victim" in Faith's conundrum is a delicately pretty blonde with charming manners, while her "tormentor" is an unattractive man with a loud voice and a pedantic manner, so it's difficult not to be affected by appearances. Apart from those two they seemed the usual mixture of boring academics, self-obsessed students and raving loonies.'

'It's good to hear you've lost none of your objectivity,' said Roz drily.

'Well, you should have seen them! You'd have agreed with me that most of them were off their heads. I'm glad you didn't entrust *your* only daughter to mad people like them.'

'You've dropped the chip you've been carrying round on your shoulder about not going to university, have you?'

'I think I may be getting a little old to be jealous of students, certainly.'

'Well, that's a relief.'

It was Kate's turn to get to her feet to indicate that she'd had enough of the subject of conversation. 'Let's take these plates out to the kitchen, shall we?'

'Good idea. Then we can move into the other room, if you like. It's more comfortable in there. Shall I make coffee?'

'Better make it a peppermint tea for me or I'll be awake half the night. I need to be up early again tomorrow.'

When they had settled down in the cosy chairs in the other room, Kate said, 'I can see you've cleared more stuff from in here, too. What have you done with your books? You haven't thrown everything away, have you?'

'That's the trouble with writers: they can't bear the idea of getting rid of that sacred object, the book, however old and useless. But don't worry. I've put most of them away in boxes. I'm renting a small storage space for my surplus possessions. I've not de-cluttered my life to an extreme degree. Now, tell me how you're getting on in Cleveland Road.'

'I'm still at the boring stage – you know, pulling off wallpaper and removing layers of old paint. Then I have acres of wall to wash before I can think of applying any new colours – except for the hall, that is. I couldn't stand the sight of it any longer when I walked into the house.'

'Very commendable. I'm glad to hear that you've inherited none of your mother's slapdash tendencies.'

'At the moment I rather wish I had.'

'You're not getting too settled in Cleveland Road though, are you?'

'Of course I am! I have no intention of moving out again in the foreseeable future. This is where I intend to live for at least the next ten years, if not longer.'

'I thought you and Jon were getting very friendly these days.'

'What's that got to do with it?'

'Positively connubial, I thought.'

'So?'

'Aren't the two of you thinking of moving in together?'

'Not at the moment, no. And you aren't usually as interested in my affairs as this.'

'You're about to tell me to mind my own business.'

'I wouldn't dream of being so rude.'

'Well, before you dismiss the idea of living with Jon out of hand you should reflect on the fact that you're not getting any younger, are you?'

'Thank you, Mother.'

'You have to face these facts, Kate. It's time you settled down. And Jon seems as good a bet as anyone, I should have thought.'

'You sound as though I have to get married before I'm forty or turn into a dried-up old spinster. Women these days aren't like that!'

'Maybe not. But you don't want to turn into a lonely old woman with no children and no stake in the future either, do you?'

'That doesn't seem a good enough reason to jump into marriage – or even living together – with the person who just happens to be around at the time.'

'And you think Jon's happy with the way things are?'

'We see each other pretty frequently. Why should we change an arrangement that suits us both?'

'Because relationships don't stand still. Either they develop or they quietly disintegrate.'

'Rubbish.'

'Believe me. I'm your mother, remember. I know about these things. The least you should do is involve him in some of the decisions you're making at the moment.'

'I'm not making any decisions. I'm just turning my house into a place fit to live in.'

'For one person.'

'There are three bedrooms. I think I'll have room for an occasional visitor.'

'One of those bedrooms will be your study, surely?'

'I call it a workroom. Study sounds too academic. And as a matter of fact I'll probably use both the rooms at the back of the house to work in.'

'And Jon doesn't mind about that?'

'Why should he? He has his own flat in London.'

'That's the problem, isn't it? From what I can gather, Jon's work will always be in London and Oxford's a long way to commute on a daily basis.'

'You think I should move to London?'

'You shouldn't rule it out, certainly.'

'I have no plans to move again, believe me, but that doesn't mean I'm excluding Jon from my life. I've told him about Faith's problem with her student, for example.'

'And what was his reaction?'

'He told me not to get involved.'

'How sensible of him. How did Faith persuade you into it, anyway?'

'Did I tell you I was taking a literature class this term?'

'Possibly.'

'Faith's our tutor, so after the class we went out for a coffee and she convinced me that I could help,' Kate finished lamely.

'It's time you learned how to say "no".'

'But did I tell you my one good piece of news?'

'What's that?'

'Susanna has turned up again. At least, she didn't just turn up, she was returned by one of my new neighbours. It made a good excuse to get acquainted.'

'Is this a little grey-haired old lady?'

'A beautiful young man, as a matter of fact. He works from home, like me, so I'm being a touch wary to begin with. I don't want too many interruptions when I finally get round to writing the new book.'

'Very wise.'

'And do you remember my friend Emma Dolby?'

'Who could forget her!'

'Well, she appears to have had a makeover, so that she now looks slim and stylish. And from a conversation I've had with her son, it seems that she's had a personality transplant as well.'

'About time too! I thought she was a very irritating person.'

'I have a certain fondness for Emma. After all, if I'd taken the wrong turning in life – gone to university, got married, found myself a sensible job – I, too, could now be the owner of fifteen children, a dull husband and an appalling wardrobe, couldn't I?'

'I very much doubt it.'

'Is that really the time?'

'It's not very late, is it?'

'Late enough for someone who is going to get up at dawn to scrape off yet another layer of paint.'

'Are you walking home, or would you like me to drive you over to Jericho?'

'Would you mind?'

Roz was waiting to turn right at the traffic lights in the High Street when Kate said, 'There! He's unmistakable!'

'Who is?'

'That's Joseph Fechan. The man I was telling you about.' She pointed to a tall figure in a dark overcoat, striding up towards South Parks Road.

'The ogre? The man you went to Bartlemas to meet this evening?'

'Yes. He must have left the college and be walking back to his own place.'

'Or to visit a friend. Or to buy some cigarettes. From what you were saying, people make too many assumptions already about Joseph Fechan.'

'I wonder where he lives,' said Kate, curious as ever. 'I can't imagine him in a modern semi with a neatly-trimmed garden. I see him living in gothic splendour, somewhere in North Oxford, with hanging cobwebs and skeletons in every cupboard.'

The lights changed and Roz turned into the same street as

Fechan. He had crossed to the opposite pavement so that he was on her side as she drove past him. A street lamp lit up his face and hair.

'He looks perfectly normal to me. I don't know what you're making such a fuss about,' she said.

'You haven't heard him speak. And you can hardly judge someone's character from seeing him at a distance, in the dark.'

'True. I still think that Faith's college is too inward-looking. I'm sure an outside observer would soon sort out that problem of hers.'

'Well, that was Faith's opinion, too. But I haven't done conspicuously well yet, have I?'

'I don't suppose anyone could, then.'

When Roz had drawn up outside Kate's house, Kate asked her whether she would like to come in for a coffee.

'Some other time. I'll give you a ring and then pop over to see how you're getting on with the decoration.'

'That's a good idea.'

'And if you need a good carpenter, or plumber, or electrician, I can recommend three good, reliable tradesmen.'

'Thanks.'

As she walked into the house, Kate reflected that her mother must be serious about improving her house to sell at a profit. She just hoped that Roz knew what she was doing. In the past, her choice of friends with money-making ideas had been disastrous.

xiv

As I look around me, at my colleagues, at the Bartlemas under-graduates (I have to admit that I know little of the lives of my neighbours in Park Town, so I am unable to generalise about them), I have come to believe that morals – at least *sexual* morals, since this is what most people mean by the term – is largely a question of physical appearance.

The good-looking man is a seducer who loves and then departs from the scene. The ugly man is faithful because he fears that no other woman will look at him. Similarly, the plain woman cleaves only to her husband in the manner of her wedding vows; the attractive woman moves from lover to lover.

Is it true that even someone like me would be a faithless Lothario if only he were given the opportunity? But would I still be 'someone like me' if I had grown into a handsome man, like my father? And could I ever believe that any approach by me to a woman would be met with anything but scorn?

But it explains my mother's behaviour, at least to me. Now I seem to understand it, though at the time I could not. She was not an immoral woman. She was merely a good-looking one who had many opportunities to take lovers, and so she did. I doubt that she ever took a lover while my father was alive, but once she was widowed she saw no reason to remain faithful to him. She had, after all, promised fidelity only 'as long as ye both shall live' and no longer.

And what of my father? Did his evenings spent in Chambers mean that he was seeing other women? Possibly. Men might have found my mother alluring, but I doubt whether that brittle – I was going to add *selfish*, but who am I to accuse another of such a fault? Let me call her *cool*, rather – and that cool nature of hers was ultimately unsatisfactory to a passionate man.

Perhaps, after all, sexual morality is less a question of physical appearance than of courage, the taste for taking risks. I cannot say that I have ever enjoyed taking a risk, if indeed anything as exciting as a risk is something I have ever taken.

There I go, analysing people and their actions, believing myself in possession of a superior intellect, able to understand others, while my own psyche is too complex, too deep for them to understand in their turn. This is my besetting sin: to believe myself more intelligent, more perceptive than other people, whereas, in reality, I have been used and manipulated by the people I despise. I have been outwitted at every turn. I have been blind to what was happening until it was too late.

Is there some good reason why I have been fooled and bamboozled by women? Not just by young and beautiful ones, but by women of all ages. It is as though I read them awry. A woman smiles; I believe she likes me. She frowns; I displease her. She has an innocent and open countenance, so I believe what she tells me. Why is it that I, who might untangle the most subtle of meanings from a sixteenth-century text, am baffled by the everyday utterances of an unsophisticated young woman?

14

In his flat in West London, Jon Kenrick poured himself a small whisky then, looking again at the heap of luggage sitting in the middle of his usually minimalist space, he sloshed in another half-inch, added just a dash of water, and swallowed a large mouthful.

'Alison!' he called. The sounds of someone enjoying a long, hot shower, washing their hair and singing Scottish songs had ended a few minutes ago.

The door opposite crashed open and a small, dumpy woman in a pink towelling robe, and with an untamed shock of wet, curly brown hair, appeared in the doorway.

'Would you like me to give you a hand getting your stuff into the spare room?' he asked. 'I'm sure you'll be needing your clothes, at least.'

'I like to relax in my dressing-gown in the evening. It's cosier, isn't it? So that's all right, I don't need anything else at the moment. And anyway, I'm not sure we'll fit it all in,' she said doubtfully. 'My room isn't very big, you know.'

Jon managed to avoid pointing out that it wasn't *her* room, or at least only for a brief period. And, as a matter of fact, once he'd removed his tie and shoes, personally he preferred to stay more or less fully dressed in the evening.

'You'll get cold feet if you walk around in your socks like that,' said Alison. 'Where are your slippers?'

'Really, I don't want to wear them. I'm quite happy in socks.' He was starting to feel like one of Alison's children.

'I suppose you know best,' said Alison doubtfully.

'Yes,' he said firmly, reminding himself that he was her *older* brother. Alison seemed to think that the possession of a husband and children gave her the right to tell him what to do. And if she'd made such a spectacular success of her own life, what was she doing in his flat rather than back home in Scotland?

'Well, maybe I will need this suitcase this evening,' Alison said helpfully, indicating one of the smallest cases in the heap. 'Why don't we move that table and then stack the rest of my belongings over there by the window? There's plenty of space in here.'

'This is the sitting area,' pointed out Jon. 'And the table is over by the window because that is where I like to take my meals, enjoying the view. I think of it as the eating area,' he explained, and swallowed another large mouthful of scotch.

'You look out on another block of flats. You won't miss a view like that.'

'I can see a portion of sky and a distant tree,' insisted Jon. 'Please leave the table where it is.'

'Is that whisky you're drinking?' asked Alison.

'Yes.' Surely she wasn't going to start commenting on the amount he'd been drinking. It was only one scotch, even if it had been an unusually large one.

'Pour me one too, would you? I've had a tiring day.'

'Not half as tiring as mine,' muttered Jon, but he obediently poured his sister a drink and handed it to her.

'And I'll put my cases behind the sofa if they'll be in the way by the window,' she said obligingly, sitting down on the black leather sofa and knocking back half her own whisky. Jon was sitting in the armchair that he usually offered to visitors.

Alison leaned forward and established firm eye-contact. 'Now, I don't want to cause any fuss, Jon. I don't want to get in your way. I shall just tiptoe my way around you. You must carry on as though I wasn't here. I know you've got your own life, after all – what's the name of this new girlfriend of yours, I'm sure you must have told me? – so you and she must come and go as you please and take no notice of little me.'

Jon watched the water drip from her wet hair on to a grey silk cushion. 'Thanks,' he said faintly.

'It must be an awful bore for you having your little sister descending on you out of the blue, but I don't expect you to alter all your arrangements just because I'm living here for the moment.'

'No, of course it's all right,' said Jon, feeling guilty that perhaps he hadn't made his sister feel welcome. 'It's no bother at all having you here.'

But why had she used the word 'living'? Didn't that imply an extended visit? Fond as he was of his sister, he wasn't sure how much of her company he could stand. She did fill the place up so! He tried not to look at the pile of luggage. Why did she have to travel with quite so much gear, and *why* did her cases have to be purple?

He would cook her a meal in a minute, and then offer to stow at least some of her possessions in the spare room. Kate always managed to keep all her stuff in the spare room when she stayed, and she used up only a small shelf in the bathroom. But Alison seemed to have spread out all over the whole flat, and he had the nasty feeling that his bathroom would be draped with wet towels and there would be puddles of water on the floor. He had tried to explain that there were empty spaces in the flat because that was the way he liked to live, but she seemed to think that space was there to be filled, preferably with some of her belongings.

'You won't want to stay away from the children for too long though, will you?' he said, trying to voice his doubts in an acceptable form.

'I'm not so sure about that,' she replied sharply. 'It will do

Iain good to find out just how much there is to do with so many children in the house. I'm in no hurry to rush back to Scotland, Jon, I can tell you. Now, where's your television set? It's a great treat for me to be able to choose what programme to watch instead of fitting in with what everyone else wants. It'll soon be time for our favourite soap, won't it?'

Jon handed across the remote and sat for a moment staring gloomily into his empty glass. 'I'd better get on with the supper,' he said, and went into the kitchen area. As he chose a packet out of the deep freeze and put it into the microwave he could hear the title music of one of his least favourite programmes booming out from the television.

'No, don't get up. You enjoy the programme,' he said, as he set two places at the table. And then he angled one of the chairs so that Alison could continue to watch while she ate her supper. Afterwards, he removed their plates and washed them up. At least her hair had stopped dripping on to his cushions, he thought, though she might have encouraged it into a more becoming shape before it dried completely.

'You're a really thoughtful man,' said Alison when the television was at last silent. 'Iain would never have looked after me like this after a hard day's work. He's quite happy to sit back in a chair and let me get on with it.'

Jon remembered how Kate would let him settle back into one of her comfortable chairs while she produced a meal for them. Was he taking her for granted, he wondered. And did she ever sit around like this, in a shapeless old dressing-gown, with her hair looking a fright? Somehow he couldn't see it.

'Yes, I just wish Iain was more like you,' Alison was saying. 'Maybe you could give him a few pointers. You know, take him down to the pub, draw him on one side, and then tell him how to be more thoughtful.'

'No. I don't think that would be at all a good idea.' Iain was, in any case, taller than Jon, and with all the physical work of the farm, was probably a lot stronger. 'And I'm not sure how patient I'd be with a house full of children,' he added. He'd probably be down at the pub with his mates, he reflected. He'd be worse than Iain.

'Isn't it time you decided to have a family?' asked Alison, breaking into his thoughts.

'What? But I'm not married.'

'You don't have to be these days.'

'It's not something I've thought about,' he said. He wondered what Kate's views were on the subject. Had they ever spoken about it? They both had such full lives that the question of children simply hadn't arisen. He wouldn't mind a child, or maybe even two. It was something he intended to get around to eventually. Perhaps he should talk to Kate about it next time he saw her – if he ever did get his flat to himself again, or if Kate managed to get her house into a civilised state. Alison looked all too settled on his sofa for his liking.

'So, what prompted this trip to London?'

'I told you. I just had to get away from them all,' she replied.

'But why just now? Was there anything in particular?' he asked tentatively.

'Iain's being quite unreasonable. Or even more so than usual, I should say. And Sandy and Fiona are simply backing him up because they want to defy my authority.'

'We all know that teenagers can be a bit of a handful. You still haven't told me what this is all about, though.'

'Iain wants to sell up and emigrate.'

'That does sound rather drastic, admittedly.'

'He says there's no future for any of us in farming in the UK. We should go somewhere with more space and where our efforts would be appreciated.'

'But you don't see it that way?'

'I certainly don't! I was born and brought up in England

and now I've moved to Scotland. That's quite far enough for me.'

'It does seem to be something that the two of you should talk about,' said Jon reasonably. Apart from offering to spin a coin, there didn't seem much that he could add, certainly.

'But he won't listen to me,' said Alison tearfully.

Jon wanted to point out that she and Iain wouldn't be able to hold much of a meaningful conversation when they were several hundred miles apart, but knew that all his sister wanted at the moment was reassuring words and a little brotherly sympathy.

He did ask, eventually, 'Who's looking after Elspeth? Won't she be missing you?' Three, after all, was rather young to be left on your own without your mother.

'She'll be all right. I have a girl to help me, and Elspeth's very fond of her. And Fiona will give a hand, and read her a bedtime story. It's time Iain did his fair share of looking after the children, anyway.'

Poor old Iain, thought Jon, but he only said, 'Do give him a ring if you want to. You can take the phone into your room if you'd like to be private.'

'He can just stew for another day or two,' said Alison. 'It will do him good. I'm nothing but an unpaid servant in that house.'

Well, an unpaid servant with a woman to come in and keep the house clean and another to help her look after the youngest child. It didn't sound too onerous to Jon, but he wasn't prepared to argue with Alison over it. He decided that, unusually for him, he would pour himself another large whisky.

It was nearly eleven when the phone rang and Alison had at last retired to the spare room. There was really only one person this was likely to be.

'Hello, Kate.'

'Hello. Are you feeling all right?'

'Yes. Why?'

'Your voice sounds husky.'

'I was trying to whisper.'

'Don't tell me. Your sister's arrived.'

'With a huge heap of luggage. God knows how long she's planning on staying!'

'And have you discovered why she's done a runner?'

'I think she considers she's taken a few days' break, so that her husband can come to his senses and see things from her point of view.'

'Oh dear.'

'Exactly. I gather that he wants to emigrate and she doesn't.'

'That's rather a basic disagreement, I can see that.'

'And I don't see how forcing him to look after their children, all on his own, is going to solve it, myself.'

'Possibly not,' said Kate, not wanting to join in someone else's argument.

'It does mean I'm going to be fully occupied though, for a week or so at least. Unless, of course, you'd like to come up to London for a couple of days and see if you can talk some sense into her.'

'I don't think she'd welcome that, do you?'

'I thought women liked talking their problems over with other women.'

'But not with some total stranger. She's probably discussed it with her own friends already. I doubt very much whether she'd welcome *my* presence in your flat.'

'I expect you're right. She'd probably take no notice of your sensible arguments, but I think she'd like the chance to look you over, ask you some intrusive personal questions and then give me her unalloyed views on your character and appearance.'

'If you raise your voice like that she's going to hear what you're saying.'

'I think she's fallen into a deep and self-satisfied sleep,' said Jon gloomily. 'I just hope I don't get Iain on the phone tomorrow, selling me *his* side of the story.'

When she had finished her conversation with Jon, Kate lay on her bed, thinking about the situation. Was she being sensible in refusing to get involved in Jon's problem with Alison, or was this one more indication that she was unable to form a close relationship with a man? Would any other woman have waded in and taken sides and argued her adopted side of the argument? There was really no telling.

Last time Jon had come to Oxford he had stood in front of her distorting mirror in the hall and they had laughed at the tall, thin man with the lugubrious face who stared back at them. But was it such a joke? He had sounded pretty lugubrious on the phone this evening.

Suppose they did as Roz suggested and moved in together. Would she really be expected to join in with family squabbles, not to mention being judged – and possibly found wanting – by the members of Jon's family? Kate had lived too long on her own for this prospect to be at all pleasing.

XV

Before the death of my father – no, it's time I stopped calling him that. He died when I was six years old. Unless I had the family photographs to remind me, I doubt whether I could even recall his face in any detail. I do remember the sound of his voice, the orotund phrases that filled the room and addled my brain, but his appearance has left me. All I have is the face in the pictures, the expression he put on for the eye of the camera. The scowl, the anger, perhaps the amusement and the fond affection of a father, these are gone for ever. He is past, he is the man who was married for fifteen years to my mother, he is simply Greville. Arthur Greville, as the vicar referred to him at his funeral.

After Greville's death, my mother made one or two women friends. I believe that she was shunned by some of the couples she had once known because the wives were nervous that she might alight upon their husbands and steal one of them for her own. In the past she had never sought the company of other women. To her they were simply the appendages, or the belongings, of their husbands. Unmarried women she disregarded entirely unless they were hired to provide some service for her, such as manicuring her nails or polishing her furniture. But after Greville's death, the situation changed.

To begin with her new women friends were of her own age, but soon she viewed their greying hair and spreading hips with dismay and, fearing that she might be associated with women who displayed such obvious signs of middle age, she started to make friends with women who were younger, and in public she treated those of her own age with deference and formality as though they were old enough to be her grandmother. I don't think it occurred to her that she might appear even older in comparison with her young friends, and to be fair to her, she didn't, at least on her good days. She had quick, youthful movements, though her hands had stiffened and sometimes there was an expression on her face as though her joints and muscles were protesting at their treatment. But she was determined to belong to the younger generation.

One of these younger friends – perhaps in her late twenties when my mother was in her early forties – was a pleasant-looking woman who had the good sense not to overshadow Celia. Celia simply didn't think of her as good-looking, though Pamela had mid-brown hair cut in a bob that emphasised the oval of her face. I think she could have made more of herself, and probably did when she was not in Celia's company. She had large, dark eyes, fringed with exceptionally long lashes. 'We'll have to call you Bambi,' my mother would joke, though there was always a sharp edge to her humour. Luckily the suggested name didn't stick, for I remember her as Pamela. Pamela Mooney.

I addressed her as 'Miss Mooney', of course, for I was a polite child, with more formal manners than are usual nowadays. But her response was to laugh, and say, 'For goodness' sake call me Pamela! I'm not as old as all that!'

Pamela. She was always happy, and I think her presence did my mother good. When Pamela was around she came out of herself, as they say, and was less irritated with things in general and me in particular.

Pamela could persuade her to get out of the house and do things. They explored country pubs for their lunch, they visited antiques centres, they even went to the cinema or the theatre.

What did Pamela get out of this friendship? I believe that my mother usually paid the bills, though Pamela didn't strike me as a grasping kind of person. I imagine she was simply not as well off as my mother.

And, in the school holidays, she made an excellent friend for Selina. I believe that at that time she was the only person my sister would confide in, and she must have been in need of such a friend.

My mother would show occasional flashes of jealousy if Selina and Pamela spent too much time together, gossiping. But Pamela was easygoing and refused to be put out by my mother's moods.

I only wish that Pamela could have been in the house more often. But as she reached her thirties inevitably she became interested in some man or other and after that she had less time for my mother and sister. I don't think my mother liked this young man much – later he became Pamela's fiancé, and eventually, her husband. Perhaps Pamela's husband didn't approve of my mother. Who knows? At all events, the friendship lapsed just when my sister needed an older, wiser friend.

It is difficult for an adolescent to judge accurately the character of an adult. We form our opinions in such an arbitrary manner. Appearance is important to us then, perhaps even more important than it is later in life. We notice the details of a person's mannerisms, and make fun of them. We don't value such mundane virtues as kindness, which to me now seems the most important of all.

I was mistaken in my judgements, I see that now.

I did my best, but of what use is a fourteen-year-old boy?

15

Later that evening, Joseph Fechan left his flat in Park Town on foot, as usual, and crossed the Banbury Road. He took one of the streets that joined the Banbury Road to the Woodstock Road, a little further to the north.

His Park Town flat spread over the first and second floors of an elegant eighteenth-century house. His furniture was in keeping with the style of the house, since it came from his own parents' home and, however faulty her judgement of people, Celia Fechan had known a good piece of furniture when she saw it. He had kept only those pieces which he knew he would find useful, or which were particularly beautiful, so that the rooms were neither cluttered nor over-powered by their contents. Joseph did not conform to the stereotype of the absent-minded academic, either. His study was tidy and organised and there was no dust on the polished surface of his desk or on top of his filing cabinet.

The house he was walking to was very different in style, however. It was small and modern, and it belonged to Rhona Trent, the junior partner of Joseph Fechan's dentist.

They had met a year previously when Joseph had suffered from an abscess beneath one of his lower molars and needed an emergency appointment. His own practitioner was unable to fit him in that day and so he was passed on to the junior partner, Rhona Trent.

'Come and sit down, Dr Fechan. Tell me what seems to be the trouble,' she had said.

She had a low, warm-toned voice with a trace of the local accent. She pronounced his name correctly. She used his title. Joseph was immediately impressed by Miss Trent. He looked at her. She had honey-blonde hair drawn back neatly into some kind of a chignon. Her eyes were blue-grey, magnified by the lenses of her rimless spectacles. She wore pink lipstick and had flawless skin.

He sat on the chair, he reclined, he relaxed as she tipped it into a near-horizontal position, then wriggled himself comfortable on the bone-pale, slippery surface. Her face came so close to his that it went out of focus. He blinked. She spoke.

'Just open your mouth, please.'

He felt her competent fingers in their latex gloves pushing his lips apart, probing the depths of his oral cavities.

'When did you last visit the hygienist?'

He watched, fascinated, as she demonstrated the use of dental floss. He listened as she advised him to give up drinking red wine and coffee. She quizzed him on his brushing technique and showed him how to improve it. Then she gave him a prescription for antibiotics and told him to make an appointment in three months' time with his usual dentist.

'So I'm not, strictly speaking, your patient?' he asked, when his mouth was at last free from metallic instruments and the plastic suction pump.

'Not after today,'

He said, 'Good,' which she might have construed as an insult, but she understood what he was saying and she smiled.

He knew that they understood one another. He rang her a week later and invited her out for dinner on the following Saturday evening. Their relationship, such as it was, had proceeded very slowly, since she was already involved with another man, albeit a married one. But Joseph persevered. At least, he told himself, his teeth had improved, as had the state of his gums, even if he and Rhona were no more than friends. But she was worth it.

For Rhona was so entirely different from every other woman he had ever known. She was no intellectual, for a start. She was neither devious nor manipulative. She disliked introspection. She could produce an edible meal, if she had to, but much preferred to eat out. She enjoyed long, breezy walks at the weekends, and she taught Joseph to enjoy them, too.

At the end of August she had finally realised that her married lover would never leave his wife and children and she had told him it was over. And then she carried on seeing Joseph, as before, and on the same platonic terms.

The door to her house opened almost as soon as he reached it and he went inside.

'White wine?' she offered, after she had hung up his coat and shown him into the sitting room. The room was, as usual, neat yet homely, the wooden surfaces dust-free and polished, the cushions on the sofa disarranged just enough to appear welcoming, yet not so much as to look untidy.

Rhona herself fitted the room perfectly. She was well-groomed, yet relaxed. Her face bore the traces of the day's make-up but with the glow of a person who has walked briskly home from work.

'White wine would be most welcome. I'm afraid it's been a hell of an evening.'

'You're looking rather upset, Joseph. Is everything all right?'

Joseph sat further back on the sofa and stretched out his legs. He was afraid that he still looked awkward and ill-at-ease, but it was the best he could manage at the moment.

'Things are no worse than usual,' he said, making an effort to smile at Rhona. 'I'm really not complaining.'

Rhona frowned. Joseph realised that his attempt at a smile had been a mistake.

'What's been happening? You've been at some sort of reception for the students, did you say?'

'A couple of hundred people herded into an over-heated room.'

'All talking about sixteenth-century verse forms?' she suggested.

'All competing over their descriptions of where they went for their summer holidays.'

'I'm sure you could ignore that.' She waited for him to say something more about the evening.

'We were drinking nasty wine and trying to make ourselves look more intelligent and more important than we ever could be in reality.'

His own voice, here in Rhona's house, was quite normal.

'It's over now,' she said comfortably, but he had the impression that she didn't believe he had confided his real reason for being upset. Perhaps he should tell her about it, but the thought of talking about himself made him feel even more uncomfortable.

'Why don't you take off your jacket and undo your tie,' she suggested. 'Then you can begin to relax. I'm sure you don't need to take things so seriously. They're only students, after all.' He had the feeling that she was about to add the word 'dear', but then stopped herself in time. He saw that his hands, resting awkwardly on his knees, were clenched, the knuckles white through the faintly purple skin. He stretched out his fingers, forced his muscles to relax.

'It's getting late,' he said apologetically. 'I shouldn't have imposed on your good nature, just dropping in out of the blue like this.'

'Nonsense. What are friends for?'

Joseph had no answer to this, since he had never before considered the question.

xvi

Inevitably, too, my mother acquired male admirers. After all, she was only a year or two older than I am now, so barely entered upon middle age. It is only too possible that she craved romance in her life, or affection, or even sex, though I was as appalled as any other child by the idea of my mother's involvement in any such activity. Perhaps, out of my sight and hearing, she unbent towards one of the gentlemen in dark suits, white shirts and sombre ties who came to share a glass of sherry with her on Sunday evenings.

Certainly there was one occasion when, inadvertently, I stumbled across the reality. I'm nearly sure that the scene involved Mr Evans. At the time I was too shocked to take in the details of his appearance, and anyway, I rarely stared at his face, or noticed the details of his features. I used to recognise the man by his neatly-parted greasy hair, by the dandruff on the shoulders of his dark jacket, by the length of cuff that appeared below his sleeve.

As well as the sitting room, at the front of the house, there was another smaller room at the back, overlooking the garden and enjoying the mellow evening sunlight. This was a less formal room than that in which my father had died, with three low, deep sofas upholstered in faded rose velvet and scattered with a selection of embroidered cushions, witnesses of times in my mother's life when she felt in need of such employment for her hands. The curtains were usually pulled three-quarters of the way across the tall window, framing the view of lawn, perennial border and flowering trees. As the light faded in the western sky and the artificial lamplight took its place indoors, the room was lit up like a stage and seemed to invite the gaze of the observer to what was happening within.

I don't know why I was out in the garden that evening. Perhaps I was playing one of my solitary games. Perhaps I had been reading a book, sitting on the wooden bench underneath the apple tree. But as the light went from the sky and I was no longer able to see the pieces of my game, or the words on the page, my gaze was inexorably drawn to that lighted window and the occupants of the room.

Everything in my mother's house was tidy and well-ordered. The scatter of cushions on the three sofas had been carefully chosen so that their colours enlivened the room and yet blended with the overall scheme. They were placed apparently at random, to give an impression of informality, but I had seen my mother twitching at a cover, or moving one of them a few inches to left or right before she was satisfied with their placement.

My mother, too, was an orderly person. She never left her room in the morning without putting on her make-up, or 'her face' as she called it. Her clothes were spotless, were pressed every time before she put them on, and never had a hanging thread or a missing button.

And then I saw her. For a moment I could not believe that this was my mother. Her hair was dishevelled. Even at that distance, and in the half-light, I could see that her clothes, too, were out of place. The lamplight glowed on a white shoulder. And there, too, was a darker shadow, a more substantial form. Surely she would break beneath the weight of that stocky male body!

But she didn't. Instead, she bent. She swayed. Then, moving to the same rhythm, entangled so that it seemed that no one would ever be able to disentangle them, they moved slowly out of my view, sinking on to the sofa, or perhaps even to the floor.

I stared at the empty window for a while, half-expecting them to reappear, as though nothing had happened. After a long time I turned and walked away. I didn't look back.

16

On the following morning Kate set off for her literature class, hoping that she wouldn't be buttonholed by Faith again. She would invent an urgent lunchtime appointment, she decided, and escape. She hadn't, in any case, come to any conclusions about Faith's colleague and her troublesome student.

As it happened, Faith appeared promptly at ten minutes to ten and started the class by telling her students that she would have to leave them at twelve, as she had a meeting to attend. So that solves *my* problem, thought Kate.

Faith led the discussion on the second half of *The Mill on the Floss* as competently as ever, but there was no sparkle, none of her usual liveliness. She came out with no teasing suggestions about the relationship between Maggie and Tom Tulliver. She looked pale, Kate thought, and her mind didn't seem fully occupied with the students before her and the text they were analysing.

At the end of the class, she reminded them that they should have finished reading *The Girls of Slender Means* by the following Wednesday, then she gathered up her books and papers, urged them all out of the room without chatting to anyone, and disappeared, practically running, down the nearest staircase.

There was no reason to believe that Daisy Tompkins was her only problem student, of course. And there were enough plots and machinations poisoning the air of Bartlemas to keep any normal academic stressed. Kate was only glad that it had nothing to do with her.

* * *

It was while Kate was crossing the corner of Cornmarket that afternoon, on her way to Blackwell's to meet Emma, that she noticed the headline on the local newspaper:

STUDENT FOUND MURDERED

She quickly bought a copy and skimmed down the front page. No name was given, but the victim was a young woman. Surely it couldn't be one of the lively young people she had met the previous evening? Don't jump to conclusions, she told herself. There are thousands of students in Oxford, what with two universities and the language schools. The chances that it was someone she knew were slight. It was a tragedy, as the death of any young person must be, but she couldn't assume that it affected her personally.

She wished that they'd given the student's name, though, or at least the name of her college. She dropped the paper into a bin before continuing on her way to Blackwell's. She had to concentrate on Emma Dolby and the concerns of her likeable son, Sam.

It was noisy in the coffee shop and Kate walked through a crowd of the young and loud to reach the counter to order her latte and florentine. She found a table for two in the corner and sat with her back against the wall so that she could watch her fellow customers. She was resigned to the fact that Emma would be late. Emma, with the constant calls on her time and attention from her family, always was and Kate didn't expect the new slimline Emma to be any different.

She sipped her coffee and hoped that Emma wouldn't be too much longer. She wanted to find out what she was up to, and put young Sam's mind at rest about his mother, but it would be tedious making herself heard above the general noise. She wished that she'd suggested somewhere a little quieter.

She'd forgotten how noisy it could be in term-time. It would be difficult to insist that Emma should unburden her soul in such an atmosphere. In the past they'd met in Emma's untidy but homely kitchen, or occasionally at Kate's smaller but neater place. But now it seemed that Emma enjoyed escaping from her domestic background, and Kate's new house was currently far from neat.

The young people around her reminded Kate of those in the Lamb Room the previous evening. Many of them were attractive, all were stylishly dressed, at least one in each group was obnoxious, in her view. And here they were again, no different from the previous evening, filling the coffee shop with their sprawling limbs and loud voices. Each one of them was putting on a performance. Blackwell's coffee shop was, presumably, this term's place to be seen. The girls all had shining hair, with stripes of a lighter colour added at one of the expensive hairdressers in the town. They had bright red lips and wore skimpy black skirts and long, tight boots on their plump legs. Bosoms were on display this year, pushed up by underwiring and allowed to spill out of low-cut tops and unbuttoned jumpers.

A sudden burst of conversation to her right was answered by an even louder burst to her left, as though the young people were competing for attention in the room. I suppose they are, at that, she thought. Then she remembered the story on the front of the newspaper. It might have been any one of these young people, or one of their friends, who lay murdered.

Kate was halfway through her coffee before Emma turned up, and even then she didn't notice her until she reached the table and put down her cup and saucer. No latte and cake for Emma: she had opted for a cup of peppermint tea. No cake, and no biscuits, either. This was definitely Emma Mark 2. The original Emma would take one biscuit from the new packet, then absentmindedly eat her way through the lot – and *then* complain that she couldn't fasten her waistband.

'Hello, Kate,' said Emma jauntily, as she sat down. 'I hope you haven't been waiting too long. The traffic was awful, I'm afraid.'

'Only for a minute or two,' said Kate, who didn't want to get off on the wrong foot by pointing out that Emma had kept her waiting for nearly twenty minutes.

'You're not eating *chocolate*, are you?'

'Yes. Why? Is something wrong with it?'

'It will make you fat and give you spots.'

'I think that only applies to teenagers,' said Kate. 'But *you're* certainly looking very trim. I can see you've been saying "no" to anything at all fattening recently.'

'I have lost weight, haven't I?' said Emma smugly.

'And you've done something to your hair, too.'

'It was time it was taken in hand. My new man does quite a decent cut.'

'I can see that.' And Emma was wearing a very attractive jacket that brought out the blue of her eyes, noticed Kate, as well as a pair of shoes with impractical heels. Emma's usual outfit looked as though it was designed for dragging a recalcitrant toddler around a muddy park, but that certainly didn't apply to today's ensemble. Kate forced herself to remember that she was here because Sam was worried about his mother, and what she might be up to, not to embark on a fascinating discussion about boutiques and hairdressers.

'So, what's brought all this on?' she asked casually. Unfortunately her words were drowned by raucous laughter from the group just behind her.

'I think it's time *you* paid your hairdresser a visit, Kate,' Emma said. 'You've got a streak of white gloss paint across the crown of your head.'

'Perhaps I'd better wait until I've finished decorating. I'm sure to get more paint in my hair. But, Emma, tell me, why the makeover?'

'What?' Emma's face was tinged with pink.

'Don't tell me you've hit a milestone birthday!'

'No. I'm no nearer forty than you are, as you well know.'

As a matter of fact, she was at least one year nearer, if not hovering right over it. 'So?'

'I had been letting myself go a little. I thought it was time to do something about it.'

'Emma, you've been bringing up a huge brood of children. You're allowed to let yourself go after the third or fourth, it's official. Did Sam say something unkind about your looks?'

'Sam? He wouldn't notice if I painted my face green and wore a bin liner.'

As Emma concentrated on her mint tea, Kate decided to try a different approach.

'I hope you're managing to get out to the right places to show off your sexy new look.'

'Sexy?' Emma sounded startled.

'Yes. Don't tell me you hadn't noticed.'

'As a matter of fact I have been going out a bit more recently,' confided Emma.

'I'm glad to hear it.' Maybe Emma's husband was starting to notice that she needed occasional entertainment. 'Sam's been taking you out to dinner, has he? Or the theatre?'

'No. Sam only wants to slump in front of the television, or read a book all evening – not that there's anything wrong in reading, of course.' Kate thought that a judicious silence on her part might encourage Emma to unburden herself, so she waited for her friend to continue. 'No, the thing is, I've made friends with this, um, person, and we go out together, doing cultural things – you know, just occasionally, when it isn't inconvenient for the family.'

'Are you telling me that this "person" is another man?'

'Yes. But you're making it sound quite unsavoury. Really, there's nothing wrong in what we're doing.'

'I'm sure there isn't. Who is he? Is it anyone I know?'

'I doubt it. His name's Peter. He's five or six years older than me, and we have a lot of interests – literary and so forth – in common.'

And presumably this Peter had the advantage of not being the father of six or seven children.

'Is he an academic?'

'No. He's in the book trade.'

That could mean almost anything, thought Kate. 'Really?' she said encouragingly.

'He buys and sells modern first editions. And other interesting books, too, of course.'

'Does he have a shop?'

'He trades on the Internet, mostly. Now, Kate, tell me what *you've* been doing recently.'

'I'm still painting my house, as you've guessed from the streaks in my hair. And I'm taking a literature course on Wednesday mornings. As a matter of fact, you know the tutor: it's Faith Beeton.'

'Oh, yes. From Bartlemas.' Emma didn't sound very interested.

'Do you still teach there yourself?'

'Not really. I might help out with the summer school again this year, if they want me to.'

'I wondered whether you saw much of the Fellows there.'

'Is this really what you wanted to ask me about? You said there was something you needed my help over. So far we seem to have been talking about my affairs.' Emma stopped at this word, as though embarrassed, then continued: 'Do you want to know about someone in particular? Who is it? Do I know them?'

'Well, yes, actually. Do you know Joseph Fechan?'

'Not very well. He isn't exactly convivial.'

'That's putting it mildly.'

197

'Though he's very sound, of course.'

This, Kate recognised, was high praise from Emma. 'So you don't know him, as a person, as it were?'

'I'm afraid not. Why do you want to know about him? I really wouldn't have thought he was your type.'

'He isn't. And, anyway, I'm not looking out for anyone new. No, this is all Faith Beeton's fault – you know what she's like when she wants a favour.'

'That woman can be tiresome, certainly.'

'My mother would agree with you. But Faith wanted an unbiased opinion of Fechan, and I don't think I'm capable of giving one.'

'He isn't easy to get to know. He's a very private man,' said Emma. 'But, Kate, I really can't tell you very much more about him since we only met, briefly, as colleagues at Bartlemas—'

'—but that's what I want to know. What's he like as a professional teacher?'

'I don't know anything about his teaching skills. And now—'

'No, I'm talking about his professional relationships.'

'He's always very correct. I would describe him as punctilious: an old-fashioned word, but then, he's an old-fashioned man.'

'Thanks. That's really all I wanted to know.'

'Good. And now you're going to have to excuse me. I have to get back to the children. The younger ones will be home from school shortly and I must be there when they get in.'

Emma rose to her feet in one fluid movement – and when did she learn how to do *that*? Kate asked herself.

'You won't go round gossiping about Peter and me, will you?'

'I wouldn't dream of it,' said Kate. Reporting back to Emma's son didn't count as 'gossip', after all. And it wasn't as though young Sam would talk to his father about Emma and

Peter. As far as she could make out, he didn't confide in any of his family about the things that concerned him.

She thought of what Emma had said about Fechan. She really hadn't been specific enough, had she? She was sure that when Emma referred to Fechan's behaviour as 'punctilious' she was talking about his relationships with his colleagues. But Emma hadn't said anything about Fechan's reputation with students, and female ones in particular. Perhaps she genuinely didn't know.

She had found out a little more about Emma's personal life, though. And even if it wasn't what Sam wanted to hear, it was at least intriguing.

When she reached home, she sent Sam an email.

Hi Sam

Emma has a new friend called Peter, who runs a book-selling business on the Internet. She assures me that they are just friends and that they go to cultural events together, occasionally.

It all sounds very innocent. I think she enjoys going to the theatre, or to a concert, from time to time, and your father is usually too tired to accompany her, so this Peter goes with her instead. It might be best to keep this info to yourself, though. We wouldn't want your father to get the wrong idea.

Cheers, Kate

She read it through and had to admit that it sounded reassuring rather than convincing. Some time later that evening she received a reply:

Good try. Kate, but if it's all so innocent, why hasn't she told us about him, or brought him back for a meal or something? If he's dealing on the Internet, I can try to find out more about him, though. Emma's not very worldly-wise, is she? He could be a crook or something, or even after her money. Sam.

Unfortunately, she reckoned that Sam was right about Emma's lack of worldly wisdom. In Kate's opinion she also lacked common sense on any matter that didn't have to do with her children. Thinking back to the slimmer, sleeker Emma with the sharply-cut hair and new-found confidence, she wondered how long the effect of excitement in her life would last. Wouldn't she – sooner rather than later – revert to her normal, plump self in her mismatched clothes which, as Kate knew, were habitually held together with at least one safety-pin?

At ten o'clock she turned on the television to watch the news. It was then that she learned that the student found dead that morning, although still not identified by the police, had been discovered in Bartlemas College. Although it wasn't stated in the report, it did seem likely that the victim had been a member of that college.

It was impossible for Kate not to think again of the party in the Lamb Room the previous evening. Could the unnamed student be one of those she had seen or spoken to at the reception, or one of those she had seen later, on her way out, making their way to Bartz, the union bar in the old cellars beneath the hall, for their own, less formal celebration?

She could no longer tell herself that this was something distant, unrelated to her own life. Bartlemas, whatever its faults, was a small, close community. Anything like this would affect every single member of the college. Everyone she had seen in the Lamb Room must be devastated by what had happened.

xvii

I see that I have written nothing about my own sexual encounters.

What is there to write? I was not the kind of young man who at fifteen or sixteen attracts a pretty girl of the same age, or even an older one who is eager to draw him into the labyrinth of sexual experience. At eighteen, I was invisible to women. Then, at nineteen, I met Laura.

It is a pretty name, and it should have belonged to a pretty girl. Her mother chose it, I believe, simply because it was a name that she liked. She had read some book where a character called Laura was the heroine.

Laura was a fair-haired, pale-skinned girl. She was by no means fat, but her hips were wide and her legs were heavy, and she moved with a slow, determined gait that caused her head to bob up and down as she walked. She favoured sensible, flat-heeled shoes with laces that she tied into neat, tight bows. She was a year or two older than me, and in her final year at a provincial university.

In spite of her looks, from my point of view, Laura was as strange and exotic a creature as any in a romantic novel. She was the younger sister of a friend of Selina's. I think that Selina had at one time been interested in her elder brother, but that was in the past. In any event, the families had kept in touch, and we met at a summer party, in their garden.

We found that we were both interested in sixteenth-century music. I should have invited her to a concert, I know that now, but in fact it was she who telephoned me and pointed out that Emma Kirkby would be singing in the Sheldonian Theatre the next week. After a few minutes of embarrassed stammering I managed to suggest that we should attend the performance together.

After that, it wasn't quite so bad. Laura was easy enough to talk to. She even allowed me to hold her hand on the way home. She chewed her fingernails, and when she had done that, she started on the sides of her thumbs. I looked away. My own fingers, I have no doubt, were damp with nervousness.

Sex? Such a messy business, I've always thought. Damp, sweaty and inelegant. I remember that it seemed to take for ever for her to untie the laces of her shoes, and then she had to remove an inordinate number of unappealing underclothes.

The act itself was undignified, and not even particularly exciting. It was a long time before I came to know what all the fuss over sex was about, and that was only after I met a woman who was utterly different from Laura, different from my mother, from Selina, and from any other woman I had ever known previously.

17

Next morning, after she had worked on the notes for her new book for an hour, Kate put on the kettle for coffee and pushed a couple of slices of wholemeal bread under the grill. She felt vaguely uneasy, and realised it was because she still didn't know the identity of the student who had been found dead in Bartlemas.

She had allowed Susanna outside, hoping that she had learned her lesson and wouldn't get lost again. Sure enough, the cat-flap crashed open and Susanna entered with a yowl to announce her return. She wound herself round Kate's legs, rubbing her head against them and calling loudly for breakfast.

'You'll have to wait for a moment,' Kate told her. 'My coffee takes priority over your cat food.' She picked Susanna up and gently scratched the top of her head before setting her down to wait in her basket.

She had made progress with her sitting room and decided at last where her workroom would be and how it would be laid out. She had even read the necessary book for her literature class. After breakfast she would be ready to write another couple of pages of notes on the characters for her new novel. As she buttered the toast, Kate turned on the radio to listen to the news. A bomb had exploded in Baghdad. There were floods in southern Europe. And then the newsreader said: 'The twenty-year-old student found dead in Oxford early yesterday morning has been named as Marguerite Tompkins, known to

203

her friends and family as "Daisy". The police are treating her death as suspicious.'

Kate waited for further details, but there were none. The day would be mild with a risk of showers everywhere and outbreaks of heavier rain in the north. It was almost possible to believe that she had imagined it. There had been no mention of Bartlemas this time, but this had to be the same person. Marguerite. When did she decide to call herself 'Daisy'? Or had it been a name given to a pretty little blonde toddler by her family? She couldn't get away from the fact that Daisy Tompkins, the young woman she had spoken to the evening before last, was dead, and 'in suspicious circumstances'.

She poured herself another mug of strong coffee. Then she opened a packet of cat food and put it down in Susanna's bowl.

How? Why?

She needed to know more. The *Oxford Mail* wouldn't be out until midday. The national papers wouldn't know any more than had been on the news. Who *would* know about it?

Susanna, her breakfast finished, jumped up on the table a few inches away from Kate and started to groom herself. Kate, finding her presence comforting, didn't tell her to get down on to the floor.

Faith Beeton was a Fellow of Bartlemas. She should know something, if anyone did – more than Kate, in any case. And from her manner in the literature class, she certainly had something on her mind. Kate picked up the phone and dialled the number. She listened to the engaged tone for several seconds before cutting the connection.

She emptied the grounds from the coffee-pot on to the compost heap and put the kettle on again. She had just poured the water on to fresh grounds when there came a tentative knock at the front door. When she opened it, she saw a young man. The smell of coffee had followed her out and surrounded her like an inviting, invisible cloud.

'Hi, Kate.'

For a second or two she couldn't place him. In the background she heard Susanna's cat-flap closing.

'It's Brad – from next door,' he said helpfully. 'Remember me?'

'Of course – sorry.' It was hard for the moment to return to the present time and place.

Brad had raised his nose, like a dog scenting a rabbit. Oh yes, the coffee.

'Why don't you come in?' Kate said. Then she added unnecessarily, 'I've just made some coffee. Would you like some?'

'Oh, thanks,' he said, just a little too eagerly. She'd have to watch it or she'd find her working morning regularly interrupted by a coffee-seeking Brad.

As she led the way into the kitchen Kate remembered that Brad had mentioned that his partner, Patrick, used to work at Bartlemas, in the Development Office. And the Development Office, at least when Kate worked at Bartlemas, had been a hotbed of gossip.

She poured their coffees. 'Would you like a biscuit?'

It was rather early in the morning for chocolate biscuits, but she had forgotten to eat the toast and was hungry. And chocolate was always welcome at times of stress, she had found.

'Did you hear the news?' she asked, when they were sitting at the table.

'Floods? Suicide bombers?' he answered, without enthusiasm.

'The death of a student at Bartlemas,' explained Kate. 'I saw it in the local paper yesterday, then this morning it was on the news. Her name was Daisy Tompkins. Did you hear about it?'

'No, I missed that. What happened to her? Not another suicide, surely? They've been doing their best to provide more support for the students so that that sort of thing doesn't happen any more.'

'The local paper said she'd been murdered, I'm afraid.'

'I don't suppose they'd make a mistake over something like that.'

'No.'

'I can't believe it had anything to do with anyone in the college, though. It must have been someone breaking in, don't you think?' said Brad hopefully.

Kate remained silent. She was remembering her feelings of unease after attending the Lamb Room party. And Brad knew nothing of the contents of the file Faith Beeton had lent her, so she couldn't refer to Fechan.

'How did Patrick find the atmosphere in Bartlemas when he worked there?' she asked.

'He wasn't very happy – I think I mentioned that when we were talking the other day.' Brad sounded relieved at the shift in the conversation. 'Patrick didn't fit in with their, well, their *ethos*, I suppose you'd call it. He described them as very competitive – as though being more successful than the next man was the most important thing in their lives.'

'They were well known for raising a lot of money for college funds, certainly,' said Kate judiciously. 'But did this competitiveness extend to the students and senior staff, as well?'

'He seemed to think that the sort of student who chose Bartlemas for their college – and who was accepted, naturally – was aiming for a salary of thirty thousand in their first year after graduation.'

'Thirty thousand?' Historical novelists had to work for some years before reaching such heights, and only then if they were lucky.

'As a minimum,' confirmed Brad.

'So not too many of them would become schoolteachers, or solicitors taking on Legal Aid work,' mused Kate.

'Look, I may be exaggerating. Perhaps it was only a minority who looked at life that way. You should talk to Patrick. He was the one who worked there, not me.'

'Maybe you'd both like to come in for a drink after work,' Kate suggested. She'd prefer to see Patrick on his own, but it seemed rude to invite him without Brad, especially since she'd never actually met Patrick.

'Why the interest?' asked Brad, helping himself to the last chocolate biscuit while Kate poured more coffee.

'It just happens that I met Daisy Tompkins the day before yesterday. She wanted to become a writer and we were going to get together to talk over her future. I was horrified when I heard on the news that she had died, as you can imagine. She was only about nineteen, after all, and just at the start of her life.'

'It's the way when someone dies unexpectedly,' said Brad. 'You have to talk it over, don't you? You have to try to make sense of what's happened.'

'You have to convince yourself that there wasn't something you could have said or done that would have prevented it from happening,' said Kate.

'You have to know you don't share in the guilt,' said Brad, as though he knew what he was talking about. 'But you can hardly blame yourself, Kate. You say you'd only just met her.'

'That's true.' But suppose she'd read Faith's file more carefully and spotted some vital point that would have solved the problem with Joseph Fechan? She couldn't confide in Brad, though. She'd have to wait until she could get hold of Faith before going into that aspect of Daisy's death.

'Look,' Brad was saying, 'I think you're blaming yourself for something that isn't your fault. And you don't even know what happened yet, do you? When Patrick gets home, if you like I'll ask him if he'd talk to you about what he knows. I've got a choir practice, so the two of you can gossip about Bartlemas to your hearts' content. Let me write down your phone number and I'll ring you at about six.'

'Thanks,' said Kate, and passed across a ballpoint and notepad.

At this moment the cat-flap was pushed open and Kate's cat reappeared.

'Hi, Susanna!'

Susanna ignored Kate and walked straight across to Brad, who bent down to stroke the fur behind her ear. She sprang on to his knee and rubbed her head against his shoulder.

'She remembers you, then,' said Kate, trying not to feel jealous.

'She's recovered, I see,' said Brad.

'I don't think there was anything much wrong with her, except hunger.'

'She looks as if she's ready for her breakfast right now.'

'Take no notice. She's already eaten it. This cat tells terrible fibs about how I starve her.'

'And has she settled in to the new house yet?'

'She's getting there. It will be better when I've got the place straight. I can't say that I'm really feeling at home here myself yet.'

'I could see quite a difference since the last time I was here,' said Brad kindly.

'It's true that I've done quite a bit, but it's the final day or two that makes all the difference, doesn't it? Till then you're just creating more chaos.'

'I spend quite a bit of time on building sites, so I'm used to applying my imagination,' said Brad. 'But Kate,' he said, putting Susanna carefully down on the floor before standing up, 'I really have to leave you now. I must have disturbed your working morning and I know that's unpopular with someone who works from home.'

Protesting that she had enjoyed his visit, Kate saw him to the door.

'I'll give you a ring,' he promised, as he left.

Kate tried to phone Faith Beeton again, but there was still no reply. She had just replaced the receiver when the phone rang. Maybe Faith had read her mind and was calling her from college.

But it wasn't Faith.

'Hi, Kate!' cried a bright, enthusiastic voice.

'Estelle?' Kate wasn't used to this new, excessively upbeat version of her agent. 'You're sounding very chipper this morning.'

'Chipper? Well, yes, I suppose I am in a good mood these days.'

She's found herself a new man, thought Kate. That would explain her mood. 'I expect you have a full social life at this time of year.'

'As a matter of fact, yes, I have. And Kate, believe it or not, I'm coming down to Oxford on Friday. Shall we meet up for lunch?'

'That would be . . . nice,' said Kate cautiously.

'I might have a friend with me,' said Estelle.

'Would this be a *new* friend?'

'Fairly new, yes.' Estelle giggled. 'You know me too well, Kate. I can't keep anything from you, can I? I do hope you'll like him. He's an Oxford man himself so I'm sure that you and he will have loads in common.' By this time Estelle was positively gushing.

He must be an exceptionally presentable man this time, thought Kate, after she had replaced the receiver. Estelle is longing to show him off. Maybe she really has found the right man for her this time. Give Estelle her due, she never stopped trying.

Kate knew she should get on with some work, but she was

feeling too restless. She would walk across Oxford – she needed the exercise, after all – and visit her mother. Roz was a good listener, as long as she wasn't immersed in her own affairs, and she might even have something useful to say about Daisy Tompkins.

xviii

But, long before I met Laura, I had to face what happened to Selina.

Will I ever know the truth of it? Of course, there was an inquest, and a verdict, and we buried her, as we had buried my father, in the same corner of the churchyard. There is a plain headstone in that place, with her name and the dates of her birth and death – nothing more. The ending was neat. My mother wore black; the same unfamiliar relatives arrived, looking mournful in their dark clothes. The vicar was a different, younger man, but he sounded just the same.

Selina, my sister, that fair-haired, blue-eyed angel of a girl. She was my star. She took the place of my inadequate mother. Indeed, she became the mother I had longed for. She was perfection. I know she was, in spite of what I learned about her later. None of it was her fault, that was clear. She was a victim. She was used.

Personally, I blame Mr Evans, and Owen Salter, and all the other men who looked at her and, just as I did, fell in love with her. She was so innocent, so untouched, so lacking in knowledge of the world and the wickedness of the men who lived in it. Perhaps it was not love they fell into, but some baser, cruder emotion. I might call it lust, if I knew what that was.

I was fifteen or sixteen when things fell apart, too wrapped up in my own concerns to notice what was happening. I had my sights set on an Oxford scholarship. It was all I thought of in those months.

I saw Selina at Easter, I remember, and she was radiant. Her skin glowed. Her hair shone. There was something in the way she moved, even the manner in which she sat down in a chair, that told me she was happy. She was more than happy; she was ecstatic.

And she spread her own happiness over the rest of us. She had so much to share that it spilled out of her. She had time for our mother. She had time for me. She had time for everyone in the world. Her joy covered us all like a raiment of gold and sparkling diamonds.

Then came the summer, and I was off on my bicycle, searching once more for interesting specimens of vernacular architecture.

I have never been able to look at an old cottage since that time and recognise the box end or the cruck beams without being reminded of Selina. These days I turn my head away from a Norman church or a Saxon tower. Why should I now be so absorbed in *them* when I ignored what was happening to my sister?

I *should* have noticed. Even her hair had lost its shine and hung, dull and lifeless, on her hunched shoulders. Her complexion lost its glow. All her enthusiasm for life had left her. Her figure thickened. That, at least, should have given me the clue. But when it came to people, I was an unobservant and ignorant boy.

And what of our mother, whose job it was to look after us? She was sunk into her own pit of despondency, looking to the men of her acquaintance to drag her out of it. She never learned to rely on her own inner resources. Besides, she had pitifully few of them.

Selina was pregnant. Of course, I know that now. It should have been blindingly obvious. If I had known it then, what would I have done? I like to think that I would have given her my love and support, whatever that might mean. At least she would have had someone to whom she could talk.

But she didn't talk to us. She sat in a hopeless silence, talking only to herself, until one evening she simply stole all the pills she could find in my mother's bathroom cabinet and added to them the painkillers that she had persuaded the doctor to prescribe her. She swallowed them all, washing them down with a bottle of white wine she had bought from the supermarket that afternoon.

Why did she need to take that way out? Pregnancy wasn't the end of the world! She could have kept the child, lived at home, having me and our mother to help her. No, I suppose that that is an unlikely scene. Certainly it was a situation she was unable to face.

It was simply the end of her world.

She should have vomited after swallowing all those pills, but she alternated wine and water to hasten the drugs through her system, and some time in the early hours of the morning, she died.

My mother made me go into her room and look at her. I don't know why she did this. Possibly it was that she wanted someone else to feel the pain and degradation of the sight. And not only the sight: it was the smell that first hit me when I edged into Selina's room with such unwillingness. And then the sight of her body. It can't have been an easy death. I'm only surprised, now, that none of us heard her. But the house was large, the walls thick, and we were heavy sleepers, my mother and I.

We buried her on a summer's day of sunshine, with an azure sky and tender white clouds harried by an insistent breeze. The grass in the churchyard was long and lush and insects hummed on the splashes of red valerian that spilled over the grey stone walls. My mother had chosen a plain coffin for her daughter, as though she was ashamed of what she had been.

It was those who had mistreated and used her who should have been ashamed.

Dry earth thudded on to the coffin lid. I stepped forward and tossed in a small posy of white roses. I don't think my mother liked that. She would have judged the gesture ostentatious.

After the funeral, my mother hardly ever mentioned Selina, and then only with a note of complaint in her voice.

And for me, Selina was the goddess who was tipped off her pedestal. She changed from the virginal, untouchable, golden girl to something that had dabbled in the gutter. For her to be pregnant, she had to have had sex with some man. How could she have done it? The sweating and the panting. The grunting and the squirming. The mess. Hot, damp skin and the thick, nauseating smell, like crushed vanilla seeds.

She was lost to me. Whatever it was that she had done, the result was that she was lost to me. I had always thought she was perfection, and now I knew that she was simply human. Now, I know that to be human is the highest aspiration we can have, but in those days I saw her as a fallen woman, quite literally: my own Selina, lying broken on the ground. My sister, no longer the sweet innocent.

But it wasn't her fault. She *is* still innocent. She was led astray by the men she knew. They ignored the pure essence of her, and saw only her human side. They were interested only in sex and they imagined that she was, too. They fooled her with protestations of love. I'm sure of it. Without them I would still have my untouched, untouchable sister.

18

Kate took a detour through the Covered Market on her way to East Oxford. She picked up an interesting loaf of bread, a pot of venison pâté and a few ripe tomatoes, just in case she and Roz were still talking when lunchtime came around. She hadn't phoned ahead, but if Roz was out she would at least have taken some exercise, and that, she found, improved both her circulation and the efficiency of her thought processes.

When Roz opened the door, Kate noticed at once that she was looking rather more formally dressed than usual. Not a bead, a sequin or a fringe in sight, in fact. Her hair was held back from her face with combs; she had applied a little make-up. What did this mean? The appearance of a new man in her life? Kate did hope not. Her mother's taste in men was not good, judging by past experience.

'Hello?' Roz didn't immediately invite her in, but stood with her arm leaning on the half-open door.

'Are you busy? Shall I come back later?'

'I think we've just about finished talking shop. Why don't you come in?'

'I've brought our lunch with me,' said Kate. 'If you're free, that is?'

'I shall be by lunchtime.' Roz was in one of her moods where she was giving nothing away, or perhaps it was because she knew that Kate was incurably curious about people's affairs, and so was determined to tease her daughter.

'Good. I was hoping we would have a chance to talk. I'll just pop these in the fridge then, shall I?' said Kate, passing through to the kitchen. Her mother was showing an unusual lack of interest in Kate's concerns.

When she'd put away the food, she walked into the sitting room to find a strange woman, also rather smartly dressed, already installed on Roz's sofa.

'This is a friend of mine, Avril.' Roz didn't explain who Avril was, Kate noted, nor did she elaborate on what the 'shop' was that they had been talking before her arrival.

'Are you interested in doing up houses, too, Kate?' asked Avril, which gave Kate a clue. She took a good look at Avril. This was the woman, apparently, who was encouraging Roz to invest hundreds of thousands of pounds (did Roz even have that kind of money?) with the dubious prospect of making a profit out of their endeavour. Avril was of medium height, rather dumpy, probably around fifty, and had the air of being shrewd rather than an intellectual – which made a pleasant change from Faith Beeton and all her acquaintance.

'I've improved only my own house, so far,' Kate said. 'I've just moved in to a rather rundown place in Jericho, and it's taking all my time and energy to bring it up to scratch.'

'But such a worthwhile project,' said Avril. 'Have you taken time off work?'

'Kate's self-employed,' said Roz. 'Her time is her own.'

'Well, I have to do enough work to pay the mortgage and finance the work on the house,' pointed out Kate.

'Coffee?' offered her mother.

'Yes, please.' Kate followed her mother out to the kitchen.

'What's up?' asked Roz. 'You're looking rather flustered.'

'I never look flustered! I'm concerned, certainly, about something unpleasant that's just happened. I was hoping we could talk about it.'

'I expect so. What is it?'

'You remember I told you about Faith Beeton and how she had a problem with a student?'

'Vaguely.'

'The girl is dead. On the news this morning they said "in suspicious circumstances".'

Roz poured water on to coffee grounds. 'I didn't think you knew her. Did you?'

'I met her the day before yesterday, at the reception that Faith invited me to.'

'Oh yes, I remember it. You said the place was full of loonies. I didn't think you'd done more than pass the time of day with either the girl or the bullying tutor.'

'We had quite a long conversation, as a matter of fact. She wanted to become a writer.'

'I hope you explained what an uncertain profession it is.'

'Well, I wasn't going to advise her to become an accountant, was I? But it doesn't really matter now what I said, does it?'

'You *are* in a bit of a state, aren't you?'

Roz placed three mugs and the coffee press on a tray and walked back into the sitting room. Kate followed her in.

'What did you say the girl's name was?' she asked as she poured out the coffee.

'Daisy Tompkins.'

'Excuse us,' said Roz to Avril, 'but Kate's upset herself over some item on the news this morning and she wants to talk about it.'

'You don't have to make excuses for me,' said Kate. 'A young girl has been murdered – a student from Bartlemas. I think it's perfectly normal to be upset.' She glared at her mother. Roz could be quite callous, sometimes, she thought.

'Of course you're upset,' put in Avril. 'It's only natural. It must have been a dreadful shock for you. Who did you say she was?'

'She was a local girl,' said Kate. 'She came from a village somewhere near Oxford, as far as I remember from what Faith told me. Wheatley, I think it was. It's not a place I know.'

'Daisy Tompkins?' broke in Avril. 'From Wheatley?'

'Do you know her?' asked Kate.

'I used to live just near Wheatley. My son was at school with the Tompkins boys – her brothers, they would have been. Daisy's quite a bit younger than them, though. Oh my God! You don't mean that she is the student who was murdered! What happened?' asked Avril.

'I don't know much about it, apart from what I heard on the news. I haven't been able to find out the details yet. I was telling Roz just now in the kitchen, I met her the day before yesterday for the first time, and we were talking about her future as a writer. It's an awful shock.'

'Yes. Oh, my goodness! I remember her very well. I watched her grow up, you might say. She was a sweet little thing when she was a child: blue eyes, fair hair, and always so clean.'

'So unlike my own dear Kate,' said Roz.

'As a matter of fact, if I'm perfectly honest, she seemed *unreal* somehow,' said Avril. 'My daughter was never that *good*, if you know what I mean.'

'Oh, but I do know,' agreed Roz.

'It made you wonder how genuine she was – what was really going on behind those innocent blue eyes. Sometimes you felt you were being outmanoeuvred.'

'Yes,' said Kate thoughtfully.

'But I'm being uncharitable!' said Avril, suddenly recollecting herself. 'I'm sure any mother would have been overjoyed to have a little girl like Daisy. There was nothing tomboyish or rowdy about her, you know. And later, so clever with her schoolwork! I don't suppose Helen Tompkins ever had a day's worry with that child, though she was a hard enough woman to please, everyone said.'

'She sounds almost too good to be true,' said Kate.

'You say that poor little Daisy is dead? Are you sure?'

'I couldn't reach my friend Faith Beeton, who is Dean for Women Students at Bartlemas – that's Daisy's college – and she should know, if anyone does. But it was given out on the news that it is an Oxford student who has died, and that her name is Daisy Tompkins. Oh, and they mentioned that her real name was Marguerite, but that she was known as "Daisy" by her friends and family.'

'That's right. Marguerite – I'd forgotten about that. We all thought it was an awful mouthful, and so old-fashioned, to burden a child with a name like that. I don't know what the other children at her school thought. They can be such cruel little monsters, can't they?'

'They certainly can,' said Kate.

'She was named after her grandmother, I think, poor little soul. She announced that she would be called "Daisy" when she must have been about – oh, thirteen or so. She could be quite determined when there was something she really wanted.'

'Did you know the family well?' asked Kate, hoping for some useful background information.

'*Everybody* knew the Tompkins boys. The two younger ones, Luke and Martin, were both a bit of a handful, but the eldest boy – "Spike" he called himself, though his name was really Steven – now there was something really nasty about him, I always thought.'

'Nasty?' prompted Kate.

'I shouldn't be talking about them like this,' said Avril. 'It's not nice, is it, with Daisy not even buried yet. And they were a very respectable family, really. Helen took care of that, though she could never manage to keep the boys in clean clothes for more than an hour a day.'

'I'm sure we wouldn't dream of saying anything unkind about Daisy,' said Kate, 'but it sounds as though her family might have been a bit of a problem.' Especially, she thought, for an ambitious girl with her sights set on Oxford.

'Oh, I wouldn't call them a problem family,' said Avril, who seemed, in spite of her protestation, only too eager to gossip about the Tompkins family. 'I think they were quite, well, *rough*, a generation or two ago, but Helen Tompkins brought them all up very strictly. She liked them to be well-dressed and well-behaved. But there's not much you can do with three boys, is there? They're bound to be a handful. And Steven, he was the ringleader. I expect the other two, Luke and Martin, would have been quiet enough lads without him to lead them into mischief. I must say I always worried when my boy was with that crowd. You were never quite sure what they might get up to next.'

'How very interesting,' said Kate.

'Now don't get me wrong,' added Avril. 'None of them was ever in *trouble*. And dear little Daisy, always so nicely dressed, so well-spoken. I can't get over it, really I can't.'

'It's difficult to take in, certainly,' said Kate. 'I always find with this sort of tragedy that it does help to talk things over, though. It puts it in perspective, don't you think?'

'You may well be right, Kate.'

'Perhaps the Tompkins boys were too bright to get caught when they were out breaking the law,' suggested Roz.

'They were certainly bright kids,' said Avril, 'though Daisy was a hard worker, too, as well as being bright. And I'm not sure that they ever actually broke the law. The boys just wanted *things*. You know, fast cars, flash clothes, wide-screen telly, little miniature computers.'

'Gold medallions?' suggested Kate.

'I don't think so,' said Avril doubtfully. 'And Steven – Spike, should I say? – had his good points. He wasn't always out making trouble. He had an allotment where he grew vegetables for his mother. That was thoughtful of him, wasn't it? He was a good little gardener, I'll say that for him, so he wasn't all bad. Though he lost interest when he got to about seventeen. But then, boys do, don't they?'

'I believe it can be difficult to keep their minds on vegetables,' said Kate.

'Well, I really mustn't keep you talking like this,' said Avril, rising to her feet. 'I'm sure that you and Roz have lots to talk about without me going on about some family you've never even met.'

'It's been really interesting,' said Kate sincerely.

'Well, Roz, shall we go house-hunting again tomorrow, or are you getting tired of it yet?' asked Avril as she picked up her handbag and turned towards the door.

'I think we made distinct progress this morning,' said Roz, following her visitor to the door. 'I'm starting to find my way around and really understand the different streets as well as the different areas of this city. I'll call round at your place at nine, shall I?'

'What was all that about?' asked Kate, as Roz came back into the room.

'I told you I was interested in doing up houses to sell at a profit,' said Roz. 'Well, Avril and I are in a loose kind of partnership.'

'You mentioned one house,' said Kate. 'One house, not houses in the plural.'

'You have to think big if you're going to make decent money.'

Kate heard herself groan, but Roz ignored her.

'Now, what was it you brought for our lunch? Venison pâté? Delicious! I'll put a salad together for us. Those look like very nice tomatoes.'

Five minutes later, as they sat down to their lunch, Roz asked, 'Now, why on earth did we have to hear all that detail about Daisy Tompkins's family? If I'd realised that Avril was such a chatterbox I'm not so sure I'd have considered working with her. Still, she does know about houses, so I suppose I can forgive her the attack of logorrhoea. But why were you pumping the poor woman for all her information on the Tompkins family?'

'Partly because I thought it might help her to process the information about Daisy's death, but also because when Faith was talking to me about Daisy Tompkins, she said that the girl gave out contradictory signals, or some such thing. On the surface she appeared to be sweet, innocent and truthful, but Faith thought she was sly and manipulative and was lying about the harassment by Joseph Fechan. When I met her – briefly and in public, admittedly – I simply couldn't make up my mind about her. I think she was genuinely interested in writing, but I'm not at all sure about anything else. I just thought that your friend Avril might help to put me straight about her.'

'But the subject is academic now, surely? If Daisy Tompkins is dead, she can't pursue a complaint again that oddly-named man.'

'But if she *was* telling the truth, then Fechan shouldn't be left to bully any other shy young female students, should he?'

'True, but I hate to point this out to you, Kate: it really isn't any of your business. What are you, a novelist or a private investigator? I'm sure that Bartlemas College is quite capable of looking after its students, and its staff, however shy any of them might be. It's Faith's job, not yours.'

'Well, that's me put in my place,' said Kate. 'You'd better blame my natural curiosity, I suppose. And I wonder where I got *that* from.'

'I can't imagine,' said Roz. 'And now, shall I make us another pot of coffee?'

Kate phoned Faith again when she returned home, and this time she answered.

'Yes,' she said tersely, in reply to Kate's enquiry. 'Daisy Tompkins has been murdered. It must have happened on the night of the Lamb Room reception, but her body wasn't found until the morning.'

'Who—'

'A couple of unfortunate engineering students, I believe.' Although Faith's tone indicated that engineering students weren't expected to have delicate feelings about finding the dead body of a fellow-student.

'How was she killed?'

'We don't know any details yet.'

'Perhaps someone broke into the college,' said Kate, hearing how weak the suggestion sounded.

'It's possible, but hardly probable. And they've taken Joseph Fechan down to the police station for questioning.'

'Oh, my God! You don't—'

'No, I don't think he killed her. I'm sure he's incapable of such a thing.' But, hearing Faith speaking so adamantly, Kate wondered whether she was trying to convince herself of Fechan's innocence. 'The college is in a state of shock, as you can imagine, The undergraduates, especially those who were Daisy's friends, are being very caring and supportive of each other.'

'And the Fellows? How are they taking it?' asked Kate.

'They, too, are expressing shock and outrage, but there is an underlying feeling of . . . well, *triumph*.'

'What? How do you mean?'

'You know: "We always thought there was something wrong with Fechan. Now we've been proved right".'

'Surely not!'

'It would solve their problems with the man, wouldn't it?' said Faith bitterly. 'No more pinpricks. No more the awkward voice of conscience when they come out with yet another crass proposal to lower standards and raise money.'

'And what about Fechan? Has he got a good lawyer? I don't suppose he could—'

'No. I don't suppose he could have killed her either,' said Faith flatly.

'You'll let me know if there's anything I can do to help?'

There was a brief pause while Faith doubtless considered what on earth Kate could do that would be remotely helpful in this situation, and then she said, 'Of course.'

She rang off.

xix

When Daisy Tompkins walked into my room for her first tutorial, it was a mild October day. She arrived before Miss Rooling and so I had time to notice her. She was a quiet, well-mannered girl, dressed in a fresh-looking summer dress and plain white shoes. She seemed shy. She sat down on the chair I indicated, keeping her knees pressed tightly together in a way I interpreted as modest.

Yes, that was my first impression of Daisy Tompkins. A well brought-up, modest young woman. She had soft, fair hair that inevitably reminded me of Selina's, and when she finally raised her eyes to mine I saw that they were blue, with a hint of green, the transparent turquoise of the Mediterranean on a sunny day in June.

I heard the accents of rural Oxfordshire in her voice, but the voice itself was low and pleasant, and what she had to say was intelligent enough. Or, at least, so it seemed to me on that first morning.

For the whole of that first term I believed her to be what she at first appeared. It wasn't until I had good reason to revise my opinion of her that I did so.

Michaelmas term ends in December, of course, two weeks or more before Christmas. But the undergraduates like to celebrate the forthcoming festival with their friends before returning home to the doubtless staider familial gatherings arranged by their parents. These student parties are often held in the college union bar, which has been converted from the cellars beneath the medieval hall. This underground cavern is referred to as 'Bartz', as though it were a vulgar night-club. But then, I suppose that a vulgar night-club is exactly what these young people wish to frequent. Certainly their music is loud and strident enough for such a place.

Some of the Junior Fellows like to show their solidarity with the undergraduate body by attending these parties, at least during the early part of the evening. I, naturally enough, would never dream of doing so, even if I were guaranteed instant popularity as a result.

On this particular evening I had been working in my room, putting the final touches to a paper for publication in a learned journal, until just on midnight.

The night was a fine one and I savoured the walk from my staircase to the lodge, passing through Pesant Quad. Unfortunately, I had inadvertently timed my departure to coincide with the end of the undergraduates' party. Young men and women were ascending the staircase in the corner of the quad and spilling across the grass towards the lodge, laughing and calling to one another as they went.

The bar is licensed, of course, and the prices are considerably lower than they are in any of the city's public houses. This, I am afraid, means that our undergraduates often drink more than is strictly good for them, or that they are capable of dealing with in an adult manner.

Many of them were drunk, to put no fine point on it. Drunk, and amorous as well. One couple came crowding behind me as I passed into the narrow confines of the lodge. The vaulted ceiling and narrow walls amplified their voices so that there was no possibility of avoiding hearing their words.

I don't like to use such crude language. I do not wish to see it on my page. But what the young woman was proposing to her partner was a specific form of sexual congress (with which she seemed very familiar, I might add). I don't know why it should be more shocking for the female partner, rather than the male, to propose this sort of thing, but I am afraid that it is so.

I entered the lodge in order to check whether I had any post. And through the glass I could see the couple who had been walking behind me. I didn't know the young man, but the girl was Daisy Tompkins.

Her face was flushed with alcohol and her dress, even on this December night, was revealing. She clung to her companion's arm, her hand like a claw on his sleeve, her nails painted black. Her lipstick, too, was so dark a red as to appear black in the subdued light, and it glistened as though she had just moistened it with her tongue. As she opened her mouth to speak again I saw that she had been drinking red wine, for she had a black stain on her tongue, like the fanged head of a snake.

A moment later they were gone, doubtless to his lodgings, to indulge in the practice which she had so recently described.

At that moment I saw that I had been wrong about her. She was nothing like my sister. I could see it now. The girl was no better than a whore, and a stupid one, at that. Inside that blonde head there lived two women: one of them, the diffident and modest young virgin, she brought to her tutorials; the other, the voluptuous and foul-mouthed harridan, was the real, the genuine Daisy Tompkins. I had been sadly deceived.

The following term, I looked at her with my newly-opened eyes and saw her for what she really was. She had scrubbed off the make-up and removed the black varnish from her nails, but I could still see the temptress beneath the innocent skin.

I pointed out her faults, as was my duty, immune now to the manipulative tactics she had used during that first term to make me think her more intelligent, more hard-working than she really was.

She didn't like it. She knew I had seen through her, knew that when I looked at her I saw right through to the rotten core. I don't know whether she recognised me that night in the lodge, though I believe she was too inebriated to recognise anybody at all. But she knew that I had seen her for what she really was and that there would be no possibility of pulling the wool over my eyes in the future.

After two more terms, she put in her formal complaint about me. There was no foundation in her accusation, but that didn't stop her. I had been scrupulously fair in judging her work, but that counted for nothing. Discipline in this establishment, as in so many others, is non-existent today. Her friends and some of the younger Fellows will take her side. Faith Beeton may stand by me, but I know that she will not wish to be seen to be taking my part since it will ultimately damage her own career. I have every expectation that I will be found to be at fault and will subsequently be unjustly punished.

That little trollop, Daisy Tompkins, will walk away, laughing, while my career lies in ruins.

19

Kate arrived at Brad and Patrick's front door, holding a bottle of red wine, early the next evening. The door opened as soon as she rang, as though someone had been waiting for her.

'Hello. I'm Kate,' she said. 'Have I called at the wrong time?'

'Hi. Of course this is the right time. Come on in. I'm Patrick.'

Patrick blinked turquoise lids and smiled with glossy lips.

So this was Brad's partner. Patrick was taller and slimmer than Brad, with light brown hair and hazel eyes with long, dark lashes.

'Come and make yourself at home. Brad's told me all about you.' He turned and led the way into the sitting room. Kate felt her back straighten and her shoulders drop as she followed his graceful form. His long, sea-blue sarong fitted snugly on his narrow hips and the beaded hem glinted as he swayed into the sitting room.

In spite of the early hour, the blinds were down and the lights were on. The lighting here was dramatic, with spot-lighted pools and shadowed depths. The room smelled of cinnamon and sandalwood.

Kate sat down at one end of a long, pale sofa, while Patrick arranged himself on its twin, opposite her. The room was admirably clear of clutter and there was a large abstract painting on one wall. She wondered which of them dusted and polished and kept the windows gleaming.

'Brad said you wanted to talk about Bartlemas,' said Patrick, plunging straight into the topic that interested her.

'You've probably had enough of the place, but one of their undergraduates has died, suddenly, and I was trying to make sense of it all. You may have heard about it on the news. I don't know any details yet, but whatever the story, I feel I have to try to make sense of it.'

'It leaves you feeling guilty, doesn't it?'

'Yes. It's irrational, but that's how it is.'

'Did you know her well?'

'No. I met her for the first time a couple of days ago. But a friend of mine, who's a Fellow there, had asked me to talk to her as she had a problem with the girl.' Oh dear, this was getting complicated, and difficult to talk about, too, without giving away too much confidential information.

'I did speak to her and I came to no firm conclusion,' she finished lamely. 'I was interested to hear your impressions of the place,' she added.

'Do you know much about Bartlemas?'

'I worked there one summer,' she said, 'helping with a summer course. But I don't suppose we overlapped since it was a few years ago. And, of course, my knowledge of Bartlemas is out of date now. My friend Faith Beeton gave me her version of what's happening there now, but I'm not at all sure how accurate her information is. She talked about little other than the great feuds and jealousies that are going on there at the moment.'

'I was in the Development Office,' said Patrick.

'I believe Brad mentioned it. But—'

'You sound surprised.'

'In my time the Development Office was full of over-confident Old Bartlemaniacs.' She suddenly thought how rude this sounded, especially if Patrick, too, had been an under-graduate there. 'Not at all like you,' she added hurriedly. 'They

229

were young men in suits and ties who were cold-calling alumni and squeezing large sums of money out of them for the college.'

'You make them sound like double-glazing salesmen.'

'Did I? I'm sorry.'

'But yes, it was rather like that when I was there as well, I must admit.'

'How long did you stay?'

'I stuck it for a year: the pay was good and it meant I could stay in Oxford with Brad but . . .'

'You didn't fit in?'

'I tried, believe me. But I'm sure they would have fired me if I hadn't moved on. I couldn't raise nearly as much as they could in a morning.'

'Where are you working now?'

'At Leicester. I'm working in the Bursary while I study for my accountancy exams.'

Patrick blinked so that Kate caught another flash of the turquoise eye-shadow. But, lovely as he was, she could see that he did have more of the accountant about him than the fundraiser. He just wasn't pushy enough. It did make him a much better prospect as a neighbour, though. And he had the kind of soft voice that would never boom through their communal walls and disturb her as she worked.

'I went to a reception at Bartlemas the other evening,' said Kate. She wondered whether to go into details about Daisy. Brad might be like Avril, and with a little encouragement he might tell her everything he knew about her. On the other hand, he was unlikely to have come across a young, female undergraduate, and Kate would sound as though she wanted to indulge in ghoulish reminiscence. It was better to keep it general, she thought. 'The party was in the Lamb Room—'

'I remember it well!'

'We were celebrating the return to college of the second-years, apparently, and most of the Fellowship appeared to be there, too.'

'It sounds hot and crowded.'

'It was.'

'What did you think of the company?'

'Well . . .'

'Oh, go on! You don't have to be diplomatic with me.'

'There were plenty of students, showing off to each other. Maybe it was just a college courting ritual, but they were very *loud*. And then there were the teaching staff.'

'I'm sure you're not supposed to call them that!' Patrick was laughing. He was starting to relax in Kate's company, and she was feeling more at home too.

'Why can't I call them teaching staff? That's what they are, surely?' said Kate.

'Shall I open that lovely bottle of wine you brought?'

'I'm not sure how lovely it is, but yes, what a good idea.'

'Any wine is lovely if one receives it as a present,' said Patrick, producing a corkscrew and pulling the cork.

'It's not bad,' said Kate after she had tasted it.

'Now, drink up and tell me all about the gruesome Fellows.'

Kate felt she had been right to move away from the subject of Daisy. She might find out more about Joseph Fechan and his colleagues now.

'Some of them *were* gruesome, I have to admit. There's a particular kind of ageing male academic who thinks he's irresistible to young women.'

'Faded blue denim or grubby tweed?' Patrick had already finished his first glass of wine, drinking it down greedily, while Kate had hardly started hers. He filled up his own glass and drank some more. There was a becoming wash of pink spreading across his cheekbones.

'Denim and tweed both. You obviously know them well,' said Kate.

'Should I find some little cheesy things to go with this wine, do you think?' interrupted Patrick.

'Not for me,' said Kate. Patrick topped up both their glasses. 'And then I met a man called Joseph Fechan. Do you know him?'

'I think everyone did. What did you make of him?'

'An unusual man,' said Kate, hoping this would cover it. From what she had heard from Faith, she would imagine it was quite an understatement. 'I didn't know what to make of him at all, in fact. Is he mad, or simply gauche? I suppose that if he's a genius he might be forgiven for his peculiar manners.'

Patrick laughed, but it might have been the result of drinking nearly half a bottle of wine in so short a time rather than Kate's wit.

'I was wondering what *you* thought of Fechan,' asked Kate.

'I'm not sure that anyone could sum him up,' said Patrick thoughtfully. 'He is very clever, though probably not in the genius category. He has very rigid ideas of right and wrong, or maybe he just believes in conventions, and traditions, and of always doing things in the approved manner. He's intolerant, certainly.'

'So, not a very nice man at all.'

'Well, I know he seems to have no social graces at all, but in spite of that he *is* a very kind man, believe it or not.'

Kate remembered the sweet smile that Fechan had bestowed on her, and the way he hadn't made her feel a complete idiot in that academic company.

'He was certainly very kind to *me* when I needed a friend at Bartlemas,' Patrick went on, 'and that's why I'll stand up for him now. Some of those tweedy Fellows are really homophobic, you know. I should be used to it and manage to rise above it, but it was depressing, especially when I wasn't very good at raising funds.'

'And Fechan supported you?'

'Yes, and needless to say it didn't improve his popularity with his colleagues.'

'But I thought you said he was conventional and intolerant?'

'He is. But he also has very strong beliefs about good and evil, right and wrong, and he won't be moved from what he believes is the "right" view, however unpopular it makes him.'

'Not a simple character at all, then.'

'Sometimes I think that that is exactly what he is. He doesn't employ the subterfuges and the compromises that the rest of us do, to ease our way through life.' He leaned across to fill Kate's glass and then his own. 'I do seem to have gone on about him at length,' he said. 'It must be very boring for you. You'll just have to blame the wine. Now, that's enough about *me*. Tell me how you're enjoying living in our lovely Jericho. How's your redecorating going? Can I come in and inspect your place soon? I know that Brad's just longing to see how you're getting on. The old bat who lived there before you had preserved the 1950s style intact, as far as we could tell. Brad used to talk himself inside her kitchen just to check out the period details. It must be quite an undertaking to bring the place within spitting distance of the twenty-first century.'

'I'm not doing too much modernisation,' said Kate. 'I'd prefer to allow it to reveal its essential nature, I suppose.'

'Oh, now you're sounding just like Brad.'

'Since he's an architect, I'm flattered! Give me another week or two,' said Kate. 'Then I'll invite you both round for a tour of inspection.'

'We'll look forward to it.'

XX

They look at my hair. I see them staring at it, wondering about it. Admittedly, it is very thick, very black, and it grows irregularly, in clumps, sticking up on the crown of my head, standing out on the left side, lying flat on the right, sticking close to my scalp at the back so that my head looks misshapen. It should be turning grey by now, perhaps with distinguished touches of silver at the sides, but it isn't. No, I still have the kind of hair that properly belongs to a small boy. In a child it might be endearing; in an adult it is merely laughable.

It fascinates them. Is it real? Is it all mine? No wonder they think I'm 'weird', whatever meaning they have ascribed to that word.

Weird! How dare they talk like that about me! How dare *she*! Who do you think you are, Daisy Tompkins, sitting in my room with your short skirt and your long legs and your nipples pushing through your skimpy, damp T-shirt? You elbow your way into my world, thinking you can succeed here with your blonde hair and your pretty little face, but they're not enough, whatever you may think. You need brains and insight and thought, Daisy. That's it: you need to sit at your desk and spend hours just thinking instead of going down to the bar with your friends, talking your obscene, nonsensical talk. It's no good, Daisy. You just don't belong here, in the world of the mind. You haven't really got a mind, have you, Daisy? You have a body, a firm, shapely body, which you flaunt in front of every man you meet, and look where that will get you!

20

Next morning, Kate's phone rang while she was eating her breakfast.

'Kate? It's Faith.' Faith sounded even more brittle than usual.

'Yes? What's happened?'

'The police are still questioning Joseph Fechan.'

'They can only keep him for twenty-four hours though, I believe.'

'Unless a senior officer gives them permission to keep him longer. And I expect that's what will happen. Look, Kate, I need to talk to you. I have a committee meeting to prepare for just now, but could we meet in Blackwell's at ten-thirty?'

Kate was about to tell her that it wasn't really convenient as far as she was concerned, but Faith was already saying, 'I'll see you there. Ten-thirty. We might just be able to find ourselves a quiet corner.'

'But—'

It was too late to argue. Faith had hung up.

Kate stared crossly at the receiver. Who did Faith think she was? She shouldn't assume that Kate was always at her beck and call. But it was, after all, a friend of Faith's who was being questioned by the police, so she could be a little accommodating, in the circumstances. The thought that if the police were questioning Fechan it was because they believed he knew something about Daisy's death, or was even implicated in it, did also occur to Kate, but Faith evidently believed that he was entirely innocent.

She looked at her watch. She had time to write a few more pages of notes on her new novel. It didn't seem worthwhile starting to apply Polyfilla to the walls of her workroom in the time before she met Faith. She had been reading *The Girls of Slender Means* the previous evening, though goodness only knew if Faith would ever manage to teach the Wednesday-morning class again. Still, it had given her some ideas for her own novel.

She leafed through the pages of notes she had written so far. They weren't so bad. There were one or two usable ideas. It was really quite exciting; she was going to take a completely different approach.

She picked up the phone and dialled Neil Orson's number. It was a bit early to expect an editor to be in his office, but Neil was keen and she knew he would be at his desk and working hard by now. He probably counted on this first hour to achieve some progress without being interrupted by the ringing of the telephone. Still, this was important.

'Hi, Neil. I just wanted to run a new idea past you.'

'Fire away, Kate.' Neil, too, sounded as though his life was going well at the moment.

'Let me know what you think about this: I was working on something quite short and dense, maybe not more than sixty thousand words. No padding, nothing flabby about it. I'll take a small group of people and look at their lives in detail over a brief period of time. You could describe it as a series of epiphanies, I suppose.'

There was a short but unflattering silence at the other end of the phone.

'I think I see what you're getting at, Kate, and it sounds very interesting. The problem from my point of view is the reader, the buyer of books, as it were. It's all a question of perceived value. Give the buyer a hefty book and he – or she, of course – thinks they're getting value for their money. Slim volumes just don't seem so good to them, do you see? Do you think you could bring it up to a hundred thousand words? That would be really helpful, if you could manage it.'

There was a hint of a query in his last words. 'I'll have a rethink, Neil,' said Kate, deflated. Then she added, quickly, before he could ring off, 'I could write it in a series of first-person narratives, each with a different perspective, a different voice.'

'You haven't been studying Graham Swift in your literature class, have you, by any chance?'

'It's possible.'

'Why don't you stick with your own voice. We at Foreword really enjoy reading it, you know. Personally speaking, my spirits rise at the sight of a new manuscript with your name on the title page.'

'Really?'

'Yes. Really.'

'I'll come with another idea and get back to you as soon as I can.'

'It's always good to hear from you, Kate.'

When Kate reached the coffee shop she saw Faith sitting at a corner table, hunched over as though she was cold. She didn't look up until Kate had bought herself a coffee and joined her at the table.

'Everyone thinks he did it,' Faith said, without preamble. 'And even those who don't would like to think he's guilty. It would fit in so neatly with their prejudices.'

'You don't think there's a possibility—'

'No, I don't.'

'I don't understand what I can do to help. I only met Fechan on that one occasion. I really don't know him at all, do I?'

'But you didn't dislike him. You didn't think he looked like a murderer.'

'Really, I—'

'No. The man is obviously innocent.'

'Why did the police pick him up for questioning?'

'Apparently there were people, both Fellows and students, who contacted the police and complained about him.'

'What did they complain about?'

'I don't know. I'm just quoting what I heard in the buttery yesterday lunchtime.'

'I still don't know what it is that you want me to do to help Fechan's cause.'

'The problem at the moment is that I have to go and see the Tompkins parents,' said Faith.

'Oh my God! Really? Why?'

'Daisy was my responsibility. I'm Dean for Women Students, remember?'

'Oh yes. Can't you palm this chore off on the Master? Surely he should be the one to visit Daisy's family.'

'But they knew about her complaint against Fechan. They want to hear what I have to say about it.'

'I expect they want to hear that Daisy was completely blameless and that Fechan will be found guilty and then flayed alive by the Bursar in Pesant Quad as a punishment.'

'But seriously, they have the right to hear my report, don't you think?'

'In that case, you'll just have to go.'

'And I'd like you to come with me.' There was a note of pleading in Faith's voice that was difficult to ignore, hard as Kate tried.

'Oh, no. I don't think that's at all suitable,' she said. 'I'm not even a member of your college. I would simply be intruding on their grief. Don't you agree?'

'I need a lift; you own a car,' said Faith baldly.

'You could hire one.'

There was a pause, then Faith said shamefacedly, 'I've never learned to drive.'

'What? How did that happen?'

'It's just one of those skills I've never acquired. And I can't play tennis either, by the way,' she added.

'That's all right. Neither can I.'

'Please, Kate. I need you to give me a lift. They live out in the sticks somewhere. I'll never be able to get to them unless someone drives me there.'

'Isn't there anyone else? Someone from Bartlemas? Someone who knew her, if it comes to that.'

'No, there isn't. And if you won't take me, I'll just have to ring up and tell them I can't make it. I'll see them at the funeral. Is that what you want?'

'Nonsense. You're being ridiculous. Wheatley isn't that far. I'm sure it has a perfectly adequate bus service.'

'Please, Kate. I'm not feeling up to sitting on a bus with a crowd of strangers. Couldn't you just drive me over there?'

'When do you want to go?' Even as she spoke, Kate realised that she had agreed to give Faith the desired lift.

'This afternoon, if at all possible. If it fits in with your own arrangements.' For Faith, this was positively humble.

Kate thought about her wasted day. Oh well, she'd just have to make up for it tomorrow. Faith had worked her into a corner and she couldn't escape without being excessively rude. Faith herself, in the same circumstances, was probably capable of being very rude indeed, but Kate knew that she was not as tough as that. 'Very well. What time shall I pick you up?'

'Would half past two suit you?' Faith had perked up immediately. There was nothing in the least humble about her demeanour now.

'Fine. I know where you live, so I'll see you then.'

'There is one other thing, Kate.'

'Yes?'

Kate must have looked horrified, for Faith rushed quickly on. 'Look, you know how good you are at asking questions and interfering in people's lives . . .'

'I wouldn't put it quite like that, but go on.'

'Can I get you another coffee? How about a slice of carrot cake?'

'No, thanks. I have to leave in a minute. I think you'd better tell me what it is you want me to do.'

'You've met Fechan. You've spoken to Daisy. Well, can't you look over her family and see if there's anything there that will give us a clue as to who killed the girl?'

'But that's a job for the police. They wouldn't want an amateur getting in their way.'

'They think that Joseph killed her. Everyone's told them how weird he is, and they've come to the conclusion that he's a murderer, too.'

'I'm sure that's not necessarily so. And anyway, these days they have to collect all the forensic evidence. If he didn't do it, then there won't be any, at least none that implicates him.'

'But suppose they're not looking any further? Suppose he gets into one of his awkward moods and refuses to answer their questions, or answers them, but insults them all while he's doing so.'

'That's a lot of "ifs". I think you should trust the legal process.'

'Just think of the number of wrong convictions there are!'

'Just think of the number of times they get it right!'

'And you could ask around at college, too, couldn't you? There must be more to Daisy Tompkins than is apparent. There *must* be other people in college who know something about her or her background that's relevant. For goodness' sake, Kate, there may be a murderer at large in Bartlemas itself!'

'That is a possibility that has occurred to me, certainly. If it wasn't your friend Joseph Fechan who murdered her, it must have been someone else. That's only logical.'

'So, will you do it? Will you take it on?'

'I'm not a member of your world,' said Kate.

'What's that got to do with anything?' Faith sounded impatient.

'And I'm not a detective. I'm a novelist. I don't even write crime fiction. And, contrary to popular opinion, I don't have unlimited free time. What is it you think I can achieve?'

'You can watch. You can listen. You can chat to Daisy's family on their own level.'

'Thanks.'

'What? Oh, you know what I mean! I'm not trying to be insulting.'

'You think I can walk into a house where the parents have just lost their only daughter, thrust a microphone under their noses, ask them what they know, then come back and analyse the answers?'

'Forget the microphone, just use your ears and eyes.'

'And how many of your colleagues are going to confide in me – a stranger, a simple novelist?'

'You underestimate yourself.'

In fairness, Kate really couldn't disagree with this. She said, 'I still don't think I'm the right person.'

'*I* think you are. You don't take us academics at our own evaluation. We think of ourselves as special, as superior to everyone else. We don't mean to be like that, but we just are. Whereas you, Kate, you're very ordinary in many ways – please, take it as a compliment! – and underneath our gowns, behind our qualifications, we're quite ordinary people, too. We live privileged lives, but we don't really come from some top social drawer.'

'You're all quite brainy,' Kate pointed out.

'That's true,' said Faith without false modesty. 'But it isn't brainpower that murdered Daisy, is it? It must have been *feelings*, and emotions like love and rage, jealousy and pride. Stuff like that.' Faith looked slightly embarrassed at using such language.

'You sound as though you could write an essay on the subject.'

'Exactly. And that's not what's needed, is it?'

'Let me get this right. You want me to spy on Daisy's family and report back to you. You want me to look at them as fellow human beings, not as specimens or texts to be analysed. You want me to intrude into the home of her bereaved parents and see if I can find something to discredit her so that Fechan is vindicated. And do you want me to find out who murdered Daisy Tompkins, while I'm at it?'

'I want you to confirm that Joseph Fechan didn't do it. Finding out who actually did do it would be a bonus.'

'Why don't you just leave it to the police?'

'I told you, they're sure that Joseph did it. I don't believe they'll look any further.'

'You don't know that. And what if I agree with them?'

'Start with an open mind. Give him a chance.'

Kate saw no point in telling Faith that she was the one who was far from open-minded. If she *were* unbiased, Faith would be keeping Joseph Fechan in mind as a suspect. But then, the two of them were friends, and Kate knew only too well that it was difficult to consider someone you knew and trusted to be a murderer.

In the case of Daisy Tompkins, however, it looked all too likely that the murderer wasn't someone from 'out there' but one of their own rarefied society.

xxi

I think of October as being misty and dank, with the wet brown leaves decomposing on the pavements of North Oxford and dark grey clouds hanging low over the equally grey stone of the colleges. But this year we have had a golden autumn, the sky an unbroken blue, the leaves still attached to the trees and changing to unlikely shades of buttercup yellow, of amber, scarlet and sienna. The hint of white mist in the early morning has dispersed by the time I cross the Parks and reach the college.

And so, that evening, after the atrocious party in the Lamb Room, after I had completed my work and left my room to stroll across the park back to my house, the night was a velvety black, with the red glow of Mars visible in the south-western sky and a faint smell of woodsmoke in the air.

Behind me I could hear the blare of popular dance music as someone opened a door and then, just as abruptly, it was cut off again as the door closed. Small groups of undergraduates passed me, the men carrying cans of beer, the young women with bottles of wine. Jones, Persse, Bullen, Posner. Their raised voices indicated that they had already visited at least one public house. Shaw, Eaves, Kettleby and Rooling. I didn't think those last two were friends, but I suppose they both know Tompkins.

Every year in October the solid, expensive cars drive on to the pavement outside Bartlemas, ignoring double yellow lines and cobblestones with equal insouciance, and deposit their young charges, their laptop computers and their duvets, their table lamps and stereo equipment, hockey sticks and skis, outside the porters' lodge. The parents of these new undergraduates drive off soon after, disappearing in a puff of blue exhaust smoke, back to their now peaceful houses in the better suburbs of the larger cities.

Each generation thinks itself unique. (I suppose that, twenty years ago, my contemporaries and I thought the same.) It doesn't occur to them that the things they do have been done before – that almost identical bright repartee has been heard in the town's coffee shops since the day they opened.

Certainly this year's intake does indeed appear very similar to last year's, and to that of many previous years, though Faith is inclined to put this resemblance down to our advancing age. And anyway, if I am honest about it, they aren't identical: each generation seems a little worse prepared for an academic course, and rather weaker in grammar and spelling than its predecessors. At the beginning of each academic year Faith makes an effort to correct such failings, and urges her charges to equip themselves with a dictionary. She even recommends simple textbooks on English grammar (our students, hers and mine, are, after all, supposed to be studying English Literature) but she tells me that she rarely sees any improvement in their grasp of syntax and punctuation, and the sometimes surprising misspellings are, she is sure, the result of putting their work through their computer's so-called 'spell-checker' without confirming the results for themselves.

Faith had mentioned that some students were holding a party this evening to celebrate the reunion after the long vacation, and I imagine that it will be a jollier affair than the gathering in the Lamb Room – that exercise in toadying to the future generators of wealth. But then, I recognise the fact that if the young are not disposed to donate something to Bartlemas, it will be impossible for us to survive in our present form through this barbarous twenty-first century.

Faith tells me that I should stand up for what we both believe in, that I should fight the forces of ignorance that are taking over the college. Fight? When have I ever won a fight, I ask her.

There's always a first time, she replies. And since she speaks with such belief in the rightness of our cause, for a moment I am swayed by the cliché. It is when I am alone again that I lose heart.

Our opponents are in tune with the music of the present time. Faith and I are still listening to Monteverdi's madrigals.

21

Kate wished that she could get in touch with Jon and discuss the situation with him. But Jon, last time they had spoken, had been in the middle of some sort of family crisis. He had sounded as though he would like to escape from his sister for a day or two, but thought it would be unkind to do so.

'Kate, she's talking about leaving Iain. She can't do that, can she? What about the children?'

'Where would she go? Would she move down to London?'

'That's what I'm afraid of. She might want to stay with *me*.'

'It would be somewhat crowded in your flat, wouldn't it?' Certainly there'd be no room left over for Kate Ivory.

'She seems to like being surrounded by large numbers of possessions,' Jon said gloomily.

'Can't you talk her out of it? I'm sure you'll be able to put a reasonable case for returning to Scotland.'

'I expect I could. But she isn't acting rationally, is she? This is just some whim of hers. I think she wants to teach her husband a lesson. You know the sort of thing: "Just look how kind and thoughtful Jon is, Iain. Why can't *you* be more like that?" I'm sure you understand what she's doing.'

'I do?'

'You're a woman, aren't you?'

'And you think we all react in the same way?'

'Well . . .'

'Just don't say it, Jon. I'd rather keep at least some of my illusions about you.'

245

'I don't know what to do about her, Kate,' he pleaded.

'Neither do I, Jon. She really needs to get back up to Scotland and talk to your brother-in-law. This problem of theirs isn't going to be solved by manipulation.'

'You think she's manipulative?'

Oh dear. What had she got herself into?

'Perhaps she just needs a new perspective on it all,' she suggested.

'I do miss you, Kate,' he said sadly.

'I miss you, too. But I think I'll wait till Alison's returned home before I come up to London.'

As she put the phone down she wondered whether she'd done the right thing. They had been on less than good terms by the end of the conversation, but she'd done the only thing she knew she could cope with; she certainly didn't want to add to his problems just at the present. She would have valued his opinion about the Daisy Tompkins affair, though – even if she was sure he would disapprove of what she was being pushed into doing this afternoon.

Kate took the London road out of Oxford. Faith sat in the passenger seat, rigidly upright, staring straight ahead. She was wearing a black suit with a blue shirt and very restrained earrings.

'You'll have to give me directions when we get to the village,' said Kate eventually. 'Do you know where we're going, or will we have to ask for information in the post office?'

'What?'

Kate repeated her question.

'I already have the directions. After you take the Wheatley turning, just go straight over the small roundabout and turn left at the bottom.' Faith returned to her own thoughts while Kate rehearsed silently what she was going to say when they reached the house.

They were passing a row of 1950s semi-detached houses when Faith said, 'It's here. Number thirty-two, there on the right.'

Kate was just saying, 'It really wouldn't be right for me to come inside, would it?' when Faith said at the same time, 'You could come with me to the door, couldn't you?'

They walked together towards the front gate. Everything was clean, and well-painted, and the small front garden was neat and unimaginative, with a small hybrid tea rose-bush on either side of the door. There were net curtains at the windows on the ground floor.

Kate walked a pace or two behind Faith as she walked up the narrow path and rang the doorbell.

'I'll be going now, shall I?' she said. 'I'll wait for you in the car.'

But just then the front door opened and it seemed rude to turn and make her escape at the same moment.

'Is your friend coming in, too?' asked the woman who stood in the doorway.

'Yes, she is,' said Faith firmly. 'Mrs Tompkins?'

'Yes. And you must be Dr Beeton.' She gave Faith her title with a slight hesitation, as though disapproving of a woman who called herself 'Doctor' and yet didn't practise medicine. Behind her, the hallway gleamed with polish and smelled of synthetic lemon spray. The carpet was dark red and patterned with large, abstract flowers, and the wallpaper was striped in olive green and cream. The effect was of a very clean and hygienic institution.

In the silence, Mrs Tompkins turned to Kate and stared at her until Kate said, 'My name's Kate Ivory. I'm just the chauffeur, really. And I could wait in the car.'

Mrs Tompkins had an impassive face, well-powdered, that showed the shadows of stress around the eyes, but no sign that she had given way to bouts of weeping. Her hair was a uniform reddish-blonde, set into the rigid, puffed-out waves of the early 1980s, when she presumably had been at her peak. Her eyes were pale blue, with the protuberance of astigmatism. She wore a matching blue knitted suit with a string of large red beads. Kate found the jauntiness of this outfit at odds with the solemnity of the occasion.

Faith caught Kate's eye over Mrs Tompkins's shoulder and sent her urgent messages which Kate interpreted as meaning that she shouldn't leave Faith on her own, so she said, 'Unless, of course, Dr Beeton wishes me to stay.'

'I don't think that will be necessary. My business with Dr Beeton is confidential,' said Mrs Tompkins.

'If you say so.'

'Who is it, Mum?' A man's voice came from inside the house, and Kate saw a large male form outlined against the light from a doorway.

'It's all right, Steven. It's only the lady from Daisy's college. I'm dealing with it,' said Mrs Tompkins.

Steven didn't move though, Kate saw. From upstairs came another male voice: 'Everything all right, Mum? Do you need me?'

'Don't you worry about me,' called back Mrs Tompkins. She was well supported by her sons, and they weren't going to give Faith an easy time, guessed Kate.

'Why don't you go into the kitchen and get yourself a cup of tea?' Mrs Tompkins said to Kate, unbending a little, and she led the way through into the large square hall. The tall, well-built man of about thirty who was standing in the doorway to their left looked Faith and Kate over carefully before moving back into the room. Mrs Tompkins opened another door and waited for Kate to go inside. 'You'll find the makings for your tea on the side there.'

So that's *me* dealt with, thought Kate, grateful that she was spared the interview between Faith and this stern, humourless woman, but feeling guilty that she had left Faith to face it on her own. Although Faith had always seemed tough, and efficient, and in control, she looked like a lightweight next to Daisy's mother. Mrs Tompkins was only a few years older than Faith, but she seemed to belong to another, more formidable generation. Although she was too young to have lived through the Second World War, she gave the impression of having coped with bombs, and food shortages, and all without the support of a man.

The kitchen door snapped shut and Kate was on her own, though she could feel the glowering presence of the Tompkins sons in the house. She wasn't going to learn much about the family from their kitchen, she thought, apart from the fact that they were excessively neat and tidy and their kitchen was as hygienic as any well-run hospital.

She heard the two women cross the hall, and the door to the sitting room, where Steven was presumably waiting for them, close behind them. Deciding that she might as well do as she was told, she looked around her obediently.

The kitchen was not only clean but rather bare. It had been modernised in the 1980s, Kate guessed, with pine cupboards and white worktops. She could see the kettle, and the tea-bags were in a glass jar on the counter.

It wasn't until she walked across to the sink to fill the kettle that she noticed that she wasn't alone.

'Hello,' she said, with surprise. The small, thin woman in the flowered pinafore must have been observing her for several moments. She had white, curly hair and a face covered in a network of lines. There were liver spots on the back of her hands, and knotted veins.

'Hello, dear. Who are you?' She accepted Kate's presence with equanimity.

'Kate Ivory. I've just driven my friend Faith here to talk to Mrs Tompkins.'

'I'm Mrs Tompkins, too,' confided the old woman. 'She's Helen. I'm Margaret.'

'Daisy's grandmother?'

'Yes. Poor little Daisy.'

'I'm so sorry about it.' It sounded trite, but she had to say something.

'It's all wrong, a lovely girl like that, murdered by some madman. You shouldn't outlive your grandchildren, should you?'

'That's too hard, yes. I am so sorry.' Kate found herself holding the old woman's hand in both hers and repeating herself in her effort to express her sympathy.

'Still, you have to carry on, don't you? You can't give in.' Mrs Tompkins used a small white handkerchief to wipe her eyes. 'She was named after me, you know.'

'She was?'

'Helen thought "Margaret" was too plain though, so she called her "Marguerite" instead. Poor little thing. Such a big name for such a little girl.'

'Perhaps "Daisy" suited her better? It's a pretty name, and delicate, like Daisy herself.'

'I'm glad you think that, and perhaps it did. But there was no pacifying her mother. She said it was a name for a servant, and we'd never been in service. She said it was a silly, fashionable sort of a name, and her daughter should have a proper, serious name, especially since she was going to college and could look forward to being in a profession. But she's a hard woman, my daughter-in-law.'

'Daisy was certainly doing very well, wasn't she? You must be very proud of what she achieved.'

'I'm proud of all my grandchildren. Would you like to see my pictures?'

'Pictures?'

'Snapshots of my family.'

'I'd love to. Would you like me to make us a cup of tea first, though?' she asked.

'Not with those tea-bags. I like a proper cup of tea, made in a teapot.'

'I'm not sure—'

'We can go round to my place.'

'What about Dr Beeton and Daisy's mother?'

'Oh, Helen will be arguing with her for a long time yet. She was working herself up about it all morning.'

'Whereabouts do you live? Is it far?'

'Less than five minutes away,' said Margaret Tompkins, taking a grey tweed coat from a hook on the back of the door, putting it on, and adding a red woollen hood that she tied beneath her chin and which made her look paler and older than she had before. 'Come along, dear,' she urged.

Kate picked up her handbag and followed her out of the back door, hoping that she wasn't letting Faith down, but feeling a sense of relief as soon as she left that oppressively clean and tidy house behind.

xxii

Oh, God. The girl is dead.

22

Margaret Tompkins was right. Her house was less than five minutes away, even walking at the pace of an elderly woman with arthritic knees. But its style was quite different from Helen's. For a start, it was over a hundred years old, and built of dark red brick, with a slate roof, a wooden porch and coloured glass panels in the front door.

When Mrs Tompkins Senior opened the front door Kate was greeted, not with a smell of lemon-scented cleaner and furniture polish, but by a maturing aroma of onions and bacon that might have been that day's lunch, or even last Sunday's supper. She could smell a cat, too, or at least its litter tray.

'Come in here,' the old lady said, leading the way along a narrow passage to the back of the house. Here the carpet was dark red, and the walls covered in a trellis of brown and cream flowers. A green-painted door with a brass handle led into the kitchen.

This kitchen had certainly not been refurbished in the 1980s, if ever, and there were more original features than the keenest estate agent could ever expect to find in a house of this date.

Mrs Tompkins opened a cupboard door and took out a tin canister patterned with pink roses.

'Do you like it nice and strong?' she asked.

'Well—'

'You need it nice and strong when there's been a death in the family,' she said, spooning black leaves into a brown pot. 'And lots of sugar,' she said, taking a matching brown bowl out of the cupboard and placing it on the scrubbed pine table. She pulled up a Windsor chair for Kate. 'Sit you down,' she said. 'Make yourself comfortable.'

The floor, Kate noticed, was covered, not with vinyl tiles, but with genuine lino in a geometrical star pattern. The pattern was worn in places – in front of the stove and by the square stone sink – and its colours were a dark olive green and orange, outlined in black. It looked as though Mrs Tompkins had the same ideas on interior decoration as the erstwhile owner of her own house in Cleveland Road.

'Helen's very upset about that man at Daisy's college,' said Margaret Tompkins as she filled the kettle and set it on the stove. 'It wasn't right, what he did to her.'

'Do we know what it was?' asked Kate. She could hardly ask whether they were sure that Daisy was telling the truth.

'She was a sweet little thing. There was nothing wrong with her,' insisted Mrs Tompkins, obliquely.

'Surely no one ever suggested that there was?'

'I don't know about that.'

The kettle was humming on the stove. Mrs Tompkins shuffled across to the teapot and carried it over to the stove and stared at the kettle until it suddenly shrieked and let out a burst of steam.

'Only ever use freshly boiling water,' she admonished Kate as she poured a stream of water on to the tea-leaves. She stirred vigorously with a teaspoon with a brown bowl and a bent handle, apparently used for just this purpose for many years.

Mrs Tompkins moved from cupboard to table, setting out cups and saucers, a milk jug and teaspoons in front of Kate. Finally she set the teapot and strainer down, too, and then poured the rich brown liquid into their cups. Kate thought it impolite to point out that she normally took hers weak – *very* weak by Mrs Tompkins's standards – with only a dash of skimmed milk and no sugar. The milk in the jug had a thick layer of cream on top and when Mrs Tompkins poured a generous amount into Kate's cup she could see globules of oil shining on the surface. Ah well, the sugar – two heaped spoonfuls – might take away the taste.

'I've got some biscuits, but I expect you'd rather have fruit cake, wouldn't you, dear? I made it myself.'

'Fruit cake sounds delicious. Yes, please.'

Mrs Tompkins opened the cake tin and cut each of them a thick slice. The cake was dark and moist, and packed full of fruit.

'Thank you. This is absolutely wonderful,' said Kate, tucking in.

'They all love my fruit cake,' said Mrs Tompkins. 'Even little Daisy, though she was never what I'd call a hearty eater.' There was another pause as she sat silently, remembering her granddaughter.

Kate sipped her mahogany-coloured liquid. 'The tea's delicious, too,' she said. Roz would be proud of her, she thought, as she repressed a shudder.

'A bit better than that tea-bag rubbish, anyway,' said Mrs Tompkins, with satisfaction. 'She doesn't appreciate a good cup of tea, that daughter-in-law of mine.'

'And your son, what about him?' Kate asked. She was curious about the invisible Mr Tompkins.

'Him? He was emasculated by that woman years ago, if you know what I mean,' said Mrs Tompkins. 'She's ruled that family, all of them, since the day she married him.'

'Daisy has some brothers, hasn't she?' asked Kate.

'Lovely lads, the lot of them,' said their proud grandmother. 'Would you like to see their pictures now?'

'I'd love to,' Kate answered. Normally she wasn't keen to look at other people's photographs, but she was curious to see what Daisy's family looked like. She had received a general impression of the brother, Steven or 'Spike', but this wasn't the time to see him at his best, after all. She could understand that he would be protective of his mother.

'Bring your tea into the front room, then.' And Margaret Tompkins showed the way into a cool, darkened room that smelled of dead flowers and, once again, of cats. She switched on the light, even though it was daylight outside.

Kate sat on a hard sofa covered in some flocked material in brown and cream (presumably to match the wallpaper in the hall). The corner of an even harder cushion dug into a sensitive spot on her back. The central hanging light in its cream parchment shade cast uncompromising shadows on to the carpet – dark green, this one, with large golden sunflowers scattered across it.

'Will Dr Beeton know where I am?' she asked. 'She won't be waiting for me, wondering where to find me, will she?'

'Don't you worry about her, Kate. Like I said, Helen will have her pinned to her chair and answering all the questions on her list. She'll know where to find us when she's done, never you mind.'

From the walls, framed photographs of what she could only suppose were the younger members of the Tompkins family stared down at her. Margaret Tompkins disappeared for two or three minutes and then reappeared with an armful of red photograph albums that looked as though they might be covered in leather, but which smelled inescapably of plastic.

'Here they are,' she said, laying them out on the low table in front of Kate. 'This is the three boys at the beach at Folkestone, back in nineteen seventy-eight.'

Three dark-eyed boys, with heavy brown hair hanging over their foreheads, scowled at Kate. They were somewhere between two and seven years old, she calculated. The largest one held a bucket in his left hand and a spade in his right as though he had beaten off his smaller brothers for their possession.

'Lovely,' she said. 'Such nice-looking boys. Which one is that?' She pointed at the one holding the bucket and spade.

'That's Steven. He's the eldest,' said his grandmother. 'He's at Helen's place at the moment. The boys are taking it in turns to look after her, make sure she isn't left on her own at all.'

'That's good of them.'

'They're very fond of their mum. And they were devoted to their little sister.'

On the pages of the album a small, fair-haired baby had appeared in their midst, as the boys grew progressively taller and heavier. They formed a barrier around the little girl, protecting her from all dangers. Daisy looked up at Kate from out of the photographs with a sweet, trusting smile on her face and a pale blue bow in her fair hair. As she grew older and her brothers grew larger, there was something else in her expression, too. Is it something calculating, Kate wondered, or am I simply adding that from my own assumptions?

'I did meet your granddaughter once,' she said. 'It was only a few days ago, in fact, at her college. We talked for five minutes or so, but she told me about her ambition to become a writer and I asked her to come and see me if she thought I could help her.'

'Why should she do that?'

'Because I'm a professional writer,' said Kate with as much modesty as she could muster. 'She seemed very keen, I thought.'

'I though you said you were a chauffeur,' said Mrs Tompkins, staring at Kate suspiciously.

'Only for the afternoon. Dr Beeton doesn't have a car, and I agreed to drive her over here.'

'That's a funny thing to do. But you say you're a writer the rest of the time. What is it you write?'

'I write novels. Historical fiction.'

'What did you say your last name was?'

'Ivory. Kate Ivory.'

'I must say I've never heard of you,' said Mrs Tompkins dubiously. 'But our Daisy was always writing little stories, and she was going to be famous one day, she was sure about that.'

'Yes. That's what she told me.'

'And she was going to come to see you for some advice on getting published?'

'Well . . .'

'I can show you them if you like.'

'What's that?'

'The stories she wrote.'

Kate's heart sank. If there was one thing she dreaded, it was being asked to read the stories written by someone who was sure they were going to be a famous writer.

'I've got all her notebooks. All the little things she used to write down.'

'Well, of course, I'd be very interested to see them. But are you sure the police don't want them?'

'They've taken away all her stuff from her bedroom. These were just the little bits and pieces she gave her old granny. They wouldn't be interested in them.'

'Could I look through them at home?'

'I don't want you taking them away and then losing them.'

'Of course not. I wouldn't do a thing like that. I'd read them very carefully,' Kate said earnestly, 'and if they showed any promise at all, I could pass them on to my agent. She's very good,' she added. If anyone could market Daisy's stories, she considered, it would be Estelle Livingstone. She could just see how Estelle would want to put that wistful, blonde head on the back cover, smiling dewily out at the reader.

Daisy Tompkins, the young, fresh novelist, struck down in her prime. Estelle would just love to sell Daisy, no problem.

'I'll leave you to look through these,' said Mrs Tompkins, passing across yet another red photograph album, 'while I find those things of Daisy's for you.'

Kate dutifully turned the pages, looking at yet more photos of the young Tompkinses, growing larger and more impressive with the passing years, Daisy poised like a delicate flower in their midst.

Did she enjoy the protection of her brothers, or did she find it stifling? Not having any brothers of her own, Kate found it difficult to imagine being the only daughter in such a family. It must be pleasant to feel that you belonged to such a close, loving group, but did it stop you from doing the things you really wanted to do? And was Daisy the only one who wanted to go to university? Did she have anything in common with these beefy young men in their leather jackets and bulging jeans?

'Here you are,' said Mrs Tompkins, returning with a brown cardboard box in her hands.

It appeared that Daisy, at least in her teens, went in for notebooks strewn with – wait for it! – *daisies*! Well, having chosen the name for herself, and in opposition to that formidable mother of hers, Kate supposed she would have to do just that. She favoured pink, too, with silver and gold embellishments.

'Such a clever little girl,' said Mrs Tompkins fondly.

Kate took the notebooks and leafed through the first of them. Daisy had neat, legible handwriting, she was glad to see, even if she did favour green ink.

'Of course, she used her computer this last couple of years,' said her grandmother. 'She still liked to write in one of her pretty notebooks, but mostly she just sat and tapped at the – what did she call it? – oh yes, at the keyboard.'

259

'But I don't suppose she gave you any floppy disks, did she?'

'What, dear?'

'Never mind.'

'She gave me these,' said Mrs Tompkins, reaching into the bottom of the box and pulling out a sheaf of pages of typescript.

'Oh, excellent. That's very professional of her,' Kate assured Mrs Tompkins.

'And you're sure you're a proper writer?'

'Of course I am! You can check me out in the public library.'

'Oh, I shall, dear, don't you worry. Now, you'd better write down your name and address for me on this bit of paper. I don't want you disappearing into the blue with my Daisy's stories. You might even publish them under your own name, for all I know.'

'Really, I wouldn't dream of doing that. I'll give you a receipt for them,' said Kate. 'There's no way I would ever attempt to pass them off as my own, I can assure you, Mrs Tompkins.'

She wrote an imposing-looking receipt, and added her full name and address, as well as her telephone number.

'And, of course, I'm an old friend of Dr Beeton's,' she added.

'But we don't know we can trust her, do we?' said Mrs Tompkins.

'Of course you can! Faith Beeton is nothing if not absolutely fair and even-handed,' said Kate.

'But then again, she's a friend of that Joseph Fechan's, isn't she?' Mrs Tompkins pronounced his name 'Feckan', and Kate really couldn't blame her.

And then there was a knock on the back door and a large young man walked into the room.

'Gran? What are you doing, hiding away in here?'

Then he stopped, seeing Kate. 'And what's *she* doing here?'

'She just came round for a cup of tea while she's waiting for her friend,' said Margaret Tompkins. 'Is that what you'd like, Steven? A cup of tea and a slice of my fruit cake?'

'You know I always like a slice of fruit cake,' he said, still staring at Kate. 'If she's a friend of the Beeton woman, you shouldn't trust her.'

'I'm just the driver,' said Kate. 'Don't mind me. And I'm leaving in a minute, anyway.'

She smiled at Steven, who looked big and tough enough to remove her forcefully from the house if he felt like it. He was still wearing jeans and a leather jacket, as he was in the photographs she'd been looking at, and a black T-shirt stretched across impressive muscles. He was much darker than Daisy, and it was difficult to see a family resemblance between him and the delicate, fair-haired girl at the Lamb Room party.

'I'm not sure about *her*,' he was starting to say when there was another knock at the back door and two more people entered the house and walked through to the sitting room. Faith Beeton was there, Kate was relieved to see, and Mrs Helen Tompkins, grimfaced as ever.

'Thank you so much for the tea,' said Kate, picking up the cardboard box and hoping that neither Steven nor the younger Mrs Tompkins would notice what she was holding. But Steven's attention was on Faith, now, and the two women extricated themselves as quickly as possible from the threatening situation. Kate clutched the box under her arm as she and Faith walked the short distance up the road to her car.

'Let's get out of here,' said Faith.

'Not a happy conversation with Mrs Helen Tompkins, then?'

'She wants her pound of flesh,' said Faith.

'You means she wants to slice it out of Joseph Fechan?'

'That was the impression she gave, certainly. The odd thing is that she seems more angry than saddened by the death of her daughter. Her mind is set on getting her revenge. *Her* revenge, you notice, rather than Daisy's. She sat there, surrounded by cards expressing sympathy at her loss and you'd have expected her to be weeping, or griefstricken, but she was rigid with *rage*.'

'And what about the boys?'

'Boys? Oh, you mean the brothers. I didn't like the look of the one we saw. He looked quite violent.'

'The three boys were very fond of their sister. And Steven, the eldest, thinks that you're trying to play down the situation with Fechan instead of supporting Daisy. You can't blame him for being furious.'

'Have you met him?'

'Only briefly, but I have now seen so many photographs of the Tompkins children at every stage of their development that I feel I know them all intimately. Tell me about your meeting with Daisy's mother.'

'It was grim. I was expecting it to be, of course. I tried to tell her how sorry I was, how sorry we all were about Daisy's death, but she just brushed my condolences aside.'

'I can see that you wouldn't be her favourite person.'

'And what could I possibly say to a woman whose daughter had just died? I simply felt inadequate. To be honest, I wouldn't have been there if she hadn't insisted that someone should come and talk to her about Daisy's complaint against Joseph. Do you know, I think she might even have believed that he was the murderer.'

'Are you absolutely sure he isn't?'

'Don't be ridiculous. He sounds loud and frightening, but there's not an ounce of violence in him.'

'We all need a certain amount of aggression to survive, don't we?'

'But not violence.'

Kate was silent, wondering whether to believe Faith on the subject of Fechan. She did seem to have a very high opinion of him. Maybe she'd given up good-looking young men and had taken up with her own intellectual equals after all.

'And was there no Mr Tompkins in the photos?' asked Faith, changing the subject.

'I imagine he was the one with the camera, as Mrs Helen Tompkins was sometimes present with her children.'

'Why have your teeth turned orange, by the way?' asked Faith as Kate drew away from the kerb and headed towards the A40.

Kate ran her tongue over them; they felt furry. 'Just blame it on Granny's tea,' she said.

'So that would be the other Mrs Tompkins, would it?'

'Helen Tompkins's mother-in-law, the mother of the invisible Mr Tompkins, and keeper of the family archive,' replied Kate.

'And you've removed a large chunk of it, have you?' Faith asked, shaking the box that Kate had placed on her knees to see what it contained.

'No. Granny pressed some of Daisy's writings on me, as I confessed to being a writer of fiction. I gather they're mostly adolescent short stories. And anyway, the police will have removed anything of importance to them from her bedroom, won't they? I can't think they'd be interested in this juvenile stuff.'

'I shouldn't think you're looking forward to ploughing through it, either.'

'You're right, but it seemed only courteous to promise Granny that I would. If there really is anything that's any good, and publishable, I'll pass it on to Estelle.'

'Your agent?'

'Yes.'

'I never managed to find myself an agent. I might have done better with my novel if I'd been taken on by someone like Estelle.'

'Not necessarily,' said Kate, remembering some of her agent's sharp comments about her work.

They both lapsed into silence as Kate reached Oxford and navigated them through to St Clement's, where Faith lived. Presumably they each had things to think about, following their visit to the two Tompkins's houses. Certainly Faith looked pale and strained after her ordeal with Daisy's mother, Kate noticed.

23

There was a phone call from Faith the next morning.

'They've let him go.'

'What? Who?'

'Joseph, of course.'

For a moment Kate had forgotten about Joseph Fechan. She had been working on her own novel, and the people who lived in the places of her imagination seemed more real than those of Bartlemas College.

'That's good, isn't it? It must mean that they agree with you that he had nothing to do with Daisy's death.'

'Oh, they believe he was involved but they just can't get him to admit it.'

'It must be a relief for him to be out of the police station though,' said Kate, trying to get Faith to take a more positive attitude.

'But what's he going to do? They won't let him near any of his students until this mess is cleared up.'

'I don't think I can help you, Faith.'

'I thought you might at least *try*.'

Kate tried a new tack. 'Last night I looked at a few pages of the notebooks that Daisy's grandmother lent me,' she said.

'I don't suppose they told you much,' said Faith, determined to be gloomy.

'I'm not so sure about that. Much of them is in the form of a dialogue between Daisy and a friend of hers called Magz, though whether they're a report of conversations that actually

265

happened, or whether she invented them, isn't entirely clear yet.'

'So?'

'I think she's writing about herself, but in a fictional form.'

'Not much help there, then.'

'There just might be if I go on working at it. I used to do that sort of thing, too, when I was a teenager. It was more interesting, more arty, than writing a straightforward journal. I thought I was practising the craft of the writer, I suppose. I imagined I was turning my life into fiction, but I doubt whether it would have been that difficult to decipher.'

'I suppose it's worth a try,' said Faith, sounding more cheerful. 'Why don't you read the whole lot and see if it tells you anything about her that we didn't know before?'

The cardboard box containing Daisy's papers was in Kate's bedroom and she went up to take another look inside it. She had tried to sort the contents into roughly chronological order. It made more sense to read them in reverse order, but she had started at what she thought was the beginning.

Luckily, Daisy's handwriting in the earlier notebooks was round and legible. The printed pages were in an informal font, but it could have been worse; it wasn't too difficult to read.

When she'd finished reading the first dozen pages, Kate decided to phone Roz.

'Are you busy today?' she asked her mother.

'What would you like me to do?'

'I'd like you to look at the stuff that Daisy was writing and give me your impressions. I want to know whether you agree with me about it.'

'How much of it is there?'

'Quite a bit, but I'm talking here about ten pages.'

'Well . . .'

'Why don't you come to lunch? I'm sure I can find

something tempting in the deli. And a glass of Pinot Gris?'

'It's time I took a look at your progress on the house,' said Roz. 'I'll see you at twelve-thirty.'

Kate cleared their lunch away and used the space on the kitchen table to place the box containing Daisy's writing in front of her mother.

'Here it is,' she said. 'Read this, and then tell me what you think.'

Roz took the pages and skimmed through the first three or four of them.

'Look, Kate, I know the poor child is dead, and I'm really sorry about it, but I'm afraid the tragedy doesn't make her a good writer. This is boring,' she said. 'How much of it do you expect me to read?'

'What do you think about the two characters?'

'The two who are having the long, tedious conversation?' She picked a page and read aloud,

' "*We're going to escape, aren't we Magz?*"

' "*I don't know about you. I'm certainly going to. In fact, compared to you, I escaped years ago.*"

' "*You can't have done. We're bound together, the two of us. One can't leave without the other.*"

' "*That's what you think, Daisy Tompkins. But then, you're just a naïve little dreamer, aren't you?*"

' "*I'm a writer. Writers have to dream. Where else do their stories come from?*"

'Honestly, Kate, how much of this is there?'

'Didn't I write this sort of thing when I was a teenager?'

'No. You had too much sense.'

'Why's it written in the form of a dialogue, do you suppose?'

'I think she's trying to explore the two sides of her personality. Daisy's the good little girl, and Magz is the wicked one. It's not exactly original, is it?'

'Maybe not. But I've just remembered, her real name was Marguerite. That explains it.'

'I did notice that she doesn't seem very fond of her mother,' said Roz, handing another page to Kate. 'Take a look at this bit.' Kate read:

There is the sound of heavy footsteps tramping up the stairs. They stop outside Daisy's door. Magz has already run across the room and turned the key in the lock. The doorknob turns and rattles, but the door doesn't open.

'That's fooled the old bitch,' she hisses at Daisy. And then, 'Sod the stupid cow, I've ruined my nails. I'll have to start again.'

The person outside the door hasn't moved away though. A voice, bleating like an old ewe, comes wavering through the narrow crack of the doorframe.

'I can hear you,' it whines. 'I can hear you wasting paper. Just doodling away. Wasting time, writing rubbish. Haven't you grown out of all that nonsense by now? You're going to be a student. You're going away to college. It's time you grew up, Miss Tompkins. Stop being so childish. Get serious *And remember, I can hear you.'*

'Can't you manage to speak to her? Would you like me to send her away for you?' asks Magz. 'I could give you a lesson in how to do it. I could show you how. OK?' She has black hair which she has waxed so that it hangs over her forehead in stiff spikes, like a giant sea urchin.

'She'll go away all by herself in a minute,' replies Daisy.

'But she'll come back again. I can get rid of her.' And Magz applies her lips – painted purple, and glossy as fat black olives – to the keyhole. 'Drop dead, you old bitch. You've had your life and now you're finished. You're a has-been. What are you good for? Lie down and die, why don't you!'

'I see what you mean,' said Kate. 'But I did meet her mother, and I didn't find her a warm and sympathetic character either.

Her old granny was OK, though. I got on with her all right.'

'She mentions that Magz turned up when they were both six years old.'

'So she's been around for years!'

'I expect Daisy didn't need her for much of that time. She seems to use her as a sounding board,' said Roz.

'Or for distancing herself from the bits of her personality – or behaviour – that she's ashamed of. Sex, for example,' said Kate.

'Yes, but more than that. There's a delight in well, flaunting herself, that's natural enough at that age, but which she seems to have taken to extremes.'

'Magz wears black nail varnish.'

'Scarlet hair.'

'Naughty clothes.'

'But why is she so worked up about it?' asked Kate. 'Why is everything so extreme?'

'Maybe she's just a neurotic teenager.'

'But that's not what her grandmother said, or Avril, if it comes to that. It isn't even what Faith thought about her.'

'Perhaps we'll learn more if we take a look at another few pages. Though I expect she witters on in the same vein for volumes on end.'

'Here, let's have a look,' said Kate, delving back into the box and coming up with another sheaf of papers.

'Put them here, on the table,' said Roz. 'Like that, we can both see what she's written.'

'Here, take a look at this page,' said Kate a little later.

'*If you want to know what hard work is, just be here on Sunday when "the boys" come to lunch.*'

Daisy speaks with such bitter intensity that Magz looks at her curiously.

'*The boys? What are you on about now?*'

'*That's what she calls them still:* the boys. *Steven must be twenty-eight by now, Martin's twenty-five, and even Luke's coming up for twenty-three. Can't she see they're adults? But no. "They'll always be* my boys,*"she says!'*

'*If she could have her way they'd be coming home for their tea every day and expecting her to do their washing and ironing for them. She'd wipe Martin's snotty nose for him if he'd let her,' says Magz. 'And does Steven know you refer to him as "Steven"? He won't like that at all now, will he? We're all supposed to call him "Spike", didn't you know that?'*

'*Stupid name. I call him "Steven",' says Daisy huffily.*

Magz has walked away from the computer where Daisy's working and is sitting on her favourite spot on the carpet with her back against the foot of Daisy's bed. 'The sun shines out of their proverbial arseholes as far as she's concerned.'

Daisy laughs. 'What's so proverbial about an arsehole?' she wants to know. Magz's way of talking is catching, she finds.

'*What I can't understand,' says Magz, 'is why they go along with it. There's nothing more gruesome than one of Helen's traditional dinners, complete with roast potatoes and boiled cabbage, boiled carrots, boiled peas and thick gravy. Why do they come?'*

'*I reckon it's the only square meal Luke gets all week,' said Daisy. 'Martin's just a wimp and does everything his mother tells him.'*

'*And what about Spike? I thought Spike was his own person.'*

'*Steven has his own agenda,' says Daisy shortly. 'His own hidden agenda.' This is a term she has recently come across in an instruction book on creative writing.*

' *"Own hidden agenda"! Just hark at you!' Magz is working at her fingernails today, removing the old varnish and pushinq down the cuticles to angry red crescents, before deciding what colour she'll paint her nails today. Whatever she chooses it is likely to be dark, and ugly, and possibly iridescent.*

'The brothers,' said Kate. 'Two of them were at the house yesterday, when Faith and I were there. And Steven, the eldest, came round to Granny's house to make sure I wasn't corrupting her, and to eat a large slice of fruit cake.'

'They sound like nice boys,' said Roz.

'Well, they were protective towards their mother, certainly. And towards their sister, from the look of Granny's photos.'

'I can't see anything extraordinary in Daisy's writings,' said Roz. 'I don't think you're going to find the answer to her murder there, certainly, if that's what you were hoping for.'

'Faith thinks the police believe that Joseph Fechan killed her. I was hoping there would be a suggestion of someone else in her notes.'

'I'll leave you to it,' said Roz. 'I'm afraid that I've read enough.'

'I think she's about to launch into an actual story.'

'Thank you very much for my lunch. It was delicious. Give me a ring if you come across anything more promising.'

Kate saw her mother out, then returned to the kitchen and the box of Daisy's writings. As she had said to Roz, the girl had at last embarked on an actual story.

24

Once upon a time there lived a beautiful princess called Lucy.

'Is that the right sort of name for a princess?' asks Daisy.
'Maybe not. But never mind, I'll just get on and write until I reach the end. I can always change it later,' replies Magz.

So, this Princess Lucy had beautiful blonde hair and big blue eyes, and at her christening her fairy godmother heaped every virtue and talent necessary for a successful princess upon her small, golden head.

And what would the most important one be, you're wondering? Well, personally, I think it's choosing the right parents. Clever and successful people make sure that their parents are really useful human beings. Forget the narrow-minded, mean-spirited, penny-pinching, untalented, insensitive shits that most of us get landed with as family.

Has your fairy godmother arrived in time to make the right choice of parents, Lucy, or is it too late by the time she gets her invitation to the christening?

Let's assume you made it through to the age of sixteen, doing everything that was expected of you, Princess Lucy. What happened then? Oh, yes. You had to choose a husband, a prince who would take over from your father when the time came, and rule the country with wisdom.

'We're not allowed to help you in your choice,' said the Queen sadly.

'You're on your own this time,' said the King.

'We've guided you through all the tricky decisions up to this point,' said the Queen.

'So just remember what we've taught you.'

'I'm sure you'll make the right choice,' said the Queen anxiously.

'It's a prince we're looking for, not a frog,' said the King.

'You're sure you can tell the difference?' asked the Queen, making eye-contact with Princess Lucy and looking seriously caring and concerned.

'Of course she can, dear,' said the King. 'She's been prac- tising for ten years so she must know the difference by now.'

'You'll be given a choice of three,' said the Queen. 'Princesses always get three princes to choose from. It's all part of the tradition.'

Princess Lucy nodded but said nothing since nobody seemed interested to hear anything she might have to say.

'A prince,' her father was repeating.

'Not a frog,' her mother reiterated.

'Choice of three,' confirmed her father.

'Yeah. I'm getting the point,' said Lucy, but too quietly for her parents to hear.

It was true that she had sat through long and wearisome lessons about how to recognise a genuine prince, but this was not a subject that interested her very much and she found that the odd facts that she retained were even now fading from her brain. She had been more interested in finding out how the world worked. Why was the sky blue, and was there any chance of voyaging to the moon? Why did oil float on the top of water, but stones sink to the bottom of the pond? And was there any hope of attracting the attention of the young man who was painting the ground-floor window-frames and who had removed his shirt to display his manly six-pack in the warm summer sun?

She had been taken to the pond in a far corner of the palace grounds in order to observe frogs, but no one told her anything interesting about them, like why they started out as tadpoles instead of miniature frogs. No, this lesson, like so many others, had been about recognising a prince. She furrowed her brow and tried to bring back the salient points. Did a real prince have green skin and round, protuberant eyes? Or was he the one with the blond curls, the jewelled tunic and the elegant legs?

Lucy did recall that kissing came into the solution somewhere and so she determined to kiss as many young men as possible: frogs, princes, the lot. Something should result from it, she thought optimistically.

And so she set off into the great world outside the castle. Her parents waved their embroidered handkerchiefs at her from the battlements as she disappeared down the long road to the borders of the country. Her mother had attached a fine silken rope to the waist of her gown so that she would always be able to know where her daughter was and what she was doing, but Lucy snipped this off with a pair of golden scissors as soon as she turned the first corner on her road. She attached it to the rear bumper of the bicycle belonging to a scholarly-looking female with a pannier-full of textbooks, and doubtless her mother was duly impressed with her daughter's intellectual pursuits and clean-living habits.

'No, that's no good,' Daisy muttered. 'I have to get back to the story about the princess choosing herself a husband to rule the country with her.'

Princess Lucy dressed herself in her best satin gown, her gold circlet on her head, and sat on an uncomfortable brocade chair, waiting to interview the three princes.

The first one came in, sat in the chair opposite her and

talked about himself. After a bit she grew bored and stopped listening. He was all right to look at, she supposed, in a dark and handsome kind of way, with brown eyes, short hair and neat, round ears.

After a while he left and the second applicant came in. He sat down in the same chair as the last one and started to talk. This one talked about football, and once again she stopped listening to him after a short time. She looked at him as he sat there on his small gilt chair and thought, You're just the same as the last one: brown eyes, short dark hair, neat, round ears. How am I supposed to tell you apart?

After a while the second prince left and the third came in and sat down opposite her. This one told her about his motorbike. He seemed to have several of them, or perhaps he just told her about the same one several times over.

Short dark hair, she thought. Brown eyes. Neat, rounded ears.

Eventually the third prince left and the committee entered the room to ask her for her choice.

'How can I choose?' she asked them. 'The three are identical. Nothing to tell them apart except for their topic of conversation.'

'Give them time,' said the chairman of the committee. 'I expect they all own motorbikes and support some football team or other. And all young men, whether princes or not, like to talk about themselves.'

They looked at her expectantly.

'Who cares?' she said. 'It's all the same to me. One of you can toss a coin.'

'Oh, no. That's not the way we do it,' said the chairman.

'Take three white feathers and blow them into the air. Let the breeze take them where it will, and cause each prince to follow his feather.'

'That's the sort of detail that gets fairy tales a bad name,' pointed out the Princess. 'You might as well ask each of them to plant a magic bean.'

'Good idea,' said a short, stout member of the committee.

'I was only joking,' said the Princess. 'You find the coin. I'll toss it.'

Kate thought about what she had read for a few minutes. She wished she knew more about fairy stories. Roz hadn't read any to her when she was little, as far as she could remember. She'd been keener on adventure stories than romances, in any case.

She glanced down the pages. There was another story here, this one ostensibly written by Daisy's alter ego, Magz. She carried on reading, though it didn't look very promising.

The storyteller is waiting to begin her tale. Word of her arrival has sped around the village, passed on from hut to hut. Now that their day's hard toil is finally ended, the people drift into the clearing and settle themselves on the cold, stony ground. Above them soars harsh grey granite, while mist eddies and swirls around them, threatening to extinguish the spluttering fire where the storyteller sits, silent and waiting. She is Griselda, the Grey One, and her hair is like the smoke from a funeral pyre, her skin like a dead grey pearl, her eyes the deep grey of the winter sea. The feeble light from the fire reflects back from her face, cold and grey.

On the outside of the circle, the wild beasts prowl, and their howling sends the listeners huddling closer in to the fire, waiting for Griselda to begin her story. They believe in the power of words: words are their weapons against their unseen enemies, forcing the wild beasts back to their dark pits under the earth.

Among the crowd around the storyteller are two children, a brother and a sister. The girl loves Griselda's stories and can't wait for tonight's offering to begin. She has found herself a patch of soft grass, has removed her shoes and curled up comfortably, ready to listen. The boy would rather be off with his arrows and knife, hunting for game in the forest.

Griselda is speaking: 'In the City the trees are loaded with ripe golden fruit.'

'She's talking crap,' says the boy. 'Let's go. You won't be missing anything.'

Kate had to admit she agreed with the boy. She wasn't interested in Griselda's story either.

25

Kate pushed back her chair and looked at the clock. It occurred to her that it was about the time in early afternoon when Emma reckoned she was relatively free of children and had a little space for herself. And if there was one person who should know about fairy stories, it was Emma Dolby. She must have read thousands of them in her time to her brood of children, and all in the original Grimm versions, Kate guessed.

She went to the phone and dialled Emma's number.

'How about popping over for a cup of tea?' she suggested. 'I've got some chocolate biscuits. Or rather,' she added hastily, remembering Emma's new slimline body, 'slices of raw carrot and celery.'

'Oh, I'm not sure . . .'

'I suppose you're meeting your friend Peter,' said Kate, trying to keep the disapproval out of her voice.

'No, I'm not,' said Emma sharply. 'I'll come straight over.'

And she even forgot to ask Kate what it was she wanted from her.

Kate looked curiously at Emma when she opened the door. Her friend was no longer quite as smart as she had been. The haircut was still sharp, but her hair was looking flatter, since Emma had not used any styling gunk that day. She was wearing a new pair of trousers, but had added an old pullover on top of them, and a comfortable pair of shoes, designed for running for a bus rather than standing around looking fashionable.

Kate swiftly made the tea and the two of them sat at the kitchen table, Daisy's box of writings in the middle.

'It looks like a bomb,' said Emma. 'What is it?'

'It belongs to the murdered Bartlemas student, Daisy Tompkins. These are her adolescent writings, as far as I can tell.'

'Shouldn't the police have them?'

'According to her grandmother, they weren't interested.'

'How did you get hold of them?'

'Her grandmother thought that I'd like to read them, since I am a professional author. I told her I'd hand them on to my agent if they're any good.'

'I won't ask you to explain,' Emma said. 'It all sounds far too unlikely. And are they any good?'

'I'd say they were written for her own amusement rather than for sharing with a wider public. There's nothing suitable for publication in the pages I've read so far, certainly. But what I wanted to ask you about was fairy stories.'

'Fairy stories! From what aspect?'

'I suppose I'm interested in their deeper meaning.'

Emma sighed. 'We could go on for hours. Have you read Bettelheim?'

'No.'

'That's a pity.'

'Would you like to look at what Daisy's written? I'll spare you the long conversations with her alter ego, and the rants against her mother, but I'd like you to take a quick look at a couple of the stories she's written. And don't worry, they're not very long.' She said this last as she saw Emma glancing at her wrist-watch. Emma, who taught creative writing in evening classes, was probably not keen on reading yet another amateur's short story.

'Very well. Do you want me to do it now?'

'If you wouldn't mind.' Excellent Emma! And Kate handed over the relevant pages.

Emma had the advantage of reading extremely fast. It was all the practice she had had with students' homework, Kate reckoned.

'Let's just have a look at that last page,' Emma said, a few short minutes later.

'Here you go. You're a star, Emma.'

You wave goodbye to the King and Queen standing on the battlements, Princess Lucy, and you turn your back on the world of your childhood.

You climb high walls and ford deep rivers, you journey across ravines, you scale the mountain heights, you find a few dragons and get lost in a morass or two, but eventually you come to the great city of Oxford. Dreaming Spires. Lost Causes. Shangri-La. Paradise. Or so they tell you.

Unfortunately, it's not quite as far from the castle as you'd been led to believe. Less than ten miles, in fact. Nothing like *a distant country*, is it? The King and Queen, not to mention the three hopeful Princes, can all travel those ten miles with no trouble at all, driving in their stately Ford Cortina. They can climb your stairs and knock on your door and come piling in, trampling all over your dreams and desires.

When she had reached the end of the pages, Kate said, 'I never really enjoyed fairy stories. The only worthwhile females are the beautiful princesses, and they just have to sit around and wait for the handsome prince to turn up and cart them off. It's not much of a life for a girl, is it?'

'But children do not necessarily identify with the character in the story who is of the same gender as themselves,' replied Emma seriously. 'You could have been the hero in *Sleeping Beauty*. You could have hacked your way through briars, or been turned into a white bear. The choice was yours. There's really no need to accept the gender stereotyping that is offered to you.'

'I must have been a very unenterprising child, then,' Kate said. 'I just remember looking at one or two of them, turning up my nose and then picking up some unlikely adventure tale.'

'I should think that Daisy, from what I've seen so far, happily identified with all sorts of characters, and different ones at different times, whatever she needed,' Emma stated.

'And the meanings?'

'The meanings are always personal. Different readers – or listeners, rather – will apply the stories to their own lives and take from them what they need at a specific time.'

'So, however carefully we analyse the stories, we're not necessarily going to know what they meant to Daisy?'

'I don't know. There are some recurring motifs.'

'But only standard fairy-tale ones, like the three princes who want to win the princess, and the children walking off into the scary forest.'

'She has taken standard elements, but she's woven them into new stories. That should tell you something. And scary forests, full of wild animals, usually stand for difficult periods of life, by the way.'

'Like adolescence?'

'Could be. One of the problems that fairy stories address is the difficulty of separating from your family, especially your mother; the fear, in fact, that you'll be on your own for ever and ever.'

'Great stuff for little children at bedtime!'

'But they always have happy endings.'

'I don't think Daisy's do.'

'That's because they're not real fairy stories. Stories collected by the Grimm Brothers, for example, demonstrate to the listening child that by overcoming difficulties he or she will come to find an adult love, and live happily ever after.'

281

'Helped along by an old crone or a magic bird, as I remember it,' said Kate.

'There you are, you're getting the hang of it. You could look out for instances of the fear of separation in her stories, though. What sort of family did Daisy come from?'

'Conventional, respectable. She had three brothers, as a matter of fact.'

'And disappeared off into the forest with one of them?'

'What's that supposed to mean?'

'I'm making wild guesses. Take no notice.'

Kate realised that their tea had cooled and she hadn't even produced the biscuits. She wasn't looking after her guest very well at all. 'Shall I make some fresh tea?' she asked.

'No, I shall have to be going soon,' said Emma despondently. 'Back to the daily grind.'

'I thought you'd cheered your life up a bit recently,' said Kate, fishing.

'You're referring to Peter?'

'Yes. Isn't he taking you somewhere interesting this week?'

'No. That friendship has come to an end, I'm afraid.'

'What happened?' Kate wondered whether young Sam knew about this development in his mother's affairs.

'We wanted different things from the relationship,' said Emma evasively.

'Yes?' Kate encouraged her.

'Oh, you know the sort of thing. He was getting too *intense*. I enjoyed the admiration, of course I did. Who wouldn't? I enjoyed dressing up and looking good. And most of all I enjoyed the fact that someone noticed me when I wore something new, or had a sharp haircut. He was so sweet. Do you know, he actually brought me a geranium in a terracotta pot because he said it was his favourite flower. But I didn't want our friendship to lead anywhere further than a little mild flirtation over dinner.'

'Men are like that, I've found. Always wanting something more,' said Kate sympathetically. She didn't tell Emma that that was one of the things that she, personally, rather liked about them.

'So, it's all over,' said Emma finally. 'And now I really must go home. I've enjoyed reading young Daisy's stories, though. And thanks for the tea, Kate.'

But, as Kate reflected when Emma had left, although it might have provided a break from domesticity, it had hardly been as exciting an afternoon as the ones with Peter.

Still, Emma had given her some useful pointers about fairy stories. She picked up the last few loose sheets from the bottom of the box and started to read.

'Daisy?'

'Yeah? Is that you back, Magz?'

'Sure is. I just wanted to talk about that man. You know the one. He's really weird, isn't he? That hair! Those teeth!'

'Now you're sounding just like Kim Kettleby. What do you want to copy her *for?'*

'I don't. I'm just saying. Like, he's weird. *What do you think you're going to learn from* him*?'*

'Enough to get me through my exams.'

'Well, I think you should get rid of him. Even better, get him booted out of Bartz.'

'Stop using that stupid slang. It's only people like engineers, or rowing freaks, who call it that.'

'Bartlemas, then, if you insist.'

'How do you suggest I should do it?'

'You're the ideas person. You'll think of something.'

'But you're the evil *ideas one. You'll have to tell me how to do it.'*

'Now you're just being ridiculous. Or mad. Or both.'

'*Come on, Magz. The old team's back in business. Only this time* we're *choosing what game we're going to play.*'

'*If you say so. You didn't enjoy the old one, that's for sure.*'

'*This one will be different, I promise you.*'

'*What put this into your head? It's very sudden, isn't it?*'

'*He looked at me like I was some kind of scum. He thinks I'm dirty. Spoiled goods. Ruined. But it wasn't my fault, was it?*'

'*No, you're the good little girl who said "no". I'm the wicked one who enjoyed it.*'

'*He thinks I'm you.*'

'*He's got it coming to him, then.*'

26

When she'd finished reading, Kate phoned Faith Beeton.

'Just a couple of queries, Faith. Did you meet Daisy's father when we went to the Tompkins's house?'

'He was there in the living room during that awful interview.'

'What was he like?'

'Grey. Colourless. Silent. He sat in a corner and said virtually nothing. He left everything to his wife. After a bit I forgot he was there.'

'The invisible man.'

'I think he was simply grief-stricken, quite literally. Mrs Tompkins was full of anger, but he was overcome by the grief of his daughter's death. I don't think he wanted to keep on with Daisy's complaint against Fechan.'

'Thanks. I was interested to know something about him.'

'Was there anything else?'

'Did you meet any of the brothers, apart from Steven?'

'No. He was in the sitting room when we got there, but Mrs Tompkins soon got rid of him. I got the impression that she stands no nonsense from any of her children, however old they are. There was one upstairs, too, but I didn't meet him or the third brother, wherever he was – at work, probably. Oh, there was one odd thing that cropped up that might interest you.'

'What was that?'

'Mrs Tompkins went to Daisy's room in the student flat she shared with some others, to pack up her belongings. And, according to her, half the clothes didn't belong to Daisy.'

'Whose were they?'

'She didn't know, but she said that whoever owned them must have been a little trollop.'

'What did the others in the flat say?'

'They insisted the clothes belonged to Daisy, but her mother wouldn't have it, and left them behind.'

'All very strange,' said Kate, who had her own ideas on the clothes and who they belonged to: Magz, she was sure. But she wasn't going to confuse Faith with that conjecture just yet.

'Have you heard any more about how Daisy died?' she asked.

'We know now that she died on the Tuesday evening, probably just before midnight. And she was strangled.'

'That should let Fechan off, then.'

'Why's that?'

'Because there must be physical evidence of whoever did it. You know the sort of thing: hairs, fibres, skin, body fluids.'

'That's quite enough for my imagination, thank you, Kate. You needn't go on.'

'Sorry. But if Fechan is innocent—'

'He is. I told you.'

'Yes. Well, what I'm saying is that there'll be no evidence against him.'

'They've left him alone since they let him leave the police station, certainly.'

'There you are, then.'

'But they don't seem to have picked up anyone else.'

'Give them time. And, by the way, do they want to speak to those of us who were at the Lamb Room reception? I've been waiting for a knock at the door and a constable with a notebook to ask me what I could remember.'

'We've provided them with a list of people who were invited, and you were included. But the list was a long one, and I don't suppose they've got as far as you yet.'

'I doubt if I know anything useful, but I'll be as helpful as I can.'

When Kate had rung off she thought about the clothes that belonged to 'the trollop'. Poor little Daisy, condemned to wear her clean white socks and flower-sprigged dresses for ever. No wonder she kept Magz around to liven her life up a bit and let her express the darker side of her personality.

Oh God! Now I'm really talking like a popular psychology manual, she thought.

When she checked her emails a little later, she found that she had arranged to meet Estelle and her new male friend the following lunchtime, in Oxford. She had forgotten all about it, with everything that had been happening. She sent a message back, confirming the arrangement.

Then she wrote a message to Sam Dolby.

Hi, Sam

No need to worry about Emma any longer. You may by now have noticed the subtle change in her: her new, cultured friend is well out of the picture, and Emma is slowly returning to her former self. I'm sure the friendship was only that, by the way, a platonic relationship, nothing more.

Cheers, Kate

A little later she received a reply:

Hi, Kate

Yeah. I had noticed, and I was wondering about it. I hope she keeps up the cool clothes and sharp hair, though. And

*I think Dad liked them, too, though he didn't say much.
Thanks for letting me know.*

Sam

Kate hoped that Emma would keep her appearance the way it was, too, but feared that she would soon look as comfortably plump and untidy as ever.

Time for some exercise, she decided, if her hips weren't to go the same way as Emma's. She needed to think about the things she had heard and read, and exercise was very conducive to thought, she had always found. There was something about the rhythmical thud of her shoes on the pavement that activated her creative brain cells. She put on her running gear and left the house, heading down towards the canal.

As she approached the house where the students lived, she looked up at the window, just in case Rebecca and Tom had started a new argument. But the window was closed and she could see no one at home. Then, just as she was about to run on, a red Fiesta drew into the kerb beside her, a crowd of students tumbled out, and she was surrounded by Rollo and Dan, a young man whose name she had forgotten, and the dark girl, Jan Rooling.

'Hi!' she said.

'How are you?' asked Dan. 'Have you recovered from the mattress-assault?'

'I'm fine. I'd forgotten all about it.'

They were subdued, she noticed, and Rollo had put his arm round Jan's shoulder in a protective way. Like one of Daisy's brothers in the photographs, thought Kate. They were all obviously upset by their friend's death, but she felt she couldn't let the opportunity to talk to Jan Rooling go by. She might never have another chance.

'Could I have a word?' she asked.

If they were surprised, they didn't show it, but invited her into the kitchen. They moved in a single tight group, as though they were travelling together for protection.

'I'll make the coffee,' said Rollo, and the rest of them sat down at the table with Kate.

'I know it's a lousy time to intrude,' she began, 'but I really wanted to ask you something, Jan.'

'Yes?' The girl looked puzzled.

She could see no way of being diplomatic so said outright, 'Why didn't you put something in writing when Daisy made her complaint against Joseph Fechan? You must have been there in the tutorial and seen what was happening.' Too late she realised that she wasn't supposed to know anything about this.

'What's it to you?' the girl wanted to know.

'I just wondered. I'm interested in people and how they think, and this niggled when I heard about it.'

'You're a friend of Faith Beeton's, aren't you?'

'Yes.'

'She's been talking.'

'Only to me, no one else. She was worried. That's why she discussed it with me. I know she shouldn't have done, but I haven't spoken about it to outsiders, and neither has she. She wanted to be sure that she was coming to the right conclusion. So, what do you think?'

'No one can come to the right conclusion,' said Jan after a moment's thought. 'Daisy was a complicated person, not at all the simple country girl that she pretended to be. At least, she wasn't really pretending. That's what she was a lot of the time. But Fechan said or did something that just got on her wrong side, and she changed. It was really embarrassing. She started to wear short skirts, and long boots, and too much make-up when she came to tutorials. Anyone could see that Fechan hated it. It made him feel awkward. Some of the male tutors would have taken advantage. You know, they'd have leaped on her. But Fechan's not like that. God knows what kind of sex-life the man has, but he just couldn't take what Daisy was throwing at him.'

'So she had no complaint against him? It was fabricated?'

'No, that's not quite true either. The more vampish Daisy became, the more uptight and difficult he got. Nothing she said or did could please him. He was really vicious to her. I just sat tight and hoped he wouldn't notice me.'

'Why didn't you put this down on paper?'

'Because it doesn't make sense. It wasn't cut and dried. Kim wanted me to say that he was an old lecher and had been harassing Daisy because she turned him down. That's the way she wanted it to be. It fitted in with her theories. But it wasn't like that, so I couldn't say it was, even to please Kim. And then Faith Beeton wanted me to say that Fechan was a saint, a wonderful teacher, a tolerant, understanding tutor. And that wasn't exactly right either. I couldn't help either of them. The truth was somewhere else, but nobody wanted to hear that. One lot wanted to get rid of Fechan, the others wanted to clobber Daisy.'

'So how do you see it?' asked Kate.

'Fechan was picking on Daisy, and he shouldn't have done. But she was encouraging him. She was teasing him, winding him up. She must have had some traumatic sort of childhood to make her behave like that. It was really weird, I can tell you.'

Once she got started, Jan seemed to enjoy telling Kate how it had been in the tutorials. It was a pity she hadn't said something at the time though. People might have understood Daisy better, in spite of what Jan thought. Faith Beeton wasn't a black-and-white person, after all. She would have listened.

'You won't go talking to Beeton about it, will you?' asked Jan.

'Not if you don't want me to. I suppose the complaint against Fechan will be dropped now, anyway.'

'He's a weirdo all right though,' said Rollo. 'They shouldn't let him loose around students. It's about time they got rid of him.'

And this was the student of Psychology, was it, wondered Kate.

'But we all saw how Daisy could be, too,' said Dan reasonably. 'It wasn't all down to Fechan, was it? Look at how she treated poor old Yan.'

'Daisy just liked men,' said Rollo.

'As a matter of fact,' said Jan, 'I don't think she did. She liked to attract them, and tease them, and feel she could boss them around. But I don't think she *liked* them much.'

Which was another new slant on Daisy Tompkins, thought Kate.

'Thanks for talking to me,' she said, and got up to leave.

'Have they arrested anyone for Daisy's murder yet?' asked Dan.

'No. Not as far as I know,' said Kate.

But she was starting to get some ideas about who might have done it.

27

Estelle had opted for pre-lunch drinks in the end, rather than lunch, to Kate's relief, and the three of them met in the bar of one of the comfortable hotels in central Oxford.

'Kate! How are you!' gushed Estelle. 'Come and meet my friend Peter Hume.'

Peter was tall and tweedy, a few years older than Estelle and rather less sharply-dressed than her usual choice of men. There was something familiar about him, but she couldn't place him exactly. He looked weathered, and rather warm and cuddly, Kate thought with surprise. Estelle, she was pleased to see, was dressed in her familiar style of black suit, cream shirt and one expensive piece of jewellery, in this case a modern piece pinned to the lapel of her jacket, featuring a very large diamond.

'Kate's one of my promising young authors, Peter.'

Peter looked politely non-committal, and Kate guessed that Estelle had been a little less complimentary about her before she arrived.

'And Peter was here at Oxford, so I'm sure you'll have lots in common.' She turned to her companion. 'My usual g and t please, sweetie. And Kate will have a glass of white wine, won't you?'

'Yes. Thank you.'

Peter went dutifully off to the bar.

'Do you know, when he came to pick me up this morning he'd brought me a geranium in a pot! A red one! Don't you think that was lovely of him?'

'Lovely.'

Kate had a sudden memory of someone else enthusing about a lovely man who brought her a present of a geranium. Emma. And Emma's manfriend was called Peter, too, she remembered.

'What does your Peter do for a living?' she asked.

'He's in the book trade.'

'Like you, then.'

'More on the buying and selling end,' said Estelle.

'And does he live in Oxford?'

'No. In a village near High Wycombe.'

So, halfway between the two. How convenient. He could get on to the M40 and turn left for London and Estelle, or right for Oxford and Emma.

'Why all the questions?' asked Estelle.

'I wanted to know more about a man who was lovely enough to bring you a potted geranium.'

'Oh!' And Estelle laughed uncertainly.

Kate had the impression that Estelle was more of a cactus person, somehow. She could see her loving the thin, dry spikiness of them, rather than the rich red flowers and peppery scent of geraniums. Or perhaps Estelle was changing. Perhaps this one really was the right man for her. According to Emma their relationship had ended. She could see that Emma would be no competition for Estelle, unfortunately, even with her smart new haircut and sleek new clothes. Still, Emma had her half-dozen children and her reliable husband, so she'd probably soon get over it.

Peter returned and handed them their drinks. They thanked him and Kate tried hard to think up some sparkling and interesting small talk. Peter had started on the subject of gardening, which left her feeling ignorant.

They were sitting at a table in the window and Peter had the seat that looked out on to the street. Estelle was just launching into an optimistic description of Kate's career, when Peter suddenly exclaimed, 'Good Lord! There's Joseph Fechan!'

Estelle looked blank, but Kate said, 'Where?'

'I haven't seen him for nearly twenty years, yet he looks just the same.'

Kate peered across his shoulder. Yes, he was right. There was Fechan, slouching along, hunched over as though hiding from people, walking right past their window.

'Were you at Oxford together?' she asked, while Estelle now looked bored with the subject.

'He's much younger than me,' said Peter, 'so we weren't really contemporaries here. But he was keen on my young sister Laura at one time. God knows what she saw in him! He was one of the worst co-ordinated men I've ever seen, with long, gangling limbs. And so clumsy! We were always expecting him to send a small table flying, or to spill his drink down your shirtfront.'

'I don't think he's changed much,' said Kate.

'No. I can see that, poor man. But do you know him? How is he getting on these days? Underneath the gaucheness, I'm sure he was really very pleasant. And of course, a real needle-brain. What our tutor would describe as "sound".'

'I'm not entirely sure I know what that means,' said Kate.

'Aren't we going to eat, Peter darling?' put in Estelle. 'I'm famished!'

'You know you'll only pick at a green salad, Estelle. I want to hear what your young friend has to say.'

Kate was sure that Estelle wouldn't appreciate that 'young'. She knew she should make an excuse and leave Estelle to her lunch with Peter, but she wanted to hear more about Joseph Fechan.

'I've only met the man once,' she said, 'but that was quite enough. He does have a rather unfortunate manner. And voice. And lack of social know-how. Oh dear. I didn't mean to run on about him like that. He was a friend of your sister's, after all.'

'We had little in common, I'm afraid, and we didn't keep in touch after he and Laura split up. But I'll tell you one extraordinary thing about him.' He leaned across the table, placing his hand over Estelle's, drawing her back into the conversation. Kate could see why Emma had enjoyed his company. He was the sort of man who really listened to you when you spoke to him.

'What was that?' Estelle asked dutifully.

'The man had the most prodigious memory. He could remember absolutely anything and everything. Had some system, he told us. Laura used to make him show off his ability as a kind of party trick. I don't think he enjoyed doing that, you know.'

'No, he wouldn't,' said Kate. And then she remembered how Fechan had reeled off the shelfmarks of the letters she might be interested in at the Bodleian. His memory hadn't deteriorated much over the years, apparently.

'Well, that's all very fascinating,' said Estelle, who clearly thought it wasn't. 'But tell me, Kate, have you started on the new book yet?'

'I'm just gathering together a few ideas,' she said vaguely.

'Don't leave it too long, will you? You know that your readers will forget you if you don't give them a new book every year.'

'I'm working on it.' And then she remembered her manners and got to her feet. 'It was lovely seeing you, Estelle, and meeting you, Peter. But now I really must be going.'

She would have liked to stay, but Estelle would never speak to her again if she did – or else, she would fail to achieve a decent advance for her next book, which would be worse.

As soon as she had left Estelle and Peter, Kate's mind moved on to other things. The moment she got home, she was going to make a phone call.

* * *

Kate wasn't looking forward to making that particular phone call, but it had to be done, so she rang Bartlemas College and asked to be put through to Dr Fechan.

'Dr Fechan? This is Kate Ivory. We met at—'

'Yes. I remember you perfectly, Miss Ivory. What is it that you want?'

'I wondered whether I could come to see you about—'

'About the nineteenth-century correspondence we were speaking of?'

'Yes, that's it.' She'd have to rush down to the Bodleian and find out what she was supposed to be talking about. Room 132, she remembered. 'Are you free at all this afternoon?'

'I am free all the time, Miss Ivory,' he said drily, and she remembered that Faith had told her that he had been relieved of all contact with his students.

'Half-past three? At Bartlemas?' she suggested.

'Yes. That will be fine. Just ask the porter at the lodge to direct you to my room.'

Kate wasn't entirely sure whether to be glad that he had fallen in with her proposal so easily. So far he had treated her with great politeness, but she certainly didn't wish to see any other side of him.

28

Kate presented herself at Bartlemas lodge at twenty-five minutes past three, since she was sure that Fechan was just as much a stickler over time as he was over everything else. She had changed her decorative earrings for plain gold studs and was wearing nothing that could remotely be described as 'vampish'.

The porter gave her directions to Dr Fechan's room, and so she crossed two quadrangles and climbed a narrow flight of stairs to arrive at a door with a small painted sign, gold on black: *Dr J. Fechan*. She knocked.

'Come in.'

His voice sounded quite normal. She turned the door handle and entered.

Fechan's room was clean, polished and tidy. She shouldn't have been surprised, she realised. He wasn't the kind of academic who lived in chaos, with tottering piles of papers and the dust of decades all over his books. His desk was neat, and clear of work. She was sure that all the papers in his filing cabinets were in order, too.

'Won't you sit down, Miss Ivory?' he said, indicating a comfortable-looking sofa, where presumably the students sat for their tutorials. She tried to remember that she was not in the position of one of his undergraduates, but sat up straight and concentrated on feeling confident and alert.

'Is there anything I can offer you at this time in the afternoon?' he asked.

'That's very kind, but no, thank you,' she replied, hoping she wasn't breathing too many fumes of white wine over him.

'You wanted to speak to me about the manuscripts—'

'No,' she said abruptly. 'I'm afraid I don't, Dr Fechan. At least, only indirectly. The correspondence we spoke of was just an excuse to come to see you.'

'You'd better explain. Why on earth would you wish to speak to me otherwise? Faith mentioned that you were a writer. You're not a journalist, by any chance, are you?'

He didn't sound friendly, but at least he hadn't started to shout at her yet. Kate was very glad that she was a novelist rather than a reporter.

'Certainly not,' she replied truthfully. 'I write fiction.'

'And so do most reporters,' he replied. 'So, Miss Ivory, tell me why you are here.'

'You have an extraordinary memory,' she began. 'At the party in the Lamb Room, when Faith mentioned the nineteenth-century letters she thought would interest me, you immediately told me their shelfmarks – quite long and complicated ones, at that.'

'I have a trained memory,' he stated.

'So I've heard. But when you say "trained", what do you mean exactly?'

'Don't you think your question is impertinent?'

'I expect it is. But when I want to know something I tend to ask straight out, rather than going round the subject in a polite and ladylike way.'

'I have always been an admirer of the polite and ladylike,' said Fechan.

Did the man have a sense of humour, or was he stating a simple fact? His was not an easy face to read.

'And was Daisy Tompkins ladylike?'

'I thought so, to begin with. But I was mistaken in her.'

'I don't suppose that many of her generation would consider that "ladylike" was a compliment.'

'Possibly not. But is this what you came to ask me about?' Fechan had leaned back in his chair and was staring at her. He wore small, rectangular glasses, she saw, a more fashionable shape than she would have expected. 'I really have nothing to say about Miss Tompkins. I am, of course, very sorry indeed that she is dead. That is a tragedy. The death of any young person is tragic – the life cut short just at the point when every future seems a possibility.'

'Is that how you felt about your own future when you were twenty?' she asked.

'Possibly. I knew what I wanted to be. The alternatives were of no interest to me. But I was hardly a typical twenty year old. However, you were about to tell me why you are here in my room.' He tipped his chair forward again and leaned across the desk. 'I thought you said you were a direct person, Miss Ivory.'

'Your trained memory,' she said hastily. 'I thought people were born with a good memory, or a bad one. I hadn't realised that you could do anything about what you had inherited. How exactly did you train it?'

'I used the classical method,' he said simply. 'The method that has been used since antiquity. I came across it when I was a child, and it fascinated me.'

'How does it work?'

'Why do you wish to know?'

'For one thing, I'm a naturally curious person.'

Fechan thought for a moment. 'I am simplifying, of course. If you are really interested in the technique there are books you can consult. But the principle of the method is to associate each item you wish to remember with a place and an image.'

Kate tried to look intelligent and attentive. Fechan stared at her for a moment, then continued.

'You build for yourself an imaginary, detailed *place* – a house, a garden, with door and windows, colonnades and pathways, corridors and rooms. You get to know this place intimately. You know how many paces there are to reach the end of the path, you know the size of the windows, the colour of the curtains. Every time you make your tour of this place, you do so in the same order. And then, each idea, or object, that you wish to remember is given an *image*, something that you can associate with it with some facility. You place the image on a door, in a niche in the corridor, on a tree in the garden, in the order in which you habitually visit them in your imagination. And then, when you wish to remember, you take your mind for a walk. Do you understand?'

'A little, perhaps. I can see that it would take an enormous amount of practice.'

'I used to practise every day. I still do, as a matter of fact. And now, will you tell me your second reason for wishing to hear this?'

'I believe that your memory of events could be important.'

'Why is that?'

'Because, whatever you see, you remember, in detail and with absolute accuracy.'

Fechan bowed his head to acknowledge the truth of what she said.

'And, Dr Fechan, you were here in College on the Tuesday evening after the party in the Lamb Room,' continued Kate.

'I was. But how do you know about it?' If he also remembered that it was the night that Daisy Tompkins had died, he made no sign.

'My mother was driving me home after dinner. It was late, well after eleven o'clock, and we saw you as you crossed the High Street and walked towards Parks Road.'

'How very observant of you.'

'The thing is, has anybody asked you what you saw?'

'I beg your pardon?'

'You must have seen the students going into Bartz for their own party. You probably saw them as they were straggling out again. What time does the bar close? It must be eleven, or eleven-thirty, surely?'

'By "Bartz" I assume you are referring to the Students' Union bar in the cellars beneath Hall.'

'Yes, that's it,' said Kate impatiently. 'Well? What time does it close?'

'It would be eleven o'clock on a Tuesday evening, unless the students had requested an extension.'

'Has anyone asked you about that evening?'

'The police were quite exhaustive in their questions.' His face was impassive, but Kate could feel the suppressed anger beneath his reply.

'But they don't know you, do they?'

'They are quite sure that they do.' Again, there was the undercurrent of violence in his voice. Kate felt that at any moment he would shout at her.

'What I mean is that you don't just observe and remember things – you make connections, too, don't you? Something that you saw or heard months, or even years ago, will pop into your mind if you see the connection.'

'That might be correct, yes, even if rather inelegantly expressed.' He was sounding calmer again. Perhaps he was just like everyone else: he just needed someone who listened to him and tried to understand.

'And I think you did see something that evening that you could connect to something that happened in the past.'

'What category of "thing" were you thinking of?'

'Something to do with Daisy Tompkins.'

'So we're back on the subject of that young lady.'

'She's dead – murdered. Remember?'

'How could I forget? I'm the person that the police believe

to be responsible for her death. Have *you* forgotten *that*?'

Suddenly, it seemed a very reckless act to be sitting here, alone, with Joseph Fechan, discussing a girl who was murdered.

'If anyone holds the key to the problem, it's you, isn't it, Dr Fechan?' She had the feeling that he liked it when she stood up to him.

'If you say so.' He sat looking at her, his hands steepled in front of his face, something rather like a smile on his face.

'So what did you see?'

'You want me to tell you everything?' He sounded amused.

'Yes. Please,' she added.

'At eleven o'clock the Oxford clocks began to strike the hour. I gathered my papers together and placed them in their folders, ready to resume work on them the following morning. It was a fine evening and there was a gibbous moon which had risen early in the south and which now hung over the Tower of Grace. I descended the staircase – twenty-seven steps – and crossed Pesant Quadrangle, then passed through the archway into the Front Quad. The students were leaving the Union bar and making their way towards the lodge. I recognised Jones, Persse, Shaw, Bullen,' said Fechan, watching her. 'Have you met them?' Kate was sure that he had noted the people she had spoken to at the Lamb Room party. 'They are known to their friends as Dan, Rollo, Rebecca and Tom. They are all second-year undergraduates who share a house in Jericho. Then I saw Posner and Eaves, known as Ethan and Holly, also Rooling, called Jan, who used to come, as you doubtless know, to the same tutorials as Daisy Tompkins. Is that enough to be going on with?'

She understood why he had looked amused. 'Thank you. Perhaps I didn't mean *everything*. Perhaps I meant *everything that was relevant to the death of Daisy Tompkins*.'

'Now you're asking me to make a value judgement.'

'I should have thought you were good at those.'

He laughed, honking through his nose.

'Very well.' He sounded as though, at last, he was going to stop teasing her. 'You want the connections? Well, when I first saw Daisy Tompkins I thought she was a simple country girl – virginal, untouched. I was a fool, of course, to believe that.'

'Not a fool,' said Kate. 'Idealistic, I would say. But half right.'

Fechan smiled at her. He really did have a charming smile. 'And then, after some weeks, she changed. She changed into a vamp, a seductress, a whore.'

'That's a bit strong, isn't it?'

'I'm sure you are aware that my use of words is perfectly accurate.'

'Oh yes – of course, it would be. Sorry. Please go on.'

'I disliked it intensely. It made me feel uncomfortable, and I know that this is unusual in the present climate. But I cannot change what I am.'

'Few of us can.'

'I hated Daisy for what she was, but on another level I recognised that she was not entirely responsible for what she had become.'

'Those who are abused become abusive in their turn?'

Fechan ignored this.

'Daisy Tompkins wanted to become a serious writer. Did you know that?' he asked Kate suddenly.

'As a matter of fact, yes, I did.'

'In the early days of our relationship as tutor and pupil, she confided this ambition in me. She even showed me some of her work.'

'Would that have been one of her modernised fairy stories?' Kate asked.

'You've seen them?'

'One or two.'

'And you've come to a conclusion, no doubt, as to their meaning.'

'At the risk of sounding like a popular manual of psychology, yes.'

Again, Kate was given Fechan's charming smile. 'You asked about connections, and those are the connections that I made. On the night of Daisy's murder I saw her in the company of several young men. I should say that she was amorously involved with them. Yes.'

'And?' Kate had already learned that Daisy enjoyed the company of men, and liked to play off one against another.

'I was not the only person to notice such things.'

'And you saw someone in the college. Perhaps someone who wasn't a member of Bartlemas?'

'That's possible.'

'Have you told anyone what you saw, and the connections you made to Daisy's past?'

'No.'

'Why not?'

'Would they believe me? Or would they, on the contrary, think that I was attempting to avert suspicion from myself on to another, unlikely person?'

'I don't think he's unlikely at all,' said Kate.

'Who?'

There was a short silence, and then Kate said, 'You know exactly who I'm talking about. Tell me the name of the man you saw in college that night.'

'Very well, if you insist. You seem a very determined woman, so I shall indulge your fancy.'

'Thank you.'

'He was rather older than most undergraduates.'

'That's what I would expect.'

Fechan spoke in a precise voice, as though giving evidence in court. 'Much later, when most people had left, I saw a man

304

I believed to be one of Miss Tompkins's brothers crossing the quadrangle and entering the Union bar. There was a light on down there, but I imagine that the bar staff were clearing up by then.'

'And was Daisy Tompkins still in there?'

'I don't know. I only know that I hadn't seen her leave, so it is a possibility.'

'And do you know which of her brothers you saw?'

'It was the eldest. His name is Steven.'

'How do you know him?'

'I was introduced to the entire family of Tompkinses during the first week of Daisy's Freshman year.' Fechan looked as though he had not enjoyed the experience. 'As you will appreciate by now, I do remember their names and faces.'

'I believe Steven likes to be known as "Spike",' said Kate.

'That, luckily, is no concern of mine.'

Fechan sat quite still in his chair, staring at Kate with very little expression on his face. The effect was not pleasant, but she refused to be intimidated.

'I think you should go to the police with this information,' she said.

'Why should I assist the police in finding the killer of a particularly foolish young woman?'

'Because if you don't, everyone at Bartlemas will go on believing that *you* killed her. And anyway, you know yourself that she wasn't "foolish", as you call it. She was a victim – a victim twice over: once as a child, and then again last Tuesday.'

'I see that you don't expect me to respond to any appeal to my civic duty.'

'I thought that self-interest was a safer card to play,' said Kate. 'It is with most people, I find.'

'What will you do if I decide not to tell what I saw? And, by the way, even if he was present at that time and in that place, I don't see why the police should believe that it was Steven

Tompkins who killed Daisy, rather than any other of the young people who were present in College that evening.'

'It just happens that some evidence – obscure and oblique, admittedly – has come to light. If I do my own civic duty, and pass on to the police some of Daisy's notebooks and writings – which her grandmother gave me, by the way – I think they may well come to the same conclusion as me – and you. And if you don't want to tell them what you saw, I expect they will eventually find someone else who noticed Steven Tompkins's arrival.'

'It was dark and the undergraduates in the vicinity were mostly drunk and immersed in their own affairs,' said Fechan.

'But I'm sure there's some physical evidence of his presence. Once they have a suspect, they can start matching his DNA to any other they may have found.'

'What an expert you are!'

'No, not really. I just watch too much television.'

'And why would her brother wish to kill her?'

'I think he was jealous.'

'And this is what you will tell the police. Do you think they will believe you? Will they understand what you are telling them?'

'I expect they come across incest quite frequently in their work. I don't suppose it will raise an eyebrow down at the police station.'

'What a very depressing world we live in, where such things are taken for granted instead of treated with the horror which they deserve.'

'So, will you do it? Will you go to the police?'

'Very well. But I have to tell you that even if Steven Tompkins is found guilty of his sister's murder, most of the members of this college will continue to believe that it was I, in fact, who was the perpetrator of the crime.'

'I'm sorry about that.'

'I have grown accustomed to the idea. Do not concern yourself about it.'

'I think it's time for me to leave.'

'Yes. It is.' He rose from his chair and walked across the room to open the door. You had to admire his manners, Kate conceded.

'I believe you know your way out.'

29

That evening, Jon phoned. Kate hadn't heard from him for a couple of days. She'd missed him, she realised.

'I tried you this afternoon,' he said, 'but you must have been out.' He was sounding very cheerful – more cheerful than he had since before his sister came to stay with him.

'I had to call in at the police station,' said Kate.

'What's happened to you now?' he asked, alarmed.

'Nothing. It's just that I had some material that could help the police with an enquiry.'

'I won't ask!'

'It's all very dull, certainly,' said Kate, 'but you'll be glad to learn that I have done my civic duty. Now, tell me about your day. You sound as though you have good news.'

'I have! Alison's gone.' Then he realised how unkind this must have sounded. 'She was very welcome, of course, but I'm glad that she and Iain have decided to talk things over. I think he'll manage to persuade her to move to Canada, eventually. She wants to be cajoled, I told him, when we spoke on the phone. He sounded as though he didn't know what the word meant, but I expect he'll get the hang of it eventually.'

'It must have been a bit crowded in your flat while she was there,' said Kate.

'And that girl is so *messy*!'

'Other people's habits get on your nerves when you're used to living on your own, don't they?'

'It depends entirely who the other person is,' he said firmly.

'Would you like to come up to London this next weekend?'

'As long as the police don't need to ask me any more questions.'

'Do you think they will?'

'Probably not. I've told them everything I know.'

'I'll see you then?'

'Yes.'

She would ask Brad and Patrick to feed Susanna for her while she was away. They were cat lovers, after all, and if she gave them the key they could come round and look at the improvements she had made to the house. It was good to think that she had neighbours who were interested, and concerned, and who loved Susanna almost as much as she did.

'I can't wait to see you,' she said. 'We might think about planning a trip in your boat before the weather closes in.'

'I'd like that,' said Jon.

'It was Emma who spotted it, really,' said Kate.

She and Faith were sitting at Kate's kitchen table, drinking Italian coffee and eating Belgian biscuits.

'I thought she was a domestic goddess who had transformed herself into a fashion victim,' said Faith. 'Incapable of spotting anything of any use.'

'You know that's unfair. Emma has a very good brain. She teaches at Bartlemas summer schools, after all.'

'I'm just jealous,' admitted Faith. 'But at least they've arrested the awful brother now, haven't they?'

'Yes. So you were proved right about Joseph Fechan.'

'And everyone underestimated his intelligence,' said Faith. 'He understood more than any of us about Daisy and her situation.'

'I did find him scary, though, when I went to see him.'

'He's marshmallow inside, really.'

'I doubt whether Daisy Tompkins believed that.'

'Tell me why her brother killed her.'

'It was in the fairy stories. There was lots of stuff about brothers and sisters, and separating from the parents, and three princes who come calling to win the Princess.'

'How does that tie in?'

'Daisy had three brothers, remember?'

'And the eldest was screwing her. Is that what you're saying?'

'Yes. She was such a pretty little thing, and they were her big, protective brothers. But he was over-possessive.'

'That's putting it mildly! And how do you know, anyway?'

'I have to admit that I'm guessing this part of it.'

'Not entirely,' said Faith. 'Apparently there was a phone call to her flat earlier on the Tuesday evening, and one of the young male students answered. He told the caller, who was Steven, naturally, that Daisy had gone to buy some more food for the party, or some such thing. Steven was incensed because he hadn't been invited, and Daisy would be indulging in lascivious dancing with other, non-Tompkins young men.'

'Now *you*'re indulging your imagination.'

'I bet I'm right.'

'Poor old Daisy,' said Kate. 'She never did come to terms with it, did she? On the one hand she was being sexually abused by a brother who was ten years older than her, and yet another part of her wanted it. No wonder she split herself down the middle.'

'Spare me the psychology!'

'But she was two different people. Even her clothes were different, depending which one she was being. And her mother refused to recognise the "evil" clothes. She knew only her pure little Daisy.'

'I don't believe that, do you? Helen Tompkins must have known something was going on, at some level. She just didn't want to see it. And what about the father?'

'You told me he was devastated by Daisy's death. It sounded as if he was completely dominated by the frightful mother.'

'Maybe. Or maybe he knew, too, and condoned it.'

'She called the other half of her personality "Magz",' said Kate.

'You mean she had an imaginary friend?'

'Yes. She'd been around for years, apparently.'

'I used to have one of those,' said Faith. 'I called her Albert.'

Kate laughed.

'It was all very serious between us,' said Faith. 'She didn't leave home until we were both thirteen.'

'One of my friends had a flock of imaginary sheep that lived in the cupboard under the stairs,' said Kate, remembering.

'Leaving this ridiculous subject, let us return to the unfortunate Joseph Fechan. In spite of the fact that he had nothing whatever to do with Daisy's death, do you realise that his career is shot to pieces?'

'He told me it would be. He said that even if it was proved that someone else killed Daisy, everyone would always wish that he'd been found guilty. It seems so unfair.'

'The adjective "weird" is being used about him all around us.'

'What is he going to do?'

'Well, apparently, he has a lovely girlfriend, a dentist, and the two of them are going to elope to the West Country, where she will join a dental practice, and he will teach English Literature to some lucky students at the new local university.'

'God help them!'

'Exactly. But I do hope that Joseph and his ladyfriend will both be very happy.'

'And so say all of us. Is it time to pour us both a celebratory glass of white wine, do you think?'

'I'm sure it is.'

'I'll fetch the bottle; you get out the glasses.'

XXiii

How do I feel, leaving my old life behind in Oxford?

I have lived here since I was nineteen. Nearly twenty years. A good proportion of anybody's life.

But I am looking to the future. I can walk away, at last, from the jealousies and the pettiness of Bartlemas and its Fellowship. Perhaps my new students will be no better than the old. Perhaps they will laugh at me behind my back and describe me as 'weird'. But there is just a chance that I might make a new start and that there will be, somewhere, a spark of originality in the sullen faces seated before me.

And this time I have Rhona with me. The cool hand in the warm latex glove. We even talk of getting married one day: the apotheosis of normality!

It is, of course, ridiculous to imagine that everything from now on will be perfect. I know that nothing is, nothing can ever be, at least in this world. (And I do not believe in any world hereafter.)

This is the first time in my life that I have looked forward to what is to come with a degree of confidence. I do believe that things will change, and for the better.

It is Rhona who has made the difference to my life. Yesterday, at her invitation, I went to her house for the evening. She cooked us a meal – a very good meal. We drank most of the bottle of wine that I took with me (a very pleasant French Viognier, I might add). It was a wonderful evening, and yet there was one small cloud to spoil its perfection. I have noticed an unwelcome change in Rhona. Not a very great change, but a difference, nevertheless.

She was wearing lipstick. Of course, Rhona usually wears lipstick, but this was *red*. A bright, lustrous red. Her dress was in

OXFORD REMAINS

her usual style, with a high neck and long sleeves, though it was slightly shorter than usual. I could see her knees, and even an inch or two of her thighs, glossy in shiny black tights. She saw me looking at her thighs, and she blushed.

She reminded me of Selina.

I'll have to tell her how uncomfortable it makes me feel and ask her not to do it again.

It reminds me of my sister, Selina, I will tell her.

I see her in the churchyard, straddling the youth in the stained jeans.

I see her holding Mr Evans's jacket out for him to put on, smiling at him.

I see her lying on her bed, stinking of vomit – and worse – her limbs in disorder.

I remind myself that Rhona is a good woman, a dentist – and who could be more respectable than that? She didn't do it intentionally, I understand that. But when I tell her how I feel, she will understand.

Now you can buy any of these other
books by **Veronica Stallwood** from your
bookshop or *direct from her publisher*.

FREE P&P AND UK DELIVERY
(Overseas and Ireland £3.50 per book)

Kate Ivory series

Death and the Oxford Box	£5.99
Oxford Exit	£6.99
Oxford Mourning	£6.99
Oxford Fall	£5.99
Oxford Knot	£6.99
Oxford Blue	£5.99
Oxford Shift	£6.99
Oxford Shadows	£5.99
Oxford Double	£5.99
Oxford Proof	£6.99

Other novels

Deathspell	£5.99
The Rainbow Sign	£5.99

TO ORDER SIMPLY CALL THIS NUMBER

01235 400 414

or visit our website: www.madaboutbooks.com

Prices and availability subject to change without notice.